PICTURES IN BLUE

A BLUE GROVE MOUNTAIN NOVEL

BLUE GROVE MOUNTAIN SERIES
BOOK ONE

KELSEY SCHULZ

ALSO BY KELSEY SCHULZ

Witchhunter; The Realm of the Isles

When Fate Steps In

Edited by Kristen Hamilton @kristensredpen

Cover Illustration & Design by Sam Palencia @InkandLaurel

❀ Created with Vellum

For anyone still discovering their path in life, keep believing in yourself.

AUTHOR'S NOTE

Content and Trigger Warnings:
Panic attacks on page, verbal abuse (parental), body dysmorphia, sibling death (flashback), gaslighting (parental)

This is an open door romance, so the content may not be suitable for some readers. There are multiple scenes depicting consensual sex and intimacy. There is also coarse language and swearing throughout the book.

CHAPTER ONE

AVERY

"*This* is honestly absolute shit."

My editor's words echo in my ear, an annoying buzzing sound ever present like gnats on a hot summer day. I risk a sympathetic glance at Charlotte and meet her hazel eyes. We speak with subtle eye movements and wait for James to continue with his critiques.

I know what it's like to be reamed by our editor. Even though Charlotte is the newest employee, she's already used to these meetings spent picking apart our work, bit by bit until there's nothing left but a page covered in red ink.

Her eyes shift downward to her blue Converse, but she doesn't let them linger there. She lifts her chin, folds her arms over her bright pink sweater and crosses her legs that are wrapped in yellow leggings. Quiet is one thing my friend is not and her wardrobe reflects that.

"Absolute shit," he repeats, slamming the copy of Charlotte's article down on the conference table. The staff around the table flinch. They've all been exactly where Charlotte is now. We all know how it goes when James isn't happy. It's like he wishes for all of us to be just as moody as he is.

Most of the staff believes he needs to get laid. I just think he's a jerk. No excuses needed. He's a jerk and he likes to treat others around him like they don't matter. He thinks he's better than everyone else because he's the editor of the paper. The "boss man" as he reminds us time and time again. I'm not kidding. *"I'm the boss man, you have to listen to me when I give out assignments"* is something we hear all the time. It's the worst kind of ego.

"Honestly, Cheryl," of course he doesn't know her name. "You've been here long enough. I expect more from you."

Apparently, "long enough" means barely three months.

When Charlotte first started here back in February, she had just graduated with her master's degree in Journalism and I suspect at this point, she may be regretting her career choice. She wouldn't be the only one, considering I am in the same boat, oar in hand, navigating the rapids right alongside her.

"You were brought on for the potential you showed," James continues in a tone that practically drips with pompousness, the words trickling from his lips. "There's none in this article and I expected better. I expect your best every time and this certainly isn't it. Tim," the short, balding man next to me stands at attention. The class brownnoser. If James asked him to swim in the ocean, Tim would ask how far and wouldn't even question it when he told him to the other side of the world. He'd buy a cap, goggles, and god forbid, a speedo and jump in the ocean right away. "Take this article over from here. Rewrite, edit, do whatever you need to do to get it ready for tonight's copy."

James starts gathering his notes, signaling the end of this horrid meeting. I don't even remember the last time we had a staff meeting that didn't end with him calling someone out for "shit" writing that usually isn't even that bad.

In fact, I don't think I have ever heard a word out of his mouth that wasn't criticism pointed at someone in the office. Or some negative comment about how they could be better. It was the same way when we were together for an unfortunate period of time. Two years of my life I wish I could steal back, smuggle them in the dead of night when he isn't looking and stash them at the end of my timeline.

You could do better, Avery.

Avery, you know I like you but...

You're so beautiful when you put in the effort.

I like when you dress up for once.

And here I am, still working under him a year after we broke up. Well, not *under* him, under him. Under him in the professional sense. The professional sense that is in a completely platonic way. You get it.

He pulls out his phone and starts walking toward the door when he looks up and realizes we are all still sitting. He zeros in on me, "Avery, will you tell me why everyone is still sitting down?" At least he got my name right. He doesn't give me a chance to answer before he motions to the door, "Well? Let's go. Don't you have shit to report? Get to work."

He sighs in frustration and walks out. The rest of the staff starts gathering pens and reporter's notebooks, empty coffee mugs and uneaten scones, heading to their desks for yet another fantastic day of news writing.

I grab my empty coffee mug with a bear on the side hugging a shiny, red heart with *Have a Beary Good Day* that Charlotte gave me last Christmas. She gave me another for my birthday that featured a dancing waffle, a smile spread across it with the words, *Don't be a Twat Waffle* surrounding it. If I could bring that one to work and drink coffee from it right in front of James, I would. But I don't have that kind of backbone. I walk around the table to where Charlotte is still sitting and take a blueberry scone, sliding it her way as I sit in the chair next to her.

"Here," I say in a soft tone. I hate watching people being talked down to. I've dealt with it throughout my whole existence and I let James' words affect me more than I care to admit, in more ways than I want to remember. My mother was never the nicest person either when it came to talking to her kid. Or about her kid. Or anything to do with her kid really. If condescension were an Olympic sport, she'd be the Michael Phelps of that event. And the runner-up would be James, standing proudly on the podium, chest puffed out in arrogance.

"Thanks," she takes the scone and holds it for a second before she brings it to her lips and takes a large bite.

"Don't listen to him," I say. "James is an asshole. And he only has this job because of his asshole father who also doesn't know what he is talking about."

"Honestly, fuck him. That article was good. And it was good because *I* wrote it." She starts to pick at the scone, blueberry by blueberry, staining the tips of her fingers a faded blue.

"You're right," I agree. "They don't get to make you feel like this. You are good enough. And your writing is good enough. They just like to make people feel small. No one can make you feel inferior without your consent."

She cracks a small smile. "Did you just quote the Princess Diaries to me?"

"Damn right I did. Listen to Joe's wisdom and put what dickhead James said behind you. You're good at what you do. You wouldn't have landed this job if you weren't. Believe in yourself. I do."

"Dickhead James?" she asks.

"Yeah, it's his name around the water cooler," I joke.

It really is though. Marly and Jason started calling him that the first week we all started at the Malibu Gazette five years ago. They did a huge overhaul of the staff when James took over, so we all came in at the same time and commiserated together over the mutual dislike of our boss.

"Fitting," she says.

"We thought so," I put my arm around her shoulders and give her a slight squeeze. "Are you going to be okay?"

"Always. You know me. I'm never down for long," she responds and lifts up the pastry with half the blueberries missing. "I have a pastry and will feel better with fresh coffee and a new assignment to focus on. Thanks, Avery." She stands and leaves me behind.

I look around the now silent conference room and remember the first time James reprimanded me for what he deemed to be "shitty writing". It was literally his favorite phrase to describe any writing that wasn't his own.

Who knows when the last time was that he put pen to paper. Or, I guess, fingers to keys. The point is, he doesn't write. Ever. But he will never hesitate to take the credit. He's the editor, so he thinks he owns everything we write because he's our boss. And since his father owns the company, we've gotten used to being steamrolled. Especially if we want to keep our jobs.

He once yelled at me because I wrote a news article about a puppy who got stuck in a manhole when there was a horse running loose who ended up totaling a car. He thought the horse story was more newsworthy and would have gotten more views than the puppy, because, and I quote, "Everyone loves reading about car accidents." I genuinely have no idea what I saw in him. He thinks he's the rarest gem in the world when in reality, he's just a common rock found on the side of a creek bed. Put him in a rock polisher and he'd still come out as a dirty clump of earth with no chance of coming out the other side smooth and pristine, shining with color. He will always be dull, rough around the edges with nothing shiny on the inside. Just a dirty, hard rock that no one wants.

The sound of the police scanner pulls me from my thoughts, and I rush out of the conference room to hear the end of the call. ". . . fire at 11 North Avenue. No injuries reported. Suspect is in a green Range Rover."

So much for a slow news day, which rarely exists in Malibu anyway. The newsroom becomes a flurry of activity as Jason grabs his camera, Marly and I grab pens and notebooks, and we all head for the door. Before the elevators close, I see Charlotte grab her phone to call the fire chief to try to get a statement. News like this happens so often, we never know where the day is going to take us.

"Avery!" A sigh escapes my lips before I realize and I brace myself for what's coming. After the fire emergency, the staff came back to the office to edit their photos and write their stories. Currently, I'm sitting at my desk, staring at the collection of pens and highlighters resting in the wooden organizer I bought from an ad I saw one night when I couldn't sleep. I handed my work over to James a few minutes earlier and I would be lying if I said I'm not sitting here waiting for his feedback. Well, his criticism.

I straighten my spine, my features calm and collected, a state that is warring with the pounding organ inside my chest. Even with all my experience in the journalism industry, I never quite got the hang of being completely confident in my work. I went to school for journalism because I was good at writing and when I graduated, this job was there so I applied, knowing it was something I could do. Even if it was something I wasn't entirely sure of.

I look up and James is standing just outside his door looking in my direction. Before I can say anything, he turns and goes back into his office. I guess he's expecting me to follow. It would have taken two seconds for him to tell me what he needed but time is money and apparently those two seconds would have cost him.

My heart continues pounding like the fingers on keyboards clicking away around me. I know exactly why he's calling me into his office. I did the job *I* wanted to do, not the one *he* wanted me to do.

I take a deep breath, hold it for five seconds and exhale before lifting my chin up. A technique I learned years ago to help with my anxiety. I won't let him phase me. At least, I won't let it show on my face. When I open the door, he's already seated at his desk, my article spread out in front of him and I don't think there is one paragraph that hasn't been violated by his red pen. There are lines scratched out, paragraphs rewritten in his indecipherable handwriting.

"Yes?" I say from my place at the door.

"Sit down," he says without glancing up from the papers.

I sit in the chair on the other side of his desk and fix my gaze on the window behind him overlooking the city. A few minutes pass, the only sound is the papers being rustled as he continues to look through my article. Finally, he looks up.

"What is this?" he asks.

"The article on the fire," I say, refusing to let my voice show how nervous I really am. The truth is, no matter how many times people critique my work, I have never gotten rid of the anxiety that comes with it. My hands are sweaty and my heart won't stop racing, my anxiety rising to the surface. I remember the other techniques that I've learned and start to open and close my hands, squeezing them briefly into fists before opening them again. Repeat.

I know what he's going to say, because it's nothing he hasn't already said to me a handful of times.

"No, this is *your* article on the fire. This is not what you do. You are not a features writer," he scoffs as if being a features writer was a piece of trash billowing in the wind on the city streets. "And you are fully aware of that," he continues.

"I just thought readers would want to read what the family had to say about losing their home t—"

"No. Readers care about the facts. You talk to the chief, the firefighters, the police. You get the facts and you report those facts in your article and we publish it in the paper. And *you* don't take the photos. Jason does."

"I know, but I just wanted—"

"I don't care what you wanted," he interrupts. "This is *my* paper."

It's your daddy's paper, I think and manage to stop myself before I roll my eyes.

"You will do things *my* way. I don't want your photos," he holds up the photo I took of a firefighter that had been on the scene outside of the burning house. His profile is featured in front of the structure. His helmet is placed on his head and he has soot smeared on his left cheek, right arm wiping the sweat from his brow. I snapped the photo without even thinking, really. I just saw him and the look of pure exhaustion on his face and knew it was a moment I didn't want to pass without documenting. I didn't intend to step on Jason's toes. He's the best photographer I've ever met and his photos are always impressive. My idea was to convince James to run the interest article beside the breaking news article in the next day's edition. But clearly, that is not going to happen, nor is it ever going to. At least not in this century; not with him running this paper.

"And," he continues.

Perfect, there's more.

"I don't want an article about the family. News is straightforward. It's not that hard."

It *is* hard though because he is completely and utterly wrong, which he would know if he actually understood how a newspaper runs. I don't think he sees the potential this newspaper has. It could be so much better if he allowed it to be. But I am not about to tell him that. He wouldn't hear what I had to say anyway.

"Tim wrote an article worthy of the paper." Of course he did. "And Jason's photo of the actual fire will run with the story. Next time, if you're going to go to an emergency that comes across the scanner, cover the emergency."

He tosses the papers in my direction, turns to his computer and begins typing. I guess that's his way of dismissing me. I gather my things and head back to my desk, tamping down the gnawing feeling in my gut that I don't belong here anymore.

Charlotte is leaning against it with her hands curled around a cup of coffee. She takes a sip and turns to my desk to grab a second mug with a pink donut on the side covered in sprinkles with the words *I do-nut give a fuck,* scrawled around it. Charlotte, unlike me, has no hesitations about bringing her profanity mugs to work. She also has a thing for puns on mugs. I don't think there is a mug in her house without some kind of pun scrawled on the side.

"When he yelled your name, I figured I'd return the favor," she sympathizes, extending the mug to me.

I set the marked-up papers on my desk and grab the mug from her. "Thanks." I don't bother keeping the disappointment out of my voice. I don't know why I even tried with the article. I knew he wouldn't run the story I wrote no matter how much work I put into it. I should have listened to my intuition on that one.

"For what it's worth," she continues, grabbing for the photograph I discarded. "Jason's photos are great, but this," she holds up the photo. "*This* is newsworthy. And I'm sure your article was too."

I let out a long sigh. "I don't know why I tried," I said, voicing my thoughts. "I knew he wouldn't publish it, but I just can't help it. I'm so tired of writing about bad things. There's a fire today, a robbery tomorrow, and a car crash the next day. I just wanted to write about real people with real stories and take pictures of happy moments. Preserve them in time. I'm over reporting about all the bad things that happen."

"I may not have been here long, but I get it. Stuff like this gets to you when all you see every day is tragedy. Even though I do features, I've had experience with breaking news reporting and it was never my thing."

"I wish he'd just let me do features, but even then, he doesn't believe they should even have a place in the paper. *Fluff pieces aren't news* and all that, he says. Such bullshit."

Charlotte scoffs and waves her hand like she's trying to wave off the essence of James around us. "Ignore him. I'd much rather read a story about a Christmas tree farm than another breaking news article about someone's home burning down."

"A Christmas tree farm?"

"What?" she exclaims. "They exist! I grew up about twenty minutes away from one. We always went as a family when we were kids and picked out the weirdest tree."

"Not the perfect cookie cutter one found in every Hallmark movie living room?"

"No," she laughs, taking a sip from her mug. "My mom always wanted to save the trees no one else picked. She said the ones that were different deserved to be loved too. Those were the ones that often needed it the most."

An ache in my chest reminds me how much I wish my mom could have been like that. Could have loved me the way I needed, instead of the way she wanted. "She sounds wonderful."

She looks down with a sad smile. "Yeah, she was." Her features change, not allowing the sadness to linger. She straightens and steps closer, "Anyway, don't listen to James. Your writing is great and so are your photos."

"Thanks, Charlotte. I appreciate it." I reach out and give her arm a squeeze.

"Anytime." With that, she makes her way back to her desk, leaving me to figure out what to do about a story for tomorrow's issue. Without James using my article on the fire, I'm going to have to come up with something different before I leave for the day or I am going to be subject to yet another office visit that I don't think I can handle.

I'd end up quitting on the spot, which may be much better for my mental health if I am being completely honest. But like everyone else in this world, I have bills to pay. If I quit, I'll be late on my rent, end up homeless with nowhere to go, and my mother will be right. She always said I would amount to nothing and most of the time, I feel like I am worth the same.

I've been at this paper, at this job for five years. I took it when they offered because I wasn't sure what else to do at the time. I had no other options and I already had mounds of debt to pay off. Thank you to the education system of America. I never really wanted to be a news reporter, but it was a job. I'd much rather write stories that interest me over breaking news, but with the job that it is, I'm stuck with what I have, no matter how hard I have tried over the last few months to break out of it.

But, I'm tired. I'm tired of hearing the bad things that happen every day and writing about them. I hate knowing the way people feel while they read my articles. No one feels happy when reading about someone who got shot a street over from their house or a car crash that ends in someone's death. And if they do, well, that's a whole other problem I don't want to think about.

My work ends up in the recycling the same day people pick it up to read. If I wrote important stories, memorable ones, my articles wouldn't end up with an empty jug of expired milk in the recycling bin. They'd end up on someone's fridge or in a folder with other collected feel-good stories. They would be the source of someone's smile that day rather than the reason for their tears or their heartbreak. One day I will tell those stories.

Today is not that day though. Today, I have a story to write for an unfair boss who inherited this paper from his unfair father in this unfair life.

CHAPTER TWO

AVERY

A few weeks pass without any other visits to James' office. The news never sleeps and most of the time neither do I. I started to seriously question what I am doing with my life weeks ago. And since then, I haven't been able to get a good night's sleep. Half the time, I end up just getting out of bed and going for a run with my camera to catch the sunrise and take some photos. Running has become my own form of therapy over the years outside of my actual therapy sessions. I used to hate it when I started, because I was doing it for all the wrong reasons. I was doing it because of my mother. Her not-so-subtle comments of me gaining weight or needing to exercise. I was never good enough unless I was small enough. But over the years, I learned to look at everything differently...with the help of my therapist. She reminded me that my worth isn't tied to my weight and running should be a form of stress relief in a way. The end goal shouldn't be to lose weight, it should be to feel healthy and to make my body stronger, not skinnier.

The only good thing to come out of the last few months is my growing friendship with Charlotte. Shortly after she started at the paper, we bonded over our mutual dislike for our boss and my ex which then turned into a lot of wine nights. Movie nights quickly followed and focused on fawning over the men in the main roles, discussing just how many hours it would take in the gym to grow a physique like theirs.

Unlike me though, Charlotte actually likes her job, even if James comes with the territory. She enjoys writing features and compliments my introverted personality with her bright colors and sunny outlook.

I look over at her now curled up and sunk into the other side of my gray sectional. One foot under her, she is dressed in a bright, orange sweater that compliments her red hair, a half-eaten egg roll between her red manicured fingers.

"You need a break," she says. Empty Chinese takeout containers litter my coffee table and we are settled onto my couch, glasses of white wine in hand, *The Little Mermaid* playing in the background.

"I don't even know the last time I took a break," I reply, draining the bottom half of my glass and reaching for the bottle to refill it.

"Then it's the perfect time to take one!" She reaches for my laptop on the coffee table and starts typing. Rubbing my eyes, I sigh and wonder if she's right. I have been completely burnt out at work, not to mention completely miserable. Miserable enough that I know I haven't been the best person to be around lately.

"Oh, this is perfect," Charlotte says as she continues to type. She pauses to pull out her wallet from her purse on the floor and grabs her credit card.

"Wait," I stand and go to her place on the couch, practically sitting on top of her to see the screen. "What are you doing?"

She waves me off. "Shoo. I'm doing what I know you *won't* do."

I try to grab the laptop, but she beats me to it by standing up rapidly, clutching the laptop close to her chest as she navigates around the coffee table. She looks down before tapping a few keys. "Aaaaaaand booked," she says as she hits the touch pad.

"What do you mean 'booked'?"

"I mean, you are booked for a three-week stay at a cute little inn in Blue Grove, Oregon!" She squeals, as the neck of her sweater falls off her right shoulder. Adjusting it, she smiles at me, all her teeth showing.

"Blue Grove?" I ask. "Oregon?"

"Yes! Have you ever been?"

"To Oregon?"

"No, to Blue Grove? It looks like the perfect place to get away. Get some clarity and all of that existential bullshit. It's a small town, quiet; it has the cutest shops, and most importantly, it's a place you need." She sounds genuinely worried about me and honestly, a getaway does sound nice. And I have never been to Oregon.

The city has seemed so overwhelming lately and every time I step outside, I get total sensory overload. There's too much noise, too many people, buildings and too many things happening all at once. A quiet town might be something I could benefit from. She gives me a sultry glare as she pushes her shoulder to her chin like she's trying to flirt, but I know she's joking. Plus, her last girlfriend was totally out of my league and the guy she dated before her would probably never come within two feet of me. "Maybe you'll find a hot lumberjack and you can get laid. Finally relax a little. Shut off that ever present brain of yours," she says, tapping my temple a few times. Her eyebrows raise, a teasing look crossing her features.

"I cannot believe you just did that!" I exclaim. Grabbing the laptop from her, I scroll through the inn's website. The inn is painted a bright red with white shutters and blooming wild-flowers in windowsill boxes that hug the bottom of the french windows. A large porch wraps around it with wooden rocking chairs and benches scattered for seating. I don't hesitate to picture myself rocking in one of those chairs, a steaming mug of coffee curled between my hands as I look out to the pine trees and mountains behind the inn. It does look peaceful.

"Avery?" I forgot Charlotte was here for a split second. Daydreaming of being at that inn.

"You totally want to go," she states at my hesitation.

"No," I deny. "Yes... I don't know. I shouldn't. I have way too much to do here at the paper."

"And I can take over for you there. Next issue."

My job is really the only thing I am worried about, and Charlotte does know how to cover my responsibilities. Am I really going to just drop everything to go to some random small town in the middle of nowhere? Will it really make a difference?

Before I can say anything else, Charlotte jumps up from her place on the couch, glass of wine in hand and makes her way to my bedroom. I set the laptop down on the coffee table and follow her. When I reach my room, she's somehow found my suitcase and is rummaging through my closet picking out clothes and packing them.

"Char, why did you put all these in here?" I say, holding up a few pieces of lingerie.

"Honey, you never know when you are going to need matching underwear, okay? It's for emergencies!" she giggles. I'm cutting her off. No more wine.

I put the items back in the suitcase because what the hell, Charlotte might be right. I resign myself to help her pack the rest of it, picking a variety of clothes. Sweats, t-shirts, hoodies, mostly comfortable clothes. If I'm doing this, the only person I am doing it for is me. I'm not going there to impress anyone, and I'd rather be comfortable while trying to figure out the next step in my life. I know I don't want to stay at the paper forever, so where do I go from here?

"I can't believe you're making me do this."

We finished packing my bags an hour ago and I have moved them from the front door to my bedroom and back again more times than I care to admit, changing my mind every few minutes.

"I already sent James a message from your email. So, yes you are," Charlotte hides a smile behind her wine glass as she takes another sip.

I shoot her a glare, "You did not!"

"I maybe, definitely did."

"Charlotte!"

"Whaaaaaat?" she drawls, picking up one of my bags and taking it outside to my car. She opens the trunk, placing the bag inside before turning toward me. "You have been such a grump around the office and kind of a drag outside of the office too."

"Hey!"

"Well, it's true! You needed a push, and I'm your friend. So I'm giving you a push."

"More like a shove," I mutter, copying her movements and put my other two bags, one containing my camera equipment, in the trunk and straighten up next to her.

She nudges my arm with her elbow. "A good shove though."

I know she's right and I'm not sure why I'm being so stubborn about leaving, but something is nagging me about doing this for myself. I've spent years trying to build my career, while navigating relationships that always turn out horribly, especially the shattered one with my mother.

I don't count on that one ever being repaired, though. Ever. It's shattered like baseball-through-the-window shattered. She can try to patch it up with plastic wrap and tape, but that's a solution that only works for her. Which is the only one she cares about. My whole childhood, she made it seem like taking care of me was something that wasn't necessary. It was something that came in last place when competing with her and her life. While most parents put their kids first, Sharon did the opposite and I always came in last.

Charlotte closes the trunk, startling me back to the present. "Alright, you are set to go tomorrow morning."

"I guess I'm running away to the mountains," I finally say out loud. As soon as the words permeate the air, my brain begins to quiet for the first time in a long time.

"To find your lumberjack!"

I roll my eyes and place my arm around her shoulders. We walk back into the house and finish off the bottle of wine. Charlotte falls asleep soon after sprawled out on the couch. I cover her up with a blanket and tiptoe back to my bedroom, careful not to wake her. I realize later when I stub my toe loudly on the leg of my bed, I don't need to tiptoe. The woman sleeps like a toddler worn out from a long day outside. I can probably have a dance party and she wouldn't even stir. I curl up in my down comforter and think about what it will be like to have no responsibilities for almost a month. No boss, no editor, no breaking news, no articles. Just me, my camera, and my running shoes. I fall asleep with images of the mountains, mist from an early morning masking a field of wildflowers.

CHAPTER THREE

AVERY

*B*lue Grove, Oregon is the smallest town I have ever been to. Well, way smaller than what I am used to at least. But it's arguably the most beautiful. I drove through the day only making occasional stops for fuel and crappy gas station coffee. My original plan was to rest at a hotel at one point along the thirteen-hour drive, but my nerves were on edge and I didn't want to waste any more time. Once I was on the road, I had the urge to get to my destination as soon as possible.

I pray to any gods that might be listening that this town has a coffee shop of some kind because I am *desperate* for a good peppermint latte. Gas station coffee can only go so far, and it has officially reached the end of its journey.

It feels weird being in a place that isn't constantly on the go. It almost seems as if Blue Grove is moving in slow motion, waiting for the rest of the world to match its pace.

I quickly find that I'm okay with slow.

I'm excited for slow.

Malibu is filled with people at every corner. Everywhere I turn, there's a new face. I don't think I came across the same face twice in one week, and if I did, it was a miracle if I even remembered them. Or their name, if I had time to talk to them. Which, again, was a rare occurrence. I like to keep to myself, so something like this isn't my go-to. Introverted mindset at its finest.

But this trip is going to be different. I'm here to meet people. Push myself out of my comfort zone even though I'd much rather grab pillows and blankets, build a fort, and burrow myself so far into my comfort zone, no one could ever find me. I'm here to discover what might be next for me or whatever clandestine bullshit it is that Charlotte wants me to do. In conclusion, this trip is exhilarating and terrifying all in one. A thing of nightmares, while also something out of one of my romance novels. But I am determined to defeat the monster under the bed, while also still searching for a weapon. My anxiety keeps me in the dark.

I feel that familiar spike at the idea of traveling to a brand new place filled with people I don't know. I've dealt with strangers as anyone does throughout my life and it has never gotten easier. I feel that all too-familiar pressure in my chest spreading to my lungs. Seizing them until my breath is stolen. I count to ten in my head and focus on the road ahead of me. Count the senses.

Sight. The long yellow lines speeding past.

Sound. The whipping wind from my open window.

Smell. Pine and fresh air.

Taste. Stale coffee from the last gas station I stopped at.

Touch. The chipping leather from my steering wheel cover digs into my palms as I grip the wheel, my knuckles turning white.

I clench my hands. Unclench. Clench. Unclench. Repeat. Until I feel the panic and the pressure in my chest start to fade. I take a deep breath and roll down my windows further, the smell of fresh pine fully invading my senses and instantly calming my spiraling thought pattern. I look at the trees and wonder how quickly I can manage to find a good hiking trail. Something I haven't really done since I was a kid exploring the woods in my backyard.

My body relaxes. There... better.

I'm no stranger to panic attacks. I was only eight years old when I had my first one and I was convinced I was dying. My mother told me I was being dramatic and acting for attention. But I really thought the pressure in my chest would crack me open. Expose me from the inside out, my guts spilling on the floor like a broken egg.

When the doctor explained that I had a panic attack, she laughed. "See? I told you. You were overreacting."

The doctor suggested counseling to talk about my anxiety and figure out what caused it, but mom laughed in her face and took me home. She never talked about it or asked me anything relating to it, so I never brought it up to her again. I learned to cope in silence and always hid in my closet when I felt an attack coming on.

There was one thing my mother was right about though. I didn't need a therapist to tell me where my anxiety came from. The source was sitting right next to me in that doctor's office. Perfectly wrapped in her pepto bismol colored pants suit, bleach blond wig in place on her head, not a strand out of place. She held herself on the highest pedestal, and her daughter had to be on an even higher one, balancing to meet her expectations.

She didn't care that my balance was shit.

I shake my head, making the image of my mother disappear from my mind. Nothing good ever comes out of thinking of her. Ever.

Hiking trails. Right. I'll ask around at the inn to see what trails are close by. That was one thing Charlotte didn't consider when she booked this trip. Then again, she doesn't strike me as the outdoorsy type. I don't think I can picture her hiking and getting her shoes scuffed up, covered in mud. But that's how you know it's been a good hike, when barely any surface of the shoe is showing beneath the dirt and mud.

I pass a faded blue and white sign with the words, *Welcome to Blue Grove Inn. Est. in 1895.* The inn is tucked off the edge of a remote country road with pine trees on one side and a decent sized barn on the other. I can spot the mountains behind the inn, three peaks prominent in the distance.

The red paint covering the exterior is faded, the white shutters slightly worn. The wood beneath peeks through the chipped paint showing the passage of time since it last resembled the pristine picture Charlotte showed me on the website. Rustling from the horses in the barn and the squeak of the porch swing fills the air. Birds singing in the background, a slight breeze, swaying the flowers in front of the inn.

Too perfect. Too good to be true.

My heart surges as I step up the creaky stairs to the front door. The main door hangs open behind a screened one, letting in the mountain air. When I step inside, I am greeted by soft chatter coming from what looks to be the dining area. People are crowded at tables, some with coffee in front of them, others with plates half covered with food.

A younger boy with sandy hair runs from one of the tables to my side. "Hi!" He says, startling me with the amount of enthusiasm he puts behind his greeting.

"Um, uh, h-hi," I stutter.

"Where are your bags?" he asks. "I gotta take your bags," he pauses. "Oh…uh, ma'am," he adds, like he remembers it's something he's supposed to say.

I smile at him. He can't be more than ten years old, and I really hate being called ma'am, even if I am a year away from 30, but I'll let it slide.

"They're in my trunk," I point my thumb in the direction of my car. "I thought I'd get checked in first."

"Sure!" He exclaims and promptly makes his way behind the check-in desk. A wall of keys with numbers etched on the side covers the surface. He starts pressing the keys in front of him, kneeling on the chair so he can see the screen better.

"Name, please?" He asks with a professional tone that's at least ten miles above James'. I wonder how angry he was this morning when I didn't show up. Charlotte sent him a short email from my computer letting him know I wouldn't be in, and not to expect me for at least three weeks.

JAMES,

I am using my vacation days that I have and won't be in the office for three weeks. I won't be reachable by phone or email, but Charlotte will pick up any slack.

Avery

THAT WAS IT. No one can say Charlotte doesn't get straight to the point.

"Avery Reid," I answer.

I look down at the boy who is now sticking his tongue out between his teeth in concentration and slowly types in my name with his index fingers, saying each letter out loud as he goes.

"A...V...E...R...Y." He hits enter, the screen lighting up with my check-in confirmation and his eyes brighten. "Granny, I did it!"

Wait, who's he calling granny? I know I probably look ancient to him, most people about 25 and up do to little kids. But I know I don't look old enough to be called granny.

Before I can respond, an older lady with long silver hair, one side pinned back, appears next to him. Her gaze goes from him to the computer. "Oh, great job, kiddo!" She offers him a high five before he jumps from the chair and heads outside in the direction of my car. Assuming he's off to get my luggage, I turn to the woman.

"Cute kid," I chuckle. "Very grown-up."

She lets out a sigh.

"If he could, he'd make himself older in a heartbeat. I always remind him to just enjoy being eight, you know? But what can I say? He really loves helping around here when he can."

Suitcases thump against the door frame as the sandy-haired boy struggles to get all my luggage inside. Setting it all down just inside the door, he collapses right next to it.

"Ethan, you could have just taken two trips, you know."

"This…was…faster," he says in between breaths.

She holds out her hand to me, laughing at Ethan, "I'm Cordelia, by the way, but you can call me Cordie. Or Granny, like everyone else. That heap on the floor is Ethan," she points to Ethan who is now completely sprawled out on the floor like he's about to make an imaginary snow angel. He's still working on catching his breath.

Ethan raises a hand above him and gives me a slight wave before letting his hand collapse with a thump beside him.

"Nice to meet you, Ethan. I'm Avery."

"I know. I checked you in like two minutes ago." He suddenly sits up and looks me dead in the eyes. Suspicious. "Do you have short term memory loss?" He asks like it's the most important question he's ever asked in his life. "Like Dory?"

"Uh, no. I just wanted to properly introduce myself to the young man who has been so helpful."

"Dang, that's too bad," he hangs his head and I see a hint of sadness in his eyes. I glance over at Cordie hoping she might give me some kind of direction as to where I should take this conversation, but she just looks at me and shrugs her frail shoulders. Clearly, I am on my own. It's been so long since I have had any interaction with kids, so I am not sure exactly where Ethan is going with this, but I decide to try to play along.

"Oh? And why is that?" I ask, wondering why he wishes anyone would have short term memory loss.

"Because, then you could have a lot of adventures over and over!" He exclaims like it's the most obvious answer in the world. To be as innocent as a little kid. A dream.

"Tell you what," I say, considering. "Next time I see you, I'll pretend I haven't met you and we can meet all over again. Deal?"

He jumps up, acting like it is the best thing he's heard all day. "Okay! Thanks, Dory!" Collecting my bags, he starts to go up the stairs to where I assume the rooms are located.

"Thanks for indulging him," says Cordie.

"Yeah, thanks for the help," I say sarcastically. I give her a shrug after a beat of silence. "He seems like a good kid though."

"He's a great kid," she pauses as if she's contemplating whether she should say more. She decides against it and hands me my room key. "Here you go. You're in room number three. Just follow the loud noises of an eight year old trying to be the hero and take all your luggage in one trip."

I climb the deep brown wooden stairs, creaks from my footsteps filling the air. I suddenly feel the exhaustion in my legs from being cramped in the car all day and all I can think about is burrowing in whatever blankets are in the room. Ethan is leaning up against the door of room three waiting for me, his elbows perched on his knees and his butt firmly planted on one of the suitcases.

"Thanks, Nemo," I wink and unlock the door. "I can take it from here."

"Okay! Later Dory!" He waves and races back down the stairs leaving me to explore the room that is going to be my home for a few weeks. Three weeks to be exact.

I grin at the room number. A gold-plated three screwed into the wooden door. Charlotte is going to lose her shit when I tell her.

"Your lucky number," she had said before I left. "Three weeks to find your lumberjack." I rolled my eyes, knowing she wasn't going to stop with the lumberjack jokes. She is nothing if not a very determined person. Or a very determined matchmaker.

I let her have her fun though. I may not know exactly what I need, but I don't think Charlotte's imaginary lumberjack is one of them.

As soon as I get settled in the room, I crash. The thirteen-hour drive has finally caught up with me and being in a car for that long at 29 years old isn't as easy as it was in my early twenties. I remember going on weekend road trips with my college friends for hours and hours, and still somehow managing to have the energy to stay out drinking, dancing, and doing everything we could fit into one night. Now, I am lucky to get my shoes off without making a face because of my back.

After a full night of sleep and one hour of staring at the high wooden ceiling with exposed beams, I decide it's time to explore. It's what I came here for, but I can't bring myself to move. The down comforter and the pillows have me in their embrace and I don't want to break from it just yet. I continue my staredown with the ceiling, determined to win a game that doesn't exist.

The ceiling reminds me of an unfinished ship with the beams crossing at integral parts. The beams are the start of something bigger. Each one with a purpose. A job. One that if it wasn't done, if one beam broke, the whole thing would collapse. I'm afraid that's what my life is becoming. There's one beam that holds it all together, becoming unsteady and I'm unsure of how much longer I can keep it stable and in place before it cracks, bringing the whole ship crashing down in a pile of broken pieces. The ship being me.

I swipe the thoughts away like a windshield wiper swiping away the rain during a downpour and jump from the bed. I throw on my joggers and a tank top, a crew neck tied around my waist in case I get cold later. One thing I have learned over the years is no matter how warm it is outside, I'm always cold. Always bring a sweatshirt.

It's amazing how much the weather can change over an 830-mile drive. I think I hit every type of weather possible on the way here. I glance outside before leaving and see dense fog and no blue sky, so I just might need the sweatshirt earlier than planned. I'm so used to the heat in Malibu, being able to cozy up in sweats for an early morning walk will be a nice change. I grab my camera and sling it over my shoulder before closing the door behind me, locking it with the key.

I skip down the stairs and find Cordie and Ethan at the front desk, heads together and what looks to be a small orange scarf between their hands. Their whispering stops as soon as they notice me coming and Ethan quickly hides the scarf behind his back.

"And just what are you two up to?" I offer a mischievous grin. Ethan looks at Cordie who gives him a shrug, leaving it to him to decide whether to include me in their shenanigans.

He looks around the corner to his left and then around the desk to his right. When he is satisfied the coast is clear, he motions me closer. "I'm only telling you this because you won't remember. Okay, Dory?"

"Got it, Nemo." I tell him while doing my best to hold back my laughter. I love this kid. I don't care if I just met him yesterday. The magic in his small child eyes is infectious.

"It's a game between me and my uncle."

"Oh?" I say with extra excitement to match his tone.

He leans even closer, his nose almost touching my cheek. "Ever heard of capture the flag?" He whispers.

I answer with a nod and wait for him to continue.

"Well, we have a game that never ends around town. He hides his flag. I hide mine. And whoever finds the other person's flag first gets a point. I'm *at least* ten points ahead of Uncle Hud. He *never* finds my flag...because I'm a good hider," he adds.

"And where are you going to hide it this time?"

"That's what me and Granny were just whispering about. I have the perfect place."

Without waiting for a response, he heads for the dining room, the silence the complete opposite from last night. He zig zags in-between the tables until he reaches the one in the furthest corner of the room. The table is clean and set for the day's meals with a small round piece of wood covered with a doily and a mason jar of wildflowers on top. Ethan picks up the jar and doily and spreads his orange-colored flag on top of the wood. He places the items on top of his flag obscuring it from view almost completely. No one would know it's there unless they were specifically looking for an orange flag.

"Now *that* is the perfect hiding place," I tell him.

"I know! Uncle Hud will never find it. If you see him, you better play dumb."

I hold up my right hand, "Scout's honor. My lips are sealed." He looks at me dumbfounded.

"You're strange, Dory. I like you."

"I like you too, kiddo."

The bell above the door chimes as I step out of Cordie's inn and onto the sidewalk, camera in tow. There is something about this town. A presence I can't shake, similar to trying to recall a memory and it slips away on the cusp of recollection.

Before I head to find the coffee shop Cordie mentioned, I take a photo of the front of the building, documenting its weathered appearance. I wonder if there is something I can do for her while I am here. The inn definitely needs some updating on the exterior and I don't think it's something Cordie can do on her own. I'll have to remember to ask her when I come back later if there is anything I can pitch in with while I'm here. My stay isn't expensive, and I have a feeling Cordie hasn't adjusted her prices since she opened.

Taking the ribbon I chose this morning, white with yellow polka dots, out of my back pocket, I tie up half my hair to keep it out of my face. That was one thing I couldn't leave California without: my box of ribbons. I've been collecting them for years and lost count of exactly how many I have a long time ago. There's just something about actually tying my hair up that is satisfying, and seeing how many unique patterns I can find is a fun game. Stripes, polka dots, flowers, sometimes animals. Hedgehogs being my favorite. Sometimes hedgehogs with flowers. The cutest.

After walking down the long gravel driveway, I look around main street and see that it is lined with a collection of businesses. A few doors down from Cordie's driveway is an outdoor shop with a deep blue sign, white letters striking against the background. *Sky's the Limit.* I walk slowly past the windows and get a glance of the merchandise. From the window, I spot canoes, fishing and hunting gear, a big fish tank and what I hope is hiking gear near the back. Making a mental note to stop by later, I take a quick picture of the front door covered with loopy lettering displaying the store's hours on it. They don't close until six, which gives me plenty of time to familiarize myself with the town and my surroundings before coming back to get hiking gear for tomorrow.

Just the thought of being among the trees on a path I'm not entirely certain on where it ends fills me with so much joy; more joy than I have felt in years. Losing my connection with the woods and the creeks is one thing I do regret about my move to California, but it's also one I can fix over the next three weeks.

My phone buzzes in my pocket and I pull it out to see Charlotte's face, tongue sticking out, looking back at me. She must have changed her contact picture the other night.

"Hey!" Enthusiasm coats my voice and I find that for once, I'm not faking it.

"Hey Mountain Girl! How's the trip so far?"

"It's good," I say. "Everyone in town is really sweet. I feel like I'm in Stars Hollow, to be honest. Huge small town Stars Hollow vibes."

"Is there a grumpy diner owner who only wears flannel and a backwards baseball cap? Or have you met your lumberjack?"

I laugh. She's never letting that one go.

"No and no," I continue walking across the street and spot a wooden sign in the shape of a coffee mug sitting on top of a stack of books with words scrawled on the spine, *Books & Beans Coffee Shop*. Coffee, finally. Peppermint latte, here I come. Summer weather be damned. My craving for a hot latte comes first.

"I'm actually out exploring the town right now. First stop, coffee." I flip the camera so she can see the sign.

"Books *and* coffee? Can I join you on your trip and live there please?"

"Maybe next time," I laugh and turn the screen back to my face.

Charlotte's mom used to own a bookstore and I know she tried to convince her mom for years to combine it with a coffee shop, but she never got the chance to before she died. I don't know much about her mom, but I know enough to know she was the complete opposite of mine.

The bells above the double glass doors chime as I enter. This town clearly has a thing for bells. The overwhelming smell of espresso fills my senses and I take a deep inhale of the bitter roast, the best smell in the entire world.

"Flip me around, I want to see! I need to take my mind off work stuff and live vicariously through you."

I flip the screen again and scan my surroundings with her. The shop is filled with chatter of nearby customers, some sitting and reading with half full cups of coffee or half eaten pastries in front of them. A few people are sitting by themselves with their laptops on and headphones in to block out their surroundings. The display case in front of me is filled with an assortment of pastries, muffins, pies, cookies, a few cakes, and some scattered cupcakes. I think I found my new favorite place.

An older woman behind the counter greets me with a warm smile. Her silver hair is tied up into a knot on top of her head reminding me of Dame Maggie Smith in *Downton Abbey*. She adjusts her glasses, a simple gold chain hanging from the frames that snakes around her neck. A crocheted shawl that looks to be handmade, probably by her, hangs loosely around her shoulders with a floral-patterned button-up underneath.

"How can I help you, dear?" she asks in a voice smooth as butter.

"Do you have peppermint lattes?"

"It's actually one of the things this little shop is famous for. That and our blueberry scones. And my cinnamon bread."

I give her a genuine smile. One that hasn't been present on my face in a long time. Most of my smiles are there to just get me through the day.

"I'll take a peppermint latte for now with an extra shot of espresso and skim milk if you have it, please. Maybe I'll come back for some cinnamon bread tomorrow."

"I'll add it to my list to make later and set it aside for you, honey."

Stunned by her kindness, I look up from my wallet where I am fishing out some cash I stuffed in there before I left my place and give her the warmest smile I have ever given anyone.

"That's so sweet of you—"

"Fran," she says.

"Fran. It's nice to meet you. I'm Avery. I'm visiting for a few weeks. Staying at the inn a few blocks down."

"Cordie is my roommate, so I kind of already knew who you were before you came in here. I didn't want to scare you off though. I'm glad you came in so I could see what you looked like. 'Stunning' is how Cordie described you and I'd have to say I agree."

I hear Charlotte let out a whistle, cat-calling me from the phone.

Before I can thank her or say anything for that matter, she gets to work making my drink. It seems all second nature to her. Pouring the syrup in one of those metal cups I see baristas use all the time. Pulling the shot, except hers is an automatic and all she has to do is press a button and let the espresso trickle down into the cup. While she waits for the shots to finish, she pours the milk into the cup not bothering to look at the measurements like she's done it a million times before and can tell how much milk she pours from the weight of the cup alone. Once the milk is steamed, she pours that into a paper cup wrapped in a sleeve with the sign on the front pictured, and adds the espresso on top, careful to not disrupt the foam too much.

"Thank you," I say as I place the money I grabbed on the counter, but she waves it off with a wrinkled hand.

"It's on the house, sweetheart. First time customer and new to town. Enjoy."

Sweetheart. The third endearment since I've walked in. It's been a long time since anyone has called me anything other than my name. I like it, I decide. I like *her.*

Fran embodies everything a grandmother should be. Warm smiles, long hugs and by the looks of the pastries and other baked goods in the display case, baking skills that would give Paul Hollywood from the *Great British Bake Off* good competition. I instantly feel better in her presence, her warm glow infectious, invading my senses like the smell of fresh apple pie right out of the oven.

"Well, she's the cutest. Can you ask her to adopt me, please?" Charlotte says.

I take a sip of my latte... nope. I don't like Fran. I love her. This coffee is the best thing I have ever tasted. Angels have broken out into the hallelujah chorus. I used to worship the coffee gods, but now I worship Fran. She's secretly a coffee goddess sent down to create the one thing that keeps the world going. Grandmotherly love and the world's best latte.

I go to take another sip, completely lost in my new obsession with Fran when a man stands up from where he must have been crouching behind the counter. The coffee cup stalls halfway to my lips.

Grease coats his palms, and he repositions the other espresso machine next to the one Fran used to make my latte. "There yah go, Fran," he says, wiping his hands on a rag hanging from his back pocket.

A red flannel covers his broad shoulders and I find myself wondering what muscles it hides underneath. Strands of dark hair fall from the bun perched on top of his head and into his eyes. He casually brushes it back with his hand, leaving a single smudge of grease behind on his forehead.

"Thank you, Hudson. These frail bones can't fix much anymore. Especially when I have to move it like that. I can never get the damn thing working."

"No worries," he responds. "That'll at least hold it over until Elias gets back in town."

"God willing," she muses. She bends down and grabs a scone out of the display case and hands it to him. "For your trouble."

"Ah, Fran, you know the way to my heart," he places a kiss on her cheek, and I suddenly wish I was Fran. Are his lips as soft as they look? Does his short beard feel scruffy? How long is his hair when it's down? What would it look like with my fingers tangled in it? A soft laugh escapes Fran's lips.

"And your stomach. Is there anything else I can get you, darlin'?"

It takes me a moment to realize she is talking to me and I have been staring at their exchange this whole time. Hell, I've been staring at *him*, my brain apparently short circuited and I forgot to look away. Still, I stand transfixed to my spot. My feet are glued. Or nailed to the floor rather. Whatever they are, they aren't moving. I'm here for good. Call Cordie and cancel my reservation, because here I'll stay, staring at the man in front of me. Ogling him for all eternity while Fran supplies me with an endless supply of peppermint lattes.

I swallow as my gaze drifts to his bare forearms and the veins that stretch up to his elbows like vines snaking up a tree. Who knew forearms were my kryptonite? I'm a sweet tooth and he's one of those huge rainbow lollipops wrapped in clear plastic, tied closed with a neat little bow.

"Holy shit," I hear Charlotte say. I forgot I still had the camera flipped in front of me. I switch it back. "Avery, you should see how deep you are blushing right now." I glance at her, eyes wide warning her to shut up. "Don't give me that look," she says. "If you don't try to jump on that, I am getting in my car and driving there right now."

She's laughing so loud eyes are starting to turn my way. "I'll call you later Charlotte," I say quickly before pressing the red button, silencing my phone once again. "Sorry, um…uh," I glance at the display case and then back at the man who is eating his scone, no care in the world. If he noticed my stare before, it didn't faze him in the slightest. "One of those scones, please. They look really good." Good in the display. Definitely not talking about the one inches from the man's mouth. Nope. Not that one.

"Because they are," Fran says proudly, but she looks back at the man she called Hudson and gives me a knowing smile.

"Hudson, have you met Avery? She's staying at Cordie's during her stay." She wraps the scone in a napkin and holds it out for me.

I mutter my thanks as Hudson takes a step forward to discard his now empty napkin into the bin. "No." His tone is clipped. Sharp. Grumpy. He clearly doesn't care about Fran's introduction.

"Don't take offense," Fran reassures me. "He's like that with everyone. The town grump. That's what Sky calls him anyway."

Hudson rolls his eyes and retreats to the back without

another word or a glance in my direction. It's difficult not to take offense considering how perfectly pleasant he was with Fran just minutes before.

"It's okay." It isn't, but I'm not here to make friends. "Thanks for this." I gesture to the coffee and scone.

"Anytime. Come back tomorrow and I'll have that cinnamon bread. I'll also have fresh lemon bars in the morning!" She calls before I make it all the way out the door. I smile. I have no idea how she knew, coincidence or sneaky grandma intuition (I'll go with the latter), but lemon bars are my favorite.

CHAPTER FOUR

HUDSON

*N*o.

That's all I said. That's all I cared to say. I don't know if she noticed, but I caught her staring at my forearms while talking with Fran. The hair on my skin rose like it could sense her gaze the moment it landed on me.

And when I looked at her... *damn*. When I looked at her, I felt all the air leave the room and I needed her voice to breathe. I escaped to the back because I knew nothing good would come out of my mouth. If I keep it shut, I can't stick my big foot in it.

I'm not good with words and I'm sure she didn't come to town for someone like me. No one does. And no one stays for someone like me either.

But, dammit, I wish she had. I haven't thought about dating for a long time. I've had flings here and there, but nothing long term. I don't care to deal with relationships. Especially after what happened to my sister.

Her death became a dark rain cloud over us and I haven't managed to escape from under it yet. Not that I have really made an effort to. After she died, my brother-in-law, Elias, and my nephew, Ethan, became my priority. They deserved some sense of normalcy when they moved back here and I was—and still am—determined to give it to them.

So, why did my heart start pounding at the sight of her? Why did my mind jump to wondering what her hair would look like if I tugged on the ribbon holding it together, slowly untying it, letting it cascade to the floor in my bedroom to join the rest of her discarded clothes?

The sound of Fran's shuffling footsteps pull me out of my thoughts and I brace myself for what I know is coming. I feel the sting of a damp rag on my shoulder blade, leaving a wet spot behind. "Boy, what was that?"

"What was what?" I play dumb. I may know exactly what she's talking about, but it doesn't mean I have to give her the satisfaction of having a conversation about it.

"You know better than to treat people with disrespect. Your parents brought you up better than that," she states. "I know you've been through the ringer, but we all have and that doesn't give you the excuse to act any other way besides decent."

I look down at my boots thinking about her late husband, Henry, and let out a long sigh.

"I'm sorry, Fran. I didn't mean to be rude. I just wasn't sure what to say."

"Oh, I don't know, maybe, 'Nice to meet you?' You act like you've never had any kind of social interaction with a woman, sheesh."

The oven timer dings, and steam escapes when Fran opens the door and pulls out the fresh cookies. A sweet, sugary smell invades the air around us and I let out a groan. "Fran, is there anything you can't bake?"

She swats my hand away from the mint chocolate chip cookies and places them on the counter. "No," she responds. "But my sugar cookies always need work. Henry was the best at those." She goes quiet as she uses a spatula to move the cookies to a cooling rack. Her features soften as she remembers her husband.

Henry had a bulky frame, contrasting Fran's small one. He was loud, boisterous and never went a day without having a conversation with everyone who came in to buy a cup of coffee or a book. He always knew the exact book you needed after one conversation too. He was magic and he took a bit of that magic with him when he died. The shop hasn't been the same without him and neither has the town. Fran still has his recommendations featured on a display under *Henry's Picks* so people who come in can remember him and maybe read some of the books he loved so much.

"I miss that man," she says softly.

"We all do," I say.

After she's done with the cookies, she levels me with the look she gives when she's about to tell me something she knows I don't want to hear. "Don't be stupid."

Without another word, she brushes past me with a soft pat on my bicep and shuffles back up front.

I grab a latte and pastries for the road and get in my red pickup truck. I pull away from Fran's, ignoring the woman walking down the sidewalk, hair tied up in a white ribbon with yellow polka dots that look like miniature suns.

Don't be stupid.

I have a feeling those words are going to be the opposite of what I do.

MY TRUCK SPUTTERS to a stop in front of my parents' house, reminding me I need to take it to Axel's to get it fixed.

Axel. A little on the nose for a mechanic, but his dad was adamant about it. He's been my best friend since high school and we're probably the most troublesome pair to ever go through Blue Grove. There usually wasn't a time one of us wasn't in detention. We grew up just down the street from each other and he's been a pain in my ass since.

I gather the pastries and coffee, let out a long sigh and prepare myself as much as I can for the ribbing I know is coming. It's Sunday, which means breakfast from Fran's at my parents' house with Elias and Ethan, and Sky if she ever decides to show up again. The whole family will be ready to gossip the moment they know there's someone new in town, but it isn't going to come from me. If it was up to me, they'd never even know about her, but this town is filled with way too many busybodies more invested in everyone else's life.

Before I can get up the steps leading up to the porch, the front door flies open revealing my mother, dressed in her "Sunday best" as she calls it. A long, navy blue skirt that reaches just below her knees with a white and blue striped button up, her sleeves rolled to her elbows. Her blonde hair is held up by a small clip, a few strands of gray coming loose around her face. She wipes her hand on the apron tied around her waist and grabs the pastries from me.

"Tell me about her," she says as she walks to the kitchen. I shake my head as I follow her. This town wastes no time. She moves a few ingredients for the cookies she makes on Sundays to make room for the box of pastries.

"I left Fran's less than five minutes ago," I tell her. "Which one called you?" It was either Fran or Cordie. Town gossipers. The whole town gossips, but those two are the worst. Or the best at it. I swear, the gossip fuels their souls in a way that is going to make them outlive us all.

Both widowed, they decided to live together after their husbands passed away to keep each other company. They didn't see a point in living alone; didn't like the idea of waking up to an empty house after having a partner for so long. I'm the opposite. I like solitude. I prefer my space and have never liked the idea of someone else in my house, taking it up.

Before she can answer, the door flies open again, followed by quick, thundering footsteps. Ethan appears around the corner and makes a beeline for mom. I'm convinced the day she became a grandmother was the best day of her life.

"Nana!" He yells, jumping into her arms like he doesn't see her almost every day. When he and Elias don't stay with me, they're usually with my parents.

"Hi baby!" She wraps her arms around him and squeezes, planting a kiss to the top of his head. I swear that kid grows an inch every week. Not long ago, his arms hugged her around the thighs rather than the waist. He's grown up a lot in the last three years. More than he should have.

"Grab the flour and help me finish these while your uncle tells me about this girl." Ethan follows her directions and ignores the second half of what she said. So do I.

I grab a pastry from the box, another blueberry scone, and shove half of it in my mouth so I have an excuse not to answer.

A hand claps my back followed by a low chuckle. "You're not getting out of it that easy," says Elias. "You're the only one here who's met her, so spill." My brother-in-law is just as bad as Fran and Cordie. Busybody. He sits on the stool next to me and perches his elbows on his knees, his chin on a closed fist and fans his eyelashes at me like he's a Disney character begging for more chocolates.

"C'mon, what does she look like?" He's baiting me. He knows I hate talking about anything to do with town news, town gossip, and new people. I can't help it. I like the familiar. My cabin, my dogs, my parents, Ethan, sometimes Elias, definitely not right now though. At this particular moment, he is crossed off my list of people I like.

"No idea. I met her at Fran's for two seconds. I didn't pay attention," I lie. I know exactly what she was wearing, the color and length of her hair—blonde ponytail reaching just below her shoulder blades—and the fact that she was talking to a friend on FaceTime. Hell, if he asked, I could tell him the color of shoes she was wearing. Navy, with bright white laces. I shake my head, emptying it of all thoughts of her. I don't need someone new in my life. My family is my priority and I want to keep it that way.

"Liar," Elias mutters back. He drops the conversation for now, but I know it won't be the last I hear of it.

I bring the coffee and pastries to the long kitchen table where my dad is sitting, the Sunday paper spread open in front of him. One indication of the world coming to an end would be if Dad didn't have the Sunday paper open to the crossword puzzle, sitting at the breakfast table, pencil in hand.

"What's a wildflower species that is eight letters long?" He asks, zeroing in on me.

"Dad, the point of the crossword is to do it yourself," I say. It never matters what clues are on the crossword, every Sunday he asks for help. Last Sunday, he asked me for the answer to a nine-letter dog breed. Wildflower species and dog breeds. Apparently that's all the knowledge I'm good for. That, and the appearance of a new, beautiful face in town. *Nope.* Not going there. Not today.

"Ahh," he groans, waving a hand in my direction. "Help your old man out."

"Dad, one of these days, you need to finish a whole cross-word by yourself."

"Oh, c'mon," he pleads.

"Nope, figure it out yourself."

"But I don't know any wildflower types," he answers stubbornly.

"How can you live in this town all your life, just a few miles from the mountains where there are *thousands* of wildflowers nearby, *multiple* species, and not know a single name for them?"

"Wildflowers are wildflowers. They're all the same," he pushes his thick-framed glasses up his nose and returns his eyes to the paper. "It starts with a 'b' and ends with an 'x'. How am I supposed to know that?"

"Blue Flax!" says a voice from the kitchen. Damnit, Ethan. I can't count the number of times he's asked the name of every plant we walk by on a hike. He loves nature and is a bottomless pit of questions.

"Hah!" My dad gloats. "At least someone in the family is willing to offer a helping hand. Thank you, my favorite grandson!" he shouts back to Ethan.

He giggles, "I'm your *only* grandson!"

"Well then, my favorite young man currently in this house."

"Hey!" exclaims Elias. "What about me?"

"Ethan wins, sorry," Dad says in a voice that doesn't come across as apologetic whatsoever.

"Eh, he wins in my book too, I guess." Elias looks over at Ethan with a fondness in his eyes that only a father can have for his son. A warm smile spreads across his features, followed by a sad one. A look that has been ever present over time. It has been that way for the last three years since Sarah died. My sister left a void behind in our family that can't be filled. An emptiness we have all felt over the years. The kind that is always present. Never leaving. Waiting in the darkest corners of the room for us to let our guard down so it can creep in, reminding us of what we have lost.

Her breast cancer diagnosis was a shock to all of us. Her and

Elias moved back home from Seattle to be closer to family so we could help them. She died a year later.

When she and Elias got married, they moved to Seattle and she opened a coffee shop, a dream she had held onto since she was a kid. Her coffee could give Fran a run for her money. Then again, Sarah spent most of her free time, summers, weekends, any time after school that she wasn't doing homework, at *Books & Beans* learning everything she could from Fran. Sarah wasn't made for the small-town life. She always talked about leaving. Doing bigger things. Running her own coffee shop in Seattle was her bigger thing. Her dream. She lived that dream for four years until she was diagnosed. She was forced to sell her shop so her and Elias could afford the chemo she needed.

She was in remission at one point even, but it came back more aggressive, and she didn't have a chance.

Her final summer, she spent as much time with us and Elias and Ethan as she possibly could. Small hikes, fishing in my lake, playing fetch with Ethan and the dogs, late-night scrabble sessions with me when she couldn't sleep. I couldn't sleep either. Not while knowing she could be gone the next morning. Sleep still didn't come easily for me. And when it did, it was often interrupted by nightmares of waking up that morning. Seeing her. Knowing she was gone as soon as my eyes opened. There was a change in the air and something in me just knew when I looked over, my sister wouldn't be there anymore. And she wasn't.

Elias spent the majority of his time taking care of her. A sick wife and a five year old weren't easy to manage alone and Elias knew that. He wasn't stupid. He knew the odds when the doctors told them it was stage four. Sarah knew the odds too, but all she said when her doctor listed them was, "fuck the odds." And did everything she could to beat it. But in the end, the odds won out.

Images of that last night filter through my head, playing

Scrabble, the black and white movie, the sadness, the laughs, the dark feeling I had when I woke up, and the nightmares that have plagued me ever since. Cold sweats, hyperventilating, and uncontrollable shaking take over and it takes hours to finally shake it off, and I am still never able to go back to sleep.

Ethan's nearing footsteps bring me back to the present, drawing me out of temporary grief. "Uncle Hud, guess what?"

If he says "chicken butt" I'm throwing him over my shoulder and into the pool in the backyard. I raise my eyebrows signaling him to go on.

"I hid my flag and you'll never *ever* find it," he brags with the biggest, most mischievous grin on his face.

"Oh, really?"

"Really!" He says, confidently.

"I bet I'll find it by Wednesday."

"No chance! I'll find yours by tomorrow morning. You probably haven't even hid yours yet."

"Hey, I still have," I tip my wrist up and glance at my watch. "Two hours to hide mine, kiddo."

"Well, you'll never find mine. It's in the *perfect* place. Only Granny and Dory know."

"Dory?" I ask. I know everyone's name in town and there definitely is no one called Dory.

"Yeah, but she won't remember, because she has short term memory loss."

Thoroughly confused, I shake my head and make a mental note to visit Cordie sometime this week. Preferably at a time when Avery is out, but I'll chance it. *For the game,* I lie to myself. I've been on a losing streak for weeks and it isn't on purpose. Ethan is either really good at finding my flags or I am really shit at hiding them.

Either way, it's a game that started a few months after Sarah died. Ethan was really struggling and he didn't fully understand what happened, only that his mom was gone and there wasn't a way to bring her back.

He always had an interest in hiding things. Elias often told stories about him hiding his toy cars around the house. Him or Sarah would open drawers, cabinets, closets, and more often than not, there would be a little toy car nestled there, waiting to be found. It never bothered them to find the cars. They'd just find them and laugh like it was the most adorable thing in the world.

After a while, I knew Ethan needed some kind of distraction. Something to take his mind off of wondering where his mother went. And our ongoing capture the flag game was born.

Ethan fell into it faster than I expected and immediately started coming up with ideas for hiding places around town. Every Sunday, a new game starts. We have until noon to hide our flags and whoever finds the other's flag first gets a point. If one of us doesn't find the other's flag by the end of the week, then the loser owes the winner a book of their choosing. Which is a prize I came up with, because Ethan is also a huge reader. He's either at Cordie's helping out with the guests, or he's at Fran's curled up in the corner with a book that's more than likely far past his grade level.

I think he also finds comfort in the sound of the coffee shop. Sarah opened one in Seattle and he loved working around the shop with her. I think spending time at Fran's helps him connect with his mom in his own way.

"Oh, I'm winning this week. I feel lucky," I said, rubbing the top of Ethan's sandy-blond head, hair sticking up.

"Wonder why," Elias mutters and I shoot him a glare, aware he's trying to hint at our newcomer. They act like my solitude isn't by choice. But it very much is. I like my life. And I have my dogs. That's all I need. They're good snugglers.

After the scones are mostly gone and the cookies are cooled from the oven, I pour a fresh cup of coffee from the pot Mom put on and say my goodbyes. I have a flag to hide and dogs to take out. And a woman to avoid.

THE UNIVERSE IS AGAINST ME. Fully, completely, and utterly against me.

Avoiding her is apparently not in the cards for me today.

I walk into Skyler's and there is Avery, looking at the hiking boots. I groan internally keeping my eyes fixed on the short, dark haired woman at the desk in the middle of the store. She's wearing her usual wardrobe of jeans, black converse, and a black tank top with a black and white flannel tied around her waist.

My sister is the definition of "edgy" in her own way. When she opened the store, she decided she wanted to change her appearance to what felt "more like her," as she put it. So she cut her long hair, shaved it at the sides, raided my closet for flannels instead of buying her own because it was more "cost friendly"— pretty sure she still pilfers from my closet when she comes over —and slowly added to her tattooed sleeve on her left arm over time to cover as much surface as possible. Her tattoos are always visible stretching from her left shoulder down to her wrist. Mountains, wildflowers, wildlife, her store's logo. She could be a walking advertisement for Blue Grove, but it all suits her. This life suits her.

I pass the rock climbing gear and a display of some of my carvings, coming to a stop at the desk. Sky doesn't even bother to look up from whatever outdoor magazine she's flipping through. She knew I was going to come by. I do every Sunday.

"Save it," she shoots my way.

"You knew I was going to show up," I retort.

"You always do," she sighs and turns away from me, leaning her back against the edge and pretending like she has other things to do behind the counter. She's avoiding me. Avoiding the conversation like she always does.

Sarah's death was hardest on her. It was hard on me too, but something about the relationship between sisters, I think makes it more difficult for her to deal with and I can't pretend to know her pain.

"You know I don't do family brunch. Not my thing. I say it every week and you don't listen."

"No, *you* don't listen," I say, throwing her words back at her.

I'm trying as hard as I can to not let my frustration show, but she makes it difficult. I've been trying to get her to come back to Sunday brunch since Sarah died. Three years and still, she refuses to come.

Even if she showed up, grabbed a pastry and left, it would be better than not showing up at all. Like me, she prefers her solitude. But, at least I actually leave the house to regularly see people. If there were a loft on the second floor, Skyler would pack up everything she owns and live there.

"I know it's hard without her there. It's hard for all of us. But we miss you, Sky." Last week I was stern with her, trying everything to get through to her. This week I'm pleading with her. But neither method works. She's stubborn and refuses to see any other point of view.

"Brother, we do this every week. I don't want to. I'm not going to. Not right now. Not anytime soon. Now, please leave my store and I'll see you in a week. I have a customer."

She moves around the counter and starts walking toward Avery, but I grab her arm, spinning her back toward me. "Please, Sky."

Tears start to pool in her eyes and I know I've pushed her too far. I try to be gentle, as if I'm coaxing a scared fox out of its hole. Nice words, calm voice, gentle touches. But Sky scares easily. She's tough, but she runs fast and she tends to run far. She's been running for three years now and we've all let her. But enough is enough. I've missed my sister and I am determined to get her back. For all of us. I let her go and drop my hand with a soft pat against my thigh.

"Look, I'm sorry for pushing you. We just miss you." Calm voice, nice words.

Her teary eyes avoid mine and she shoves her hands in her front pockets. "Hudson, I'm just—" she looks up like she's searching the high, wooden ceiling for answers, words she doesn't know how to speak. "I just... it's hard," she finally admits, shoulders deflating in defeat.

I place a hand on her shoulder. Gentle touches. "I know. It's still hard for me too. It's still hard for everyone that she's not there next to Dad giving him all the answers to his crossword," I let out a soft chuckle.

"She was such a suck up," Sky tries to mask it, but a smile tugs at the edge of her lips.

"Oh she was the worst," I agree and squeeze her shoulder. I pull her in for a tight hug and let her dry her eyes on my sleeve, because that's what I do. I'm the big brother. Here to help her through her emotions while promptly ignoring all of the ones swirling in my chest. She gives one final squeeze, her arms tightening around my torso before letting go and taking a step back. Her eyes are still shining with tears, but she blinks them back and takes a deep breath.

"I'll come around, just...time."

I give her a small smile and let her walk away toward Avery.

I start to walk to the door, but stop when Avery's hands shift to her hair.

My breath catches watching her untie her ribbon and then gather all her hair to tie it up in a high ponytail, combating the heat from the store. Is it hot? I think Sky's air is broken and I make a mental note to come back tomorrow when there isn't the subject of town gossip standing in the middle of the store.

Where did she come from? Why is she looking at hiking boots? Does she hike? Or is this some touristy thing she's going to try for the first time?

A chuckle pierces the air and brings my gaze to Sky who appeared next to me when I clearly wasn't paying attention. *Shit.* By the look of her smirk, she caught me staring.

"Yah know," she whispers. "You know the trails *really* well around here."

"No."

That fucking word again.

"Don't even think about it," I warn her.

"Oh, I won't," she says slyly. No longer a scared fox hiding in its hole, but a clever one, a predator hunting down its prey. "But *you* will."

Without another word, she makes her way around the racks with a pair of hiking boots in her hands. She goes to Avery's side who is pretending to look over the boots like she didn't overhear our entire conversation. As the silence stretches, Avery looks up and meets my eye.

I catch a glimpse of blue before she quickly looks away, fiddling with the camera strap slung over her shoulder, twisting the fabric in between her fingers.

When Sky reaches Avery, I turn around and leave the store, bells jingling above me. I'll try again next week.

Maybe she will listen next time, I tell myself even though I know it's a lie.

CHAPTER FIVE

AVERY

*H*udson's heavy footsteps retreat to the door while I keep my eyes firmly on the camera in my hands. Him and Sky's conversation hangs in the air around us, like fog on a fall morning. Wispy, eerie, a warning of things to come.

"Okay, here is a style I think could work for you," Sky says, holding the boots she went to grab with two fingers at her side. "Doing some hiking while you're here, Avery?"

Does everyone know who I am already? I didn't tell her my name when I came in earlier.

"Sorry," she backtracks after seeing the comprehension spread on my face... "You'll learn quickly that Fran and Cordie are the best way to get news out around here. They live for this sort of stuff."

"This sort of stuff?" I ask.

"You. New people. City people coming to a small mountain town to escape the busy, miserable sounds of yelling and honking."

"Oh?"

"A mountain escape. A getaway to change your life. Right?"

"Am I that obvious?"

"Eh, not really. I just read people really well." She raises her eyebrows like she's waiting for me to confirm that I blew into town to climb into her supposed brother's bed.

"Uh, n-no," I stammer. "I came here for the quiet. Hiking, self-discovery, all that cliche stuff you find in romance novels."

"Ah. You're one of those. Got it," she says with a wink that I decide to ignore.

"Hiking trails. What are the best ones around? And what are the best boots?"

"Well, like I said before, these aren't going to be good for you right now," she responds, pulling the boots I picked up out of my hands and replacing them with the ones she grabbed.

"It's supposed to rain a lot this week and these aren't the greatest when it comes to traction." She sets them on the shelf with a soft *clunk.* "They are the cheapest though, so if you're looking at it that way, then they *are* your best bet. But," she pauses to look through the shelves like she's making sure every-thing is in its rightful place. "If you are looking for quality boots that'll last a long time, those are what you want." She waves a finger to the boots she brought over.

"They might be a bit uncomfortable for your first hike or two, so I'd recommend taking shorter hikes at first to break them in."

I hold the tan shoes to inspect them. They look like the typical hiking boot with thick laces and an even thicker sole for more support. The box advertises the waterproof and breath-able material they are made out of, and there's not much more I could ask for. "I'll take them."

"Perfect," she turns and I follow her to the counter, gently placing the boots on the glass case, various wood carvings and knives on display. A soft nudge on my forearm makes me jump as a black cat walks his way across the counter, his paws leaving smudged prints behind on the glass. I hold my hand out for him to sniff and he promptly ignores it and looks up at Sky.

"She's fine, Max."

With her voice of approval, he turns back to me and lets me pet him, the sound of his purrs growing with each scratch of his ears. "Well, aren't you the sweetest."

"Don't let him fool you. He's an ass." As if he understood, Max gives Sky a look that says she will pay for that comment later. I laugh and continue to stroke his fur.

I nudge my head toward the door Hudson left through a few moments ago and I level my eyes with her. "Is he always like that?"

"Who?" She asks, not looking up from the computer.

"The guy that was here...who you were arguing with?" I shouldn't be prying, but I can't help myself. The image of him at Fran's, muscular forearms, dark hair falling in his eyes has been circling through my mind since I saw him.

"Oh, Hudson," she confirms. "Is my brother always an asshole?" she questions without hesitation. "Yeah. More so than usual though. Probably just needs to get laid."

My cheeks redden. "I don't think I've seen him crack a smile at all. I mean, I've only seen him once. But he did smile at Fran. He just doesn't seem like the smiley type."

A dry chuckle escapes from her. "That's because he's not. He takes his role of the town grump very seriously," she says, scanning the boots and placing them in a reusable cloth bag with her logo embroidered on the side. "But he has a real soft spot for Fran."

"I don't blame him for that."

"We all have a soft spot for that woman. She could stab me with one of her crochet hooks and I'd probably thank her."

I let out a laugh and grab my bag, the shoes heavy inside. "So, where's the best place to hike?"

"Well, we are really close to the Three Sisters, it's three mountain peaks really close together that usually get lumped into one name." She pulls out a map and unfolds it, spreading it out on the counter in between us and smooths the creases with her hands.

"There are a lot of great trails in the area around the Three Sisters. There are some trails that are a couple of miles long and some that take a few days to hike. For you right now, I'd definitely recommend the shorter trails until you get a feel for the landscape and break in your boots. The easiest trail is the Proxy Falls Trail," she pulls out a pen and circles the area. "I think you'd love it because it's less than two miles and there's a great waterfall to see, and you can swim in the water, but I wouldn't do that one alone this week since it's supposed to rain more. It gets muddy and really easy to lose your footing even if you are a seasoned hiker."

"Oh, I'm not. But I used to hike a lot when I was younger."

"Then the Proxy Falls won't be too bad for you, but like I said, don't go alone. Just in case."

"Do you have time to take me?"

Sorry, cupcake. Can't. The store is my first priority and there's no one to take over."

By the sly look on her face, I had an inkling of where she was going with this. My gut tells me she noticed the tension in the air when her brother was here. Tension that wasn't from the two of them.

I fiddle with the business cards organized on the counter. I take one and press a corner into my middle finger and another into my thumb, spinning the card around and around. I catch a glance at the name printed on the front,

Skylar Waters

HUDSON WATERS, I think. I like that.

The way he looked in the coffee shop invades my mind and

it's not like I can deny I like the way he looks and the way his shirts hug his shoulders and biceps, the fabric snug enough to see the muscles underneath. And suddenly I wish I was that flannel, wrapping myself around his back, feeling his body, his warmth, the contraction of his muscles...

Ugh.

I can't help noticing how good looking he is. Okay, not good looking. Hot. Butter melting in a frying pan, hot. If a magazine needed a model for flannel, he would be it. Or as Charlotte would suggest, a lumberjack model.

I shake my head and make myself focus, turning my eyes back to Sky. "Mmmmkay, so who would you suggest?"

"I'll ask around and see who is up for a hike. If Fran was 30 years younger, she'd jump at the chance just to find out all she could about you."

"Honestly, a hike with Fran wouldn't be the worst thing."

She studies my features before letting out a loud sigh. "Hey, I said I couldn't take you hiking, but I *can* take you drinking."

My laugh echoes in the store and I realize Sky reminds me a lot of Charlotte. Same forceful attitude, same loud personality, but always with the best intentions. I hope. "Trying to get me drunk?" I ask.

"Oh yes," she responds in a sarcastic tone. "Drunk enough to spill all of your secrets."

I know she's joking, but my anxiety spikes slightly at the idea of unlocking the chest of secrets I keep under lock at all times. I'm not sure I'm ready to share them with anyone just yet.

"I was kidding," she says, noticing the rising panic in my face. "I promise if you get drunk, I won't let you spill anything. But if you do choose to share, your secrets are safe with me. Scout's honor," she raises her right hand in the air and I feel myself relax a bit.

"Okay," I hear myself say. A night out with a new friend might be what I need. Something new, something fun.

Something blue, I joke to myself.

"Here, hand me your phone," she reaches out her hand and I grab my phone from the side pocket in my leggings and hand it over.

"We all go to the bar on Tuesday nights," she continues. "You can come with me and my friends, Jacob and Sophie. I'll put my number in and you can let me know if you want to join us. I'll stop by the inn and walk with you."

She quickly puts her number in my phone and I leave the store with a renewed hope of friendship. And maybe hiking with someone who knows more than the word "No" around me.

CHAPTER SIX

AVERY

*B*y the time the afternoon hit and the sun was slowly lowering, I had explored most of the town and met what seemed to be most of its residents.

Margie runs the thrift shop, and while most of the items looked like they came from Fran or Cordie's wardrobe, there were some buried treasures. I bought an antique clock I thought would look perfect in my apartment at home. It was one of those classic round clocks with a wooden base and gold accents. It has an intricate design around it with gold frames that hang from the bottom. I also snagged a few oversized sweaters that looked like they were crocheted by Fran. They are cozy and cute and I couldn't resist taking a piece of that woman with me when I leave in a few weeks.

I stopped at the market for some snacks to keep in my room. The market is owned by a short, red-haired woman named Sallie. She went into a monologue about her twins and how they went off to college together in New York. They were supposed to call her yesterday to check in, but they didn't. She rolled her eyes saying "at least the mountain is out." Whatever that means.

Then I went to *Frank's Bar & Restaurant* where I met Frank. He owns the bar, where I'm guessing is the location of the town hangout on Tuesdays that Sky mentioned. He could give Hudson a stiff competition on who says less words in my presence. He took my order, served me, and placed my bill on the table with barely a grunt of acknowledgement.

This town is either filled with grumpy men or I am the problem. Whichever it is, I'm still glad to be away from the chaos of the paper. I meant to check in with Charlotte earlier to see if James' head exploded yet, but it got lost in the activities of the day.

After *Frank's*, I figured I'd head back to *Books & Beans* to see what kind of book selection Fran had and ended up choosing *Jane Eyre,* one I know I don't have on my shelves at home. After going from place to place, I am ready to settle down in my room, a peppermint latte in hand, cozied under the covers with my new book. Well, an old book, rather. Fran sells a few second hand books that people donate and this one came with an inscription of a line from the book written on the title page.

"I am no bird; and no net ensnares me: I am a free human being with an independent will."

And I couldn't help but wonder who wrote the inscription and how it came to be in my hands at precisely the right time. Serendipity at its finest. I am the bird and I am determined to not allow a net to ensnare me any longer.

I think *Books & Beans* is my favorite place so far. The love that Fran has put into it is felt in every book on the shelves, every piece of furniture carefully placed, every cup of coffee she steams and everything she bakes. There is so much love in the place. So much love that I have never experienced before in my own life.

My thoughts drift to my broken relationship with my mother. I haven't heard from her since she left with whatever guy was currently praising the ground she walks on. Thriving on praise is a trait I unfortunately get from her. A trait I also never had fulfilled by her. Criticism was her go-to conversation and rarely were any positive words sprinkled in.

I cover myself with the down comforter that I may or may not be planning to steal when I leave, and dive into my book. To no one's surprise I went immediately to the romance section and grabbed the first one I thought would make me feel something other than empty. Even though my own love life is nowhere near active, I smile at the thought of living vicariously through the pages of someone else's life for a few hours, even if it has every chance of destroying my heart along the way.

After a few chapters, I close the book and turn on my side, the light from my phone glowing in the darkness. The idea of hiking again lingers in the back of my mind and pushes its way to the front as I scroll to find Sky's number. Hope rises in my chest, a phoenix from the ashes, at the thought of spending the day outside, among the trees with a clear head and a clear path.

CHAPTER SEVEN

HUDSON

*hwunk.*
    No.

Thwunk.

No.

I swing my ax, the rhythm calming my racing heart.

No.

No.

No.

Three more swings.

That word. The only word I know around her apparently. I know she heard my conversation with Sky. Take her hiking?

No.

Thwunk. The wood splits in two, splintering at the sides. I had a few orders come in this morning while I was at Fran's fixing the espresso machine. The barn was filled with plenty of wood for me to use, but I needed to clear my head.

Of *her.*

Thwunk.

Her ribbon.

Thwunk.

Her tying it up in a ponytail.

Thwunk.

Her eyes.

I sigh, frustrated. This isn't helping. I toss the ax aside and start gathering the pile of wood I managed to chop in a short time. The sound of the ax stopping acts like a whistle for the dogs and all five of them come running, circling me and begging for dinner. Or to throw a ball. They are suckers for a good tennis ball. I've lost count of how many we've lost in the lake over the years. If anything else, Sky's business is in good hands as long as she keeps selling tennis balls thanks to the five golden retrievers following me up to the barn. I drop the wood in front of the stalls containing Cletus and Mick, two horses that belong to Ethan and Elias, but they keep them here because they don't have the space to keep them at their place. They live a few blocks away from the inn and don't have land or a barn to keep them. I don't mind though. A couple more animals to take care of helps me keep my mind off things. I try to take them out and exercise them in the middle of the day, riding one through the trails with the other following on a lead.

Cletus is a deep brown thoroughbred and Mick is a black stallion, so dark Ethan tried to name him Black Beauty, but decided Mick fit him better.

I pull out my phone to check the orders I have to start tonight and find a message from an unknown number.

A picture of hiking boots fills the screen, legs wrapped with tight, black leggings snug inside the boots.

Unknown: They fit! Thanks for helping me choose!

Unknown: Any word on finding me a hiking buddy?

As much as Sky didn't want to be involved in family life, she really likes to meddle in mine.

Me: Who do you think this is?

Unknown: Sky? You put your number in my phone earlier at your store.

Me: Not Sky.

Unknown: Okaaaaaayyy, then who am I texting?

Me: Her brother.

Unknown: Oh.

Oʜ.

Good to know I'm not the only one with one-word sentences.

Unknown: Do you have Sky's number?

Me: Yes.

What am I doing? Why am I texting her? I should be calling Sky to berate her for meddling when she *just* complained about me trying to do the same thing.

Unknown: Caaaan you send it to me?

Unknown: She's supposed to find me a hiking buddy for sometime this week and I wanted to check in before I go to bed.

Unknown: And she's supposed to take me to the bar Tuesday for some town thing.

Of course Sky invited her to that. As much as she wants to

isolate herself, she sure enjoys being at Frank's with everyone else.

I imagine Avery sitting in one of the king beds in the inn, buried in the covers, staring at her phone screen. Her face softly lit in the darkness. Hair fanned out on the pillow behind her. Does she sleep in an oversized t-shirt? Just a tank top? Naked? NOPE. Not going there. Not letting my mind go there.

> Me: No.

No. The only word I know apparently. What am I doing? I should just give her Sky's number, delete the message chain and leave it at that. Instead, my thumbs decide to save her number. I type 'Avery', but delete it instead. I think about the ribbon she was wearing the first time I saw her. White with white polka dots. I change her contact name and continue to text her.

> Me: Nice photo, by the way.

> Sunshine: Wasn't supposed to be for you.

SOMETHING about the way I can tell she's irritated with me brings a smug smile to my face. I liked irritating her. Why?

> Me: I saved it anyway.

> Sunshine: DELETE IT NOW!

> I chuckle. Now she's really mad.

Me: Don't worry. I have it saved as my wallpaper now.

Sunshine: Oh, so you have some kind of foot fetish? Good to know.

Me: Good to know?

Me: What do you plan on doing with that information?

Sunshine: Blasting it all over town if you don't quit bugging me.

Me: Might be worth the risk.

I PALM MY FOREHEAD. This isn't what I wanted to be doing. So why am I doing it? Why does the idea of her thinking of me affect me so much? I don't like her. I don't care why she's here in town. And I don't care what she would look like in just those boots and the sunshine ribbon in her hair. *Shit,* I am irrevocably fucked.

Sunshine: Delete my number. Delete my picture.

Me: Then how will you get a hiking buddy for this week?

Sunshine: I'll get Sky's number from Cordie or Fran. Or I'll just find out where she lives and go knock on her door.

Me: That would be considered stalker behavior.

Sunshine: As long as it gets me away from this conversation, I don't think I really care.

Me: Alright, alright. I get it. I'm not wanted here. But if you don't find someone to hike with, let me know.

Sunshine: Why?

Me: I might know a guy.

Sunshine: Who?

Me: A guy willing to put up with you for a day.

Sunshine: You?

Me: If you promise to behave.

Sunshine: HA! Like I'm the one who needs that reminder. This is more words than you've ever said to me and you aren't even saying them. You're typing them. I doubt you could even survive a day with me. You'd have to talk in more than one word sentences.

Me: Would I though?

Sunshine: You would stay silent the whole day?

Me: I like quiet hikes.

Sunshine: Then find me another partner because I like to talk.

Me: Maybe I like to listen.

CHAPTER EIGHT

AVERY

*W*hat in the hell is happening?

All I wanted to do was find out if Sky found someone for me to go hiking with and she decided to take it upon herself to manipulate me into texting her grumpy ass brother.

Why would I want to spend the day with someone who has no interest in being anywhere near me? I mean, the feeling is mutual, but I'd much rather navigate my own way through the trails than spend it with a man who clearly doesn't want to be around me.

Or does he?

His texts suggest otherwise. He's the one offering and he wouldn't offer unless he wanted to, right?

"Ugghhhh," I let out the longest groan of my life.

This trip was not supposed to be complicated. In fact, it was supposed to be the most uncomplicated thing I've ever done, besides the whole figuring-out-what-to-do-with-my-life part.

Clearly, the universe has other plans. Flannel wrapped plans. I was looking forward to focusing on the nature around me. The trees, the water, the crunching leaves.

But now it seems the scenery will include a six foot mountain man, with forearms that are apparently a weakness of mine. An image of him wearing his red flannel, with nothing underneath and a backwards baseball cap, completely in his Luke Danes era, comes to mind.

I shake my head, immediately chasing away what that one image does to my body and toss my phone on the chaise under the window. I'm done with it for tonight and I don't trust myself with it anymore. I burrow further into the blankets and fall asleep with visions of flexing veins and long dark hair pulled up into a bun.

THE SOUNDS of rain splattering against the window and a flash of lightning wake me. I squint against the light as it strobes in through the windows. I forgot to close the curtains last night, but the sight of rain is comforting and today might just be a day I stay in bed and enjoy being lazy.

I snuggle into the comforter, the text conversation from last night cycling through my thoughts and the idea of seeing Hudson again both excites and terrifies me.

Before I fall down that particular rabbit hole too far, my phone starts buzzing. I groan and quickly escape the covers to snatch it before diving back into the warmth I left behind.

Charlotte's contact picture fills the screen and I answer on the third ring. Her face fills the screen, white foam cascading down her chin.

"You could have waited until you were done with that," I tell her.

Her head disappears and I am stuck staring at the ceiling as I listen to her spit out her toothpaste, gurgle with water and splatter it in the sink.

"Dude, could you be any messier? You got it on the camera."

"Sorry. There's no polite way to do that." She smears a towel across the phone, blacking out the picture. "Sooooo, how's it going?" When I don't answer she grabs the phone and stares at me. "What's wrong? Why're you looking at me like that?"

"Because, *this*," I gesture around me. "is all *your* fault." I point an accusatory finger at her.

She laughs like she doesn't understand how it's all her fault. But it is. She's to blame for all of it. The trip. The town. The mountain man currently setting up a tent in my brain prepared to camp out for yet another day. "What happened?" She asks.

"I don't even know."

"Explain," she pushes.

So I do. I tell her everything that transpired from the last time we talked. I tell her about the texts and Hudson's obvious flirting and annoyance. All of it came from Mr. Mountain Man himself.

"What did you say his sister's name was again?"

"Sky."

She hums. "I like her."

I groan. "She's diabolical."

"And *that's* why I like her," she states. "So, what's the issue? Just go hiking."

"I barely know him!" Sure, *she* doesn't care if I go into the woods with a complete stranger, in a remote location where I'll probably get mauled by a bear. For all we know, he's luring me into the woods because he's an ax murderer. A lumberjack with another use for his ax. I run my hand through my hair, frustrated and confused.

"Okay and? You were dying to hike when you left. What changed?"

"*He's* apparently going to accompany me."

"Honey, I'm going to need more words here. He who?"

"*HIM!* The guy. The one you so proudly call the lumberjack." I prefer Mountain Man. Or asshole. I'm flexible.

"You're *kidding!*"

"No. I'm not. Clearly, you're not the only one that decided I needed companionship. I just don't understand," I say, rubbing a hand down my face in frustration. "How can he be so UGH one minute and then basically offering to spend the day with me the next? It's clear that he doesn't like me, so why would he do it?"

Charlotte sighs and rolls her eyes.

"What?" I ask.

"You are the most oblivious person I know. And I haven't even known you *that* long."

"What do you mean?"

"He likes you, Avery."

"HAH!" I burst out. "No, he doesn't."

"Yes….he does. Why else would he keep texting you instead of giving you his sister's number right away? He could have sent you the number and ended the conversation. Instead, he continued messaging you. He even offered to take you hiking, knowing you'd spend the day together."

"That doesn't mean he likes me," I try denying.

"Whatever you say, Ave. That man has a crush. And *you* need a drink."

"Oh, that's the other thing," I remember, and tell her about Sky inviting me to the town hangout on Tuesday.

The next thing I know, she's almost forcing me to go out with Sky and her friends, which are two more strangers. She's determined to get me killed this week. Has she ever heard the phrase *Stranger Danger?*

"Fiiiine," I draw out. "I'll think about it, okay?. But only because it'll distract me and there's alcohol involved." I don't drink often, but a light buzz sounds like just the thing I need right now. "Okay, enough about me. How's work been?"

She goes on to tell me about the last few days since I've been gone. James was furious I left without preparing him and the staff beforehand, and only let it slide because Charlotte was taking over for me. As long as Charlotte kept up with her job too, he didn't care. He just wanted articles, and Charlotte was a warm body willing to provide it.

Part of me wishes I missed my job. I used to love writing and the fast-paced environment of the newsroom, but it didn't last long for me. A year into it, I realized it wasn't something I wanted to do for the rest of my life, but I saw no way out at the time. I had a job, an apartment and too many bills to pay. As much as I wanted to get out, life got in the way as it always does.

My phone starts buzzing and I cover my face with a pillow when I see who is calling. "Charlotte, I'll call you with an update tomorrow. My mother is calling."

"Yikes. Good luck with that. And have a blast with the lumberjack!"

I roll my eyes and switch calls, my heart thundering in my chest. It has been weeks since I've talked to her. She doesn't call often and I usually never call her. Lack of communication is something she's going to complain about.

I put her on speaker and toss the phone next to me, staring at the ceiling. Deep breath.

Inhale. Exhale.

My heart doesn't slow down and I can feel my anxiety start to rise.

Inhale. Exhale.

"Hello mother," I answer.

"Avery, where have you been?"

"Where I've always been," I reply dully, throwing an arm over my face like I can shield myself from the fallout that will inevitably come from this conversation. A phone call from my mother rarely indicates anything good and my voice refuses to even try to be chipper. The flutter in my chest I felt when I thought about the possibility of hiking with Hudson subsequently died when her name came on the screen.

She has a way of making me feel bad about my actions even when they haven't happened yet. I'm not planning on giving her the satisfaction this time.

"Don't take that tone with me. I tried to reach you all day yesterday and you never answered."

"I'm out of town, mother. I probably haven't had service." A lie. I felt my phone vibrate multiple times yesterday and without checking, I knew who it was. I have a sense when it comes to her. A sixth sense called existential dread.

When it comes to my mother, I've always had it. When her name lights up on the screen, my chest automatically tightens. My limbs feel heavy and the all familiar fog of depression looms over my head. My own personal rain cloud that dumps on me any chance she gets.

"Out of town? For what? Where are you? What about your job?" Her string of questions comes out in a garbled mess like an unsupervised toddler who has just drunk their weight in coffee.

"Vacation. I needed a break. I'm away for three weeks so I might continue to be hard to reach." I close my eyes tight, knowing where she is going to take the conversation next.

"Well, don't over indulge. Just because you're on vacation doesn't mean you get to or should binge every night. Your figure is important and you have to make sure that keeps or else you'll never be able to get a man."

I sigh, and the familiar sting of tears that make their appearance almost every time my mother calls start to fill my eyes. "Yep."

"I'm just lookin' out for you, Avery."

"Mhmm," I mutter, because it's all I can manage.

"How much do you weigh right now? Make sure to check in and find a gym while you're there! Sweat out the toxins. You need it if you need a break from work. Sheesh, you act like writing articles is such hard work," she continues, bypassing the fact that I'm not even responding to any of her questions. "How hard can that be? Writing isn't stressful."

I shake my head feeling more miserable than I had before I left California. If Sharon is good at anything, making her daughter feel like the smallest creature on the planet is one of them. I am smaller than the people living in Whoville. Smaller than the smallest Who, nothing more than a speck.

"Listen, mother. I have a lot to do today." Another lie. "I have to go."

"Oh good! Get a run in! Those love handles were showing a bit the last time I saw you. Kisses!" And she hangs up.

I stare at the ceiling until I drift back into a fitful sleep to the sounds of rain pattering against the window. My dandelion careening in my mother's storm.

A FEW HOURS LATER, I wake up tangled in the covers, stomach growling, demanding to be fed. Reluctantly, I untangle myself and I know before I even look in the mirror how awful I look. I can feel the puffiness in my eyes and the undersides are ringed in red color. My conversation with my mother circles over and over in my head. A vulture waiting on the perfect moment to settle on the road to pick at my dead carcass. An endless cycle of bullying. Look up narcissism in the dictionary, Sharon is right there next to it, smiling from ear to ear.

Coffee.

I need coffee and a scone to turn this day around. Caffeine is what I need to chase away the oncoming headache and the demon that is my mother. I'm not letting her ruin the rest of my day. Half the day is already lost, because I let her trigger a negative mental spiral. The outcome of too many days have been dependent on her and I have let her have too much say in how I feel. The rest of the day is not going to go that way, because I am not going to let it.

I quickly dress in the leggings I discarded on the floor after I sent Sky, who was actually Hudson, the picture of me in my boots, and an oversized gray hoodie. Tight shirts and sweaters never appealed to me. Probably because every time I did wear one, Sharon found a way to pick apart any fat that was filling out the shirt, which wasn't really fat. But if I wasn't stick thin, I wasn't doing it right. What "it" was, I still have no idea.

I throw on my boots and grab my phone, but think better of it. I toss it back on the bed after turning it off. And it feels... liberating. No phone means no other phone calls today. I won't have to worry about Sharon calling me in the middle of a peaceful moment. More importantly, before I take my first sip of coffee. With my hair up in one of my ribbons (pink today with a white chevron pattern), camera slung over my shoulder, and water bottle in hand, I step out of my room ready to block out anything that could possibly disrupt my day.

Muffled voices carry up the stairs as I take them down one at a time, a small hop to my step. On the last one, I almost collide with a very tall, very broad-chested man. I look up to see sparkling green eyes, squinting down at me.

"Going somewhere?" a deep voice wraps around my senses and I want to burrow into it and hibernate for the winter.

So much for no disruptions.

"Uh, sorry. Took the stairs too fast." I start to make my way around Hudson before he catches my elbow gently and I turn back toward him, his warm touch scattering goosebumps up my arm. "Look, I'm in no mood to argue before I've had coffee, so, please let go so I can go to Fran's and praise the ground she walks on."

He chuckles and lets go, but abruptly stops to study my face. My red, puffy eyes doing nothing to hide the fact I spent most of the morning crying. "Hey, I'm sorry," he says softly, taking a step back to give me space. "I'll leave you alone, but are you okay?"

"Peachy," I say, not bothering to look him in the eye. My headache picks this moment to throb even harder between my eyes, and I can tell if I don't get caffeine and a round of medication, it is going to turn into a migraine fast. I turn to the front desk to see Cordie smiling between the both of us, trying to ignore the intense pounding behind my right eye.

I squint against her white crocheted cardigan, the light reflecting off it making it too bright for my sore eyes. Underneath she wears a light blue button-up and a tan, ankle-length skirt. The older ladies in this town are the pinnacle of grandmotherhood and something about that brings me a world of comfort. Every time I find myself in their presence, the urge to embrace myself in the biggest grandmotherly hug is overwhelming. Something tells me that if I did do that, none of them would even flinch.

"Do you have any aspirin or something?"

"Sure thing, honey," She says and without hesitation, she grabs two pills from an aspirin bottle from behind the desk and hands them to me. I take a swig from my water bottle and place the pills in my mouth, swallowing and hoping they kick in fast.

"Thanks, Cordie. My growing migraine appreciates you. And so do I."

"You having company?" I ask, motioning to the two cups of coffee on the desk and a bag that I am sure is filled with mouth-watering pastries from Fran's.

"No," she gives me a wry smile. "But you are." She looks in Hudson's direction and saunters off to the dining area, leaving me alone with the man whose chest I was close to feeling up just moments before.

Not sure what to do, I stand there, looking past him and try not to think about what his chest would have felt like under the hands I am now clenching and unclenching over and over, my anxiety rising.

Hudson just stares at me. I feel his eyes go straight to my boots, probably noticing I'm wearing the same leggings as last night. Most men aren't very observant, but something about Hudson tells me that if I paint my nails with a clear coat of polish, he would notice. I cross my arms, feeling his gaze roam. I don't like being looked at, not in the way he is looking at me. Which is what? Cautiously? Curiously? Is he seeing my flaws and filing them away so he can point them out later?

A flush creeps up my neck and I look toward the coffee to avoid his eyes that are about to come into contact with mine.

"So, is that mine?" I point to one of the cups wrapped in a light brown sleeve with the *Books & Beans* logo.

"The one on the right," he answers.

"Ah, he speaks!" I say, sarcastically.

"I do."

Not much, apparently. So far, Hudson is a much better conversationalist over text than he is in person. At least this time I'm getting more than one-word responses. More than the word *no.*

I don't wait for him to say more before I grab the coffee he indicated on the right and take a sip, fully expecting it to be a plain black coffee. Hudson strikes me as a plain black coffee kind of man. Nothing fancy. One who believes that lattes aren't for "real" men or some stupid testosterone-filled bullshit. Instead, I am greeted by the sweet bite of peppermint mixed with the bitter taste of espresso, perfectly blended.

I raise my eyebrows, looking at him expectantly. He picks up on my cue like I knew he would. "I heard you order it at Fran's," he explains. I didn't think he noticed anything other than the espresso machine that seemed to have a death wish. I was very, very wrong. "Peppermint latte with an extra shot of espresso and skim milk, right?"

"Right," is all I can manage to say in a soft tone. I'm not used to being noticed. Let alone noticed by someone as attractive as Hudson.

"And what's in the bag?" I ask, heart pounding, waiting for an answer I'm not sure I'm ready for.

"Lemon bars."

CHAPTER NINE

HUDSON

The shock on her face is worth the extra effort I made to go to Fran's first thing this morning before her lemon bars sold out. I know Fran mentioned keeping some aside for Avery, but she tends to forget sometimes. For some reason, I couldn't handle the thought of Avery not getting the lemon bars as promised.

She looks ready to go back to bed and the idea that she is wearing the same pants she had on in the picture last night does a lot of things to my head and other parts of my body that I don't want to think about. Ribbons and leggings she's slept in? That's what it takes now apparently. Two pieces of clothing.

Who knew? Not me.

Now I do and there's part of me that wishes I didn't.

"Lemon bars?" she repeats in a quiet voice.

"Yeah. While I was there getting coffee, Fran put some in a bag for you. Told me to bring them," I lie. She doesn't need to know I asked Fran for them specifically to bring with me. Something I could bring as a peace offering of some sort, I guess. "An apology," I continue.

"What?" She asks, surprise lacing her word. Now who's talking in one word sentences?

"For my sister," I explain. I'm not saying I'm upset by what Sky did in giving Avery my number instead of hers, but the more I thought about it last night, the more I felt like she deserved some kind of compensation for my sister's meddling.

"Youuur sister?" She repeats, drawing out the first word.

"Meddling," I answer.

"Oh," is all she says before she takes another sip of her coffee and reaches her hand in the bag for one of the lemon bars. I copy her action and take one for myself, biting into the tart flavor. Fran can do no wrong. Besides her sugar cookies. But her lemon bars are a tried and true recipe that is set in stone. It's one of those recipes that has been handed down for generations, always constant, never changing. With no kids of her own, maybe I can convince Fran to cough it up, so I can bake them whenever I want. I'm not much of a baker, not compared to Fran, but I often spent my childhood days with her husband, Henry, in the back of the bakery, when I wasn't out causing trouble with Axel.

She holds the coffee up in a cheers gesture, "Well, thanks for this, Hudson. I appreciate it."

"Y-you're welcome," I stammer, liking the way my name sounds coming from her lips.

My eyes flick to them as she flicks her tongue across her bottom one, cleaning the powdered sugar that landed there. I want to pull it between my teeth and taste the sweetness of the sugar, the lingering tart flavor from the lemon. I imagine framing her face with my hands, pulling her closer, pressing her body into me, breasts firm against my chest.

Her gaze reaches mine and it's then I realize I've been staring at her mouth, not saying anything for a full minute.

"How are you doing today?" she asks, popping the last bit of bar into her mouth and sucking the crumbs off of each finger.

An image of her on top of me watching as I draw each finger into my mouth, slowly licking and sucking the sweetness from them. She rocks back and forth sinking further onto me, our hips in sync as we...

Fuck.

She waves her hand in front of my face, "Helloooo. Are you having a stroke? Do I need to call an ambulance?"

I shake my head. "Sorry," I say in a quiet tone. "Distracted."

"Mm," is all she says before asking her question again.

"I'm, uh-good, I guess."

I shove the hand not holding coffee into my pocket, trying to keep it from fidgeting. This is weird. Being civil and friendly with her. I prefer our banter from last night, the teasing playfulness in our texts.

She gives me a tight smile and I can feel Cordie's eyes flicking between the two of us. I fidget from foot to foot, trying to shift the front of my jeans without her noticing, not sure where to go from here. Do I invite her to do something today? Is she bored? Does she want me to leave? I'm just standing here like an idiot with a boner and words have completely left my brain.

"I was just about to go grab some and was dreading the rain, so I am happy to avoid that."

I stay silent, because apparently I'm mute now. Never talking again. My lips are sealed forever and Avery probably thinks I'm insane.

"Anyway," she says, waiting for an answer I don't have. I try to smile, but it goes nowhere and she mutters another quick thanks before grabbing another bar from the bottom of the bag and retreating back upstairs, her ponytail swishing back and forth across her back. I take a step, starting to go after her, to ask her something, anything to make her stay a little bit longer, but change my mind and just watch her bound up the stairs.

There is a pink ribbon in her hair today with some sort of

zigzag pattern and I can't look away until she disappears from view. Stalkerish behavior that I am not usually prone to, but she is the sun and I am stuck in her orbit with no escape.

Cordie's eyes bore into the side of my head and I can feel the load of crap she's about to give me. "That was the *worst* interaction I have ever seen and I have been around for a *long* time," she chuckles, fiddling with the thin chain hanging from her glasses. "You've got it bad, don't you?" she asks.

I roll my eyes. "I was just making up for Sky being Sky," I say, even though we both know there is more to it than that.

"With the way you were drooling after her, I am going to call bullshit on that one."

"I wasn't drooling," I say in a defensive tone, wiping below my bottom lip for good measure.

"You were maybe two seconds away from that. Next time, just have a conversation instead of standing there like a love-struck dummy."

"I am *not* lovestruck."

Deny, deny, deny.

"Whatever you say, Loverboy." Cordie grabs her empty coffee mug and heads back into the kitchen, leaving me in the quiet lobby. I decide to walk home to try to clear my head, currently filled with pictures of blonde hair swishing back and forth, a pink ribbon holding it in place.

CHAPTER TEN

AVERY

*J*t's mid-evening and I have spent most of the day planted in one of the inn's rocking chairs on the porch. I attempted to distract myself with a book, but each time I read a page, I retained nothing and had to go back, repeating the cycle until I eventually gave up. I've been watching the continuing storm, rain still pouring from the sky, splattering the street. Very few people have walked by, heads down, too distracted with getting out of the rain to notice me on the porch. I'm glad for that in a way. I've been able to rock quietly, fill up my coffee when I need to, and take a moment to breathe.

Every once in a while though, those moments are filled with the look on Hudson's face from this morning. He completely zoned out and I have a feeling I know where his mind went, considering he kept fidgeting with his jeans. I wonder what had him so frazzled. I remember licking the powdered sugar from my lips and he seemed to disappear on the spot.

Do I really affect him that much? A simple flick of the tongue and he's speechless? And then my mind wanders to his tongue and what it would feel like on my skin as it travels from my mouth down to my stomach, lower, lower until—

I jump at the sound of my phone resting in my lap. A text lights up the screen and I feel my heart start to pick up speed.

We've had a total of three conversations, two of which I don't think we can count as conversations. They were more like run-ins. One at the cafe and the other at the inn. The only true conversation we have had was over text, the both of us hiding behind two screens and apparently that's how we are going to continue this friendship.

> Hudson: Sorry about earlier.

> Me: Two apologies in one day? I'm a lucky girl.

> Hudson: Consider yourself so, because it doesn't happen often.

> Me: Mmm, for some reason, I find that hard to believe.

A FEW MINUTES goes by with no response, so I ask a question, hoping he comes back to give me an answer.

> Me: So about this town hangout tomorrow night. What can I expect?

> Hudson: Lots of loud meddling people drinking way too much beer, it's all they can do to keep their balance while dancing.

> Me: There's dancing?

I picture Fran and Cordie forcing Hudson to dance with them, Sky cheering them on from a table nearby, laughing into her drink.

> Hudson: Too much.

> Me: I'm assuming you don't join in on that particular activity?

Hudson: No.

I roll my eyes at his answer. I have a feeling he answered that way to annoy me on purpose, but I think this time, it's done to pester me in a good way. I don't know, but this feels more natural. At least more natural than this morning, which was stilted and awkward. It's easier for us to hide behind our screens where we can think of what we want to say without the heavy silence hanging in the air like a booby trap waiting to be tripped, the deathly arrows shooting at us as we try to navigate the tension.

> Me: I didn't think so.

Hudson: Do you?

> Me: Do I what?

Hudson: Like to dance?

> Me: Depends on who I'm dancing with.

I'M TAUNTING HIM, challenging him and I wonder if he's going to take the bait or if he's going to ignore it. He doesn't seem like the type to back down from a challenge, but he also doesn't strike me as the type to go out to a bar when he knows it's going to be crowded with people. In a crowd, he'd be close enough for me to reach out my fingers and softly brush my knuckles against his before entwining our fingers, pulling him over to dance in a secluded corner, away from everyone else. His hand would be firm and strong against my lower back as he holds me in place, his other hand encompassing mine as he leads us in slow circles. I would lay my head on his chest and breathe in the scent of him as he rests his cheek on the top of my head, the nearness creating a different sort of tension between us.

And now I wish I was upstairs with my vibrator, that image firmly planted in my brain, because I think I want that. I want to dance with him and feel him slowly move with me, his hands roaming. One on my ass and the other at the base of my neck, teasing my ribbon, maybe tugging it from my hair.

The vibration from my phone startles me with another text from him.

> Hudson: I don't usually come out to those things anyway.

> Me: I don't remember inviting you.

I imagine his features changing from a soft smile to a scoff, brushing off my comment and rolling his eyes, putting his phone down to run a hand through his long hair, fingers tangling in it at the ends.

> Hudson: I don't remember asking.

I throw my head back with a laugh, because I can't help myself. The way he doesn't back down from me is intriguing and I want to know more.

My legs itch to move, so I untangle myself from the chair and start walking to the other side of the wrap-around porch, thinking of what to send next. Do I ask him to come with Sky and me? If I don't, would he show up? Do I want him to?

Yes, I answer myself.

I do want him to.

But I also don't want to be too forward. Or should I be?

I groan at my circling thoughts, clearly getting nowhere. It's been so long since I have gone out with anyone, not for lack of trying, but James was the last serious relationship I had and I don't know if I'm ready for anything like that again. Especially when this trip has an end date.

I walk around the porch passing my empty chair, the pounding rain fueling the rising energy in my chest. That last cup of coffee may not have been the best idea. When I come to the back of the inn, I stop for a second to take it in. I breathe deep, calming my racing heart, and thrive in the smell of the rain mixing with the pine trees.

The mountains peek just above the trees, three points reaching for the sky. I listen to the sounds of the rain until I feel my heart calm to a steady pace and I continue walking, wishing I could go out for a run. Technically, I guess I could, but that would also mean coming back completely drenched and that's not the way I want to spend my evening. I'd rather spend it learning more about him.

I lift my phone and hover my thumbs above the keyboard, responses filtering in and out of my head as I search for the right one.

You need a break.

Finally relax a little. Shut off that ever present brain of yours...

Charlotte's words echo in my head and before I have a chance to sabotage myself (again) I type out my reply and hit send.

> **Me: Maybe I'll see you there.**

His reply comes immediately and I bring my fingers to my lips, fidgeting with the bottom one, smiling like a love struck teenager at my screen.

> **Hudson: Maybe.**

Maybe.

I stifle a yawn and glance at the timestamp on my phone.

8 p.m.

We've been texting for longer than I realized and even though I spent most of the day relaxing, my body still feels tired and in need of sleep. It's hard to believe I used to stay up all night studying or reading. More often than not, I find myself wishing for my bed by 7 p.m. and reading until I fall asleep.

I turn back from the railing and return to my spot to gather my things, ready to head upstairs, curious to see what tomorrow night might bring. Less than 24 hours from now, I could be face-to-face with him once again, wondering if he is going to show his grumpy side or the side I can see in his texts. Something different than what he tries to give off in person. Layers I want to carefully peel back, revealing who he is underneath it all. A discovery waiting for me; these little moments in time a map leading me to the bright red X.

Comfort from the creaking stairs enters my body as I slowly climb them to my room, being careful not to make too much noise in case people are asleep by now. The inn is dark and quiet, the creaks echoing off the walls.

When I get to my room, I don't bother changing before I throw back the covers and get comfortable in the king-sized bed. I feel my eyes start to droop immediately and let my body sink into the mattress. I gently tug the ribbon from my hair and grab my phone beside me typing one last reply, the sleepy feeling making me more confident than usual.

> Me: Maybe I want to see you.

And I drift off to sleep before hitting send, leaving it in the message box, the vertical line blinking until I let my hand drop and dream about warm hands and blue eyes.

CHAPTER ELEVEN

AVERY

I wake up feeling fully rested for once. A smile on my face and adrenaline in my veins, I get up and dress for my run before remembering the text from last night. Searching through the covers, I find my phone buried at the foot of the bed and open it to the text thread.

The message I didn't send stares at me, my thumb hovering over the blue arrow to the right of it, weighing the pros and cons of pressing it.

Fuck it.

I press the arrow and watch the blue message come on the screen followed by *Read at 9:01 a.m.* right underneath it.

Three dots appear in gray, indicating he's typing for a few seconds before it disappears again. I wait a few minutes, but it doesn't show up again. Grabbing a dark blue ribbon from the box, I tie my hair up into a high ponytail before leaving my room. I stuff my phone into the side pocket of my leggings, put in my AirPods and head downstairs.

There's already a full dining room, mixed voices and laughs echoing through the air.

I stop in front of the check-in desk to peek into the dining room. Cordie is standing next to a table filled with a small family, her hand on the husband's shoulder, head thrown back laughing with a hand braced on her chest. The woman next to him is wrangling a baby who currently has a fistfull of her breakfast, syrup coating her tiny fingers.

Clanking silverware evaporates in the air, entangling with the voices and there's something about this whole scene that brings me a sense of calm. My anxiety is quiet and for once it's not a lurking in the dark kind of quiet, ready to pounce at the first sign of weakness, but it's the kind of quiet you find on a peaceful Sunday morning surrounded by sunshine, fresh coffee, and people you love by your side. The feeling that everything is okay in the world. I close my eyes and savor the sounds and smells for a few more moments before I step outside and start stretching at the bottom of the stairs.

Once my muscles feel relaxed enough, I find my running playlist and start with a slow jog down the dirt driveway past the stables toward the main road. Once I reach the end of the drive, I turn on the sidewalk, passing businesses side by side. The sidewalk is busy for the morning, but I have a feeling this is the type of town that is up as early as 6 a.m. Sure enough, each business sign I pass has hours posted starting at 6:30 a.m. or 7 a.m.

A group of people are out helping hang a sign at the hardware store. One door down, a woman puts a sidewalk sign outside her antique shop detailing the current discounts inside. Across the street, the local florist is rearranging his flower displays beneath the white window sills, contrasting with the bright blue siding of the building.

My feet pound on the ground as I pick up the pace now that my body is warmed up. The more buildings I pass, the more eyes I feel turn my way, but I just look ahead and focus on my breathing, pushing my legs to go faster.

I run past the storefronts, until I reach a four-way intersection and turn right, a part of town I haven't gotten to yet. Plus if I go straight, I'll pass Sky's and there is a chance Hudson might be there for whatever reason and I don't know if I want to run into him just yet. Considering I just sent that text, I still want to hide behind the safety of my screen in case he doesn't respond. The fact that he read it is enough to have my stomach in knots. Maybe I shouldn't have sent it. I couldn't help but hear Charlotte's voice echoing over and over in my head though, pushing me to open up and have fun. Considering she packed at least ten different pieces of lingerie, she was really pushing me. But what if he read it, thought I was crazy and that's why he hasn't texted back? Was I too forward? Did I misread all of his signals? I sort through our interactions and yes, they were a tad cringy with a dash of awkwardness, the perfect recipe for disaster, but he still flirted with me. Right? I think.

I groan and keep running, trying to focus on the air on my face and the sound of my shoes against the pavement. I'm overthinking and second-guessing everything.

As always.

I overthink until I don't know what is real and what is made up from my anxiety. I've been doing it for the majority of my life and it makes everything so much harder.

I slow my legs until I am walking, taking in deep gulps of air, trying to catch my breath. I blow out slowly and walk in circles until I feel my heart rate come down bit by bit. When I turn around again, I come face to face with a vacant two-story building. It doesn't look like it has been occupied in years and I wonder what it was before. I try to peer inside the windows, but most of them are blocked except for one corner. Standing on my tiptoes, I look inside to see absolutely nothing. The inside is empty aside from a few chairs stacked in the corner and the walls are prepped for paint, but there isn't any color on them that I can see. It's like the space was intended for something, but the owner never got around to finishing it.

Suddenly, my mind is filled with the image of a front desk to the left, photoshoot equipment in the corner, families coming to have their pictures taken...by me.

Would that be crazy?

Yes. I answer myself, but the idea awakens something long hidden deep inside me. A creative creature hibernating, patiently waiting for the right idea to plant itself and grow, luring it out of its cave.

I look around at the windows and there's no sign indicating it's for sale, but by the look of the dust coating the inside, no one has been here recently. I slump my shoulders and file away the building in the back of my head, wondering who might own it.

Maybe Cordie will know.

I turn away from the building and continue my run around the block until the burn in my legs and in my lungs becomes unbearable. I slow to a walk and start retracing my steps back to the inn.

By the time I get back to Cordie's, the breakfast crowd has dispersed and the dining room is empty. I walk around the corner looking for Cordie and catch a flash of color on the back table, Ethan's bright flag still hiding beneath the centerpiece. I take satisfaction in knowing that his flag is still safely hidden.

"Don't worry, Carl. We can order more." Cordie's voice carries from the half open door I assume leads to the kitchen in the back. The left half of her body is between the frame and the door as she continues to talk to Carl.

She must hear me coming because as I draw closer she turns her head and I am met with a bright, unwavering smile.

"Avery!" she exclaims in a tone I don't hear often when it's associated with my name. "I was wondering where you ran off to this morning."

"I went for a run," I answer.

"Ah, I used to do that when I was your age. Can't do that anymore with these knees and my bitch of a back."

It's not often I hear older people use words like that, but it suits her. I laugh and nod my head toward the camouflaged flag. "Hasn't found it, huh?"

She waves her hand. "Oh, I doubt he will even come here to look," she says, giving me a glance that has something hidden behind it.

"Mmm," I answer.

Her eyes glance down at my sweat covered clothes before wandering back up to my face, strands of hair stuck to my neck and cheeks. "Did you need something?"

"Uh, yeah. I was wondering if you had Sky's number. She said she gave me hers, but it turned out to be Hudson's, and she invited me out to the town thing at the bar tonight and told me to text her if I decided to come but I don't have her real number," I ramble in one breath.

She lets out a soft laugh. "Now *that* sounds like Sky."

Shuffling through the dining room, I follow her to the front desk where she takes out a pen and a pad of post-its. She writes down a number and hands it to me. "Here."

"Now this is *actually* Sky's number, right? Not another guy in town who you might be trying to set me up with?"

"I promise you, that is Sky's number," she says, pointing to the paper.

"Thank you," I nod.

"She means well."

"Mmhmm," I hum sarcastically before leaving the room to head upstairs. Once I shower, I have more than half the day left until the gathering at the bar. I open my phone and send Sky a quick text letting her know I want to come tonight.

I settle into the now familiar bed and dive back into my book, the hours passing quickly as the story unfolds in my head, scene by scene, until I forget I'm laying on a bed and not beside the characters, listening to them fight.

The sound of my phone ringing pulls me out of the story and I answer the call, Charlotte's face once again smiling from the screen.

"Is this going to be a daily thing?" I ask.

"Is that a problem?"

"Of course not. I'm glad you miss me."

"I am dying over here and need to know every detail. I'm stuck at work while you are blissfully tucked away in a little mountain town and I am jealous, okay?"

I laugh at her dramatics and almost tell her to come join me, but remember I am supposed to be focusing on me. So instead, I fill her in on every little detail right down to how many pinecones I passed on my run this morning, even explaining to her the plot to the book I am currently reading and the view from my window.

"So, you've gone on a run, taken a shower, and you've just been reading all day?"

"Yes," I answer confidently even though I know she's about to scold me for not doing more, but in a loving way.

"You're not supposed to stay in your room all day!" she exclaims.

A text from Sky appears at the top of my screen partially obscuring Charlotte's face.

> Sky: I'll meet you in the lobby in an hour. We can walk over together and meet Jacob and Soph.

I swipe the text away and focus on Charlotte.

"I'm not." She doesn't hear me and continues on her rant.

"You're supposed to be out of your room, meeting people, hanging out, going hiking, going on some sort of big mountain adventure! Not reading—wait, what did you say?"

There it is. I was wondering how long it was going to take her to realize what I said. I fill her in on the bar hangout the town has every week and the more I say, the more her face lights up.

"I'm going out in..." I check the time on my phone, "an hour or so."

"And you're still in bed?" She asks, yelling at me.

"Yes?"

A sigh almost louder than her yelling left her lips as she throws her head back. "You said this is something the whole town goes to?"

"Yes."

"The *whole* town?"

"I just said yes, Char."

"And you're laying in bed instead of getting ready?"

I'm not sure how many more times I can tell her I'm not moving from this spot until about thirty minutes before I plan to meet Sky downstairs in the lobby.

"And what if Lumberjack shows up?"

I'm not going to lie. I've been asking that question all day, but with the unanswered text still sitting in our thread, my answer is probably no. No, it's definitely no. And suddenly, I am thrust back into my first day in town, Hudson behind the counter at Fran's tinkering away with the espresso machine. The image moves in slow motion as he stands and I see his face for the first time, his eyes close as he runs a hand through his hair, the veins on his exposed forearms flex. My imagination takes over and he slowly tugs the ponytail from his hair, letting his long tresses cascade down to his shoulders. He shakes out his hair and levels his striking blue eyes with mine, looking and looking until it feels like he's staring into my soul and it's all I can do to pry my gaze away. Except I don't. I continue staring, unabashedly until he plants one hand on the countertop and somehow leaps over, landing right in front of me, chest to chest, breathless and staring.

"Are you done with your little fantasy there, Ave?"

Charlotte's voice breaks me from my thoughts, which I desperately wish could go on. I look at her and a wry smile is plastered on her face. Covering mine with a pillow, I groan into it and she laughs at me.

"You liiiiiike him," she teases.

"Shut up!" I yell so she can hear me through the muffled pillow. "I do not!"

"Liar, liar, something is on fire and I am one hundred percent sure it's your loins."

I remove the pillow and give her a disgusted look. "Please never use that phrase ever again in your life. That was horrid."

Her sing-song laugh fills the air and a blush creeps up my cheeks and I let a small smile show, because she's right and she knows she's right. "Avery," her tone is quiet, more serious now. "You look happy."

"I am," I admit. "This town is...I don't know."

"You do know."

"It's magic," I say, cringing at myself at how cheesy it sounds, but it is. I feel at home here. The vacant space from this morning floats through my mind and I almost tell Charlotte about it, but decide not to. If I tell her about it and what I think I can do, she will immediately be on board and push me to do it. She'd be supportive and excited and would be the ultimate cheerleader, but the idea comes with sudden pressure. Anxiety presses heavy on my chest, a weight that if I lay under it long enough, I won't be able to push it back up.

"Gross, that was the cheesiest thing you've ever said."

"Better than telling me that my loins are on fire!" I yell in defense.

We both crumple into a fit of laughter until tears are streaking down our cheeks and we can't breathe. When we finally catch our breaths she pushes me to get up and get ready for Sky. For once, I listen to her because if I didn't get up now, I would stay in the cocoon I have created for myself in bed, another night passed with a book and a warm drink. Which really doesn't sound all that bad. Better than dealing with the anxiety of socializing.

"I'm glad you're doing this, Avery. I wish I could come with you tonight, but you'll be just fine."

"I do too, but I will see you soon." We say our goodbyes and I press end on the call.

I do wish she was here with me for this. Charlotte is so much better at talking to people she doesn't know. She always manages to break the tension with random topics to talk about and she isn't afraid of small talk. Tonight would be easier with her there, but this is my thing and I have to do it by myself. Well, by myself with Sky.

I'm glad I walked into her shop when I did. A growing friendship wasn't something I expected to find while here, but her brother wasn't something I planned for either and, well, here we are. Suddenly, the interrupted fantasy of him comes back and I am hot all over, again, and my anxiety brain creeps in and I'm freaking out.

What if he does show up?

Should I dress up?

Should I shower again?

I check the time. Crap, I have twenty minutes…and now I wish I had listened to Charlotte earlier. No time to shower again. Instead, I leap out of bed and rifle through my suitcase for anything besides sweats and come up empty.

Fuck.

I start searching through the extra pockets, hoping beyond hope Charlotte shoved something, anything, in here without me noticing. Once I get to the last zippered pocket, the large one on the front, I send the biggest silent thank you I have ever sent and make a mental note to call her later with a real thank you or send her an obnoxious bouquet of flowers to work. Make her happy and piss off James in the process. My fingers brush a soft piece of fabric and I tug until it is fully out, the long red, patterned dress, flowing to the floor.

It's perfect.

Surprisingly, it's not too dressy or fancy. She didn't choose this for herself, she chose it for me and I am so glad she did. I undress quickly and throw the maxi dress over my head. The red floral pattern is interrupted by a slit up the side that reaches the middle of my thigh, showing off a little more leg than I'd like, but tonight is about embracing change. So I embrace it. I stand in front of the floor length mirror attached to the bathroom door and start brushing through my hair. Pulling half of it back, I tie a simple, solid colored red ribbon to match my dress. Once it's in a bow, I realize I'm barefoot.

Once again, sending positive energy to the universe, I return to the pocket the dress was hidden in and reach deeper until my hand comes into contact with what feels like shoes. I pull out a pair of thin brown sandals and slip into them. I finish the outfit with a necklace—also shoved into the pocket—a slightly deeper brown than the shoes, a collection of metal feathers hanging from the chain and coming to rest in between my breasts. The dress' neckline is low, like I-can't-wear-a-regular-bra-with-this low. Luckily, my breasts are small enough to remain hidden behind the fabric without having to wear any extra support. Small boob gang for the win!

With everything in place, I take one more look in the mirror and notice five things I like about myself in this moment. Another piece of advice from my therapist that I try to follow as much as I can. I remember the first time she suggested this exercise as a way of retraining my brain to love my body in its current form, rather than picking it apart, something I did way too often when I was constantly judged by my mother. Truthfully, my body image issues started with her. Flippant comments about my weight and my appearance stuck with me more than I care to admit.

The first time I did this, I was completely embarrassed even though I did it in the safety of my own home with no one else around to hear me. But talking to myself in a mirror, out loud, about how I love my body felt like the biggest lie at first. Because I didn't. And I never really did, until recently. Once I started seeing running through a different lens, I became less afraid of the mirror and everything it used to represent for me. I still feel weird sometimes saying out loud what I love about me, but it is oddly cathartic and I have a feeling I am going to need catharsis before tonight.

So, I let my eyes travel over my reflection, taking in my appearance and talk out loud.

"The red compliments my skin tone."

I turn and let the slit of the dress fall on either side of my thigh.

"My legs are strong and I love them." That one is true. I have come to really love my legs, even if they still jiggle. But everyone's do. Something that took me way too long to realize. Healthy legs don't stay still. They jiggle all the same and they have cellulite and they look bigger when sitting down. But they also carry my whole body. They let me move and more importantly run. They help me exercise. And best of all, they are the perfect surface for pets to curl up on.

I turn to the side, surveying my stomach and smile. Placing a hand on the small pooch there, I say out loud, "I love my stomach and the way it fuels my body."

I continue with two more.

"I love my hands, even though anxiety has caused me to chew my nails and pick my cuticles. My hands help me cope and carry the things I need to. They take my pictures."

And finally, "I love myself. I love my body. I love my mind."

Cheesy as it all may sound, I feel better. I cross my arms over my chest and give myself a squeeze. Half the time when I do this exercise, I chicken out and go about my day. Sometimes I am still scared to allow myself to love who I am. But today is not one of those days. Today is a day I love myself and my body, and I am ready to go out and experience something new.

By the time I lock my door behind me and get to the bottom of the stairs, Sky is leaning on an elbow against the front counter, head turned toward Cordie in conversation about tonight.

"I'll be surprised if he shows up, but who knows," comes Coride's soft voice.

Sky must have seen me appear in the corner of her vision because she immediately turns my way and lets out a long whistle. I let myself bask in it for a brief moment and grab the side of my dress without the slit, hold it out to the side and spin around. Once I do a full circle, I stop and smile at Sky. "You clean up good, cupcake," she says, looking me up and down.

"Sky is right," Cordie agrees.

"Thank you," I say, acknowledging them both and for once, taking their compliments as they are.

"Are you ready?" I ask Sky.

"I am if you are," she says, pushing herself off the counter and heading toward the door. "I'll see you there, Cordie!" she calls back before exiting.

I offer Cordie a small wave before following Sky out the door, the bells sounding their now familiar chime in our wake.

"So, who are we meeting there again?"

"Oh, my best friends, Jacob and Sophie," she answers. "The three of us always go to this thing together and watch everyone get plastered. Plus Jacob's been out of town for some vet convention thing, so it's been over a week since we've seen him."

I'll come back to the look that spreads across her face at the idea of seeing Jacob again and flash her a concerned look. Here I am thinking this was going to be just an innocent town gathering, and she's talking like everyone shows up with the goal of being so drunk, they can't walk home later.

"I'm just kidding," she nudges my arm in a teasing manner and I let out a relieved sigh. "I mean, there's always a few here and there who could definitely slow down on the drinking, but overall, everyone behaves."

I give her a smile and we continue our walk to the bar in comfortable silence.

After a few more feet down the sidewalk, there is a man walking toward us. His thick-framed glasses sit on the bridge of his nose and he adjusts them as he moves closer to us. He has light brown hair that looks like he styled it to be messy, like he ran his hands through it multiple times to get it right. A light green jacket hugs his shoulders and he has what looks to be an old fashioned pager clipped to his hip, with jeans and black and white sneakers. Sky quickens her pace the closer the man gets and when they are face to face, to my surprise, she throws her arms around him as he wraps his arms around her waist and spins her around like they are long lost lovers, finding each other once again after years of searching.

Sky may have said they were best friends, but I can see the lie for what it was from here. Shit, I could have seen it blindfolded. After Sky's feet are firmly planted back onto the sidewalk, she turns to me, one arm still around him.

"Soph is meeting us at the bar, but Avery, this is Jacob." She motions to him, before turning her palm up and reaching her hand out in the air between us. "Jacob, this is Avery. The new blood in town."

Jacob reaches a hand out to me and I take it, shaking it up and down. "The famous Avery."

I let out a shy, embarrassed laugh. "I don't think I'm famous."

"Oh, that's where you're wrong my friend. In this town, you're absolutely famous."

He moves to put one arm around my shoulders, pulling me into their group, while one arm remains around Sky. I surprise myself as I feel my arm wrap around Jacob's waist coming to rest right under Sky's and it feels...comfortable. Usually I would feel weird and reserved and very panicky, but I don't. And for once, I don't even question it.

"You're the most exciting thing to happen here since the Great Blackout of 2003."

"The what?" I ask as we continue to walk, arms around each other like I have been a part of their inner circle for years.

"Hudson and Axel," Sky says in a way of explanation. But it leaves me more confused. And flustered because I wasn't expecting Hudson's name to come up so soon tonight. I figured it would at one point, but I was hoping to have at least one beer in me before that moment.

"They somehow tripped a breaker doing something stupid and the whole town was out of power for three whole days."

"Three days?" I exclaim.

"They were young and stupid," Sky adds.

"Clearly. But how did they manage that?" I ask, while wondering who Axel is and I feel a slight pang in my chest at the thought of the person being a woman. I've never met a woman named Axel before, but I also don't think I have met a person with that name, so who knows.

"One of them dared the other to climb an electric pole," Jacob answers.

"And that one did."

"But that one also slipped and grabbed the wire and since it was probably original to the town," Jacob starts.

"Ripped it down as he fell and out went the lights," Sky finishes.

"Three days, complete darkness."

"Complete chaos more like it," Sky says, running her free hand through her hair before turning us toward the street, the sound from the bar filling the air. We all look left and right, the safety directions from our childhood ingrained in us, in perfect sync like we rehearsed it beforehand.

The closer we get, the louder the noise becomes, but it isn't an overwhelming noise you'd usually hear from overcrowded bars. It's softer, with different tones of chatter and laughter filling my senses. There's a big enough crowd inside that some people are standing and sitting around the outdoor seating.

Sky was right. This is something the whole town comes to. The string lights hanging above them cast a soft glow on their faces. I can't imagine Frank being the one to hang up lights like that and wonder who convinced him to do it. It's something I could see Charlotte pushing a grumpy old man like Frank to do.

We enter through the already open door and they search for Sophie. Surprisingly, there is a lone table right in the middle of the bar, a black-haired woman standing next to it. Sky makes a beeline for the table and hugs the woman before sitting on the high bar stool, before Jacob and I even have a chance to react.

"She moves fast," I say loud enough so he can hear me.

"You should see her in a foot race. Woman can outrun me blindfolded," he says, moving around the people standing around us, talking with their neighbors.

I picture Sky blindfolded, crouched in a runner's stance next to Jacob mirroring her, before Hudson calls *Go!* They take off and Sky leaves a cloud in her wake like a cartoon character and Jacob comically spins around until he falls on his ass, stars dancing around his head while Sky dances at the finish line.

"I'll get us drinks!" calls Jacob before turning away and heading toward the bar which is lined with people, no stools left empty. He claps a man on the shoulder as he leans on the bar with his elbow. The man returns his side hug and adjusts his glasses before returning to the newspaper in front of him that is open to a crossword puzzle. The woman beside him gets up from her stool and wraps Jacob in a hug. A smile lights up her face and he matches her energy, seemingly glad to see her.

"He's such a suck up," Sky's voice comes from beside me. I look at her and she is staring at Jacob and the older couple.

He flashes them a bright smile as he continues talking, only stopping briefly when the bartender comes by to take his order. Once the drinks are set on the bar in front of him, he hugs the woman again before gathering the glasses and heading back toward our table.

"Suck up," Sky repeats to Jacob as he sets the beers down in front of us.

Jacob gives her a sly smile. "You're only mad because they like me more than you."

She rolls her eyes and punches him lightly on the bicep and he dramatically puts a hand to his chest. "You've wounded me," he proclaims.

"Oh, please. Go back over to Isabelle if you want positive energy."

"Hey, your mother would love to hang out with me all night. It'll keep her entertained while George tries and fails to finish his crossword."

Shaking her head, Sky takes a gulp of beer before leveling her eyes with his and I am pretty sure she forgets I am standing next to her. The air charges as they continue their staredown and I am officially uncomfortable.

"Ignore them," says the woman I'm assuming is Sophie. "They're desperately in love and neither of them are willing to admit it." She ignores the penetrating stare from Sky and reaches out her hand to me. "I'm Sophie by the way."

My hand mirrors her, and we grasp hands. I am starting to turn around to leave them to whatever the hell this is when a figure starts walking toward the table. His sandy hair combed neatly to the side, some strands coming loose from whatever product he used to hold it in place. He runs a hand through it and the short strands stay up after he lets go. He's wearing blue jeans, dark brown work boots and a bright blue sweater Charlotte would die for.

"I was wondering if you were going to show up, brother," Sky says as he approaches the table.

He nudges her, wrapping an arm around her shoulders in a brotherly fashion. "You think I'd miss the town newbie being bombarded by everyone? I came to help fend off the beasts."

He tilts his head my way and reaches out a muscular arm. "I'm Elias. The honorary brother," he says with no other explanation.

I take his hand and give him a warm smile. "Avery."

"Yeah, I know. Hudson won't shut up about you—oof." Sky's elbow is so quick, I almost miss it and would have if Elias hadn't reacted. She jabbed him in the ribs hard from the look of his wince and the way he is now rubbing his side. "What?" He asks, innocently. "It's the truth."

Sky just shrugs and jumps back into our conversation. "We were just talking about my lovely, sickeningly sweet parents."

"Hah, yeah, can't relate to that," he scoffs.

"Me either," I say, my mouth moving faster than my brain.

He nods in response before leaving the table to go to the bar. So much for polite conversation, I guess.

Jacob and Sky are now talking about a few new animals that

have come into the shelter in the past week, so I take the moment to look around the bar.

"Alright," I hear from behind me and Elias is back with two tall glasses of beer with an inch or so of foam on top. I raise my eyebrows in question, glancing at my half empty glass in front of me. "I figured we needed another round of drinks for this conversation," he explains.

I laugh and take the glass from his left hand. I raise it and clink it against his in cheers before bringing it to my lips and taking two big gulps. If we were going to talk about shitty parents, I'd need more than just a few casual sips. The taste of the beer lingers on my tongue and I can see Elias watching me. The beer has a fruity element to it that is nothing like I've tasted before.

The surprise must show on my face because Elias starts explaining. "It's Frank's own concoction. He doesn't tell anyone what's actually in it, but we all know it's some kind of fruit. No one has figured it out yet though."

"He makes his own beer?"

"Oh yeah, it became a big hobby of his about two years ago and this is the beer he's adjusted the most until he perfected it a few months ago."

I take another swig and savor the fruity taste, trying to figure out what it is. "Damn."

Elias laughs and raises his own glass to his lips. "Told you. We can't figure it out either."

He sets his glass down with a *clunk* and places his forearms on the table, leaning forward. His watch glints in the lights as he adjusts the black watch band. "So, shitty parents?" He asks.

Okay, jumping right in. "Shitty mom, really." I sigh and debate on telling him more. Before I make a choice though, he continues, making it for me.

"I've had my fair share of that."

"You have?" I press. I might not be sure if I want to talk

about Sharon just yet, so I will welcome someone else's drama for once.

He hesitates before going on, eyes flitting from his beer, then to the table before settling on me. "My mom is in jail for something she did a long time ago and my dad wasn't the best father, so I cut ties as soon as I turned eighteen," he states like it's a subject he has exhausted many times. "I tried making amends with my mom, but she really didn't seem to want to try, so I stopped trying for the both of us and here I am living a life with two less toxic people," he lets out a long sigh. But I catch a glimpse of light behind his eyes. It truly doesn't bother him that he no longer talks to his parents.

I nod. "How did you do that? Stop trying, I mean." I think about Sharon and the feeling she leaves me with every time we talk or the times she visits. Empty. Alone. Worthless.

"I had to step back and look closely at the space I was giving them in my life and decide that it wasn't worth it. Decide they weren't worth it anymore, because they decided that I wasn't. So, why should I continue to try?"

Understanding washes over me as I imagine him fending for himself and deciding to break contact with his parents at such a young age. The courage it must have taken to do something like that. Courage I don't think I have.

"That...makes sense," I respond, because I'm not sure what else to say. I look up from my beer and am met with kind eyes, and a soft smile like he knows exactly what I'm thinking.

"It took a while to get to where I am now. A lot of work, a lot of therapy later on in life and a lot of space to think. It wasn't easy, but it's been the best decision I could have made for myself."

Taking another gulp of beer, I close my eyes and take a deep breath, pushing down the rising anxiety at the idea of telling Sharon she no longer has a place in my life. I let out a sudden laugh at the idea of actually cutting her out. Standing up to her and telling her to never contact me again. I wonder how many shades of red her face would turn. Or would she care? Would she put up a fight? Or just walk away from her only daughter? Her only family.

Taking my right hand off the table, I rest it at my side as discreetly as I can.

Clench, digging my nails into my palms for a few seconds.

Unclench, the pressure releasing, shallow indents from my fingernails left behind.

Clench. Unclench. Until I feel the wave of anxiety pass and I can focus on Elias again.

"It doesn't sound easy," I say so quietly I'm surprised he heard me.

"It's not," he responds, matching my tone. "But you're not alone, unless you want to be."

I give him a small, appreciative smile and raise my glass again. "Thank you, Elias."

He clinks his glass to mine, "You're welcome." Running his hand through his hair, he adjusts his sweater and lets out a small laugh. "Talk about an introduction. That was a heavy conversation for someone you just met."

I laugh with him and look to my right. "You can thank Sky for that."

She turns away from Jacob and Sophie to look at us. "What are we thanking Sky for? For being amazing? Wonderful? An utter and complete joy upon your lives?" Stepping back from the table she crosses her legs, holding out her arms on either side and bends into a deep bow. "You're welcome."

Jacob and Sophie are laughing and start to applaud her as she stands before taking another bow. "A true treasure!" Jacob says in a terrible attempt at a British accent as he places his thumb and finger between his lips and whistles for Sky who is reveling in his attention. Soon the whole bar is turned toward her and applauding along with Jacob, no questions asked. Just complete comradery throughout. Sky doesn't even flinch at the sudden attention and turns away from our table, bowing to the crowd. When she turns back, Jacob reaches his hand toward her and pulls her towards the only open space in the bar followed by whistles and more applause. They start dancing to the upbeat music as others join in around them, Sophie cheering the loudest from the sidelines.

"Always the center of attention," a familiar voice sounds from behind me and my body immediately straightens as it is wrapped up in a scent I have been craving since I first came into contact with it. I didn't think he would come considering the text I sent this morning was still unanswered.

Elias moves around the table and claps Hudson on the back. "You know Sky. She acts like she wants to be a recluse, but she secretly craves the attention of everyone around her."

"You've definitely got that right," Hudson agrees.

"Let me get you a drink. Beer?" Elias offers.

"Yes, but not the shit you're drinking."

"Killjoy. You're the only one who doesn't like that beer."

"Fruit and beer? Not my style."

Elias just rolls his eyes before disappearing behind the crowd in the direction of the bar. I keep my eyes focused on the people dancing and the ones crowded around watching, swaying to the music. Not at all paying attention to the man now standing where Elias was, but at least a whole foot closer, our forearms braced on the table a few inches from touching.

"I didn't think you'd come out," I say, eyes still focused on anything but him.

"I heard someone wanted to see me," he teases and I feel my cheeks immediately redden.

"It didn't seem like you wanted to be seen." I swallow, forcing down the embarrassment I feel from sending that text earlier only to get nothing in response.

He closes the distance between our arms and the warmth of

his bleeds into my skin. He nudges my shoulder with his gently before returning to his spot inches away, but he leaves his arm against mine. I hesitate for a brief moment and decide to leave my arm where it is.

"It's no excuse, but I got distracted."

I scoff. Typical. No explanation. No responsibility. No apology. Nothing. Deflated, I move my arm away from his and start heading toward the bar for a refill. I have dealt with enough excuses in my life from men to know, this isn't something I am going to entertain.

Before I make it two steps though, I feel his hand gently grab my elbow and tug me back to him. I am about to yank it away before I see the pleading look in his eyes. "Please, wait."

So instead of yanking, I pull my arm from his touch and look up at him expectantly. Waiting for the "excuse." Maybe I'm being rude and probably a brat, but I am not going to let him walk all over me. That's not how this is going to go.

"I really did get distracted," he says like he's…embarrassed? Why would he be embarrassed? I raise my eyebrows at him, waiting.

He starts to reach for me again, but pauses as if thinking about it and drops his hands to his sides, shuffling from one foot to the other. "Okay, okay. I was responding to your text, but the dogs got in the way while I was walking by the lake and I tripped and dropped my phone… in the lake."

I can't help it. I burst out laughing at the mental image of Hudson fully tripping over his dogs, followed by a comically loud splash as he is sprawled out on the grass, dogs fighting for his attention. Licking his face and aggressively wagging their tails as he tries to fight them off.

"It's not funny!" he protests, but the slight tug of his lips betrays him until he joins in laughing with me. "I spent all day one town over replacing my phone. I only *just* got the replacement figured out a bit ago and was going to text you, but figured it would be way too late, so I just decided to show up," his laughter subsides and he meets my eyes filled with tears from laughing so hard. "I really am sorry."

"Three apologies. We've known each other for three days and I've gotten three apologies. Some people would consider that a major red flag, Waters."

He smiles unabashedly and holds up a finger. "One of those apologies was for Sky. So really, it's only two," he lifts up a second finger.

"Two in three days is still too many."

He motions me back to the table and I follow before I can convince myself to turn and run out the door. "How can I make it up to you?"

I look up at the ceiling, pretending to be deep in thought, considering. Really, wishing he would move closer to me than he is now. He settles himself across the table from me instead of next to me and I miss his warmth, even though there are so many people crowded in here, it is plenty warm. Hot, even. Stifling. The more I look at him and think about the two fingers he held up moments ago, the hotter I get. I adjust my legs, trying to shift my stance without him noticing, but, of course, he does. And he answers with a knowing grin.

"You okay over there, Sunshine?"

"Peachy."

"See that's what I think is in the beer." He pivots the conversation, pointing to the empty glass in front of me.

"Thought you didn't like it?" I challenge.

"I don't. But I have tried it and it's peaches."

I have no idea if he's right or not. I am too focused on the blue flannel wrapped around his body that matches his eyes. A deep blue ocean I think I want to get lost in. "What are my options?" I ask.

He furrows his brow. "Options for what?"

"You said you'd make it up to me. What are my options, Lumberjack?" Charlotte would be proud.

"Lumberjack?"

"It's the flannel," I say. "Gives off the lumberjack vibes."

Chuckling, he just shrugs his shoulders and stares me down. "Alright. Here are your options," he says, holding up his hands ready to count them out. Lifting one finger, "We go on that hike." Another finger, "I take you horseback riding." One more, "A swim in the lake in my backyard."

He sits there, holding three fingers up, holding my gaze. I'm not going to lie to myself, all three of those things sound incredible. Especially a swim in the lake. I imagine him stripping off his clothes, revealing the muscles underneath, slowly wading into the water until he dips his head under, coming up and running his hands over his hair, water droplets dripping from his eyelashes.

"Avery." Hudson's voice breaks me from my thoughts and I realize he had been trying to get my attention. Or I assume that's the case just from the waving hand in my face.

I shake my head slightly, clearing it of him, well, really just moving that image to the back of my mind. Filing it away for later. "Uh, sorry," I say, trying not to tumble over my words.

"What were you thinking about?" he asks even though the look in his eye tells me that he already knows.

"Tell you what, Mountain Man." I'm ignoring his question and he knows it. I lean forward on my forearms, my face inches from his as he copies my movement. "The hike you already owe me because I need a guide. Horseback riding can make up for Sky and a swim can just be a bonus." I say it all with more confidence than I feel, because I truly have no idea what I'm doing and I think the first beer is giving me more courage than exists in my body.

"All three on one condition," he says slowly moving around the table until he is right in front of me.

"And what's that?"

"You dance with me," his tone is soft and his hand is reaching out in front of him, palm turned upward, much like Jacob's was a few minutes ago. Was that only a few minutes ago? I feel like hours have passed since then.

"Deal." I put my hand in his, reveling in the rough skin I feel there, wanting to feel it everywhere.

He pulls me by the hand, navigating his way through the crowd. Eyes follow us from every direction, heads dipping to their neighbors whispering and not so subtly pointing our way. I'm not sure what is happening, but from context, I don't think this is something Hudson Waters does very often. Even Sky and Jacob have stopped dancing together to stare at us. Elias and Sophie are staring from the bar with a supportive grin spread across Elias' face. He raises his half full glass of beer—apparently unbothered by the fact he was supposed to be getting us one—and nods his head at me before taking a long sip from it. I offer him a small smile before Hudson pulls me in front of him, completely oblivious—or choosing to ignore—the curious eyes around us.

I take his lead and focus on him as his hand comes to rest on my lower back as he pulls me closer until my chest is flush against his. I am living the daydream I had earlier of what his chest would have felt like if we had actually collided at the inn.

His chest is firm against mine and my mind wanders to what it would feel like if we were skin to skin. One hand is on his shoulder and the other one is safely encased in his, hovering in the air beside us. I follow him as he leads us in circles, feet moving in time with the beat. And I am...surprised.

Hudson didn't strike me as a dancer, yet, here we are, dancing in a crowded bar like we've been doing it for years. A couple on their 50th anniversary dancing to their wedding song. Our heads gravitate closer to one another, our cheeks almost touching as we breathe in the scent of each other. I want to lay my head on his chest and close my eyes, feeling his body wrapping around mine in a tight embrace. Part of me wonders if he is thinking the same thing, because his hands tighten and then hesitate to pull me closer. I pull back slightly so I can meet his eyes. His breath hitches and his eyes flick to my lips before coming back to mine.

For a second, it seems like he's going to close his lips over mine, but before he can, the music shifts from calm and slow to upbeat and loud, breaking our spell. Hudson leads me back to the table where Sky and Jacob are already standing, ignoring the shift in the atmosphere, playing quarters. From the looks of Jacob's almost empty glass, Sky is winning. Sure enough as we approach the table she lands her quarter into the empty glass in the middle of the table. She throws her arms up and lets out a "Woooo!" as Jacob downs the rest of his beer.

"I'll see you tomorrow," Hudson whispers in my ear and turns to leave the bar, leaving me alone with his sister and her supposed best friend.

"Bye!" Sky sarcastically calls after him. "Good to see you, prick!"

I point my thumb behind me in his direction. "Does he do that a lot?"

"Leave? Yeah. He doesn't like to linger once he gets what he wants." She raises her eyebrows a few times as if to indicate I was what he wanted.

And for once, I let that wash over me, basking in the feeling of being wanted by someone.

CHAPTER TWELVE

HUDSON

*M*y heart is racing as I leave the bar, fighting the urge to go back in and pull Avery out with me. The feeling of her body so near mine lingers, her perfume sticking to my senses. I'm not sure I want to think about how it felt to have her so close to me. The way my heart beat in a steady rhythm with her steps, her breath. *Her.*

The way she felt in my arms...I enjoyed it more than I should have. But I want to feel it again. I want to feel her again.

And suddenly, I regret leaving so quickly. Part of me wants to rush back into that bar, pull her close and never let her go again.

I run my hand through my hair, pulling it up in a bun on the top of my head and turn toward my house. There's no sense in sticking around if all I am going to do is stand outside.

I don't even resist the pull when I grab my phone from my pocket and immediately open up our text thread. Picturing her face and the way she felt in my hands, I start typing.

> Me: Thanks for the dance.

Three dots appear almost immediately and my heart jumps straight to my throat.

> Sunshine: Come back and we can do it again ;)

Oh, she's definitely flirting now and I suspect it's Frank's beer that is giving her the courage to do so.

> Me: I have to go take care of the dogs. But maybe another time.

> Sunshine: How many dogs do you have?

> Me: Five.

> Sunshine: Five?! You're insane.

> Me: No, just a sucker for them.

> Sunshine: That's a lot of fur.

> Me: They keep me warm at night though.

> Sunshine: Oh, so they're just your cuddle buddies.

> Me: I've got no one else.

I don't know why I say it. But I want to make sure, *need* to make sure she knows I don't have anyone in my life like that. I haven't wanted that in a long time and since I saw her at Fran's, all I can think about is her curled up against my side. Her being there next to me when I wake up from the nightmare. Her consoling me until I fall asleep again in her arms.

I haven't had comfort like that in a long time. But, I haven't allowed myself to have it either. No one knows about the nightmare. I don't talk about it. I suffer in silence and let the neverending pressure in my chest pass until I drift off to sleep again, only to experience the same nightmare a few nights later. The dogs nudge me until I wake up, soaked in my sheets. Once I'm awake, they snuggle closer and I distract myself by stroking their fur until I am able to fall asleep again. On the occasions that doesn't work though, I get up and go for a run. Usually that works, but lately, even then, the pressure doesn't ease and I get back home with the same feeling, but physically exhausted. My brain still spinning with the nightmare, haunting me until I am nothing but a shell in the morning.

But the first look at her and her yellow, polka-dotted ribbon, and the pressure lifted. Just a smidge and when we were dancing, it felt...freeing. Freeing from all the pain I have built up on the inside in the last three years. The pain that I have kept locked inside of myself, buried so deep, I can't find a way to get it out.

> Sunshine: That's a shame.

> Me: It is.

> Sunshine: Tomorrow?

> Me: Tomorrow. Meet me in the morning at my place. Sky can tell you how to get here.

The dots don't return and I imagine her going up to the bar to order another beer, striking up a conversation with the older couple next to her. My mom would love that.

As soon as I open the door, three of the dogs run to greet me. The other two are waiting by the back door to be let out. I head that way and they all fight to get out first before I have the door halfway open. I watch them run in the yard and my mind drifts back to Avery and the anticipation of spending more time with her tomorrow.

I slept like shit and if it wasn't for Avery walking up my driveway right now, I'd still be in bed, completely burrowed in my covers for the rest of the day. Throwing back the rest of the lukewarm coffee left in my mug, I lift my hand in a small wave that she returns. She's dressed in black leggings and a white t-shirt with a faded image of a coffee cup on it, steam rising from the top.

"Did you find your way okay?" I ask, breaking the silence first.

She comes to a stop a few feet in front of me and my breath hitches at her scent, lilac and honey. A combination I want to inhale for the rest of my life. The scent reminds me of the field of wildflowers out back.

"Yeah, Sky gave me directions. But considering you're the only huge ass cabin out here, it wasn't hard to find," she smiles and my heart beats a little faster.

I wave my hand in the air gesturing for her to follow me. "Well, c'mon, let's go ridin'." Walking toward the barn, I hear her fall into step next to me and I find that I am nervous. I feel like I'm in high school again about to go on a first date. What the hell is happening?

Once we get to the stables, Mick and Cletus are stomping their hooves ready to go. Avery goes toward Mick and strokes his broad neck, her other hand resting under his chin.

"Hey, big guy," she whispers to him and Mick is already completely gone for her.

"I planned to have you ride Cletus actually," I say, putting my hand on his nose.

"You think I can't handle a stallion?" She says and my heart crashes in my chest at her sass. Is she flirting? I think she is, but I can't tell.

"I'm sure you can, but as a first time rider, I figured I'd give you the easier one," I respond. "But, if you want to take on Mick, he's all yours. Just don't complain when you fall off," I smirk at her.

She scoffs. "I'm sure I can tame him if I need to."

"I'm sure you can, Princess."

She throws me a glare and I am pretty sure once she gets settled on Mick, she is going to turn the reins and trample me to the ground.

"*Don't* call me Princess," is all she says before she puts a foot in the stirrup and swings her leg over, settling herself in the saddle. Mick lets out a huff and I swear he gives me a look that says, "You're an idiot." I glare at him until he looks away and then feel ridiculous trying to have a stand off with a horse.

I copy Avery's movements and mount Cletus. He stills as I get settled and grab the reins, patting the side of his neck. He answers with a huff and I swear these two are out to get me today. They've automatically taken her side like she's the one who houses them and feeds them, providing a loving home for them.

"Do you need me to teach you the basics, Sunshine? Or can you handle it on your own?"

That glare again. I think I enjoy coaxing that look out of her. There's a slight wrinkle that appears right above her left brow. I wonder if it wrinkles the same when she comes.

Fucking hell, this is going to be a long ride.

"I've seen enough westerns. I think I can figure it out." To prove it, she gathers the reins in one hand, grabs the saddle horn with the other and gently nudges her heels into Mick, urging him into a walk.

As much as I'd like to deny it, I'm impressed. She must see it on my face, because her voice rings through the air. "I'm not clueless, Waters."

I roll my eyes and nudge Cletus to follow her. Once I catch up, I match her pace and we ride in silence for a few minutes. Ahead there is a clear trail, wide enough for us to fit side-by-side, our legs almost touching. I cut this path when Elias and Ethan moved back so they could ride when they wanted. Really, it was for me to keep distracted. The movements of cutting through the brush and clearing a trail helped me think of anything other than Sarah.

We fall into a quiet rhythm as we enter the woods, the soft padding of hooves, the squeaking of the saddles, and the wind rustling the leaves are the only sounds around us.

"So, dancing, huh?" Avery asks.

"What?"

"Dancing? Not something you do often?"

I let out a small laugh. "No, I can't say I ever dance, really." Honestly, I don't even remember the last time I danced with anyone. Maybe my mom at a friend's wedding when I was a kid. But other than that, I stay firmly on the sidelines. The comfortable sidelines.

"Then why?"

I shrug my shoulders as if I could possibly downplay the way I felt when we were making that deal last night. It felt like if I didn't have her near me right that second, my body was going to explode and the only excuse I had to get her close was to dance. I know everyone had eyes on us, enough to know that she noticed.

"You seemed like you needed the fun," is all I say before coaxing Cletus into a trot that he quickly decided was a sign to gallop.

"Try to keep up, Princess!" I call behind me and laugh when I am once again met with her glare. Luckily this trail remains basically flat the whole way or I wouldn't let Cletus run like this. After a few moments I can hear quickened hooves and when I look back, Avery is smiling as wide as I have ever seen and it's so genuine I can't help but smile back. She looks free and happy, and I know that feeling. There's something different about being on the back of a horse, galloping on an open trail, wind on your skin, through your hair, nature around, there's no better feeling. Other than sharing it with the person you love.

After about a mile or so the trail opens up to a clearing and we both slow down, our heavy breaths permeating the air.

"That...was...exhilarating," she says in between breaths.

"It's the best part of riding."

"Do you ride every day?"

"Not all the time, but I do when I need to clear my head," I answer.

"So every day?" She jokes. I laugh, but she's also not far off from the truth. "You seem like a man who thinks far too much."

"And you seem like a woman who reads people far too well," I admit.

"Sometimes, but not always."

We both dismount and let the horses graze. I find a flat spot on the ground and lay back in the sun, warmth seeping into my skin. Avery follows and she lies next to me, her arm touching mine. I don't make any effort to move it, enjoying the feeling of her skin.

"What do you mean, not always?"

She sighs and I look over. Her face is tilted toward the sun, eyes closed and lips parted. Squinting, she turns to me. "I'm good at reading people, but when it comes to guys I like or want to date, I am the worst judge of character."

"Meaning?"

"I've had relationships in the past and literally all of them have sucked." A chuckle escapes my lips before I can stop it and she props herself up on her elbow. "I mean it. Every single guy I've dated has been trash."

Copying her movements, I roll to my side and rest my head in my hand, my elbow sinking into the grass. "Did you ever stop to think that it's not your lack of judgment skills, but that those men were manipulative? They made you think they were good guys, when in reality, to their core, they suck. And it's not your fault they suck."

She stares at me for a few seconds before returning her back to the grass and closing her eyes again. "Thank you," she says quietly and then shifts herself closer to me, the sides of our bodies in contact again, closer this time.

"Anytime, Princess," I flinch waiting for her to yell at me, berate me, anything to break the tension.

She doesn't disappoint with a small swat on my shoulder. "*Don't* call me Princess."

I wake with a jolt and it takes a second to realize where I am. We must have fallen asleep, because the sun is setting and the air is cooling off. Luckily, I can still hear the horses wandering around behind me. As the rest of my senses settle in, I realize Avery's leg is stretched over me, her thigh resting...well, resting right where she can feel exactly what my body is thinking at the moment and part of me wishes I could wake her the way I wanted to. Her breasts are pushed up against my arm and the awareness of them there does nothing to help my mind go to other places. The hand on my chest shifts and her breathing hitches before she removes it and starts to realize where she is.

Her eyes meet mine and we are both transfixed by the other.

"We fell asleep," I whisper, still not moving. And neither does she. She must feel me against her leg, but she either doesn't or she doesn't care, because she still doesn't move.

"I'm sorry," is all she says.

Shifting my head closer, I place my thumb on the side of her jaw and trace a line down to her chin until it is between my thumb and forefinger. "For what?" I'm still whispering. Afraid to break the spell that is being cast on us.

"I don't know," she says, and shifts her leg against me. I let out a groan.

"Unless you want this afternoon to get a little more interesting, I suggest not doing that again."

"Doing what?" she asks in an innocent tone. "This?" She shifts her leg again and I can't help but press myself into her. Her hand moves across my chest and down until she reaches the hem of my shirt. Lifting it slightly, her fingers graze my skin and I inhale sharply at her touch. I continue to press myself into her leg, moving closer and closer to her center. I want to kiss her. I can pull her to me and in a second she would be straddling me, her whole body on top of mine. Moving my head closer to hers, I plan to do just that when one of the horses neighs suddenly, breaking the moment.

Avery jumps and scrambles to her feet looking around for what spooked them. I copy her movements, but see nothing around that could have made them scared. I sigh and head to the other side where they are nervously pacing.

"We better get them back before they run off scared at something else," I say, grabbing their reins and walking back to her.

She hasn't moved since she stood and I wonder if she's going to say anything about what just happened. Or what didn't happen.

"Good idea," is all she says and we ride the rest of the way back in silence, the tension way heavier than this morning.

CHAPTER THIRTEEN

HUDSON

*T*he next night of sleep isn't any better than the last and my body is exhausted. After our ride yesterday and our moment in the field, my brain is more muddled than before. And the walk to the inn this morning didn't help clear my head.

Usually a hike would help, but I have a feeling being in close proximity to Avery isn't going to help. My heart is racing at the idea of seeing her again.

I hear her light footsteps bounding down the stairs and when she comes around the corner, I am awestruck. She is in the middle of tying her hair up in a turquoise ribbon and the sight of her takes my breath straight from my lungs.

I don't think she expected me to be here on time because she stops short at the sight of me. We stare at each other caught in a contest neither one of us wants to lose. I hold up the bag filled with lemon bars and gesture to the cups of coffee on the check-in desk.

"I thought we would need fuel for our hike," I say as a greeting, holding up a coffee and the bag.

"Oh," is all she says before grabbing her coffee. She takes a sip and reaches her hand in the bag for one of the lemon bars. I copy her action and take one for myself, biting into the tart flavor.

"So," I say, breaking the silence after I scarf down my lemon bar. "Which trail were you wanting to take?"

"Oh, uhhh, I'm not sure?" She hesitates. "Sky said a shorter trail might be better with the rain and the new shoes, but I don't mind doing a longer one."

"It's going to be muddy. That okay?"

She rolls her eyes. "I couldn't care less about getting a little dirty." Realizing what she said, she quickly looks away and takes another sip of her coffee. Is she flirting? Even unintentional flirting is flirting. It counts. Why does that make my chest flutter?

"I don't mind getting dirty either. Let's go."

Coffees in hand, we both turn toward the door at the same time and bump shoulders trying to exit.

"Marx brothers moment there," she says. "Sorry," she motions me to go in front of her.

"You know the Marx brothers?" I have never in my thirty-two years on this earth met a female who has seen Marx brothers.

"*You* know the Marx brothers?" she asks.

"What's with the emphasis? They're classic."

"You just don't strike me as a 'classic' kind of guy," she says, gesturing with air quotes around the word classic.

"Classics. Black and white movies. I'm there. I like them. They're quiet compared to color. Color can be overstimulating for me sometimes. There's just something about black and white that's—"

"Comforting," she finishes.

We fall into silence as we walk down the sidewalk, passing townspeople as we go. I lose count of the number of heads turning our way the longer we walk. Suddenly, there are business owners cleaning windows that don't have streaks on them, sweeping sidewalks that have no visible leaves to sweep, even Frank is outside fixing a sign I'm almost positive isn't broken at all. Fran and Cordie are good. *Too* good.

Avery sends me a wary glance when she finally notices the extra eyes staring at us. "Ignore them," I tell her. "Don't give them any more ammo than they already have."

"Oooookay," she draws out and takes her camera in her hands to snap pictures of the people around her. I don't have the slightest idea as to why she would want a bunch of pictures of these people pretending to clean and fix things just to eavesdrop on us. All they want is to one-up Fran and Cordie and have something new to report to everyone. Those two are always five steps ahead of everyone else.

The click of her camera fills the air, and I find myself wondering what is going on inside her head. What motivates her to take the pictures she does? What makes her decide what is worth taking pictures of? And why do I want to know?

"So what do you have in your backpack?" she asks, gesturing to the pack I slung across my shoulders.

"Hiking essentials."

"Like?"

"Snacks, water, whiskey."

"Whiskey?" She laughs.

"Essential."

We finally reach the edge of town and the campground comes into view. On top of all the usual campsites to rent for trailers and tents, there are a few long-term trailers available for people to rent. Tourist season kicks off around Memorial Day, so they're sitting empty right now. Our primary tourist season runs from late spring into early fall with our proximity to the mountains, hiking trails, and campgrounds. The busy summer season helps the local businesses, but we are always talking about new ideas at town meetings to bring in more tourists late fall to early spring. I've lost track of the number of festivals we have.

Along with her outdoor store, Sky inherited the campground our parents used to run. It's where my fondness for the outdoors comes from and it's why my cabin is secluded a few miles down the road opposite from the camp. I like the quiet, and the lake nearby makes it more desirable. I never imagined settling down here, but leaving after Sarah died was never an option.

When I first opened my shop a year after she died, I never thought it would take off the way it did, but apparently people love detailed wood carvings of their animals, and it gave me something to do with my hands. Something to take my mind off of my grief. My family was never sure about my idea to do it, but Sarah always was. She saw something in me that I sometimes still don't, and she was the first one to push me into selling my work. Before she suggested it, I always just did it as a hobby. Something to pass the time—to create something with my hands—and bring people a little bit of joy and some sense of comfort.

When we reach the edge of the campground, Avery stops at the sign marking the different trails and the length of each one.

"Which one are we taking?"

"This one," I point to the one outlined in blue that stretches toward the middle peak. This isn't the longest one, but it isn't a short hike either, at least four miles or so and it isn't usually too rough. But with the rain last night, some spots might be more difficult than usual.

"Not the shortest one?" She asks, wryly. "I would have thought you'd take the easy way out and take me on the shortest hike possible. Get me out of your hair sooner."

The image of her hands in my hair comes to mind and I wonder what her fingers would feel like tangled up in it. I shake my head. "Nah, the short one is too easy. Figured you'd want a bit of a challenge."

"And why do you think that?"

"You just don't seem like the type to take the easy route," I answer quietly like I'm telling a secret I promised to keep to myself.

"Mm," is all she says and starts walking toward the blue trail.

I can't count how many times I've taken this trail in the past. Axel and I hiked it a lot when we were kids. Usually at night, when our parents thought we were in bed asleep. We'd sneak out with our packs, ready to camp out by the waterfall, hoping to spot a bear or a cougar so we would have some kind of thrilling story for school the next day. The one time we did see a bear, we almost shit our pants. Both of us scrambled up a tree and hid there until he was finished raiding our food and went along his way. I smile at the memory of how idiotic we were. Still are half the time.

"Wow," Avery says. "He smiles in my presence."

I look over and find her studying me, blue eyes scanning my face and looking for something I don't think I can give her. "Just memories of me and an old buddy being stupid teenagers."

"Oh?"

Something about the way she's looking at me makes me want to tell her every single time we snuck out and hid in these woods and every time we got caught.

"Axel. He owns the auto shop a mile or so from the inn. We've been best friends basically our whole lives. Grew up here together and got into a lot of shit together too. Detentions, pranks around town, just stupid, teenage boy shit."

"What's the dumbest thing you guys did together?"

I think about all the things we got into together and try to recall the one thing we did that was probably way too far. "There's a long list of things, Sunshine," I say, the nickname slipping from my lips before my brain has a chance to process it.

"But the dumbest thing," I continue before she can ask about it, keeping an eye on the trail ahead of us. "Was probably the time we attempted to do the longest hike without any prep. No gear, no overnight stuff, nothing. We thought we were invincible. Thought we could do the hike in half the time just because we were young and fit."

"Sky said that hike is over a day long."

"It's about 47 miles long to be exact, so it takes at least 21 hours of hiking, not including breaks and sleeping. We weren't prepared at all."

"So how long did you last?" She asks, her eyes widening with interest, and I want to stop and bask in her attention.

"About 4 hours in, we both realized our mistake when we got hungry...I have no idea what was going through our heads other than us trying to prove how manly we were. Big mistake."

"Did your parents flip out?"

"Not really. They were used to our bullshit at that point. I think my dad was more surprised we didn't stick it out longer given how stubborn we both were. But mom was making fried chicken and pie that night and I wasn't going to miss that. I remember using that as an excuse to Axel when I wanted to bow out. But he wanted that apple pie just as badly as I did."

"I would definitely not hesitate to quit for homemade fried chicken and pie," she laughs.

"I'd quit anything for my mom's cooking," I say without hesitation. Because it's true. The only reason I'm still fit is because I run regularly and fit in other workouts when I can. Her cooking would be the death of me if I didn't keep up with my routine. But in the best way.

"She sounds nice."

"She's the best."

We fall into silence as we concentrate on the trail. The further in we go, the muddier and slicker it gets. A few times,

Avery slips and I reach my arms out to catch her, only for her to grab a nearby tree to recover her balance.

Part of me wishes she would let herself fall just so I can feel her in my arms again. Every time she slips and catches herself, my arms itch for contact, coming up empty. The tension between us grows and I start to wonder if either she feels it too or if this attraction is one-sided and yesterday was a fluke created in our hazy, sleepy state.

Throughout the hike and between hills and muddy patches, Avery continues to take out her camera to snap pictures of the trees, different plants, bugs she spots on the ground, even rocks. By the time we reach the halfway mark, her knees are caked in mud from her kneeling down to get the shot she wanted. She doesn't seem to care one bit.

The hardest part of the hike is near the end when the hill becomes a steep slope we have to make our way down. Axel and I would come here after it rained all the time to slide in the mud.

"This next part is going to be difficult with the mud. Be careful," I warn.

"Don't think I can handle myself?" she asks.

"I didn't say tha—"

Before I finish, her foot slips and she starts sliding. I throw my hand out to grab her around the waist, but I lose my footing and now we are both sliding down the slope of mud. I feel a few rocks scrape their way up my back as I dig in with my boots trying to find any kind of traction. Her foot gets caught under me and I can feel it twist at an odd angle before we finally come to a stop at the bottom of the hill.

"Told you to be careful," I groan. My back is stinging, and I know without having to look there are bright red scratches stretching all the way to my shoulder blades. I hear her hiss as she tries to stand. "Shit, are you okay?" I ask.

She collapses down in front of me and holds her left ankle. "I think I twisted it. It got caught under you."

Ignoring the ache in my back, I sit up to examine her. I gently unlace her boot and slowly take her sock off, exposing her already reddening skin.

"Does this hurt?" I press gently on the side of it.

She winces again and nods.

"I think you just twisted it. You shouldn't walk on it though. C'mon," I lift her up and put her arm over my shoulder, taking most of her weight. "We're almost there."

I support her until we get to the end of the trail and stop near a rock where she can sit down. She stops short when we make the last turn, I think she has stopped breathing, the way her mouth hangs open and the movement in her chest stalls.

The waterfall to our left sparkles and reflects in her eyes, filling the air around us with the thundering sound of water hitting the creek bed rock below. The pool underneath ripples in waves from the fall; a hidden oasis the town is always proud to boast about.

Between stopping every few minutes so Avery could take pictures, the muddy trail and the fall, it took two hours longer to get to the waterfall than usual. I glance at my watch and it's a little after two in the afternoon, and I am surprised neither of us felt the need to stop for food. I sling my pack from my shoulders and start setting up the stuff I brought for lunch; sandwiches, chips, and a few extra lemon bars from Fran. She had insisted.

"You hungry?" I call to her over the sound of the waterfall.

She's still staring ahead of her, not speaking, not reaching for her camera. Just staring in awe like she's never seen anything like it.

"Uh, yeah, I could eat," she says without looking away.

I grab a sandwich and make my way over to where she's

sitting. "Here," I say, stretching my arm out to her, sandwich in hand.

"Thanks," she takes it, still looking at the waterfall. Now that I am closer, I am able to see the tears in her eyes that she is clearly trying to hold back. For whatever reason, she doesn't want me to see her crying and I have a feeling the tears aren't because of the pain she feels in her ankle.

As much as I want to reach out and comfort her, I don't. I move back to my spot on a rock a few feet away and eat my sandwich, leaving her to whatever it is she is feeling.

CHAPTER FOURTEEN

AVERY

uck. Slipping down that hill *hurt*. I don't even know how my ankle got caught under Hudson. I don't remember how I slipped, I just remember feeling his arms circle my waist, and him pulling me on top of him as we fell together. From his grunts, I knew his back got scraped on the way down, but when we reached the bottom it was like he didn't even care. All he wanted was to make sure *I* was okay.

That was different. I'm not used to people caring about *my* well-being and if they do, it is often an inconvenience for them. One they usually make sure I am aware of. So I always try to be okay. I'm *always* okay. The tenderness he showed me almost broke my heart, because it's something my soul begged for when I was a kid.

"Are you okay?" Hudson asks a few moments later. Our sandwiches eaten and our wrappers packed away in the bag, we have been sitting in silence, neither of us sure what to do next. His whisper is loud enough for me to hear a few feet away from the rock he's sitting on. It's like he's afraid the question will send me into hysteria. He isn't far from the truth though.

"You know, I used to explore the woods all the time when I

was a kid," I say. He doesn't respond, but looks at me, waiting for me to continue like he knows this is something I need to say. "There were these woods in our backyard and I would go all the time to explore and jump in the creek and try to hop over it." I look up at the trees, trying to staunch the flow of the tears now streaking down my face.

"One time I found a waterfall just like this one and it became a bit of a safe haven for me when I needed to get away from the stifling house. I always felt like I was suffocating, because she made it feel that way." I picture my little kid self soaking my shoes when I didn't make it over to the other side and I'd always come home covered in mud, which my mother absolutely hated. "I always made sure to take my shoes off and tiptoe to the bathroom for a quick shower before she caught me. The few times she did see me, she always made sure I knew how much she despised me playing outside. She *hated* it when I was dirty. When I wasn't perfect. 'You look disgusting,' she'd say. 'Have some respect for yourself and stay clean. Ladies don't go out and play in the mud and get dirty.' I was pretty sure ladies didn't smoke a carton of cigarettes a day and drink until they passed out either, but I kept my mouth shut. I knew better.

"She always went on about looking proper. 'Look proper for dinner. Look proper for my friends. A lady always has to look proper.'" I scoff at the memory. That was always her biggest concern. My appearance. The way I looked and how I presented myself in front of her and her friends. How I presented myself to the world. "She wanted me to impress them," I continue. "But I never did. No matter how hard I tried. I dressed the way she wanted me to, wore my make-up exactly the way she taught me. Not too much, not too little."

You want a natural look. Just enough. Too much and you'll look like a whore.

I don't say this, hell, I don't know why I'm saying any of this in front of a man who probably doesn't want to listen to any of this anyway. But something about being out in the woods, near the sound of the waterfall makes it feel like my secrets are safe here. Safe with him. Like if I whispered my deepest fears, they would be whisked away, never to be spoken again, a burden lifted and carried away on the wind.

"Hair pinned back, out of my face and perfectly placed, none of that mattered, I still wasn't good enough. I never was."

I'm still not. The unsaid words hang in the air, a blade waiting to drop. I'm still a disappointment in her eyes if her phone call from last night was any indication.

"She'd tell her friends I was a natural beauty. I'd smile, thinking she was finally giving me some sort of compliment, finally noticing me in the smallest capacity. But then she'd go on to tell them I'd look better if I watched what I ate and lost a few pounds. I remember being so crushed that she thought of me only in size. Like my value was connected to my weight, to a neon number on a scale. Bright and haunting. The thinner I was, the lighter I was, the better daughter I was. And she never cared if I was in earshot. Most of the time she made sure I was near enough to hear her. She'd flip if she saw my appearance now."

I look down at myself and try to block out Sharon's disapproving look that always seems to linger in my mind. I run and my legs are more muscular than average, but they're still big. I don't have a thigh gap and the stretch marks between my legs have been there since high school. I have always hated them, because I always thought the reason I had them was because my body was bigger than it was "supposed" to be. Every time I look in the mirror, the pink scars blink back at me like a flashing neon sign made to accentuate my flaws.

I let out a long, unsteady breath before pushing her to the recesses of my mind. Even after all this time away from her, I still let her get to me. A two minute phone call. That's all it was and this is the effect I was letting it have. In front of someone I barely know, no less.

Realization hits me and I gape at myself. Oh my god, I can't believe I just told Hudson of all people about the way my mother treated me. The way she still treats me.

I wipe my tears on my sleeves, waiting for him to say something. Anything. Or just run for the literal hills away from me. But he doesn't. He just sits there and stares at me, his eyes boring into the side of my face.

"She's wrong. You're strong as hell and she's bitter and took it out on you. You *are* beautiful," he whispers so softly, I'm sure I imagine it until I turn and meet his eyes. The air between us grows thick, heavy. A weighted blanket on a cold winter's night and I want to curl under it with him, mug of cocoa in hand while he reads to me from one of my books.

The silence stretches for a while and I am lost in staring at him. His eyes stay on mine and we stare, observing the other with I don't know what. Trepidation? Hope? Expectation? And I am searching through the recesses of my mind to figure out when was the last time someone gave me a compliment and meant it.

Whatever hangs in the air between us, he breaks it and stands, going to the edge of the water. To my surprise he starts taking off his boots, socks, then his shirt, leaving the heavy conversation behind us and filling my mind with something much, *much* better.

The image of Hudson Waters shirtless.

My eyes widen. *Holy shit.* If I had my phone and Charlotte on FaceTime, I'm pretty sure she would pass out. I'm unsure on whether or not I am going to pass out.

"Whoa, what're you doing?"

"What does it look like?" He says, teasing as he proceeds to take off his pants revealing the navy blue boxer briefs underneath. I must look like a fish breathing underwater, because my mouth hangs open before I close it only for it to fall open again.

"Ohmygodohmygodohmygod," I let out in a jumble, making my eyes go anywhere other than where they desperately want to go. My hands come up to my face, covering my eyes to resist the temptation to stare to my heart's content.

"Just want to wash all the mud off," is all he says before slowly wading into the pool. The water around him ripples and spreads as I peek through my fingers unable to resist. He's turned toward the waterfall and I let myself admire his muscular back and broad shoulders. Toned from whatever it is he does for a living. Long red scratches stretch from his lower back to in between his shoulder blades and he hisses the further down he sinks into the water. He reaches up and tugs at the ponytail holding half his hair back, letting it fall into his face.

"I can feel you staring," he calls back, face half turned toward me. I don't think I have ever had a fantasy as good as the one unfolding in front of me. Without overthinking, I stand on my right foot, careful about the weight I put on my left, and start undressing until I am in my black sports bra and matching underwear. I make a mental note to thank Charlotte for the matching sets she shoved into my suitcase.

My eyes travel to him and our gazes lock, green to blue.

"Now *you're* staring." I smirk, knowing I leveled the playing field and watching. If he thought he was getting away with the glances and stares he had been shooting my way during the whole hike, he was wrong. I noticed every single one and my body reacted each time. But that was nothing compared to standing here now as bare as I have been in front of anyone in years.

I wade in slowly, hiding my body beneath the water as I drift toward the waterfall. Hudson stays where he is, but I feel his gaze following me, burning into me.

The water above runs through my hair, the mud slowly

cascading down my back. My ears strain to listen to the sounds of the water, to figure out where he is standing now, if he is moving closer to me.

"Let me," his voice comes from behind and startles me. Before I say anything, Hudson gently places his hands on my head and starts cleaning the mud from my hair, his fingers moving in slow circular motions gently pressing into my skin.

"Is this okay?" he asks, just loud enough for me to hear over the water. I just nod. I don't trust my voice right now. The man has his hands... in. My. Hair. And it feels more than good. Better than anything I have ever felt. Better than sex. Okay, probably better than the sex I've had and I wonder how much better sex with him would feel. But, nope. Not going there. Although, my body really wants to go there. I close my eyes and focus on the feel of his hands massaging my scalp, his fingers combing through the thick strands.

"If I knew the noises you'd make while washing your hair, I would have asked to do it a lot sooner."

My eyes fly open and I realize I had in fact been moaning at his touch. Red floods my cheeks and I'm embarrassed. Again. How many times can I be embarrassed in front of this man? You know what, no, I'm not embarrassed. His hands feel nice. The massage feels nice. That's it. I'm not going to hide the fact that I am enjoying this moment.

I turn toward him and my breath catches at the sight of him under the waterfall. His chest is at eye level and I get quite the view. I allow myself to take my time to meet his eyes, taking in every ounce of lean muscle on his pecs, the peaks of his brown nipples with water dripping down, down, down...

Hudson clears his throat and my eyes dart up to his. His deep, green eyes. Send a search party, because I am utterly lost in them. His lashes lower dangerously, eyes landing on my lower lip. My chest rises and falls in a quick rhythm, my brain not catching up with what is happening. What *is* happening?

Hudson is looking at me like he wants to kiss me. Is he going to kiss me? Do I want him to kiss me? Yes. I do, I decide.

He places a hand on the back of my neck and slowly pulls me closer. So slowly, it feels like the slow-mo feature is on. His head dips and he draws a line from the left side of my jaw with his nose, down to my chin, over my lips, until we are nose to nose, our shared breath mingling with the water falling between us.

"What are you doing?" I ask, breaking the spell he's cast upon us. I hate myself. Why does my brain decide to catch up at *that* moment?

Hudson stalls and clears his throat again. "Nothing. Um... uh...sorry. That was out of line." He pulls away and the cold air creeps in, goosebumps replacing where his hands were, my body already missing his touch.

"No—" I start, but he's already making his way back to our stuff.

"I'll go get a camp set up."

Shit. What did I just do? And why do I feel a gnawing pit in the center of my stomach?

When the mud is completely washed off, I retrace Hudson's path to the bank and start to regret taking my clothes off. I have nothing to use to dry off and it is starting to get colder. He must notice my shiver because he pulls a blanket out of his pack that is apparently bottomless and wraps it around my shoulders, careful not to make any contact with my skin.

The pack proves even deeper than I imagined, because Hudson pulls out a sleeping bag, a thermos, more food items, a canteen, and a tarp.

"Uhhh, did you plan on staying for the week, or?"

"Always be prepared," he answers.

"For what?" I ask.

"Anything." He starts to lay out the tarp on the ground in front of the makeshift fire pit he must have put together while I finished cleaning myself.

"What are you doing?"

"Setting up," he answers.

"For?"

"Tonight."

"Tonight?" I ask, confused.

"Yes."

Apparently, I'm going to have to ask specific questions for him to actually explain in more than one word. Our almost kiss apparently reset him to factory settings and we are back to one word answers.

"Why are you setting up anything for tonight? What do you mean?"

He gestured to the ground. "Well, because of the mud, it took us a bit longer to hike and you," he points to my ankle, "are in no condition to hike all the way back and we would be trying to hike in the dark. Too dangerous. So, we camp here tonight."

Great. Perfect. Grand. Just what I need. Camping in a secluded area with a man I am insanely attracted to, but need to stay away from. And I'm sure there's only one sleeping bag.

I walk over and glance in the pack. Yep. Empty.

This night just got a lot more interesting.

CHAPTER FIFTEEN

HUDSON

I can feel her watching me. I know I shouldn't have tried to kiss her, but damn. When she undressed and came into the water with me, I could only hold back so much. I didn't want to hold back at all and I wouldn't have if she didn't ask what I was doing. I wanted to do more than just kiss her under that waterfall. The image of her behind the waterfall, perched on the rock's surface, legs spread, my face buried between them, invades my mind. And my body. I shift myself so my back is to her, hiding other parts of my body, as I flatten out the tarp as much as I can to give us plenty of space to sleep later.

"I'm surprised you know to put the tarp on the ground," she teases. I smile, glad she brought back whatever back and forth we've been doing since she came here.

"I have lived near these mountains my whole life. It's common sense that—"

"A tarp is twice as useful under you than above you," she finishes. I don't try to hide my shock.

"What?" she shrugs. "I watch *Bear Grylls*. But if you suggest we drink our own pee, I'm walking back to the inn, pain or no pain. I don't give a shit how dark it is or how many bears might be waiting in the trees to maul me."

"I'd filter it before we drank it," I joke.

She wrinkles her nose in response and I chuckle at her. I unzip the sleeping bag and spread it out on top of the tarp. My nerves grow at the makeshift bed, knowing we will be closer than either of us would like to be overnight. But, warmth and all that. Not an excuse at all to spoon her. But I find myself glad I don't own a second sleeping bag.

"So, what now?" She asks, wrapping the blanket tighter around her.

"Now, we try to get a fire going. And you, put your clothes back on unless you want this night to go a different way," I say bluntly, because I'm still hard from the image of her in the waterfall, and if she doesn't put her clothes back on now, the rest of what she does have on is going to come off.

Before I grab the matches, I gather my hair behind me and wrap the hair tie around it, tying it in a high bun to keep it out of my face. Avery hasn't moved from her spot to get dressed and I'm pretty sure she has stopped breathing.

"Then you have to put your clothes back on too. And," she swallows. "Maybe not do that again."

"What?" I ask innocently. "Keep my hair out of my face?"

"Yeah, that. Don't put your hair up again. In fact, just don't touch your hair again," she mumbles and gathers up her clothes before hiding behind a nearby tree to dress. I have a feeling we both know if she unwrapped that blanket out here, it would have been game over for both of us. I pull on my jeans and the thick flannel jacket I packed and get to work on the fire. By the time she emerges from behind the tree, blanket draped over her arm, the twigs crackle as the fire grows enough that I can sit back on the tarp and poke at it until the flames grow.

Avery wordlessly sits a few inches away from me, her own stick in hand to move the firewood around. The tension between us hangs in the air again, waiting to be broken. The anticipation building more and more, and it feels like something before a big life event.

The excitement before buying or building a house; the wait before a vacation; or, in my case before a new pup comes into the animal shelter. But this is something more than that. Something bigger. No matter how much we both want to deny it. But according to the gossip, she is leaving in a few weeks. Avery is leaving. I have to keep reminding myself of that fact. It doesn't matter how attracted we are to each other. She's going home to her life. Her friends. Her job. She's not sticking around. And I am not going to allow myself to fall when I know she's going to leave. I can't.

I grab my pack and start digging in the side pocket.

"What else could you possibly pull out of that thing?" Avery asks, clearly exasperated for whatever reason.

"Provisions," I say.

"Do you ever have more than one word answers?"

"Rarely," I smile wryly.

"I looked in there earlier for another sleeping bag and it was empty," she states.

"Side pockets," I place some chocolate in front of her followed by a small bag of jumbo marshmallows and a box of graham crackers.

"Just how long did you think we were going to be in the woods for?"

"Like I said, I like to be prepared. Plus," I add. "What's a hiking trip without s'mores?"

"S'mores are for camping. Not hiking," she says.

"Incorrect. Every time my siblings and I hiked this path, we'd always stop here for s'mores before heading back no matter what time of day it was."

Really, it was Sarah that had insisted. She was the one who always made sure her bag had contents for s'mores. She didn't care that we just ate or that we would eat immediately after getting home. A hike wasn't a hike without stopping for s'mores.

"Oh, you have more than one sibling?" she asks and I realize I used the plural.

"No," I answer and busy myself with opening everything. She must hear the sharpness in my tone because she doesn't ask anything else and grabs a marshmallow. Spearing it, she places it over the fire, lets it catch for a few seconds and blows it out. The edges are black and the inside starts to squish out as she places it between the graham cracker pieces and chocolate she readied beforehand. She hands it to me. The perfect s'more. And I grab it with a quiet, "thank you." She repeats the process for herself and we sit in silence as we eat, licking the sticky marshmallow off our fingers with dignity. I wish I was the one licking it off her fingers instead.

Fuck, s'mores may have been a bad idea. Never have I found eating a s'more sexy. But Avery is making me question everything and now I need to shift my hips in the opposite direction. Again. I'm never going to look at a s'more the same way, nor am I going to eat one without thinking of Avery licking the chocolate she left behind on her bottom lip. I don't think I want to. When she's done eating—and licking the marshmallow off her fingers, which does things to me I don't want to admit—she stands up without a word and goes to the other side pocket of the bag I brought.

"What are you doing?" I ask.

"Looking for another ponytail holder for my hair. I like to sleep with it up so it's out of my face."

She pulls out a small red head scarf and glances at me with a look I don't want to be on the receiving end of.

"And this is?" She asks.

"Nothing," I make a grab for it before she holds it up in the air out of my reach.

"Cheater!" she yells.

"What?"

"You, Hudson Waters, are a dirty cheater! And cheating in a game with your innocent nephew? Shame on you." Her face is serious, but she can't hide the humor in her tone.

"How do you even know what that is?"

"I promised not to reveal my sources. And unlike you, I keep my promises."

"Oh, please. Ethan asked you to snoop, didn't he?"

Laughing, she says, "No, actually. I really did just need a ponytail holder, but this is even better."

"I *was* going to hide it Sunday and I forgot, so I was going to do it today, but *someone* just had to go on a hike *and* get us stuck in the woods overnight. So, the game has to wait until tomorrow. I promise I wasn't hiding the flag in my bag. I wouldn't do that to Ethan, believe it or not."

"Alright," she says in a playful tone. "I *guess* I believe you. But you're definitely going to lose, because you'll never find his flag."

"I never do," I smile. "Here." I hold out the hair tie I had on my wrist for her.

She puts the flag back where she found it and carefully takes the hair tie from me. By the cautious movements of her hand, I can tell she is making an effort to avoid any sort of contact with my fingers. She doesn't succeed though and the tips of them lightly graze the skin on the inside of my wrist.

"Thank you."

After she ties her hair in a high ponytail, she goes to the sleeping bag, and lays down with her back toward me even though it's not even 7 p.m. Stubborn woman.

Just breathe.

I stand and shift my pants, forcing myself to think of anything else besides the woman in front of me and what the curve of her hip would feel like in my hand.

My dogs.

My parents.

Elias.

Ethan.

Sky.

Fran.

...Avery.

Avery and the way her light hair fans out above and around her head, her arm curled up under her. The way she looked before she came into the water with me. The way she looked after getting out, the water slowly dripping down her body, slick and wet, and suddenly I want other parts of her to be slick and wet and I want to be the one to draw that reaction from her body.

Fuck. It's going to be a long night.

Climbing in behind her, I put as much space between us as I can without giving up too much of the cover, but we are close enough I can feel the heat radiating from her, her rapid breathing louder than the crackling fire.

"You okay?" I whisper.

"Mmhmm," is all she says, her fist above the sleeping bag clenching and unclenching.

I lay on my back with one arm stretched up behind my head, and my other resting on my chest. Staring at the sky, trying to make out the constellations I can see through the trees, but all I can see is the glint Avery had in her eyes when we almost kissed. The steady beat of her heart I felt when I grazed her jaw, and the breathless way she asked what I was doing. What I wouldn't give to go back to that moment and not take my time. To catch her lips with mine before she said anything. It's good that she stopped me, because there's no way I would have been able to stop with just a kiss. Not with her.

"Tell me a story," she says so softly, I almost don't hear her.

"Mm, what kind of story?"

"A happy one."

I think for a second, shifting through the stories I've told Ethan in the past before deciding on one.

"The year Buttercup was born, the most beautiful woman in the world was a French scullery maid named Annette."

Avery starts laughing, shifting her body so it mirrors mine, her lying on her back, an arm resting under her head. "Really, Hudson? You think I wouldn't recognize the first line of *The Princess Bride?*"

"Long shot," I say with a smile. Another smile. The last time I smiled this much was... well, I don't know. Years ago probably. When Sarah was here.

"Tell me a different one. An *original* one," she emphasizes.

"As you wish," I say without hesitation before I really think about it.

The air grows thick again and I become even more aware of her heat beside me. It's taking everything in me to keep my hand where it's resting on my chest. To not reach out for her hand to still her movements, back to clenching and unclenching.

"Once upon a time," I start and she snorts. "C'mon, Sunshine, you want a story or not?"

"I'm sorry, I'm sorry," she says in between laughs. "It's just a cheesy opening."

"Cheesy? It's classic!" I argue.

"Right, you're a fan of classics. Okay, okay, continue. I promise I'll be quiet." She pretends to zip her lip and lays her arm back down, closer to mine, but still this time.

"Once upon a time," I start again. "There was a princess, beautiful as the sun. She had magic and loved to experiment with potions, finding ingredients, mixing them together to imbue with her magic, creating any potion she desired."

I look over at Avery and watch her for a moment; she's

staring at the sky, eyes lazily closing, hesitating to open longer each time.

"She could do anything. Until one day she ran out of the ingredient she needed the most. Pages. She often used pages from old books in her potions. She would tear them to pieces, cut them to shreds, or burn them using the ashes in the mixture. Any way she could think to use the page, she did it. But when she ran out, she had to visit the local bookshop in town, desperate to continue making her potions."

Her eyes are now closed, but I can tell from the motion of her breathing that she is still awake. Listening. When I glance up though, her hands are finally still, the nervous movements stopped.

"There, she met the town's grumpy, but very handsome, shop owner who knew exactly what she did with her books and he refused to sell any to her," I continue. "He was mortified by the idea of her decimating what he thought was the most precious thing in the world. So, every day the princess came back, and every day the shop owner told her no, until finally they made a deal."

I look over expecting to be met with deep breathing and closed eyes, but instead Avery's eyes are wide open, gazing at me, listening intently. Without second guessing, I remove my hand from my chest and place it on hers, tangling our fingers together, and she doesn't pull away.

"He would give her one page per day, but that was it. And he would choose how to destroy it for her potions. He knew the way it was destroyed mattered to her, but she was desperate enough to get back to her potions that she agreed. Her magic was calling and she needed to let it free before it burst out of her. What the shop owner didn't know was that she hated using pages. But it was what her magic demanded of her. She didn't know why, she just knew that's what it needed to stay under control. To stay satiated. So, every day, she went back to the shop and every day the young man was there waiting with her next page. But every day, her visit lasted longer and longer until she was often there from morning till night and she was somehow able to ignore the calling of her magic. At least, in his presence. There was something about him that changed her. And something about her that intrigued him. They continued on that path until they decided to move on and marry. And they lived happily ever after."

She sits up suddenly, untangling her fingers from mine. "What?" she yells. "That's it?"

"What?" I ask. "They lived happily ever after. Isn't that a good thing?"

"Yes, but... they just had a beginning and an end. There's no middle! There has to be a middle!" she exclaims.

"Hey, *you* wanted a story. I provided one. You can't critique it."

"It was good until the end. There's no build up."

"She went to the shop every day and they talked. There was plenty of build up."

"No!" she yells louder. "There wasn't! Build up is small touches and almost kisses."

My face heats for the same reason hers does and I wonder if she also wishes she didn't stop me earlier.

"It's realizing one has feelings for the other but not knowing how to express them," she continues, hands flying in the air. "And denying to the ends of the earth that they are in love with each other until the end where they have the kiss that leaves all the other kisses rated the most passionate and the most pure all behind!" She says, using one of the last lines of the movie, passion and irritation coating her voice.

"Now, who's quoting *The Princess Bride*."

She hits my shoulder, "Oh shut up. You completely robbed me of the middle. I demand a middle."

I smile. "When I think of one, you'll be the first to know, I promise."

"HAH!" she laughs. "I don't think I hold much stock in your promises, considering you can't even play capture the flag fairly with your *nephew*."

I chuckle. "Point taken. But I really did intend to play fairly. I just had to drag your ass on this hike."

She rolls her eyes and lays back down next to me a little closer than before.

"It's a nice ass though," I say without thinking. My mouth moves way faster than my brain around her and I'm not sure how I feel about it.

"Goodnight, Hudson," she says, rolling over on her side, facing me this time.

"Goodnight, Sunshine," I whisper.

CHAPTER SIXTEEN

HUDSON

"*H-A-P-P-Y,*" Sarah spells.

"*Mmmm,*" I groan. "*A word that's hard to come by these days.*"

"*You aren't happy?*" she asks.

I look at her with her bright red head scarf covering her now bald head and wonder how she can ask me that. How can she ask anyone that?

"*No, Sarah. I'm not.*"

"*C'mon, big brother. I'm going to be okay.*"

"*How can you say that?*" I question, anger sneaking into my tone.

"*Hudson, I'm dying. I've wasted enough time being angry about that. I'm not wasting any more days being angry at the world. I want to spend whatever time I have left being happy with my family. With you, Elias, Ethan,*" her voice breaks on Ethan's name.

"*I don't want to leave you all with the image of me being broken in the end. I am not broken. I am* whole *because of you. Because of who I have around me. Cancer may have taken the life I was dreaming of, but I have been able to live and be happy with the time I am given. You should too.*"

I give her a sad smile, not really taking in her words. She is dying. I can't be happy about that.

I look down at my letters neatly placed on the Scrabble board and spell out my word. Avoiding the heavier talk.

"P-E-N-I-S."

"Reeeeeal mature," she draws out.

"P-E-N-I-S," a small voice says from behind me. "What does that spell, Mama?"

We both collapse into laughter as Ethan crawls into Sarah's lap. "Uncle Hudson will tell you when you're older," she says. And I don't miss the glance she gives me. If she didn't have cancer she would have said she would tell him when he's older. But she can't do that. Because she won't be there. She won't see him grow up. She won't see him live a life of all the happy moments she wants us all to have.

She squeezes him tightly and ushers him up to bed after he picks another toy car to sleep with. That kid and his cars is a love story for the ages if there ever was one. When she comes back, we finish our game. She wins, as per usual, and we fall asleep watching The Shop Around the Corner, her on the couch, me on the floor next to her.

I wake up near the end of the movie when Kralik and Pirovitch are looking through the diner window discovering who the mystery woman is. "Because it is Miss Novack," Pirovitch's voice echoes through the room.

I look over at Sarah, expecting to see her smile because her favorite part of the movie is when they discover who the person behind the letters is. Instead, there is only stillness and my heart drops to my stomach. I can't breathe, because I know she isn't.

"Sarah," I say, knowing she won't answer, but my brain doesn't understand. It does not comprehend that she isn't there. I have to try to wake her up.

She has to wake up. But she doesn't.

She is gone.

My little sister is gone...and I am broken.

"Sarah!" Louder. She has to hear me. She has to wake up.

"Sarah!" I gently shake her, tears streaming down my face, falling and soaking into the blanket covering her.

"Sarah! Sarah! Sarah!" I keep yelling because I can't stop until she wakes up. I can't stop until I see her eyes open and joke about how she tricked me.

"Sarah! Sarah!" I feel arms pulling me away from her. Elias' voice is just as broken as mine, "Hudson, Hudson!"

"Hudson! Hudson! Wake up!"

My eyes snap open to Avery hovering above me, shaking my shoulders. The tears I felt in my dream are trailing slowly down my cheeks and my chest is aching. I'm hyperventilating. All I see is Sarah.

Cold. Unmoving.

Dead.

Avery places her hands on either side of my face, angling it to hers.

"Hudson, breathe," she instructs.

I can't. I can't breathe. It hurts too much. When I breathe, the air pierces my lungs like it's a foreign object obstructed in my body, stabbing me over and over until all of the blood in my body seeps out of me.

"Hudson," she says again, tightening her hold on me. I see the resignation in her eyes and without hesitating, she lifts her left leg over me resting her knees on either side of my hips.

She leans closer to my face, our eyes inches away. "Breathe," she says, softly. "Breathe with me."

"Inhale." I inhale as deep as I can, my eyes never leaving hers.

"Exhale." I exhale, my heart rate slowing to a calmer pace.

"Focus on the sounds around us." I hear leaves rustling in the trees, the waterfall, the cicadas. Avery's breath, her chest rising and falling.

"Feel your hands. Open and close them." I do. And my body starts to relax. The panic is passing and now I am fully aware of

Avery's body above me. She leans down and places a soft kiss to my forehead and settles herself next to me, her body never leaving mine. Draping an arm across my chest, she nuzzles her head between my chest and shoulder. The way she fits plants a different ache in my heart than what was there a few minutes ago.

"How did you know to do that?" I ask, breaking the silence before she has a chance to ask what just happened. Finding Sarah was the worst thing that I have ever been through and I don't talk about it. I never have. Not even with Elias.

"I've had panic attacks most of my life and I learned ways to cope. Learned how to stop them and how to work through them."

"On your own?"

She hesitates. "When I was a kid, yeah. But when I started therapy a few years ago, I was able to learn other methods to help."

"Is that what I had?" I ask. "A panic attack?"

"I think so, yeah. Have you ever had one before?"

I think back to all the nights similar to this one when I have been jerked awake by that memory, taunting me. My chest was tight, and sweat soaked my sheets. The only thing I could do was breathe until I felt the pressure lighten. But what Avery did helped calm my racing heart so much faster.

"I think so. But I never realized that's what it was." I pull her closer and kiss the top of her head. "Thank you," I whisper in her hair.

She hugs me tight, letting her fingers trace circles on my chest and after a few minutes, I hear her breathe in and I know she's going to ask. "Who's Sarah?"

My hand on her lower back stills the soft strokes I was making and I feel my mind start to go into overdrive, but my heart softens. Just a little bit. "Sarah was my sister," I hear myself say. "She was Ethan's mother. Elias's wife."

"What happened to her?" I focus on her hand, her continuous movement against me.

"She died," I say softly. "She had breast cancer. She fought it off once and was in remission for a while, but it came back more aggressive and she decided not to do any more treatments. She didn't want to live the rest of her life in and out of the hospital, weak, tired. Sarah wanted to live her last days, months, whatever time she had left with her family and for them to remember her for who she was, not what she had."

"I'm so sorry," she spreads her hand and flattens it over my heart. "And the nightmare?" My heart quickens against her palm and I know she feels it. "I'm sorry. You don't have to talk about it if you don't want to. I get it. It's personal."

Usually, I wouldn't want to talk about it. When people ask how I'm doing, I avoid the topic altogether and change the subject as fast as I can. Being vulnerable isn't something I do often. Or ever. But being here away from the town, in the woods, it feels like what I say would stay here if I asked.

"I found her. That morning," the image of her lying still on the couch creeps in and for the first time in a long time, I don't close my eyes to it. "We were playing Scrabble the night before, watching a movie. Ethan had come down to say good night, and her and Elias took him back to bed. She came back down to finish our movie and we fell asleep. When I woke up, she was gone. Worst fucking day of my life."

"I don't know what to say," she sniffs.

"Most people don't."

"I'm sorry you were the one that had to go through that. It must have been hard."

"It was. Elias must have heard me yelling her name, trying to wake her up. He came down and once he got my panic under control, he focused on his wife. I didn't know what to do. But he did. Elias always knows what to do. He's the logical one. Always has been. He took care of everything before everyone woke up, especially Ethan. We were all at my parents' house to be together as much as we could. We woke my parents and Sky before the funeral home came, but Elias didn't want Ethan to see her like that on the couch, expecting her to wake up. He was only 5 and he wasn't sure what kind of effect that would have had on him as a kid."

"I can't imagine going through something like that as a kid."

"Yeah, it was hard on him. Still is sometimes. Which is why we do the capture the flag throughout the week. It's a fun distraction for him."

"For both of you," she responds.

"I suppose."

"I can tell you love him more than yourself. No one would go through all the effort you do with him or your whole family if you didn't love them."

I shrug. "I don't do that much."

"Liar," she says and we fall into silence, the only sound is the water and the swaying of the trees. Our breaths lingering in the air.

I can hear hers deepen as she drifts back to sleep. I watch her chest rise and fall and warmth flows through my body at the image of her comforting me, helping me work through my panic. And something else. A feeling. An attraction? No. Something more fills my chest and I tuck her tighter into me, openly afraid to let her go in the morning.

I don't know how long I stay awake, but it's long enough to imagine all the ways I want to wake her up. Soft touches down her spine. A firm kiss to her lips or her cheek. A trail of kisses down her neck. Down, down, down, until I'm nestled between her legs.

Fuck, I have really got to stop making myself hard.

WHEN WE WAKE up in the morning, our legs are tangled together and her ass is pressed up against me. I am wrapped around her, spooning her and there isn't an inch of her body that isn't in contact with me. Her heartbeat picks up and I can tell she's awake, realizing how close we are. Will she break the silence first? Or will she pretend to sleep? I'm all for pretending to sleep because that means we get to lay like this a little longer. But we can't. I have things to do today, and I'm sure she does too.

I make a decision and lean forward to kiss the spot right below her ear. "Sleep well?"

Her eyes fly open and her ass twitches. My hand stills her hip and pushes slightly so she isn't touching me. At least, not there. "Don't do that again," I groan. "Unless you want this morning to get a little bit more exciting."

Avery flings the sleeping bag off of her and jumps up to make her way to the water. When the adrenaline wears off, she slows her steps until she is at the edge. As she crouches down, her ankle gives way and she falls face first into the water.

I burst with laughter as she turns and stands, wiping the water from her face. "That did *not* just happen."

I grab my stomach, my laughter filling the air around us. "Going for a swim, Flounder?"

She limps toward me with a scowl I think is supposed to intimidate me. "This is your fault."

"In what world is *this*," I swipe my hand up and down, gesturing at her now wet appearance. "My fault?" I finish. She doesn't answer, but holds out her hand, palm up. I slap it and get an even deeper scowl. She's more beautiful when she's trying to scare me. "Yes, Sunshine?"

"My clothes are wet. You owe me a shirt. Give me yours."

I don't hesitate to strip off my shirt and place it in her still open hand.

"As you wish," I say and her eyes widen, not leaving my torso. I think she realizes her mistake at the same time I give her a knowing smile. But she calls my bluff and goes behind a tree to change out of her wet shirt. Part of me was hoping she wouldn't call me on it so she had to stay in her wet shirt. Now I'm hiking shirtless, but I can tell she doesn't mind so I sure as hell am not going to let it bother me.

She's leaving, I remind myself. She's leaving and there's nothing here I want to let myself consider. She's gorgeous, sure, and I was more vulnerable with her last night than I have been with anyone currently in my life. I don't talk about Sarah. To anyone. Sky included. Then again, Sky is less likely to approach the subject than I am. And for the first few months after her death, Elias somehow managed to direct every conversation back to Sarah.

The brunch was particularly good that day. "Remember when Sarah made the perfect batch of pancakes?"

Or when he spent a week in the workshop with me, watching me carve and trying to learn for himself. "Remember when Sarah wanted you to do a carving of me for her and it looked like Freddie Kruger? Good thing you stick with animals."

Or when Ethan decided for the thousandth time he wanted a

different colored flag for the week. "Remember when Sarah made us all play flag football during brunch so Ethan could coach us from the sidelines?"

Remember when. Remember when. Remember when.

The last three years of my life have been filled with "remember whens" and every time they creep into my head it makes my heart ache. I remember all of them. I remember all of Sarah, and in the months following her death all I wanted to do was forget. It's still what I want to do. I think.

I spent those months avoiding those conversations and eventually everyone gave up trying to talk to me about Sarah. If anyone needed a heart-to-heart, they figured out I was not the person to go to. I'm still not. I don't do feelings, but the nightmare is fresh in my mind and it feels like I am going to explode if I don't talk about it. It felt safe under the cover of darkness with the moon and stars being the only light, and the waterfall drowning out the chorus of the night.

My hands tingle at the memory of feeling her skin against mine. Stroking the little bit of skin that showed under the hem of her shirt. Shaking my head, I rub my hands down my face and sigh. Resolved with my decision. I walk toward Avery where she has started packing things into my bag, ready to get back to town. What can I say to her to get her to understand how I feel? If I asked her to be with me for the time she has left, would she? It might be short, but all I know is the tightness in my chest doesn't feel as suffocating when she is near.

I rub the back of my neck, a nervous habit, and open my mouth to speak.

"Look, I appreciate you taking me on this hike," says Avery, beating me in breaking our silence.

The ache tightens again. A python wrapping around its prey, tightening and tightening until there is no breath left.

"But whatever this is," she gestures between us, "it stays in the woods. Okay? I'm here to figure out my life, and you're not in the plan. If the plan was the Cliffs of Insanity, you'd be the boat sailing in the opposite direction as fast and as far as you could."

Ouch. I flinch.

She doesn't meet my eyes, and a part of me feels like she doesn't agree with the words she's saying. But, I'll respect her wishes. Even if it hurts.

I smirk. "But who would be there to rescue you from the Dread Pirate Roberts?"

That earns me another glare. Her most daunting yet. "I don't need rescuing."

I take a different approach. "So what you're saying is, we never leave the woods?" I raise my eyebrows, hoping she takes the bait and bites back.

She gives me a mischievous look, leaving whatever thought she had behind. "In your dreams, Waters."

"Oh, I hope so." Another glare. I've pushed too far, so I backtrack, hands raised in surrender. "Alright, alright. Whatever this is…was, stays here."

"Thank you," she whispers.

"As you wish."

Heat rushes to her cheeks before she turns away and tries to shove the last half of the sleeping bag sticking out of the pack, taking the leaves that were stuck to the bottom with it. She slings the bag over her shoulders once it's packed and starts limping her way down the path, her eyes focusing on anything but my bare chest.

"You think you're going to make it all the way back limping like that?" I call after her.

She doesn't turn around. "How else am I supposed to get back?"

Right on cue, she stumbles and I rush to her side to catch her, one hand on her waist covered by my shirt and the other right under her armpit. Or, more accurately, right next to her breast. My fingers graze the side of it and it is my turn for heat to rise in my face. I quickly move my hand, just not in the direction my body *really* wants it to go and turn away from her, crouching down until my back is low enough for her.

"Hop on."

"Excuse me?"

"Hop on," I repeat.

"You're going to carry me? All the way back?" She says clearly doubting my ability or strength or whatever it would take to get her back to the inn.

"I've had to carry my dogs through worse, I'll be fine. C'mon. Hop on," I say again. To my surprise she follows my directions without any more questions. She wraps her legs around my lower back, my forearms resting under her knees and her arms around my neck.

Fuck, I wish I had my shirt. The contact of our skin sends more thoughts to my head I have to force out. She does not belong there and as much as I want to follow the direction of those thoughts, play out what her body does to mine, how mine reacts to hers clinging to my back, I am not going to let myself go there.

Not until she wants me to.

CHAPTER SEVENTEEN

AVERY

*Y*ep. He definitely got sideboob when he tried to catch me. While he carries me—on the same out-and-back trail we hiked yesterday—I try as hard as I can to not think about how good it felt to have his hand there and how much I wish he had moved it in the opposite direction. After I *just* told him I basically wanted nothing to do with him. Now, there isn't a part of my body that isn't touching his and I am aware of every single point of contact between our bodies.

With every step he takes, the muscles in his back flex and touch the very center of me, making it sensitive and driving me absolutely insane.

I try to focus on anything else. The trees. *What type are these? Pine? Oak? What kind of oak? White or red? Is that sassafras we just passed? If I crumpled it, would I smell the familiar scent of Fruit Loops and be transported back to my childhood?*

The way I completely panicked earlier and all of the sudden decided to make a deal to be just friends? Stupid. I don't want that. From the way my body is pulsating, she definitely doesn't want that either. Nope, don't want to think about it. Must invade my mind with anything other than Hudson's muscles flexing underneath me.

Uhhhhh, weeds! Yes, lots of weeds. So many weeds. Are there different species of weeds? Probably. I wonder if weeds are poisonous. This is working. Definitely not thinking about the strong grip Hudson has under my knees. I never realized how sensitive that part of my body was. But, apparently, right now, it's the most sensitive part of me. The way his fingers dig in with just enough pressure. Not enough to hurt, but enough to keep his grip firm and steady. I wonder what the pressure of his fingers would feel like elsewhere, replacing the warmth of his back between my legs, opening with one, exploring with another...

NO!

Weeds. Does poison ivy count as a weed, or is that an actual plant? Is there poison ivy around? That does it. The feeling of Hudson beneath me is quickly replaced by fear. My fear of contracting the red, itchy rash.

It has me paranoid and focusing my eyes on the ground around us. I have had poison ivy exactly once in my life from exploring the woods in our backyard, and I remember being absolutely miserable for days after. No amount of calamine lotion or aloe vera could soothe my skin and I made it my number one rule of exploring in the woods. Never come into contact with poison ivy ever again.

"You doing okay back there?" Hudson asks, adjusting his hands. "You're fidgeting."

"Uh, yeah," I continue to look around for red vines with three leaves. A mantra in my head. *Red vine, three leaves.* Like Donkey from Shrek, *blue flower, red thorns.*

I laugh at my train of thought and question how it can go from thinking of Hudson's hands on the most intimate parts of my body to thinking of a fictional talking donkey. The human brain, specifically mine, is a marvel.

"What are you laughing at?"

"Nothing."

"It's not nothing. I'm bored up here, so spill." I have a slight suspicion he is trying to avoid thoughts similar to mine.

"Is poison ivy a weed?" I ask.

"What?"

"Is poison ivy a weed?" I repeat. "Or is it a plant?"

"Any particular reason you're asking about poison ivy?"

"No," I say, adjusting my grip around his neck. "I am just curious."

"Curious?"

"*Yes.*" Exasperated by the fact he's not answering my question. "You know, inquisitive, interested?"

"I know what curious means," he sighs.

"Well, you were acting like you didn't, so I wasn't sure. I don't know you. You could be the typical burly man with nothing behind your handsome features and defined jaw."

"You think my features are handsome?" He drawls.

"You know, for someone who *just* entered into an agreement to stay away from one another, you flirt an awful lot."

"Hey, flirting wasn't part of the agreement. And *you're* the one plastered to my back."

"Through no choice of my own!"

"You have a choice."

"Sure, limping my way back sounds like a fantastic idea," the sarcasm drips from my lips.

He chuckles and zig zags his way through the trees and around the branches in the way of our path. The silence stretches between us, but this time it isn't an uncomfortable, tension-filled silence. It's...nice. The wind whistles through the trees and the leaves rustle every once in a while from whatever creature is scurrying by. Sounds of the forest and the nearby creek are comforting and calming in a way I haven't felt in a long time.

And suddenly, I find myself wishing we never left the waterfall. Wishing that the peace I feel now in the woods with Hudson could last through my stay, even though the end is inevitable. I'm leaving soon and starting anything with Hudson is just asking for more heartbreak. But the thought of staying away from him leaves an empty feeling in my stomach. A hunger that can't be satisfied unless he is near me.

I let out a long sigh and resign myself to the fact that Hudson and I are going to have to figure out a way to honor what I decided. Just friends. We can do just friends as long as he stays on his side of town and I stay on mine.

Right?

Right.

BY THE TIME we make it back to the inn, it's a little past noon. The lunch crowd fills the dining room, and when we cross the threshold, me still on Hudson's back, a hush falls over the room. I've never seen a crowd of people fall silent so fast outside of the stillness that follows people in the theater when a movie starts. But these people have a reason. I can only imagine what it looks like from their perspective.

Hudson shirtless, me hanging from his back *wearing* his shirt, both of us covered in dirt and mud from the hike back where we obviously spent the night together.

Why didn't we go back to his house to change first? I should have put my damp clothes back on. I didn't think through the ramifications of coming here, in *this* town, in our current state. To make matters worse, both Cordie *and* Fran are at the front desk, their smiles stretching wide across their faces. Both of them channeling the Cheshire Cat; mischievous, cunning, plotting.

"And just where have you two been?" asks Fran.

At the same time, Cordie asks in a suggestive tone, "What have you two been up to?"

"Hiking."

Always with the one-word answers.

The Hudson in the woods has faded away and in his place is the grump of a man I met in the coffee shop the first day I came to town. *No.* I'm surprised that's not the word he used, refusing to answer their questions. But, from what I have observed since I have been here, I know he has a soft spot for these two, especially Fran, so a little explanation is warranted on his part.

I slide off Hudson's back to the left, careful not to land on my injured ankle. Unfortunately, being careful also means going slow and I feel *everything*. The hardness of his back against my chest, his firm ass against the inside of my thighs, his hands never leaving my body even when I land on my foot. His left hand moves to my hip and remains there to help support me or just to touch me, I don't know. I'm not complaining.

"Hudson took me hiking yesterday," I explain. "We fell and I twisted my ankle, and we couldn't make it back before dark, so we camped overnight and came back when we could. But I fell in the water this morning so my clothes were soaked and Hudson offered his shirt and then he carried me back because I couldn't walk, and here we are." The words tumble out of my mouth, a rock slide careening down the side of a mountain. I take a deep breath as the two women stare at us, their smiles still plastered on their faces, ever growing, if that's even possible. Trouble is looming behind their eyes.

I turn to Hudson and lightly punch his arm. "So, uh, thanks for the hike and for seeing me back here safely and everything." I hesitate, not sure how much to say or if I should say anything else. His green eyes bore into mine, a question looming there I'm afraid for him to ask.

"Welcome," is all he says.

"I can, uh, take it from here." I move out of his grip. He hesitates for a moment, tightening the hand on my hip before he lets go and turns to the door to leave without looking back.

Fran and Cordie haven't moved their gazes from me. I give them a sheepish smile and start limping my way upstairs eager for a shower that's not in the middle of the woods.

When I get to my room, I realize I am still wearing Hudson's shirt and consequently, my damp clothes are still in his bag. As is all of my camera equipment.

Nice going, Avery.

The first day of staying away from each other and we are already failing. If it were just my clothes, I'd leave it alone. I have plenty in my suitcase. But I *need* my equipment. It's part of the reason I came here and it's part of me. It took me ages to save up for all of it. Along with the paper, I worked at a local restaurant waiting tables and all the checks and tips I made from there went to my photography equipment. It took me almost a year to save enough to spend on camera gear, on top of all the bills I still had to pay. Which meant, unfortunately, I am going to have to go to Hudson's place to retrieve it.

Lovely.

I grab my phone to send him a quick text, but am bombarded with messages, voicemails, and notifications when I turn it back on. I delete my mom's voicemails without listening to them and ignore the emails from my boss that I will get around to answering later and pull up mine and Hudson's text conversation. What should I say? The last time we texted, it was because I accidentally sent a picture of my feet. Well, my feet in shoes. Not feet pics. I don't know his picture preferences, nor do I need to.

> Me: Hi, um, I forgot my camera equipment in your bag... Do you mind if I come by and get it later? I need it to take the photos I planned to take today and I have nothing else going on, so let me know if I can come grab it.

DELETE. Way too long.

> Me: Hey, do you have my camera stuff? I think I forgot to grab it.

I hold down the backspace and watch the letters disappear from the screen. I'm overthinking this.

> Me: You have my camera equipment.

I hit send before I can once again over analyze the message, ignoring the three dots that show up on the screen. I toss my phone on the chaise underneath the window, but have to retrieve it a second later when a FaceTime call lights up the screen as soon as it lands. I had a feeling she'd be calling soon considering half of the messages I didn't respond to are hers.

I swipe to answer the call. "Hey, Charlotte."

"OMG, where have you BEEN?" she yells. "I thought you were dead. I finally just called the inn and Cordie said you went hiking yesterday and hadn't come back. What the hell, Ave! Why didn't you take your phone with you? That's like hiking 101!" She yells.

I feel a twinge of guilt at the idea of making her worry so much. I didn't think about letting her know where I was going and how I might not answer. I just wanted a day when I didn't hear from Sharon or have to think about her.

"I'm sorry. Sharon called yesterday and I just wanted a day away from my phone so Hudson took me hiking and I twisted my ankle and we got stuck and—"

"WHAT?" she yells, cutting me off.

"I said I—"

"No, nononono, I *heard* what you said. And first of all, fuck Sharon. She's the worst and I don't get why you let her manipulate you and make you feel like shit. Cut the head off the snake and leave her behind. I've been telling you this."

And she has. Ever since Sharon dropped by my apartment when Charlotte was there and not so subtly criticized everything in it, including me, she has made it her mission to get me to cut Sharon off. I don't know why I can't let go. I know she's not the greatest person, but she's still my mother and that counts for something, right? Part of me just doesn't know anymore and having a relationship with her is becoming more difficult. She makes it difficult. No matter what I do, I'm never the daughter she wants me to be.

"And two," Charlotte says, pulling me from my thoughts. "You spent the night with Hudson?" She squeals.

"Yes, but it's not like that!" I blurt out. Because it wasn't. It isn't. "Nothing is going to happen there, Charlotte. We agreed."

"Who agreed?"

"Hudson and I agreed."

"Ummm, if you agreed nothing was happening there, then something must have happened. So, what happened?"

I consider not telling her anything. Telling her what *almost* happened is just going to give her more fuel to feed the fire or whatever it is (or isn't) between us. But I need to talk about it. I learned over the years that I don't cope well when I don't talk through my feelings or what I'm thinking. My therapist has helped me realize how much I kept to myself throughout my childhood and how damaging it was for me.

I go into an explanation of the hike, the mud, my ankle, the waterfall, and the almost kiss.

"He was going to kiss you and you stopped him? WHY would you stop him?" she yells.

"Because, Charlotte. I'm leaving soon. Why would I start something when I know I'm leaving?"

"Why wouldn't you? Have you never had a fling before? Why can't it just be that?"

No, I've never had a fling. Ever. I've only had relationships. I've never even really dated before, besides James. I had my first boyfriend when I was a sophomore in high school and we dated until senior year. We broke up for the reasons you'd expect. Different colleges, different goals, didn't want to do long distance. Then I met a guy in college, which again didn't work out.

It never helped that Sharon was always in the back of my mind, reminding me that it was my fault when my relationships fell apart. Remembering James and the train wreck that turned into, I don't think I'm the best judge of character when it comes to guys anyway.

"I don't think I'm a fling type of person," I respond. I feel things too deeply and I always fall first. And it's usually face first.

"But how do you know you aren't a fling person when you've never tried? Stop overthinking everything and just have fun for once, Ave. I'm begging you."

"I *am* having fun. Just my version of it."

"Alright, alright. I can respect that. But, wait, whose shirt are you wearing?" she asks.

Shit. I realize I am still wrapped in Hudson's shirt, clearly visible to Charlotte on the screen.

"Uhhh, mine?" I say, trying to play it off, but I already know she isn't going to let it go.

"HAH, nice try. I know you. You don't own flannel."

"You don't know every shirt I own. I could have bought this recently or received it as a gift."

"You mean you received it as a gift from a hot man from a charming, Hallmark-like, small town who *carried you on his back* so you didn't have to walk back and further hurt yourself?"

Putting my face in my free hand, I groan. "Stooooop, okay? It's his shirt. I fell in the water this morning and didn't have anything to change into so I made him give me his shirt because he was being an ass about it."

Charlotte responds with a burst of laughter. Her face leaves the screen as she doubles over, her guttural laugh filling the air. "You are so in for it," I hear her voice say. I roll my eyes, ignoring just how right she might be.

EXHAUSTION OVERWHELMS MY BODY. The rest of our conversation included more teasing from Charlotte and more of me insisting I could keep up my end of the deal Hudson and I made. As much as I want to crawl under the covers and sleep the rest of the day, I can't consciously get into clean bed sheets without first cleaning myself.

I strip off Hudson's shirt and resist the temptation to inhale the scent of him. Pine, salt, and a type of woodsy scent, maybe cedar, or cherry. Whatever it is, it's intoxicating and it might just be my new drug.

After I shower, lingering longer under the steady stream of water—hot enough to make my skin look like I spent the last few hours reading on the beach with no sun protectant—I dress quickly in another pair of leggings and an oversized gray sweatshirt, and tie my hair in a red ribbon with frayed ends. My ankle throbs a little less and the swelling isn't as bad as it was this morning. Probably because I haven't really been walking on it much today. It's still sore, but the pain is manageable. At least enough to go get my equipment, come back and curl up in bed with my laptop on the empty side of the bed streaming movies the rest of the day. However, when I sit on the bed to tie my shoes, I am greeted with a soaked bed sheet.

Just what I need, I think as a drop of water hits the top of my head. "You've *got* to be kidding me."

I stand and watch as another water droplet cascades from the ceiling and lands with a wet drip on top of the wet spot. A leaky roof. Perfect. Between the hike, last night, Hudson this morning, and the teasing from Charlotte, this is the last thing I want to deal with. I'm going to have to pack all of my stuff, most of which is strewn everywhere as I made myself at home over the last few days, move into a different room, and get settled there before I can cocoon myself for the evening.

"Cordie!" I call down the stairs as I slowly make my way to the front desk, using the railing as a crutch.

"Yes, dear?" She calls back from the front desk where she is attempting to crochet either a sweater or a blanket. Maybe a scarf with extra ends? I can't tell.

"My room has a leak in the roof right above the bed."

She sets down her work and sighs. "I was afraid of that. Sometimes with heavy rain like we got the other day, the roof leaks every now and then. Your room is one of the frequent ones that suffers, but I was hoping the last repairs Elias did would hold up a little while longer."

She stands from her stool and reaches for the phone before I can ask where she wants me to move my stuff. "Fran!" She says louder than her normal speaking volume.

"Leaky roof again....yeah, Avery's room...yeah, same place....Where do you think she can stay? You got room at your place?....Mmmm, maybe? I think he has family in town...Oh, good idea! We can ask around there."

Her features change. They go from worried to scheming in the matter of seconds. What I wouldn't give to hear what Fran was saying on the other end, because they are up to something.

"Now *that's* an idea... he's got the room...Would he do it?" She chuckles at something Fran says.

"You're right, Franny...Okay, I'll let her know. See you at 6." Cordie hangs up the phone and levels her eyes with mine, light and fire behind her gaze.

"Here's what we are going to do," she starts. "All the rooms here are booked and I'm sure one or two of the others have the same leaks. The whole roof needs replacing, I just haven't had the money to do it, so Elias patches it up for me when he can, but he's out of town and even if he were here, it would take too long."

It takes me a second to register what she's saying. "Wait, you mean I can't stay here?"

She shakes her head, "Nope. Everything is booked. Fran had the idea of asking around at the town meeting later tonight to see who might have a room for you to stay in for the rest of your visit."

My stomach drops at the idea of losing my own space and staying in a stranger's home. The inn is technically a stranger's home, but it doesn't feel like that. Over the last few days, I've found myself looking forward to being greeted by Cordie, and sometimes Ethan and the other guests in the dining room. Walking up the creaky stairs toward my room where I can seclude myself and work on editing that day's photos. Now, I'll have to worry about intruding in someone else's space, not really knowing what to do with myself or my things. I sigh, this trip is starting to give me more stress than it is relieving it.

"There's no other inn in town I can stay in?" I ask, already knowing the answer.

"Sorry, honey. This is the only one here. But don't you worry," she says, reaching over the desk to pat my arm. "We will find you a place to stay where you'll be just as comfortable as you have been here."

I don't know what it is, but something about her smile makes me think that there is a lot more to her and Fran's conversation than she is letting on.

CHAPTER EIGHTEEN

HUDSON

Sunshine: You have my camera equipment.

A fact I realized as soon as I walked into the living room and set the bag down, and it landed with a heavier thud than warranted considering its contents. When I opened it to unpack a covered lense peeked out from under her damp clothes, another thing I forgot was in there.

I pull my phone from my back pocket as I move through all of my dogs to let them out back. Thankfully I was able to send a quick text to Sky last night to let her know what happened and to ask her to take care of them so I wouldn't come home to piss-covered floors. They drive me crazy most days, but I wouldn't change it. Every time Jacob at the shelter finds a golden retriever puppy or an adult someone can't take care of anymore, he calls me and I adopt them.

I don't think I could even name all of the animals we had had as kids because my family has always supported the animal shelter. My favorite was always our family dog, Margo, an old golden retriever we fell in love with at the shelter the day we went to look for a guinea pig for Sky. But Margo found us instead. We were goners as soon as she looked at us. We took her home right away and she lived her last two years in a home filled with love, belly scratches, and lots of tennis balls. Ever since then, I've had a soft spot for dogs, but the biggest for goldens. I have five of them so far: Bernard, Buddy, Judy, Hermes, and Patch. They're a lot to handle on the best day, but they are also the best cuddlers and the reason I have a king sized bed.

As the five of them take care of their business, I start typing out a text to Avery.

> Me: I noticed.

I can almost hear her roll her eyes at the short response and I smile. Walking toward the barn, I swipe away the text conversation and open up my Etsy app. I ignore the email notifications and go straight to the current orders. At least ten new orders have come in since yesterday morning when we left for the hike. I open up the first picture to a medium sized husky lab with wide brown eyes, ears perked, and what looks like a smile on her face.

Etsy Order Confirmation for: $150.00

Subject: Shiva

Message: Hi! I was referred to your shop by a friend of mine who ordered from you in the past and I am really impressed by your work. Our husky lab, Shiva, has been an amazing part of our family for years and we would love to have something of her for our mantle. I attached a few pictures of her at her best from different angles. Let me know if there's any other details you need from me.

Looking forward to working with you!

Kay

I SCROLL through the few pictures she sent and open the next order.

Etsy Order Confirmation for: $150.00

Subject: Mia

Message: Hello, I absolutely love your shop and your work. I found you through an Instagram ad and knew I had to contact you. We lost our husky malamute suddenly a few weeks ago. She had a mass on her spleen and it ruptured. We didn't know she had it and we were taken by surprise by her passing. I'd love to have a carving of her to have in our home. My husband and I have had her since she was two years old and she has been such a permanent fixture in our lives. She lived a long life and having a piece of her to see every day would make it easier. I have pictures attached as requested so you can see her profile. If there's anything else you need, don't hesitate to ask.

Marie

FUCK. Cancer. The word looms above me, big and haunting. A whisper of the past tickling my skin, reminding me of the way it felt when Sarah first told us of her diagnosis years ago.

Unfortunately, a lot of the carvings I do are for dogs that have died because of cancer, and no matter how many times I read those words, it never gets any easier. I open the pictures and a fluffy white dog with striking blue eyes fills the screen. Her mouth is open, tongue hanging out and a soccer ball sitting in front of her. I smile and hope the end wasn't too painful for her.

I look through the other orders, most of them similar to the ones before. A great dane passing from old age, a pug close to the end, a young bulldog the owner just wanted a carving of for no other reason than to immortalize their best friend.

I try to think of ideas for each dog, but my mind keeps

seeing the white ball of fluff, pure happiness shining behind her blue eyes. My hands itch to get started and the ideas circulate through my head on how to make the resemblance perfect for the owners and for Mia. Fluffier dogs are the hardest to get right, but I like a challenge. I start by sorting through the logs I cut earlier in the week when I tried and failed to get Avery out of my head after our initial meeting at Fran's. The cuts weren't all perfectly straight, so I sort through them until I find a log I think will suffice.

I secure it on the lathe and grab my tools when my phone pings with a text notification. I had forgotten I texted Avery a bit ago before I looked through my orders.

> Sunshine: Okaaaayy. Can I come get it?

> Me: If you want.

> Sunshine: Well, I have nothing else to do besides the town meeting later so do you have time for me to come get it now?

The town meeting? Why would she be going to that? It's only for people who live here and while she's obviously here temporarily, why would she be interested in something that's really just a cover for Tom, the town magistrate, to complain to an audience forced to listen? I've been attending for years and no matter what it is, he will always bring up an issue at the monthly town meeting and complain about it so the whole town is made aware of it. And more often than not the issue won't go anywhere past his complaints, but there is the rare occasion where actual town issues come up that need a solution. But very rarely do they include someone from out of town.

I ignore Avery's message for now and focus on my work. Pulling my hair in a tight knot, I cover my eyes with my safety glasses and put on my work gloves. I turn it on, the wood slowly picking up speed. Sawdust flies as I start molding the shape I want, slowly making it smaller and smaller until it resembles what I have in my head. By the time I finish making the basic shape, an hour has gone by and I remember I never responded to Avery. After some debate, I decide to deal with it later. The itch to continue making progress on this carving needs to be answered first.

The dogs perk their heads up at my movement as I start to take the piece of wood off the lathe and move to the next step of my process. They like to keep me company while I work, cuddling together a distance far enough away that the sawdust won't land on their fur. The noise never seems to bother them and more often than not, they use it as a time to rest together.

I rearrange the tools on my table and grab the knife I need to start cutting away the bigger pieces of wood to shape out Mia. The moment I sit down to carve, however, my phone buzzes a few inches away, the screen lighting up with a text notification. I see Avery's name before I pull up our text conversation.

Sunshine: I gave you an hour. I'm on my way.

I roll my eyes at the thought of her expecting me to be immediately available when she texted. I try not to be too attached to my phone, especially when I have work to do. I never really even bring my phone with me into the workshop, but I forgot to leave it in the house earlier and didn't feel like taking it back inside. Now, I'm wishing I had.

I'll never understand people expecting others to be constantly available and ready to answer a phone call or a text at the drop of a hat. I'll be the first to admit that I'm not the greatest communicator when it comes to technology and I really don't want to be. It's just not who I am. I start typing out a snarky response, but then hit the backspace button.

I think about how important my work is to me and wonder if Avery feels the same when it comes to her photography.

When I looked at the camera equipment that she left in the bag earlier, it didn't look like some run-of-the-mill camera. It looked professional. Like something you would expect a professional photographer to have. Giving her the benefit of the doubt, I type out a less grumpy text.

> Me: Sorry. Working. You can come by whenever. Or I can bring it to the town meeting later for you.

This feels far too personal after our agreement to stay away from each other this morning. Was that only this morning? It feels like it was days ago. The ache in my chest hasn't lightened since this morning and the idea of seeing her here makes it loosen. Just a bit.

My heart wars with my brain when I imagine her sitting next to the dogs, their heads and bodies snug next to her watching me work, her camera propped on her drawn up knees as she cycles through pictures she's taken from the day. She changes the settings to adjust to the lighting in my workshop to take pictures of me and instead of feeling embarrassed or closed off as is my specialty, the idea of sharing that part of me feels... comfortable. Something about it strikes a chord in me, creating a melody I can't stop listening to.

I pick up my phone and type out a text to tell her to just come here and we can walk to the town meeting together when a response from her shows up under my last text.

> Sunshine: I'm grabbing some dinner now, so I'll meet you at the meeting to grab it.

Before I can talk myself out of it or come up with another stupid excuse, I type out a text and send it.

> Me: A bit early for dinner, isn't it? Grab some for me and bring it here. We can eat, you can get your stuff, and we can go to the meeting together.

Together.

That word adds a crescendo to the melody and my heart picks up speed.

"What am I doing?" I ask out loud. The dogs all look at me, heads tilted, questioning.

The more important question is, what is *she* doing? After telling me she just wanted to be friends, I would assume she'd rather meet me at the meeting and not come into my personal space.

Rubbing my hands over my face, I let out a sigh and return to my work, ignoring the pounding in my chest and the gnawing in my stomach that definitely isn't from hunger.

CHAPTER NINETEEN

HUDSON

By the time Avery shows up, another hour has passed and I've made significant progress on Mia. Her outline is smoothed out and her profile is starting to take shape to resemble the picture Marie sent over.

I watch as Avery stops and stares at my house, probably trying to figure out how someone like me lives in such a large home. It's a two-story cabin, with more rooms than I know what to do with, but when Elias designed it for me, Sarah insisted on adding rooms for the big family she was convinced I would have in the future. It may be large with way too much space for me, but it is comfortable for the dogs and I. Plus, Ethan has plenty of room to spread out when he comes to stay with me while his dad is stuck on a deadline for projects.

I hear her knock on the door and see her step back, waiting for me to answer. Judy and Bernard sprint over to her and start putting their noses on everything in sniffing distance before she lifts her head, looking in the direction they came from. She scratches under Judy's chin as her eyes look up to find mine.

The pressure in my chest lightens as she walks toward me, brown bags in hand with the two dogs happily trotting at her heels. She is dressed in black leggings and a gray sweatshirt that is probably way too hot for the warmer weather, but she looks comfortable. And gorgeous.

"Hey," she says quietly when she reaches the entrance to the barn.

I crouch down and reach for Judy and Bernard to come back next to me. "Sorry about them. They're the ones who get a little bit too friendly with guests."

"It's fine," she says, bending down to continue showering Judy with chin scratches. "I love dogs. Especially goldens," she says. "I remember the stray I fed in our backyard when I was a kid. I risked sneaking him in the house a few times. He was my buddy."

I don't let my features change at her words; don't let the excitement I feel at her admission show. We're acquaintances. Two strangers passing in the night, oblivious to one another, buried in our own world as we continue walking. Except I'm not oblivious to her. As much as I wish I was, I'm not. The trepidation I felt earlier about her coming here lessens with her actual presence, and I feel a feathery lightness in my chest that I'm not sure what to do with.

"So, couldn't help but come by again? Stalking me, Sunshine?" I give her a sideways grin, hiking up one eyebrow. Questioning.

"In your dreams, Waters. I'm here for the dogs," she claps back.

I love it.

"I stopped by your sister's," she continues. "Her store, that is. I was bored and desperate and really wanted my camera. I was hoping to walk around town today to take some more pictures, but obviously I couldn't and ended up scouting out places to take pictures tomorrow instead and stopped by Sky's," she says, pulling the red ribbon from her hair and running her fingers through it, letting it fall over her left shoulder.

"I was too restless without my camera and then realized it had been a while since I ate and figured since I wasn't sure where I'm staying tonight, I'd get something to eat now, and well, here I am."

The words come out in a rush and I'm surprised I am able to understand. In one hand she holds the bag of food I'm assuming is from Frank's bar given the grease stains spreading on the bottom of the bag and from the scent of burgers filling the air. Her other hand rests at her side, opening and closing. I've noticed she does this in certain situations and after, she seems calmer...grounded. Since she helped me through my panic last night, I assume it's a way of coping with anxiety. Something I don't think she had planned on opening up about. I don't think either of us planned on opening up the way we did, and I got the feeling she didn't like being vulnerable any more than I did. Yet, here she is. A few feet away from me after we agreed to stay away from each other for the remainder of her trip.

Her eyes wander around my shop, landing on my shelf of projects, skimming over the pile of wood off to the side and stopping on the project I placed on the table a few minutes ago when I stood to greet her.

"What exactly is this?" She asks.

"My workshop." I don't know what it is about my answers that bother her, but for some reason, when I don't go into massive detail and just give her the bare minimum, it creates a little wrinkle on her forehead and she squints her eyes at me in annoyance. Making the wrinkle appear is becoming my new favorite thing to do.

"Your workshop for?"

"My shop." The wrinkle deepens.

"Your shop for?"

"My projects." I think I can actually see the steam coming out of her ears. It's so easy to get under her skin and part of me wishes she'd let me stay there. I'd attach myself to her forever, even if it's just to see her forehead wrinkle and the death glare she gives me. She groans in frustration and doesn't ask any more questions.

Instead, she walks over to the shelves and looks over the orders I haven't sent yet. A small poodle named Isabel whose owners wanted a replica for their son to have in his room. Next to her is a great dane, Fiona. The bulk of my customers want the carvings as they are, no paint or anything, leaving the wood to show. But Fiona's wanted me to paint her likeness and while it wasn't something I really enjoyed doing, I like how hers turned out. She had a little bit of gray in the face that was hard to replicate, but after mixing the colors a few times, I was able to get it to come across the way it did in her pictures. She's littered with black spots down her back, mixed with white and gray. I finished painting her a few days ago and I need to get her shipped to the owners either today or tomorrow, but I keep forgetting to grab packing supplies. That was my plan a few days ago after I finished fixing the espresso machine for Fran, but things changed.

Avery picks up Fiona. "Did you make all of these?" she asks, not trying to hide the surprise in her voice.

"Yes," I answer.

"This is what you do?"

"Yes." She levels me with a look I can only describe as exasperated. "I run an Etsy shop." Her jaw drops as I suspected it would. Most people's reactions are the same.

"Surprised?" I ask and she quickly closes her mouth and places Fiona back on the shelf with careful movements.

"Uh, no. Just, uh....," she stutters, considering her words. "Yeah, surprised, I guess."

"What did you think I do for a living?"

Most people guess my profession based on my looks. I have a muscular build and I have long hair, wear a lot of flannel, and people assume I work on a farm or do some kind of manual labor, which I guess is included in what I do with chopping wood for my projects, but there's more to me than what people see. They just don't stick around long enough to find out what it is I actually do.

"I don't know what I expected," she says, waving a hand to brush it off. "But it wasn't something soooo...." She searches for a word.

"Attractive? Sexy? Manly? Irresistible?"

"Creative," she finishes, not taking the bait. I give her a soft smile and silently thank her for seeing me.

"I mean, look at all of these," she continues, turning back toward the shelves. "These are incredible, Hudson. How did you get into this?"

Opening the bag, I start laying out the food on the table, avoiding her gaze.

"I started carving when I was a kid. It was always something fun to do, just small things here and there, but I really enjoyed creating dogs. When our family dog passed away, I made one for my parents and my siblings. Sarah posted hers online and it gained a lot of traction. So she convinced me to open a shop and it grew from there. I eventually got enough orders and attention, I was able to use it as my full time income."

"What did you do before?"

"I mostly helped my buddy Axel at his mechanic shop in town. I still do sometimes if his dad can't handle the workload. He has chronic pain and can't always help around the shop as much as he used to, so I step in whenever I'm needed. But mostly I do this," I gesture at the shelves behind me.

"I enjoy working with my hands." I give her a sly smile and a blush creeps up her collarbone, spreading to her neck and filling her cheeks. "C'mon," I motion to the food now spread out on the table. "Let's eat before it gets cold."

We eat in a comfortable silence for a few minutes until the

dogs realize we have food and surround us, waiting for anything to drop from the table.

She tilts her chin down at them. "What are their names?" she asks.

"There's Bernard and Judy, the two who accosted you when you got here," I point to the two closest to her. Judy has slim features and softer fur than the rest of them, while Bernard is more lanky.

"And then there's Buddy," I point to the largest one next to me. He's also the oldest and has a little gray on his snout. He's been moving slower these days and I've been feeling like these past few months are some of his last. I give in and throw him a few fries from my pile and he quickly grabs them before the others do.

"And the other two?" She gestures to the two sleeping at the back of the barn, oblivious to the food she brought in.

"Those two came from the same litter and are thick as thieves. I couldn't stand the idea of separating them." Her features soften before she continues to eat her burger and sneaks a few fries to Judy and Bernard when she thinks I'm not looking. "They're Hermes and Patch."

I can see her trying to figure out the connection of their names. No one has ever caught the reference and I'm curious to see if she will.

She bursts into laughter around her bite of burger and covers her mouth.

"What?" I ask.

"You're just not what I expected, Hudson."

"And what did you expect?"

"Well," she says behind her hand. "For starters, I did not expect you to name your dogs after elves."

"What can I say? I really love Christmas movies."

She doesn't say anything else and I think I've finally won our banter match.

Hudson - 1. Avery - 0.

"You know, you're the first one to ever put that together."

"Well, I love Christmas movies, I used to watch them with my mom sometimes. Christmas was the only time she was nice to me. Or made an effort to be nice and have a relationship with me, that is." Sadness creeps into her features and I reach for her leg inches from mine. I give her knee a squeeze, hoping it brings her some form of comfort. I wait for her to move away, but she doesn't, so I rest my hand there until we finish eating.

My thumb starts moving back and forth, a mind of its own, but neither of us make any move to stop it.

After we are done eating, I collect the wrappers and food bags and toss them in the trash can near the door. According to my watch, we have about an hour before the meeting starts which is plenty of time to walk there. It's only about two miles away.

"I'll go grab your equipment, feed the dogs real quick, and we can head to the meeting."

"Okay, thanks."

I start walking toward the house before I realize something and spin back around to face Avery. "Wait, did you walk here?"

"Yes?" she answers with a questioning look.

"What the hell are you thinking, Avery? Your ankle was swollen this morning!" My voice is louder than I intend, but the idea of her injuring herself further stirs something in me.

"I iced it, it's fine," she says, trying, and failing to hide her wince as she shifts to her injured foot. "I can walk on it, it's fine."

I rub the back of my neck. This woman. "No, it's not. You need to take care of yourself. You need rest."

"I haven't had time to rest with everything that happened since this morning," she says and her words from earlier come back to me.

"What happened this morning?"

"The roof in my room is leaking and there's no other rooms apparently. That's why I'm going to the meeting tonight. Cordie called Fran and they said they'd figure out what to do at the meeting. I guess they're sure there's someone with a room available. I just wanted to walk to clear my head since I didn't have my gear to do that."

I suddenly feel guilty for not taking her stuff to her earlier and making her come get it. I was selfish in wanting to get lost in my work for a few hours when all she wanted to do was the same thing.

"Shit, I'm sorry," I say, sheepishly.

"It's okay. You didn't know. But we should get going."

"I can drive my truck so you don't have to walk—ah shit, nevermind. Axel has it. He's doing some work for me. Let me go grab your stuff and we'll figure it out."

After I come back outside, camera bag slung over my shoulder, I stop a few feet away from Avery. "It's about two miles to town and you shouldn't walk on your ankle any more than you already did, so hop on." I turn my back toward her and motion for her to hop on my back like I did this morning.

"You're joking," she says.

"Nope, I'm not letting you walk. So, hop on or you're staying here with the elves."

"I think I'd rather take the elves over this."

"Don't kid yourself, Sunshine. You've been dying to ride me again since this morning."

The forehead wrinkle makes its appearance along with a look of dejection. I don't think I'm the only one who has been thinking of nothing else but her skin coming into contact with mine.

We said we'd stay away from each other. It's what she wants. I remind myself. Then why did my heart sink into my stomach and turn at the idea of not being near her? I don't wait for her to respond and turn around, motioning her to get on my back. My heart beats with anticipation at the thought of carrying her again, and even though my legs and back are feeling sore from earlier this morning and working this afternoon, the soreness seems to lessen greatly at the idea of touching her again. And my mind wanders to what it would be like to touch her in other places. Places a bit higher than her legs.

I come back to the present at the feeling of her hands on my shoulders as she carefully hops up and wraps her legs around me. I place my hands under her knees like I did this morning and even with her weight on me I feel lighter.

I start walking and search for something to say to lessen the growing tension between us.

"Favorite movie? Go."

"What?" She asks.

"What's your favorite movie? And please dear god don't say *Twilight*."

"What's wrong with *Twilight*? Those movies are classics."

"They're terrible!" I exclaim.

"Wait, you've seen them?"

"Avery, I grew up with two sisters, of course I've seen them. I've probably seen them more times than you have."

"Team Edward or Team Jacob?" She asks and I sigh, wondering how we got here.

"Team Charlie."

"What? That's not an option."

"It is in my book. That man goes through so much shit in those movies. He deserved better."

She moves her head closer to me until her cheek is almost touching mine. "He is the hottest one out of all of them."

I shake my head not even sure what is making me say the words that are about to come out of my mouth. "You know, I don't think I disagree with you."

She laughs, and what I would give to make her laugh like that every hour of every day. To make her smile and never feel pain or sadness again. The sound of her laugh flows through the air and mixes with mine, a melody created just for us.

"Okay, okay," she says. "Favorite movie. Mmmmmm...I guess if we are talking classics, then *Shop Around the Corner,* but if we are talking more modern films then definitely *Monty Python and the Holy Grail* or *The Princess Bride.*"

Trepidation seeps into my skin and settles there, a parasite latching on to its host. I let the silence stretch between us, trying to figure out how to form the words I want to say. "You know that movie?"

"*The Princess Bride?* Yeah we talked about it yesterday, remember? Or does Ethan need to call you Dory too?"

"No. *The Shop Around the Corner?* That's your favorite classic movie?"

"Yeeeeees," she draws out like the answer should have been obvious. "Is that so hard to believe?" She adds.

"Yes," I say. "I mean, no, it's just...anytime I've ever mentioned that movie to anyone—which isn't a lot because not very many people like classics—they've never seen it or they've never even heard of it. And now, here you are, someone from a completely different world, a woman that wants to stay away from me, which I agreed to, who knows that movie and it's your favorite."

The universe is royally fucking with me. I'm convinced. Or Sarah, if I believe in that kind of stuff, which I don't know if I do, but even I have to admit, this is weird.

"Maybe I shouldn't have made you agree to that," she whispers, so quietly I almost doubt her words.

My shoulders tense and she shifts on my back, repositioning herself. We ignore her comment and keep walking. With about a mile left to the bar I am determined to focus on anything else besides her body pressed against mine and the feeling of her warmth seeping through her clothes. A mile to keep my mind from wondering what her skin would feel like against mine and if it's as soft as it looks in the sunlight.

"How does your ankle feel?" I clear my throat, still unbelieving that she walked so far on an injured ankle. She clearly doesn't mind much pain or she is more tolerant than I previously gave her credit for.

"It's okay," she responds, quietly. "It'll be fine once I ice it again later tonight."

We walk the rest of the way in comfortable silence. Once we reach the bar around the corner, Avery starts to slide off my back, taking me by surprise. When I don't let go right away, she stumbles and tightens her grip on my shoulders.

"Sorry," I say. "I wasn't ready for your dismount."

"I just didn't think it was a good idea to arrive on your back again when basically the whole town is around the corner."

She has a point. This morning was a disaster with the whole dining room at the inn gawking at us like we were aliens sent from space demanding them to take us to their overlords.

"You're right. Sorry." I slip off the camera bag that is slung across my shoulder and hand it to her. Her fingers graze mine as she takes it and places the bag on her shoulder.

"Thanks," she takes a step back, heading into the bar. "And thanks for the, uh, ride…I guess…I'll see you around." With a small wave and her eyes looking anywhere but at me, she retreats into the bar and I am left staring at the spot in the gravel where she was just standing.

A few minutes later, I feel a pat on my back and warmth to my right as Elias leans in. "You know, you can always go in after her instead of standing here, wishing she'd reappear in that spot," he points to the tracks her shoes left.

I shove him off with a grunt and make my way inside, with Elias, Ethan, and my parents following. The bar is the only place large enough for most of the town to meet and has become a designated place for the town meetings every month, much to Frank's disappointment. He loves good business, but he absolutely hates town meetings. He thinks they're pointless and most of the time they are. Really, they are just one big excuse to get everyone together in one place to listen to Tom air out his issues, and then drink and socialize the rest of the night. I don't mind the drinking. It is the socializing I vehemently try to avoid.

The circular tables are moved off to the side to make room for the rows of chairs in front of the bar, Frank behind it cleaning glasses and preparing everything for when the meeting ends. A wooden podium stands at the front, Tom fussing with the microphone protruding from the top, Cordie and Fran on his left trying to get his attention.

"Why are you even here?" Elias asks behind me. "You never come to meetings."

"Avery left her camera stuff in my bag this morning. I came to give it back to her."

"Ahhh," he says knowingly, like he just fit the last piece of the puzzle into place and is finally seeing the full picture of me.

"What 'ahhhh?'" I ask.

"Hudson." He levels me with a look before moving closer, out of earshot from my parents who found seats near the middle of the crowd. "You may be oblivious, but I'm not. *And* as much as you wish it right now, I'm not blind either. You literally just carried that girl here. And even if you didn't, you could have given her the stuff and went straight back home."

I roll my eyes. "I'm tired, okay? I've been working all day and I don't feel like walking back, so I figured I'd hitch a ride from you after this is over."

He settles in his seat next to Ethan and without looking my way, he responds in a sarcastic tone, "Suuuuure."

Ethan leans far enough to catch my eyes and a wide grin spreads across his features. "You sulking because you're losing, Uncle Hud?"

Shit. In my rush to throw myself into work to avoid any thoughts of Avery, I haven't had time to look for his flag. Or even wonder where to start looking for it for that matter.

Before I can respond, Elias chimes in. "Nah, he's sulking over a girl."

"Shut up," I send a glare his way. Avery is sitting two rows ahead of us, but he said it loud enough for her to hear. I can tell, because at his words, she tilts her head ever so slightly and brushes her hair behind her right ear.

"What are you doing here?" I turn to see Axel bending to sit in the seat behind me.

"He's sulking over a girl," Ethan echoes.

"Oh, is he now?"

"Shut up, Axel. I will throw you to the ground. I can take you."

"You will *not*." Now my mom is chiming into the conversation. "You will behave," she says firmly. "And, stop sulking over her and ask her out," she adds with a sly smile.

"Listen to your mother, Hudson," Dad adds in a tone I'm all too familiar with from childhood.

A short laugh escapes Avery and I catch her eye before she quickly turns her head to the front as Tom bangs his gavel, waits for the chatter to die down before speaking.

"I call this town meeting to order! We have a few things on the agenda. First of them being the fence on second street. A few posts are rotting and it's dangerous. It needs to be fixed as soon as possible. Any volunteers?"

No hands go up because that fence just so happens to be separating his property from the park and it is probably on his property line and he just doesn't want to be responsible for fixing it.

"That's on your property, Tom," says Elias, echoing my thoughts.

"No, it's the town's property," Tom argues.

"I know the property lines of the town, Tom. That fence is on your side."

"Well, I don't have the tools to fix it nor do I have the hands." He holds up his aging hands and he hesitates before he adds shaking for good measure.

Elias rolls his eyes. "I'll be over to fix it later this week."

"Okay, that matter is solved. Now, the next issue is roadkill."

"Roadkill?" Cordie chimes in.

"There is an overabundance of it!" Tom responds, raising his voice. "Squirrels all over the road. Opossums. Raccoons. You name it. They're everywhere."

"And you want us to do what about it?" asks Fran.

"If you hit and kill an animal, just clean it up and throw it away."

"You're joking?" Elias says, exasperated. It never fails. Every time there is a meeting, someone gets into it with Tom's unrealistic expectations, but he always gets his way in the end. I never understand why anyone tries to reason with him.

"It's not hard to just scoop it up and dispose of it."

"You're the one who hits most of them! You can barely see above your dash and you don't pay attention. Just last week, you almost ran me over crossing the street!" Elias proclaims.

I chuckle. Elias isn't from here, so he always falls into the trap of arguing with Tom and he never comes out on top.

"He did!" Elias insists. The crowd shifts in their seats, anxious to get to the end of what I'm sure is a long list of issues Tom has to address.

A light comes from Avery's lap and she glances at the screen. She stands and leaves through the front door to answer her phone. I ignore the urge I have to follow her and stay planted in my chair.

Jacob stands, blue scrubs wrinkled and spotted with stains I don't want to know the origin of, before either Tom or Elias can say anything else. "I'll take care of it, Tom. Just let me know where they are after the meeting."

"Alright, with that settled, Cordie has something she said she needs to bring up." He moves aside and motions for Cordie to take his place at the podium.

She clears her throat and throws a not so subtle look at Fran in the front row. "As you all know, we have a visitor in town. Avery. I think she stepped out to take a call, but we have an issue. The room she's staying in has a leak and she can't stay there until it's fixed. Elias, I know you've been busy with other projects, so there's not a huge rush, but if you can come help fix it when you're free, I'd be grateful."

"Sure thing, Cordelia." He responds in a respectful tone.

"The rooms that don't have leaks are full, so Avery needs somewhere to stay."

"Tom, do you have room?" Fran asks.

He hesitates. "Uhhh, nope, I've got a few renovations going."

"Renovations?" I speak up. "I do all of your renovations, Tom."

"W-well, I, uh, I've been into a lot of DIY-ing recently," he says, unconvincingly.

Lying old man.

Cordie turns to Jacob. "Don't you have a spare room?"

"Sorry," he says, shaking his head. "I have family in town."

Jacob hasn't had family in town for years. What are they doing? I catch Fran's eyes and see the hint of mischief behind them. It matches Cordie's. The excuses cycle through the crowd. They range from carpets being cleaned to fostering animals from the shelter and it becomes glaringly obvious what their plan is. Well, the plan Cordie and Fran put them up to.

This whole town is against me.

What exactly do they expect is going to happen? Avery isn't here for an extended period of time. Hardly any time for feelings to develop, much less a friendship. Even though that's already somewhat happened, we have no plans to take it further.

Ethan chimes in finally. "What about Uncle Hudson?" he turns toward me. "You have lots of rooms not being used."

"You know, Ethan," says Fran, not even trying to hide the obvious fake surprise in her voice. "I didn't even think of that," she says with a wink that lets me know she knows exactly what she is doing and somehow roped my traitorous nephew into it.

"Traitor," I whisper and he just turns to me and gives me what I can only describe as a shit-eating grin. The kind kids give when they are about to do something they know they aren't supposed to. Consequences be damned. Like being a part of a ridiculous scheme concocted by a bunch of busy-body gossips who think this random woman from out of town will be the one I fall head over heels for. News flash…they are wrong. And I plan to prove it to them.

"You know what, Ethan?" I say with as much mock enthusiasm as I can muster. "That's a great idea."

Silence. They expected a fight that I am not going to give them. Avery can take whatever spare room for whatever time she has left of her visit and then she can leave. Be out of my life for good, and I can go back to normal in a heartbeat. I can deal with her for a few weeks. I'll just pick up more orders and bury myself in my work. I probably won't even see her much.

"Alright," says Tom, his booming voice breaking the silence. "With that settled, we have nothing else, so, meeting adjourned. Frank, start the drinks." Frank responds with a grunt, but starts handing out beers and taking food orders.

Tom bangs his gavel on the podium for good measure as some people start to trickle outside after they grab their drinks. That has got to be the fifth gavel he's gone through in the last few months. He either breaks them from being a little too enthusiastic or someone (usually Fran or Cordie) steals it. I still have no idea what they do with them. Burn them? Bury them?

Who knows. There's probably a graveyard of gavels right under Cordie's freshly planted tomatoes. *Here lie the gavels rescued from Tom's heavy hand. Safe and at peace.*

Those two are like teenagers always ready to influence the other to do something most people would deem stupid. Like sneaking out in the middle of the night to meet friends in a random parking lot to buy beer. Or into Tom's study—or wherever he keeps his gavel—to steal it. I'm surprised he doesn't sleep with it under his pillow or lock it behind a glass display case, the key hidden safely in his nightstand. Knowing Fran and Cordie, they'd still find a way to steal it. They'd somehow manage to make a copy of the key or steal his hearing aids so they can sneak into his room undetected.

Always up to something.

Speaking of, I walk toward them and look down at their small frames. "Don't think I don't know what you two are doing." I point between them.

They both place their hands on their chests like they're in grade school about to recite the pledge of allegiance. In this case, they're trying to pledge their innocence and unfortunately for them, I know better.

"Us?" says Cordie.

"We aren't up to anything other than trying to find poor Avery somewhere to stay," adds Fran.

"We're just lucky you happen to have room for her and are so graciously willing to welcome her into your home." Cordie bats her eyelashes like a cartoon character begging to get what they want or flirting their way out of the situation they landed themselves in. Definitely the latter. Always the latter with these two. They flirt with everybody. The town always says it's just their grandmotherly charm, but I've never bought it. They know what they're doing and so do I. No matter how charming they can be and no matter how much I love them, the eyelashes aren't going to phase me.

I roll my eyes. "You're lucky I love you both." I shift my gaze to Fran. "You owe me at least three weeks of free coffee and scones as a thank you. *And* some lemon bars."

"Lemon bars, you say?" She sees right through me.

"Oh dear boy," she sighs and pats my cheek in a soft, grandmotherly gesture. "I have a feeling it's you who is going to be thanking me."

She winks again and heads to the bar arm in arm with Cordie. Thick as thieves. They immediately put their heads together and start whispering, throwing the occasional glance Tom's way.

I look back at Ethan who walked up behind me. "At least warn a comrade next time there's an ambush."

"And get on Granny's bad side?" He points his thumb behind him at the bar where Fran and Cordie are now scribbling notes on a napkin. "No chance."

Smart kid.

I put my arm around him and have him in a headlock before he can reach me. "Alright, just for that, we are having liver and spinach for dinner."

He struggles to get out of my grasp, but I'm not letting him off that easy. "No way, Uncle Hud. We'll both starve if that's what's for dinner."

He's right. Liver and spinach don't sound appetizing and even if I did want to get back at him, I'm not going to make myself suffer along with him. He finally manages to free himself.

"Let's do pancakes and bacon."

I have to give the kid credit. He knows my weakness. I never say no to breakfast for dinner. "You're too smart for your own good."

"How do you think I always find your flag before you find mine?" He says without missing a beat.

With a grunt, I lift him in a fireman's carry and start to head for the doors. Elias and Ethan usually don't stick around for the after party, so I don't plan to either. He starts to squirm and can't help but laugh. I let out a chuckle and start to tickle him, making him flail even more.

"You better stop moving so much or I'm going to drop you!" I warn him, continuing my attack.

"Uncle Hud...stop it!" he says between giggles.

"No chance. This is payback for your little scheming in there."

He continues to struggle and laugh until we round the corner to head to the parking lot and bump straight into someone. I manage to catch Ethan before he faceplants on the sidewalk and I look up. I'm met with familiar blue eyes and a look of exasperation spread on my new roommate's face.

CHAPTER TWENTY

AVERY

"*O*h my gosh, I am so sorry!" I say as I bend down to pick up my phone, Charlotte's voice echoing from the ground. When I stand, Ethan is grinning ear to ear and Hudson is staring, unblinking at me.

"I wasn't paying attention." I hold my phone up to show Charlotte on FaceTime. Again. For someone who shoved me out the door, figuratively and literally, to go on this trip, she's having a hard time letting me actually do the trip. Don't get me wrong, I love her to death and enjoy our conversations, but she's going to get cut off if she continues to call me at 5 a.m.— something she's done several times since I got here.

She has insomnia and continues to tell me how lucky I am that she doesn't call me at 2 a.m. when she's bored. I'd block her number if she followed through with that plan. At least put her on 'do not disturb' until after the trip. I should stop at Fran's and hand her off to her or Cordie. I have a feeling the three of them would get along swell.

"Are you okay?" I hear Charlotte ask. I hold the phone up so I can see her.

"Yeah, I'm fine. I just ran into someone. Literally."

"Who?" She asks and I can feel my cheeks redden. I just hope Hudson doesn't notice it in the dim lighting coming from the front entrance of the bar.

"Oh, nevermind. I can see you're blushing. Hellooooo Mountain Man!" She yells louder and I can feel the heat flare in my cheeks, deepening what I am sure is a very obnoxious and now clearly noticeable blush. "Avery," I hear Charlotte say quietly. "You're staring," she says *not* so quietly.

I'm going to kill her. And then I remember I can just hang up on her, the beautiful, big red button now singing its siren song and I gladly allow myself to be pulled into its depths.

"Charlotte, I'll call you tomorrow."

"You better," she manages to get in before I hit the end call button. I swear she's going to pay. Some form of revenge is in order. Maybe I'll get Fran and Cordie to help me. They'll know what to do.

"I'm sorry again. For this," I gesture to me and them. "And for her," I hold up my phone, now a black screen.

"It's okay, Dory!" says Ethan.

Right, Dory. I almost forgot our game. "I'm sorry, I don't think we've met before. I'm Avery." I hold out my hand to him.

He laughs. "I'm Ethan." He says taking my hand, playing along. "And this is my Uncle Hudson."

I glance at his uncle who is making an effort to look anywhere but me. "We've met. He actually took me on a hike yesterday."

"Cool!" he says. "Hey, do you like dogs?"

"I love dogs. Why?"

"Because you're staying with Uncle Hud and he has five of them."

Staying with *who* now? I think I might have just had a heart attack. A heart palpitation? Heart murmur? Whatever it is, my heart has stopped beating. "Wait, what?" This kid needs to rewind.

"He has five golden retrievers. They're all super friendly and like to take up the whole bed!" He spreads his arms as wide as they can go completely oblivious to the tension in the air.

I look at Hudson, whose eyes are on the concrete below him like if he concentrated on that spot hard enough it would crack open and swallow him whole. If only it would take me too.

Finally, he lifts his eyes to meet mine and I can physically feel my stomach flip. I'm on a rollercoaster and it just went down the steepest of inclines. "The town likes to meddle," he says, in a way of explanation. I give him a questioning stare and he waves it off like it's no big deal.

It's a big deal and Charlotte is going to lose her shit tomorrow when I call her.

"Don't worry about it. The point is, you have a room at my place until the inn's roof is fixed, which most likely won't happen until you're gone. I have plenty of spare rooms and I work odd hours so you probably won't even see much of me. It'll be like your own cabin."

"Oh," I say, trying to keep the disappointment out of my voice. I may not want to start anything romantically, but having him around as a friend might be nice.

"Well, thank you," I say, still pondering the logistics of me somehow ending up at Hudson's cabin. Of all places.

"Okay, I'll see you guys later!" Ethan calls before he starts heading back inside.

Hudson grabs his shoulder. "Not so fast, traitor. What do you mean, you'll see us later? You and your dad are coming for dinner."

"Sorry, Uncle Hud," he says in a sly tone. "Grandma and Grandpa asked us to stay and help around the house for a few days so that's where we'll be."

"You just said you were having dinner with me!" Hudson exclaims.

He shrugs his shoulders. "Forgot. Sorry!" he calls back as he starts to run toward his dad.

I don't think *that* was part of the plan. From the look on Hudson's face, I'd say none of this was part of the plan.

Hudson moves to grab him, but Ethan ducks under his arm and maneuvers around his body and meets his dad by the door. "See you later, bro!" Calls Elias with a two-fingered salute and a smile that tells me this whole town is up to no good.

Hudson responds with a middle finger that holds a set of car keys. At the look of surprise on Elias' face, I'm assuming they are his and I sigh in relief that I don't have to walk anywhere else considering my ankle is starting to throb.

"Take it!" Elias calls back, laughing. "You need it more than I do right now."

My whole body is pulsing at the idea of being around Hudson, in his house, surrounded by his scent, his things, his life, for the remainder of my trip. The deal we made in the woods just this morning is feeling flimsier by the minute.

The ride to get my stuff at the inn is quiet. Hudson's grip on the steering wheel tightens the further we drive and I want to ask what he is thinking, but I'm not sure if he wants to answer.

Before he pulls the truck to a complete stop, I hop out of the passenger side and go inside as quickly as my ankle will allow. I go up to my room and grab my packed suitcase and gear. With one last look around the room to make sure I'm not leaving anything behind, I turn toward the door and jump when I see Hudson leaning against the door frame, legs crossed at the ankles, watching me. His dark hair is pulled into a low bun and his sleeves are rolled, reaching the spot just below his elbow. His stubble is a bit longer than this morning and it shades his face, darkening his features in a way that makes my lower half ache with the need to brush my fingers across it. My mind flits to an image of his face between my legs, wondering what it would feel like there; the roughness of it creating the most delicious friction.

"What are you thinking about over there, Sunshine?" he asks, darkly.

I clear my throat and avert my gaze from his. "Um... uh... nothing," I stutter.

"Mmmm," is all he says in response as he takes my belongings from me and heads for the door. He pauses before he leaves and looks back at me, waiting for me to follow.

Without a word, he reaches out his free hand for me to take. I hesitate, then picture myself losing my balance and tumbling down the stairs, further injuring myself. So I place my hand in his and use it to steady myself as we descend the stairs. The epitome of a gentleman without hesitation. I can only imagine what it looks like to an outsider.

A doting husband helping his injured wife down the stairs and into the car, making sure she is secure and safe before walking around to the driver's side to take them to their happy home and do what married couples do.

We step down the steps slowly, his grip tightening on my hip as I struggle to catch my breath. Between his arms around me and struggling to get down the stairs, my heart is racing. Once we reach the landing, I make the mistake of glancing up at him. His eyes bore into mine and my voice is barely audible. "Thank you," I manage. Hudson brushes a piece of hair back and runs a finger along my jaw like he just can't help himself and before I can even comprehend his touch on my skin, he turns away and repositions us to help me the rest of the way down.

I never thought I would be turned on by someone helping me into a car, but here I am. Hudson places one hand on my back with the other bracing the back of my knees as he gently lifts me into Elias' truck. Without a word, he grabs the seatbelt and stretches it across my torso to my hip, clicks it in place and closes the passenger door all somehow without making contact with me. My body hums with tension and I take a deep breath, trying to calm my erratic heartbeat.

He is still as he drives us back to his house and I am infinitely glad he was able to swipe the keys from his brother-in-law. I don't think I could have walked back and I also didn't want him to carry me back again. The tension in the cab of this truck is bad enough with the two feet of space between us and if our bodies were in contact again, I don't think I would be able to stop myself from touching him. Would he want me to? I shake my head at the thought.

No. I tell myself. We have an agreement.

But look where that got you. The voice inside my head argues. *In an enclosed space, in his home for days on end. Just the two of you. You and the most beautiful man you've ever seen.*

Two weeks. We can deal with being in close proximity for two weeks. Right? Right.

"Avery?" Hudson says a bit louder than his normal volume and I realize I must have zoned out for the rest of the drive because we are now parked in front of his cabin, three of the dogs peering through his front window. It's hard to believe I was just here a few hours earlier. It feels like a lifetime ago. Something in Hudson has changed. He was tense before, but that is nothing compared to how tense he is now.

He clears his throat and I realize I still haven't spoken. "Yeah, sorry. Um, thanks for borrowing the truck. I don't think I would have made it on my ankle. I probably need to ice it again before I go to bed."

"You've only iced it once?" He says in a clipped, displeased tone.

"Uh, yeah. I haven't really had the chance with the roof leaking and all."

He quickly gets out of the truck and makes his way to my side. I unbuckle my seatbelt in preparation and it's a good thing I do because as soon as he gets the door open, he scoops me up into his arms and carries me inside. The number of times this man has carried me is beginning to be too many and not enough at the same time. Without adjusting his grip, he manages to easily make it up his porch stairs, across the few feet that stretch from the stairs to the front door and then carries me inside to a large sectional couch in his living room.

As soon as he sets me down, Judy and Bernard jump up on the couch and sprawl out on either side of me, fighting for my attention. Hermes and Patch are settled in front of the fireplace —patiently waiting for Hudson to light it—and Buddy is on his heels, panting, searching for a treat in his hands. While he looks through his freezer for an ice pack, I take the opportunity to take in the rest of the room.

Across from the couch sits a stone, wood-burning fireplace with a wooden mantle littered with his carvings. A large flat screen is mounted above it and built-in bookshelves hug either side of the fireplace. The shelves are filled with more carvings in between stacks of books I plan to investigate later when Hudson isn't hovering over me like a mother bear. To the right of those is a wall of floor-to-ceiling windows with a view of the forest in the back, along with a lake I assume he owns to the left of the trees. Behind them is a striking view of the mountains, three peaks clearly visible through the clouds.

My breath catches at the wildflowers that scatter his yard. Striking blues, pinks, and purples blend together to create a painted canvas out of a fairy tale. I'm so used to seeing perfectly cut grass with straight lines and no weeds—the typical yard in a residential area—but this is the exact opposite and a complete contrast to the front yard. Where the grass is short up front, it thrives in the back. For every clean line near the walkway up front, there's lush greenery that comes to a point with buds and petals flourishing from the top. I want to sit on the back porch with a cup of steaming coffee in hand and watch the flowers sway in the wind. I could sit there all day with my camera, taking pictures and savoring the beauty nature graced his back-yard with.

Tomorrow. I tell myself. That's how I am spending my day. If I still can't walk without pain or swelling, I am going to plant myself out there on one of the deck chairs and spend the day reading one of his books, camera in one hand and coffee in the other. A dream.

"When I built this place, I couldn't bring myself to cut the back yard." Hudson appears at my side with a package of frozen peas and a hand towel. He wraps up the peas and gently picks up my swollen ankle. He motions for Bernard to move and he takes his place, sitting close enough to stretch my leg so my ankle rests on his lap. After he's settled, he puts the homemade ice pack on my ankle—the cold soothing my now flushed skin where his fingers grazed it—and grabs the remote. Buddy settles himself on the other side of him, with Bernard cuddling up to Hermes and Patch after letting out the loudest sigh I've ever heard from a dog.

"He's the one with the biggest attitude of the pack," says Hudson in response. "He's like a moody teenager half the time." To prove his point, Bernard looks back at Hudson again before lying his head down on his paws facing the fireplace, as far away from Hudson as he can be.

Hudson scrolls through the apps on the tv before landing on Disney+ and selects *The Princess Bride* without a word. As the movie starts, he grabs the blanket—with a flannel pattern, of course—and drapes it over both of us. I find myself staring at him, in disbelief that this is the same man from just a week ago, who couldn't get away from me fast enough. Now, here I am, *in his house*, sitting next to him practically cuddling with him on his couch about to watch one of my favorite movies with a gorgeous view behind me and dogs spread throughout the room. And the only thing I can think of is how peaceful I feel in this moment. In his home. With him.

About twenty minutes into the movie, Hudson takes the ice pack off my ankle and tosses it on the coffee table in front of us. He leans back and stretches his arm across the back of the couch, his hand landing just behind my head. I keep my legs draped across him seeing no reason to move them and settle further into the couch while Westley says for the millionth time "As you wish."

Once the movie reaches the sword fight scene between the Dread Pirate Roberts and Inigo Montoya, I feel Hudson's fingers brush the skin behind my ear as he twirls a strand of hair around his finger. I look his way and I don't know if he realizes what he's doing or not, but I don't think I want him to stop. The light touches feel good. More than good.

By the time the rodents of unusual size come up, his other hand is holding my good ankle firmly as his thumb traces the faintest of circles on my skin. I don't know what he's doing or what he's expecting, but I find myself wanting to reciprocate his small touches. Currently, my right hand is buried in Judy's fur, scratching and petting her. Something to keep my hands to myself. But he isn't, so why should I? If I move my left hand, I might be able to touch his torso, but I'd have to maneuver myself closer to him and I can't do that without being obnoxiously obvious. He'd see right through it.

Fuck it. I do it anyway and his body freezes as I tuck my side into his and settle my head on his shoulder, his hair brushing my cheek.

"What are you doing?" he whispers, still unmoving.

"I don't know," I whisper back, because I don't. I don't know what I'm doing here, I don't know what I'm doing in this town and I don't know what I'm doing with him. All I know is I don't think I want it to end.

Finally, he settles his arm behind me, resting on the small of my back, an inch of skin exposed between the hem of my shirt and the top of my pants. An inch of skin that feels like miles with his fingers tracing slow lines back and forth. Back and forth.

We sit like this for the remainder of the movie, hands exploring, but never crossing a line we aren't ready for. Our original agreement to stay away from each other is clearly out the window. So far out the window, it is soaring through the wildflowers outside, flitting toward the lake and diving in to sink into the deepest part of the water to hide among the seaweed.

When the movie ends, the spell that had settled over us is broken. Hudson untangles himself from me and stands to stretch.

"I'm going to go shower," is all he says before heading to the stairs behind the fireplace, up to what I assume is his room. He didn't show me the rest of the house, too busy worrying about my swollen ankle. I glance down and notice it's looking significantly better than it did earlier. The swelling has gone down and the bruising is pretty mild.

I give Judy one last head scratch before standing to grab my things and I realize Hudson didn't show me where the guest room is. I quickly change into clean clothes and slide my feet into my blue, sherpa-lined crocs to take the chill away from my toes. With nothing else to do, now is my chance to explore the books on his shelves. Stacks of small books are scattered among the shelves along with a few carvings here and there. One is placed snug against a plant in the corner while another sits carefully on top of a stack of what looks to be middle grade novels. I'm able to take my time observing the wooden figurines without Hudson's gaze watching me. They are intricate. Detailed. More detailed than I've ever seen. How the burly man in the shower could carve such delicate designs is beyond me.

I imagine his rough, callused hands slowly carving, chipping away at the wood until it transforms into his vision beneath what was a plain piece of wood before. And then I imagine what other things those rough, callused hands could do.

Our almost kiss by the waterfall and the moment from the stairs is seared into my mind and I can still feel the ghost of his breath on my skin and the way my body reacted to his.

Water. I need water. My nerves are shot and being under the same roof as Hudson isn't helping. I move across the room to the kitchen and search through a few cabinets before I find the glasses. I pour a cup of water, drain it in a few gulps and refill it. Leaning my elbows on the kitchen island, back to the stairs, I FaceTime Charlotte.

She answers on the first ring.

"Do you just wait by the phone for me to call or what?" I joke.

"Hah hah," she laughs sarcastically. "I have a life outside of you, Ave. Believe it or not."

"Oh, sorry, I thought your whole world revolved around me and my love life." I level her with what I hope is an intimidating stare, but I know it doesn't work, because she lets out a laugh.

"Pleaaaase," she draws out. "You'd be lost without me playing matchmaker."

"No, I don't think I would. I have plenty of matchmakers here it seems."

Her eyebrows raise at that. "Oh?"

I fill her in on everything that happened after our call ended during the meeting when I ran into Hudson.

"What do you mean you're staying at his house?" she asks, the shriek in her voice fills the kitchen and I shush her.

"Be quiet," I say. "Keep your voice down. He's in the shower upstairs, but who knows what he can hear from up there."

"From a whole floor above you? He can hear our conversation over the sound of a shower and through the floors? Impressive."

"There could be vents that connect to his room, you don't know." I look above me searching for anything that could indicate Hudson's ability to hear me from wherever he is upstairs.

"Sheesh, you're paranoid."

"I just don't want him listening to us."

"Why not?" she asks. "He's hot. I'm about to go there myself... So what are you wearing?" she adds before a smile stretches across her features.

I look down at my plaid pajama pants, blue crocs and over-sized sweatshirt.

"Nothing that says come and get it." *At least not tonight,* the voice inside my head adds.

"Why not go for it? What is there to lose?"

I let her words seep in and consider them. I've been so worried this whole time about losing something. But is there really anything for me to lose?

You'll fall for him, the voice inside me says.

If I let myself go there with Hudson, I *will* fall for him and in the end I won't be good enough and I'll be the one who gets hurt. Again. I've never been good enough, so what does it matter? And I am not going to let myself travel down that road. I won't let myself be shattered again.

I roll my eyes at Charlotte. "Okay, let's change the subject."

"Alright, fine," she agrees. "What does he do for a living? Is he an actual lumberjack?"

I sigh, "That's not changing the subject."

"Hey, it's either that, or you can tell me how good his ass looks in a pair of blue jeans."

"Charlotte, I am not discussing how good Hudson's ass looks in his jeans."

"Hah!" she exclaims. "So you've been looking at his ass?"

"Ohmygod," I ignore her and press on. "He isn't a lumber-jack, but he works with wood."

"Oh, I bet he does," she says in a suggestive tone.

I palm my face, embarrassed at the words that just left my mouth. "No, that's not what I meant and you know it! I do not want to talk about his masturbation habits. Now, shut up and talk about something else. How is work?"

Thankfully, the rest of the conversation revolves around work and the fact that Charlotte is over dealing with James and his bullshit. I can relate way more than I want to.

When we end the FaceTime, I listen for the sound of the shower, but find it quiet. I grab my camera from the countertop and start scrolling through the photos I've taken so far to get an idea of where else in town I can visit in the next few days. My favorites are from Fran's. There's something about capturing the cozy moment of a reader, snuggled up on one of the store's couches, a book open in their lap with a fresh cup of coffee on the table next to them. A warm hug in a picture. I make a mental note to get a print of this one to frame it when I get home.

I hear Hudson walking down the stairs, creaks filling the air, giving the cabin an even more homier feel. I turn and thank whatever entity responsible that Hudson is fully dressed. But he's dressed in gray sweatpants. Gray fucking sweatpants. Could he have put on *anything* else? Literally anything else would have been better than gray *fucking* sweatpants. I groan internally and go back to the couch, calling Judy to come over. I am not above using a dog as a shield. I'm curled into the furthest corner of the sectional, legs stretched out in front of me on the connected ottoman, Judy's body snuggled up against mine. Hudson would have to physically remove Judy from my side to get next to me and with one glance at her, I don't think she would make it easy.

I make a grab for the remote and start scrolling through the selections while Hudson busies himself in the kitchen. The theme song of the *Great British Bake Off* fills the room as Hudson sets a tray of snacks down on the coffee table. He'd give Lorelai Gilmore a run for her money with how much food he has set out. A wooden tray is filled with a variety of meats and cheeses, crackers, a few fruits, assorted nuts, a bowl of popcorn, and a small bowl of chocolate.

I look up at him, questioning.

"I figured since we didn't stay after the meeting that you'd be hungry," he says. "And what's a movie night without snacks?"

My heart thaws further and my eyes follow him as he settles on the couch a foot away from Judy.

"You'll have to crawl out of your corner to reach it though," he says with a sly smile, knowing the coffee table is completely out of my reach unless I sit up and scoot closer to him. I roll my eyes and sigh and, not so reluctantly, move closer to him on the couch. Closer, but still a few inches away from him. Not touching.

He grabs a cracker and stacks it with meat and cheese before popping it into his mouth. I watch him chew and am startled when his voice reaches my ears.

"You're staring again, Sunshine," he says, eyes never leaving the screen.

I say nothing and scoop a handful of popcorn, sneaking a piece or two—really, three—to Judy before turning my eyes to the screen.

"I saw that." Apparently, he not only has hearing that could rival a bat, but he sees everything too.

"Sorry, can't resist when she's giving me puppy dog eyes."

"I never get that saying."

"What do you mean?"

"When people say a dog gives you puppy dog eyes. They're all puppy dog eyes. All puppies have eyes, therefore, puppy dog eyes aren't something they give, they're just," he motions his hands in the air, pointing to where Patch and Hermes are still cuddled in front of the fireplace. "There," he finishes.

"But dogs can definitely give you sad eyes if they want something. They beg with their facial expressions."

"But the whole concept of them giving puppy dog eyes is ridiculous."

"How? They can totally make their faces expressive to the point of manipulation. They know they're cute and know how to get someone to sneak them a few pieces of popcorn."

"But—"

"Hudson, why are we arguing about this and how did we get here?" I say, smiling at the most ridiculous conversation I have ever had with a man. The only conversations James ever wanted to have were in-depth serious ones, which were good ones to have, but there was never any balance with him. If I showed him a post or a picture I thought was funny, but funny in a stupid way, he would scoff and ask how a person could find humor in stuff like that. And every time it happened, I'd draw into myself, chest caving, arms folding and shrink. He never noticed, of course. His attention would be back on his phone the next second and he'd go back to whatever business email that needed answering at 8 o'clock at night on a Saturday.

"You brought up puppy dog eyes, I just stated my opinion on the matter," he says, tossing a few peanuts from his fist, into his mouth. Why is that attractive? A simple action like that should not be as attractive as it is.

We sit in comfortable silence as the episode plays and each time a contestant does something out of the ordinary, Hudson mutters under his breath.

One puts their sugar cookies in the oven, "Oven isn't on. Not going to bake in time."

Another doesn't roll out the dough thin enough. "Those aren't going to bake all the way through. The middle is going to be raw."

A contestant doesn't mix the royal icing properly (apparently). "Nope, that's going to be way too runny."

By about halfway through the episode, his commentary has raised to a normal volume and I find myself once again surprised by the man sitting inches away from me.

"Okay, do you bake or something too?"

He glances over, a look of surprise on his face like he forgot I was here or he just didn't realize how loud he was talking. "I dabble."

"You *dabble?*" I repeat, eyebrows raised.

"Yeah, I help Fran when she needs it in the bakery."

The ice continues to chip away, falling down the cliff, shattering on the surface below, my resolve crumbling like one of the contestant's cookies on the screen.

"*You*... help Fran... *bake?*" I can't wrap my head around him in the back of the bakery, side-by-side with Fran, sleeves rolled up, kneading dough for bread, or gently mixing meringue for a pie topping, forearms exposed and covered in patches of flour, an apron tied around his waist, his hair tied back into a high bun, and ooohhhh turns out I *can* wrap my head around that image.

"Is that so hard to imagine?" he asks in a sultry tone like he knows exactly the thoughts that just went through my head.

"N-no," I stutter.

He moves closer to me until he is a breath away from my ear. I have never stayed so still in my life. I am a statue, hard and unmoving. I close my eyes and revel in the feeling of the warmth from his skin. "There are a lot of things I can do, Sunshine."

Hudson makes motions to leave, but thinks twice before leaning back in, this time putting his finger under my chin, his thumb resting under my bottom lip. He draws my head back to look at him and I oblige. His eyes are a dark green now. Dangerous and taunting.

"Feel free to take the couch if you're too comfortable to move or you can go to the guest bedroom I have ready upstairs. Third door on the left, but it's right next to mine and the walls are thin. Just so you know, in case you call Charlotte again to talk about my masturbation habits." He places a feather light kiss on my cheek and turns away to head up the stairs, leaving me utterly speechless.

CHAPTER TWENTY-ONE

HUDSON

*I*t's 2 a.m. and all I have managed to do since coming into my room is think about how Avery is sleeping one room over. Or I assume she is. I don't think she stayed on the couch downstairs and I swore I heard all five dogs stampeding up the stairs after her, following her into her room. Traitors. They should form a club with Ethan.

All of the beings who used to be loyal friends to Hudson Waters.

Avery's flannel pants and oversized sweatshirt circle in my head until I am dizzy with attraction. I didn't even know I had a thing for a woman swallowed by a sweatshirt, but the way she wore it, sleeves rolled up halfway to her elbows, her soft skin exposed, blonde hair knotted on the top of her head, cozy. There is something effortlessly sexy about her being comfortable enough with me to just be herself. No pretense. No expectations. Just unequivocally herself. She didn't put on a show for me. She's unafraid to be herself around me and I like that.

I like *her.*

I pull a pillow over my face and apply pressure before tossing it to the ground. The next two weeks are going to be hard. Harder than... well, harder than I am right now imagining what she looks like while she sleeps. Fuck, I sound like a stalker. I need to clear my head.

I sneak out of the house as quietly as I can and avoid the creaks in the floors. I pause outside of Avery's room to see if she is maybe awake too, but decide against it and manage to get outside without startling the dogs.

Hands shoved in my pockets to stop them from shaking, I walk down the gravel road leading away from my house and go toward the campgrounds.

Once I pass the camping spots, I can feel the familiar sensation of dread. It's why I never come here, but something is different about tonight. Something is telling me to come here and I can't ignore it. The last time I was here, there were crowds of people gathered under a tent, attempting to stay dry from the rain. I didn't care. I stood off to the side, letting the rain droplets soak into the back of the suit I knew I'd never wear again. I'd made sure of it by burning it that night in my fireplace.

I've never been one to visit graves. I never saw a point to it. What is buried there is no more than something that held a person's soul while they were alive. The idea of standing on a grave, staring at a headstone and talking to no one was not a concept I've ever understood. But here I am, going to Sarah's headstone, trying to figure out what the hell I'm doing here. Trying to figure out what the hell I'm doing in general.

I maneuver my way through the other headstones, careful

not to step on any graves and I think about kids being superstitious enough to avoid the cracks in the sidewalk. I may not get the idea of talking to a stone, but it doesn't feel right to casually stroll through the cemetery, stepping on the graves as I go.

Finally, I come to the spot I haven't seen in three years and blink back tears. The headstone isn't as bright and shiny as that day. It's worn with time and weather, reminding me a bit of myself. I haven't been very bright since Sarah died either and the years have taken their toll. I take a deep breath of the warm summer air and start talking.

"I met a girl," I say, leaving all sense of trepidation behind me and jumping in before I can talk myself out of it. "A woman," I correct and ignore the creeping feeling of embarrassment. I almost wish the stone would talk back, but then I'd have even bigger problems than the warring emotions I have felt in my chest since I saw Avery in the coffee shop. "Avery. She's... well, she's Avery. You'd like her though. She gives me a lot of shit like you used to. She actually reminds me of you."

I tell her about the last few days and the way my skin tingles, goosebumps flaring at the surface, when Avery glares at me, trying to make me cave. I wanted to give in and having her in my house makes it difficult not to.

Taking a few deep breaths, I exhale the negativity coursing through me and focus on the woman sleeping in my home. Gently, I place a hand on top of the cold stone and I feel my chest constrict at first then loosen, the pressure constantly there finally letting up on its own for the first time in three years.

CHAPTER TWENTY-TWO

AVERY

*T*rue to my word, I spend the next day out on the back porch with a never ending supply of coffee, a romance I found buried between the middle grade fiction, and a blanket draped over my legs. Every few chapters, I glance up to stare at the trees and the mountains towering behind them. I could get used to this view. Pull this blanket over my head, book in hand and hibernate for the winter, only coming out for food or coffee. A dream that will be shattered in two short weeks, but I push that thought away as soon as it comes. I plan to relish in my dreams a little while longer.

I have no idea where Hudson went in the middle of the night, but I could tell by his footsteps that he was trying not to wake me. He paused just outside my door for a few seconds before continuing downstairs and out the front door. I didn't ask him about it this morning when he came downstairs and poured himself some coffee as I continued scrambling eggs for breakfast, but I still wondered where he suddenly had to go at 2 a.m.

After I scarfed down my eggs, I retreated to my small sanctuary outside on the porch. I've only gone inside when Hudson is out of the house. I assume he is in the barn working for the day, so I'm taking the opportunity for time alone where I have to do absolutely nothing. No work, no articles to write, no pressure. Nothing but the scenes from my book playing in my head and the steam from the fresh coffee I made tickling my nose.

I count the hours by each cup of coffee I grab and by the time I get to the third-act breakup in the book, I take a break and look up at the mid-afternoon sky. Birds fly back and forth as the clouds attempt to chase them. A slight breeze bends the field of wildflowers in synchronization and I close my eyes against it, committing this feeling to memory. I grab my camera from the table next to me and take a photo. That one is going in a frame. I return the camera to its spot and grab my mug of coffee, gently curling my fingers around it before taking a sip.

The dogs scatter at my feet, lifting their heads up and turning them in succession toward the windows. I follow their heads and jerk back when I see a figure standing there. Coffee sloshes over my hand, leaving bright red spots behind. Hudson disappears from the door and walks outside with a lukewarm rag. He hesitates before bending down and reaching for my hands. Calloused palms against soft skin. The warmth from the rag bleeds into my skin as he gently cleans up the coffee from my hands, beauty taking care of the beast.

"Hey," his voice is low, soft. Different from any voice he has used with me before. I look over to him and look into his eyes, the air now charged.

"Hey," I repeat, matching his tone, too afraid to break the moment, to break whatever is happening right now.

I break first, panicking at the racing heart in my chest and what it means. I don't want to know what it means.

I turn my head back to my book and take a sip from my coffee, not caring that it is way too hot to drink and burning my mouth. I flinch and hope he doesn't notice, but automatically have a feeling he does. He's too observant for his own good.

"Need some ice in there?" He says, a laugh trapped in his throat.

"No," I reply, stubbornly, tongue stinging from the heat. "What did you need?"

"Right. I am going to make dinner and wondered if you had a preference between steak or pasta?"

"Depends on who's cooking. Are you getting the food from Frank's?"

He laughs. "Pasta from Frank's is a very bad decision. Anything outside the realm of red meat is a big risk."

"Okay, then steaks."

"I'm not going to Frank's. I'm cooking."

"You're going to cook?" I ask. This feels too much like we are creeping into relationship territory. "For me?"

He just shrugs, "If you'll let me."

I turn back to my book, determined to finish it and mutter, "Sure, why not." But only because I'm hungry. Nothing else.

Without another word he comes onto the porch and starts setting up the grill, almost like he's equally determined to not let me finish. If he keeps cleaning the grill the way he is, he's going to win this one. He pulls his hair up into a messy bun and I completely give up hope of returning to the happy ending in my book.

I don't really consider my actions before I close my book, hoping to remember the page I was on, and stand. I don't recall starting to move toward him, but I go to where Hudson is dropping charcoal into the grill, stacking them neatly.

"What is going on between us?" It comes out more bold than I planned, but I also am tired of being confused. My mind is in a million places at once and I can't begin to sort through my feelings. I want him. But I don't want to want him. "What is," I motion between us, "this?"

I had planned to leave with a clear head, a sure path. But my head is muddied and cloudy. I don't need a mountain man wrapped in flannel with hair thicker than mine fogging it up. My path now has endless forks in the road created by the man standing in front of me.

"This," he repeats my hand motion, "is physical attraction."

As much as I want to deny it, he is right. I am attracted to him and with all his subtle, small, occasional touches, there's no doubt that he feels the same way.

"So what do we do about it over the next two week because it's already torture?"

"Don't think you can resist me, Sunshine?"

I roll my eyes and punch his bicep, resisting the urge to grab it and pull him closer to me, making him shut up in a completely different way...

"You feel it. I feel it," he confirms. "Two weeks. There's an end date. So let's take the two weeks, get it out of our systems."

Get it out of our systems. I can't count how many times that line has been written into romance novels only for it to end up being the biggest lie. And here we are. Telling lies like we both expect this to remain surface level.

"No strings attached."

I let out a frustrated sigh. "Have you seen the number of movies about friends with benefits? There's literally a movie called *Friends With Benefits* and *No Strings Attached* where the main characters can't stick to the rules they made up in the beginning."

"The difference is we aren't characters in some romantic comedy. We are actual people and staying away from each other isn't working." He's right. It's not. The amount of tension we have built up in the last week has become stifling. As thick as the fog covering the grass outside. "You leave at the end of it. I stay. We go back to our lives."

No strings attached. The words bounce around in my head, a ping pong ball being volleyed back and forth. They hit the net and settle, softly bouncing on the table. Can I do no strings? I don't want to admit it, but the crush I felt when I saw him in the coffee shop has only grown.

Just have fun. Charlotte's words come back to me, convincing me to let loose and trust myself. A few short days and only one day at his place and my heart is retreating into enemy territory, betraying my determination to believe that I don't deserve something like this.

No strings attached almost never works in movies or books, and a little bit of me knows when I leave this town, a piece of me will stay behind. Not just because of Hudson, but these people. This town. It has taken me by the best kind of surprise.

It is breakfast in bed, friends jumping out of their hiding places to yell "surprise!", a gift out of nowhere just because, wrapped in paper hugged by a shiny, gold ribbon. A piece of me will always be here. And I can feel a small piece starting to break off and attach itself to Hudson.

"Two weeks," I hear myself say before I can think about it anymore. The ping pong ball rolling off the table, gaining momentum until it becomes hidden in an overcrowded garage, lost among the piled up junk.

Overanalyze. Overthink. It's what I always do. I'm done with that. At least, for two weeks I am. No overanalyzing. No over-thinking. Just doing. Just action. Just him.

I'll let myself freak out and panic about it on my 13-hour drive back to Malibu. But right now, all I want is his hands on me.

"Two weeks," he repeats before he reaches for my waist, pulling me closer, the grill behind him forgotten. There is no space between our bodies and the heat under my skin is almost unbearable. With no warning, he lifts me up and wraps my legs around his waist, carrying me through the door and into the living room. I'm getting too used to him carrying me around. After he sets me down on my feet, he starts lowering his head, his lips hovering above mine before he stops abruptly.

"Wait," he says. "Hold that thought. Don't move."

CHAPTER TWENTY-THREE

HUDSON

I rush through the back door, leaving Avery standing in the living room, confused. A look of hurt flashes across her face. "I'm coming right back, I promise. Just wait here," I reassure her before running into the backyard.

I scrape my way across the yard, through the wildflowers and to the tree line where the saplings are planted. I find one that doesn't look like it's going to survive because of its smaller size and withering branches. I pull out a pocket knife from my back pocket & cut it near the bottom beforeI run back inside and stretch my arm out to Avery, sapling in hand.

"Here."

I don't think I have ever seen a more bewildered expression on a person's face than the one on hers right now. I guess I would be confused too considering I just sprinted into my yard and cut out a tree like a crazy person.

"Before," I continue. "You said that whatever this was between us stays in the woods. Well, now, so we follow what you said, here's some of the woods," I say, sheepishly realizing how ridiculous it sounds when I say the words out loud.

Avery grabs the sapling from me. "Hudson, you did not just

go out into the woods and cut down a fucking tree to bring in here."

I shrug. "Yeah, I did. It sounded a lot better in my head."

She sets the sapling down carefully on the coffee table and levels her gaze with mine, all amusement and embarrassment gone from the room. Heat pools behind her eyes and hunger grows low in my stomach.

"Come here," I say—almost as a growl—and she listens.

We crash into each other, hands, tongues, our bodies meshing as one, hands frantically exploring. One of my hands is tangled in her hair, the other on the curve of her ass and nothing I pictured before could compare to actually feeling it. She's perfect in every way and I am done for.

CHAPTER TWENTY-FOUR

AVERY

I don't have time to react before his lips are on mine. The fiery heat in the beginning of the kiss dissipates into a slow, tender rhythm. Hesitant and calm, but sure of itself.

I wrap my arms around him to pull him closer, my hands tangling in his hair, mirroring his a second ago, tugging him closer. He groans and deepens the kiss, his tongue finding mine again.

All of our walls we spent so much time building up and hiding behind come crashing down and crumple into a pile of rubble at our feet. We've crossed the imaginary lines I tried to draw between us, and there's no going back.

His hand finds my breast above the fabric I thought was too thin earlier. It feels entirely too thick now. Too much between his hand and my skin.

He squeezes softly and I hear myself gasp beneath his touch. My body squirms as I try to get closer to him. His warmth. I need his clothes off now. I need to feel him. His skin on mine. I need the heat of him to surround me like the fire roaring in his living room, chasing the chill from my bones.

I can feel his hardness pressed against me through his jeans.

I reach my hand to grip him through the rough fabric. He tugs my shirt above my head breaking contact with me. For that brief moment the chill comes back to my body, but he wastes no time taking back his place in front of me.

His eyes burn into mine. "Let me see you," he says. A shiver snakes down my spine, leaving a trail of goosebumps.

Slowly, I grab the top of my leggings and tug them down with my underwear. Then, never breaking my eyes from his, I reach behind me to unclasp my bra, letting it fall to the floor, a whisper of fabric landing between us.

I stand under the intensity of his gaze and let him look up and down and back up again. I've never laid myself out there like this for anyone before. Never even for myself. With past boyfriends, I always crossed my arms, left partial clothes on or kept the lights off. Whatever it was, my body was always hidden in one way or another. I never wanted to fully show it in fear that it wasn't good enough.

I have wider hips than most women and petite wouldn't be a word to describe me. I have curves. Thick thighs. Broad shoulders. Love handles that stubbornly remain no matter how much running I do. Skin I can grab and pinch in the mirror, wishing to pluck it off like cotton candy at the carnival.

"Fucking hell, Avery," he says quietly, like he's afraid if he says it any louder I'll run. Usually, I would want to. Usually, I would feel like fleeing at the first sign of vulnerability, but with Hudson, it feels different. The way his eyes roam over my body, like he cannot get enough of me. And for once, I feel something other than unworthy. I feel empowered. I lift my chin, and let myself gaze at him in what I think is a seductive way. It must work, because he takes a sharp inhale and a deeper hunger enters his eyes and I want nothing more than to fill it.

It feels *good*; like my body isn't something he would pick apart, listing the ways it could be better or the way that it could be different than what it is. I have a feeling he would look at me the same way he is now if I weighed 50 pounds more.

"Your turn," I say, my eyes landing on the bulge trying to escape his jeans. Mimicking what I did a few moments ago, he slowly pushes his pants down over his ankles and stands in front of me completely open.

I push the thought aside and study him. His muscular chest. The planes of his torso and the forearms I have grown to become obsessed with in such a short span of time. The tension stretches between us, a tether connecting us together the string taut with no room to move. Our eyes continue to roam over each other until the tether snaps and we collide with one another again.

I don't even remember telling my legs to move. Maybe I didn't. Maybe he closed the distance between us. Whichever it is, it doesn't matter. All that matters is the feeling of his calloused hands running through the strands of my hair. His breath leaves a trail of heat behind as he plants kisses down my jaw and continuing to my throat.

A soft moan escapes my lips when he reaches the place where my collarbone meets my neck. I never knew that I was so sensitive there, but I'm elated that we're discovering it together. A subtle secret my body held onto just for him. I wonder how many more it's hiding and if Hudson will be the one to discover them, like gems in a treasure chest. Held close, hidden behind a hard exterior until someone gently pries it open, finding the beauty within.

My gems are hidden behind an exterior so thick, nothing short of a crane could open it. But slowly, gently, Hudson is prying it open, discovering my secrets and treasures hidden deep beneath the surface. Ones that I have kept close to my heart to avoid the pain I am all too familiar with.

I am thrust back into the moment when Hudson's hand finds the wetness between my legs.

"There you are," he murmurs against my throat. His lips find mine again as his hand works me, coaxing sounds out of me I've never heard before. His finger circles my opening. Slow, teasing. Taunting.

"Hudson, please," I beg.

"Mmmm, I like you begging," he says in a deep sultry voice. Breathless and filled with lust.

He pushes me backward, his hand never leaving the spot between my legs, until the back of my calves collide with the sectional. I sit, trying to pull him on top of me but he positions me on the couch seated as he kneels in front of me.

My cheeks heat with the realization of what he's about to do. "Hudson, wait." I stall him, hiding behind my hands. "I've never...uh—" shit, this feels way too embarrassing to admit.

"Hey, wait. Don't do that," he says, straightening up and pulling my hands away from my face. I want to hide. The familiar feeling washes over me and I want to collect my gems, build my exterior back up and wait for the tide to wash me away. "Don't hide from me," he says. The sincerity in his voice startles me.

Two weeks. I remind myself.

"If we're going to do this....no strings attached, we've got to be honest with each other. No judgment."

No strings attached.

No judgment.

Honesty. That's the one that gets me. The one that terrifies me.

I inhale deeply and exhale long and slow, like I was taught so many years ago. I look up to the ceiling to avoid his gaze. He said to be honest, but that doesn't mean I have to look him in the eyes when I do it. "I've never done that before," I say quietly.

"Done what?" he asks, his thumb traces lazy circles on my hand, leaving a trail of heat behind.

"Had anyone...umm...go down on me." I flick my gaze to his

and am met with nothing but soft features. Not a look of pity or one that says he's stifling a laugh, but one of genuine surprise.

"Can I ask why?"

"I just never felt comfortable enough?" I say it like a question, even though I know the reason. "I've just always been too self-conscious about my body...my thighs. They're big and... they jiggle. It's not something I like and I've never been with a guy who has really ever been interested in...that," I finish, embarrassed.

No answer. Just a stare from deep pools of green. "One," he says, bending down to place a kiss on the inside of my right thigh. "Your thighs are beautiful. Two," he places a kiss closer to my center on my left thigh. "All the guys you've ever been with are idiots if they can't recognize what it takes to satisfy a woman. Three," he says before placing the third kiss.

Alternating between my thighs, closer and closer.

Right...left...right.

"I plan to take my time with you, Avery. To give you what you deserve. And you deserve to feel beautiful."

Deserve to feel beautiful. I used to wonder what that would feel like, but here with Hudson, I don't have to wonder. For the first time in my life, I let go of the insecurities and let him explore.

No strings attached.

No judgment.

Honesty.

I give him a nod, my voice nowhere to be found and he takes that as permission to continue.

And I am *so* glad he continues.

He swirls his tongue around the center of me a few times before he draws my clit into his mouth sucking and licking and *holy. shit.* My nerves are so far gone. Completely obliterated by this man kneeling between my legs.

His tongue continues its rhythm as he brings a finger to my

entrance further teasing me. I buck my hips into him, seeking more friction than the agonizing pace he's giving me. He lifts my right leg and places it on his shoulder, finding a better angle before he pushes a finger into me. My hands search for grip on the couch, the need to grab something, anything, overwhelming. I lift my head and look around for a pillow or a blanket, but come up empty.

Hudson's eyes find mine and without stopping, he pulls the pony tail from his hair, letting it fall in front of his face, the ends softly grazing my skin. He grabs my hand and places it on his head. Ignoring the feeling of hesitation creeping into my limbs, I thread my fingers through his hair and pull him closer.

He adds a finger and I come undone, he moves faster at my reaction, his mouth moving in rhythm with his fingers.

I can feel myself start to clench around him and he must feel it too because he adds another finger as his other hand stretches up to find my breast.

He works my nipple between his fingers and there are so many sensations coursing through my body at once, I can't focus on any specific one. I don't know how he does it all at once, but I do know I have never felt like this before.

The feeling inside me builds as he moves his hand across my body to my other nipple, working it just like the first one.

He pinches it just slightly and finally, everything in me shatters in the best possible way. I have been broken apart from the inside out before, but not like this, never like this and I know this is the only way I ever want to break apart again. With him.

"Hudson!" I moan. He doesn't stop. His fingers keep thrusting in and out while his tongue continues to focus on my now sensitive clit.

"That's it, Sunshine," he praises. His fingers move with precision. An assassin finding its mark. I grip his hair so hard, I'll be surprised if he doesn't have a bald spot there later. His fingers continue their attack and I am dead in the water.

Drowning. I'm never coming up for air as long as he's inside me. I never knew drowning could feel so good. Could feel like this. Hudson is the oxygen in my lungs and he's all I need to keep breathing. All I want.

When my orgasm finally subsides, Hudson slows his hands, his mouth pressing a kiss to me. He kisses each thigh again before he makes his way up to my stomach, each of my breasts, my chest, up my neck, until he reaches my mouth, his hands braced on either side of me.

"I didn't realize that's what I was missing out on," I smile at him sleepily, my body beginning to feel heavy, satisfied and in utter bliss.

He lets out a soft chuckle. "Oh, honey, even if you'd done that before, you'd have still been missing out," he says.

"Mmm…so cocky now."

He tilts his head to the side, studying me. "Not cocky. Just a man who knows how to pleasure a woman."

"I can't argue with you there. Especially not after that."

I place a hand on his chest and gently push him back to switch our positions. Him on the couch, me kneeling. "Avery, you don't have to," he whispers.

I lightly nudge the muscles of his abs with my nose and sweep my gaze up to meet his. My eyelashes heavy with lust and longing. As I slowly make my way down his torso, he lets out a ragged breath each time I place a kiss on his skin. The way my touch affects him makes my knees weaker than they already are. I like seeing him come undone like this. Come undone for me.

"You're so busy taking care of everyone else around you. You deserve to be taken care of too," I say against his skin. "Let me take care of you Hudson," I add.

The further down I trail my lips the heavier his breathing becomes. I can feel his erection against my chest as I move, slowly teasing him, making him wait and prolonging his pleasure as he did mine. The length of him pulses with anticipation and without hesitating, I wrap my mouth around him, sucking him in. His head falls back against the couch with a loud sigh that encourages me to keep going.

I start moving my hand slowly, keeping my mouth still until he puts his hand on the back of my head, carefully thrusting into my mouth. I like the feel of him here; open and vulnerable. A place I never thought I would be with him. That he would ever be with me. I work him faster in my hands, moving up and down his shaft. His thrust meeting my rhythm, his groan filling the room.

"Avery," he begs. "Please."

"Mmmm, I like it when you beg," I say, repeating his words from earlier.

I answer his plea and move faster until he braces his hands above him gripping the cushions and he stills. I lock eyes with him and watch him, and all I can think about at this moment is how I want to watch him come undone over and over again. I have never enjoyed this before, but with him I would do it anytime he asked if I got to watch him react like this beneath me. I cup him, apply pressure and am met with a loud grunt that makes me more determined to coax more from him. His groans match my rhythm as I stroke and lick, my other hand gently squeezing until warmth fills my mouth and I swallow it down, coaxing one last shudder from his body.

He slumps to the side and reaches for me, cupping the back of my head to draw me closer. He kisses me in desperation before motioning for me to lay next to him. I stand to grab a blanket before returning to his side.

I sink into the couch next to him, our bodies touching from head to toe and lie my head in the crook of his shoulder and his chest, my right leg swung over him. I throw the blanket over us and I fall asleep to the rhythm of his heartbeat beneath my ear.

CHAPTER TWENTY-FIVE

HUDSON

A nudge at the top of my head pulls me from my sleep. It takes me a second to remember that Avery and I fell asleep on the couch last night which also means I forgot to let the dogs out before bed and the nudge I feel is most likely from Judy. She might be the most needy of the bunch, but I'm sure the rest of them are itching to go out. I'm just grateful they kept themselves out of the living room last night. It would have been awkward with five pairs of eyes looking at us.

I glance down at Avery, content in the spot she fell asleep in, snuggled close to my side. I tighten my grip on her and am reluctant to leave her warmth. I don't think there's any way for me to get up without waking her with the way her body is wrapped around mine though. If Judy didn't get Bernard to join in her begging, I may have tried to ignore her, but the others are patiently waiting at the back door, Patch gently scratching the glass with a whine.

I trace a line from Avery's wrist up her arm, my fingers landing on her cheek and my chest swells with an emotion I am not ready to feel yet. One I haven't felt in a long time.

I am lost. Completely and utterly lost. To her. Since the day she walked into town, I haven't been able to find my way. I've been traveling a path leading to the middle of nowhere. But my destination is her. It's always been her and I was an idiot to ever think otherwise. As soon as our lips met, I knew the two week agreement was bullshit for me. It's a fallen leaf in the wind, being whisked away and at mercy to the path the wind sets it on.

We haven't even had sex and the best sexual experience I have ever had happened last night on this couch. I plant a kiss on the top of her head and she snuggles closer to me with a sleepy moan.

"Morning," she mutters.

"How did you sleep?" I ask.

"Perfect."

Goosebumps rise on her skin as I continue my path from her shoulder to her hip, skimming her abdomen. "And how are you feeling?"

She beams up at me, a lazy smile and tired eyes. She looks content. Happy. Happier than I have seen her since she came to town. "I feel…good," she says.

"Just good?"

A small laugh escapes her. "Better than good?"

I adjust our bodies so I am hovering over her, arms braced on either side of her head. I nudge her nose gently with mine, my hair forming a curtain around us.

"What is better than good?" I press. "Great? Grand? Fantastic? The best you've ever had?"

Each word is followed by a touch to her skin, a kiss on her lips, pressure from our centers.

I kiss her lazily and she pulls me in to deepen the kiss. Slow, easy. Then, she spreads her legs on either side of me and hooks her ankles behind me.

"As much as I love this position, honey, I don't think I want to do this with them watching." I say, nodding my head to the five creatures planted in front of the windows, staring.

Avery follows my gaze and lets out a full belly laugh and I think it is the most beautiful sound I have ever heard, besides the noises she makes when she comes. I want to collect her sounds, bottle them up in a jar to save them just for me. Open them when I need something to remind me what is possible in this life.

She kisses me again long and deep before pushing me off of her towards the door.

"You could have at least let me have the blanket to cover myself!" I exclaim, the chilled morning air biting at places I'd rather it never reach ever again.

"And why would I deprive myself of such a view?" She asks, gathering the extra blanket to her chest as if it would fly away with the slightest gust of wind.

"I can't argue with you there," I say, turning to show her my ass and making a show of bending down to scoop up my forgotten clothes.

"Cocky."

"And you love it." I grab a blanket from the floor instead before letting the dogs out to do their business. Judy and Bernard burst from the door and sprint through the yard while Buddy jogs his way down the stairs, taking his time. Hermes and Patch are slower to move. Both have arthritis and take a bit longer to walk down the stairs.

I hear Avery's feet padding across the wooden floor closer until she reaches my back and wraps her arms along with the blanket around my torso. "What's on the agenda today, Mountain Man?"

"Mountain Man?"

"Just thought I'd try it out. Charlotte wants me to call you Lumberjack, but I think Mountain Man suits you more."

"And why's that?" I ask, half-turning my head and placing my hand over hers, the other holding the blanket around my waist in place.

She shrugs. "It just does. Do you have one of those mountain hats?"

"Mountain hats?" I chuckle.

"Yeah, you know, the ones with the fuzzy lining and ear flaps? You'd look good in one of those."

He chuckles. "People around here don't wear trapper hats."

"Is that what they're called?"

"Yes."

"Well, then I'll settle for a backwards baseball cap...only the cap though."

I turn in her embrace and match her teasing gaze. "Oh, will you now?"

"I will," she says confidently.

"I had no idea one evening of orgasms would make you so risque, Reid."

"Well, it was the best I've ever had," she responds. "Waters."

The way she says my name has me, and other parts of my body, jumping to full attention. Her hands find the edge of the blanket covering my bottom half and teases her fingers along the top of it before she rips it from me and sprints back inside leaving me stark naked on my back porch.

"Reid!" I call after her. Giggling like a mad woman, she stands on the other side of the shut sliding glass door holding up my blanket in one hand and securing hers around her with the other.

"Ooops!" She drops the blanket to the floor and stares at me with a wild smile. I like this side of her. Playful, light. I also like being clothed, but I am not going to give her the satisfaction of knowing that piece of information. As she continues to stare, her eyes landing below my waist, I turn and lean my elbows on the wooden railing in front of the chairs and stick out my ass in all its glory, surprisingly comfortable naked knowing she's the one with the view.

The dogs are sprinting around the yard completely ignorant of my current state. They run around chasing each other in a few more circles before making their way to the house, five tongues lolling out the side, their pants filling the air. Avery opens the door for them before letting her gaze land on me again.

"You owe me," I say.

"For what?" she says innocently, batting her eyelashes up at me.

"That has no effect on me," I lie. She lowers her eyes to my lips, a small smile tugging at hers. Her hand wraps around the edge of the blanket and she unwraps it from around her and stands tall. "*That* has an effect on me though."

Her honeyed hair rests on her chest almost reaching her nipples which are pebbled now that the warmth of the blanket is gone.

"Do I still owe you?" She whispers seductively. She lets out a gasp as I pick her up, resting her legs on my hips, my hands completely full of her from behind as I grip her tightly.

I wrap one hand around her lower back and place the other on the back of her neck just below her jaw. "You do, but I'll worry about that later."

"Taking me back to the couch to finish what we started earlier?"

"No. My first time with you is not going to be like teenagers who can't control their hormones. We are going upstairs," I kiss her throat, "to my bedroom," I trail my tongue along her jaw, "where I can make sure it's better than your last." When my tongue reaches her lips, she pulls it in and tangles it with hers.

"But you were my last."

"And you think that was all I had? Trust me, Sunshine,

there's way more we can do than what we did on that couch last night."

"Show me."

They're all the words I need as I carry her upstairs and do exactly as she says.

CHAPTER TWENTY-SIX

AVERY

"*S*how me," I say, heart beating erratically in my chest, a hummingbird's wings fluttering above a flower. Quick, but calm and steady. That's how I feel in Hudson's arms as he carries me up to his room. For the first time in a long time, the familiar anxiety I usually feel at the idea of having sex with a man isn't present. Instead, it is replaced with the most delicious anticipation. It is the mouth-watering feeling of fulfilling a craving for fresh lemon bars, the first sip of fresh coffee in the morning, the inhale of fresh mountain air on a porch that over-looks a field of wildflowers.

When we cross the threshold to his room he kicks the door closed with his foot, hands never leaving their place, and lips never leaving mine. He lays me gently on the bed, our bodies fitting together like fractured pieces of a broken teacup. The chip in my cup is filled by him and I feel whole again.

My hands knot in his hair as he shuffles his hand around in his night stand. He pulls out a foil package and stares at it, hesitating.

His gaze settles on me and plants a quick kiss on my lips before pulling away from me.

"Are you sure?" he asks. My heart aches at the tenderness in his voice and the fact that he even bothered to ask at all. When I have been in this position before, a guy has never asked, he's just taken.

"Yes," I respond firmly, nodding my head and pulling his face back down to mine. I'm more than ready.

He wastes no time ripping open the package. He settles himself between my thighs and his gaze burns into mine as he enters me slowly. I gasp at the feeling of him, hard and full. I lift both arms over my head and he traps them in one hand, the other teasing my right breast.

My body is wound so tight, like it's bound by a corset, squeezing my insides until I can't breathe. Slowly, Hudson loosens the laces, air filling my lungs and I breathe him in. Our movements are frantic, desperate and filled with longing. His grunts fill the air and tangle with my moans. Each thrust comes quicker until we are spent and slick with sweat, each of us failing to catch our breath. And we cannot get enough of each other. Again and again.

We lay on Hudson's bed, tangled in each other and the sheets, watching the wind blow through the trees visible from his floor to ceiling window behind his bed. He doesn't have a normal headboard or anything like that, but his mattress and box spring are placed on an adjustable metal frame that is close enough to the window, we can rest our feet against the glass if we want to. Hudson has his legs up and crossed at the ankles. I am afraid to leave behind prints, but I get the feeling he cleans the windows every night before bed given the state of the rest of his house.

Hudson isn't like me. He is organization wrapped up in a neat little box, topped with a professional, tidy bow. Rain patters against the window, the perfect level of white noise to fall asleep to if I had any intention of doing so, my body deliciously tired from him. The sky has darkened during our time spent in bed and there is something about the sound of the rain mixed with the fading light that brings me back to our night in the woods. The feeling of "this stays here" creeps up on me and I want to spill my secrets to this man. Everything I have ever kept inside starts to crawl to the surface, fighting each other for which one will escape first.

"Tell me about the town," I say instead.

"What do you want to know?" He asks, kissing the top of my head laying on his chest. His hand slides up and down my arm. Warm and comforting.

"Everything," I say. Because I do. The more time I spend here, the more I want to know. I want to know about the people, what they do outside of their businesses. I want to know the quirks and personalities of each one, what makes them so interesting and likable.

"Well we have town meetings as you know."

"With meddling townspeople," my voice is muffled against his chest as I plant a kiss there.

He chuckles. "Yes, we have a lot of those. But, if this is what I get out of them meddling, I think I like it that way." I don't respond and try not to think of the weight behind his words.

"Do you have festivals?" I ask.

"Tons of them. Way too many if you ask me, but it's a way to bring extra money into the town."

"You have yourselves a regular Stars Hollow here."

He lets out a guttural laugh. "Stars Hollow has nothing on Blue Grove. Trust me."

I scoff in surprise. "You've seen Gilmore Girls? You're kidding me, right?"

Hudson levels me with a glare. "Sunshine, I grew up with two younger sisters and my mom. Of course, I have seen Gilmore Girls. More times than I care to admit."

I count off my fingers. "Flannel, grumpy, a hermit, all you're missing is a backwards baseball cap to fully complete your transformation into Luke Danes."

"I have one in my closet for that" he quips.

"Mmmmm, I like the sound of that."

"Let's see, in the summer we don't have much going on with festivals. Just a lot of people coming into the area for hiking and camping," he continues, fully ignoring my comment. I'm not going to let him forget it though. No way am I going back to California without the very real image of him in that hat. Maybe I'll raid his closet later.

"But in October, we have a Halloween weekend festival and the town goes all out. We have a haunted house in the mechanic shop and Axel makes it his goal to have someone leaving screaming for their life. Elias usually. He's a big scaredy cat. But when the kids go through, he has a more mild version for them. And endless amounts of candy that the parents are never super thankful for. But the kids rave about it for at least a week afterward."

I picture Hudson dressed up as some kind of scary monster hiding behind a mask, but the image that comes to mind is him guiding a mini superman through the house, his hand completely enveloping the boy's as he whispers to him that nothing scary will pop out.

"And then there's the annual hayride around the town that Frank hosts."

"Frank?" I blurt out. "Frank from the bar? He hosts an annual hayride? Willingly?"

Hudson nuzzles me closer. "Yes. He's an old grump, but he has a soft spot when it comes to the holidays. And he knows the kids love the yearly tradition of bouncing up and down with sticks of hay up their butts."

I laugh at the image. "Who knew you took after Frank."

"I do not take after Frank," Hudson says in a mocking defensive tone. "I'm the actual town grump. He's the one who's soft around the edges."

"You like to think of yourself that way, don't you?" I ask, raising my head up an inch to meet his eyes. "I see you, Hudson." I didn't mean to turn the conversation into something deeper, but I want Hudson to see himself the way I see him. The way I know the rest of the town sees him.

He reaches down to peck a too-quick kiss on my lips and continues.

"Then there's the fall festival, which is different from the Halloween one. This one is actually in the middle of November and is filled with your typical fall stuff. Caramel apples, apple pie, warm apple cider, finding the crunchiest leaf."

"The crunchiest leaf?" I ask

"Yeah, we make it a big competition each year. Whoever finds the crunchiest leaf that year gets to take home all of Fran's day-after-Thanksgiving goodies. Almost none of the town shops for food after Thanksgiving and Fran usually stays closed that weekend, so she stocks the town's favorites and lets the winner raid the shelves. It's actually pretty stiff competition, especially among the kids, but Ethan and I have a standing win for the last two years."

I hold up my hand and start counting on my fingers. "Okay, so there's the Halloween festival, the fall festival, so I'm assuming there's a winter festival?"

"Yep, in January. We have every winter-themed activity you

can think of. Snow cones, sledding, a snowman-building contest—"

"*That* one you got from Gilmore Girls."

"Guilty," he says and his face turns somber. "It was actually Sarah's idea. We've just kept it going the past three years and all of the money we raise we donate to breast cancer foundations."

"And do you and Ethan win that one too?"

"Oh no, definitely not. Our snowmen are shit every year, but we participate anyway to boost morale. And Ethan enjoys it. The winners of those are actually Fran and Cordie usually."

"You're kidding?" I say, surprised.

"Nope. But they sabotage almost every year. Especially Tom's."

"What do you get for winning this?"

"For winning this, you get the satisfaction of putting everybody else to shame. And a year of free beer at Frank's. Cordie and Fran love their beer. I don't think those two need more though. They get up to enough mischief on their own without the influence of alcohol."

He laughs and gets lost in a memory I hope brings him comfort. I have seen the way he looks at those two women and I know they're two of the good ones. Two grandmotherly like characters in his life that he would do anything for.

HUDSON

MY HEART SWELLS with excitement as I tell Avery more about Blue Grove. And I feel comfortable giving her the pieces of me I never thought I would give anyone. This feels like a moment in time that I want to remember. The way her face lights up at the mention of the different festivals is a look I don't want to forget anytime soon. And all of a sudden I wish she was staying long enough that she would get to experience those things. That I would get to experience them with her.

I want to experience the look on her face when she sees Fran and Cordie sneaking up behind Tom's snowman with a blow-torch, slowly melting the bottom of it without anyone noticing. One year they even tossed poppers at the bottom that startled Tom so much, he tumbled into his snowman. He was fine, but we didn't hear the end of it for the next three town meetings. The two old women hiding their smiles each time, even though the whole town knew it was them behind the pranks every year.

I want to hear her laugh when she realizes the hayride is probably the most uncomfortable thing any human adult can experience, yet somehow, it's still fun. I want her to experience my world, but to do that, she'd have to stay. And that's not something I can ask her to do, is it? I don't know.

She is bigger than this town. Bigger than me. I can't ask her to give up her life for me. Even though it's something I wish I could do. More than anything. Even if I did ask her to stay, there's no guarantee she would say yes.

And that terrifies me.

CHAPTER TWENTY-SEVEN

HUDSON

*T*he next few days pass with Avery in the warm cocoon of the cabin. Ever since the agreement, we haven't had a reason to leave, so we pass the time with work, food, and *a lot* of physical activity. The more we are together, the more I start to realize that "getting it out of our systems" is something that won't ever happen. She isn't something to get out of my system. She's something I want permanently in my blood, a steady flow injected into my veins.

Avery is the embodiment of good things and her stuff has made a home in my room and there isn't a night that passes that she isn't in my bed wrapped in my arms. Being the neat freak that I am (which she has pointed out on multiple occasions), I don't even care that she leaves her ribbons *everywhere*. I like tidiness. I like clean. But her ribbons? I act like they drive me crazy, but the truth is, discovering a piece of her somewhere around my house, knowing she was there at some point in time, fills me with something I can't figure out. Happiness? Longing? I don't know, but the blue ribbon currently laying on the counter next to her can stay forever as far as I am concerned.

My phone buzzes and I am pulled back into the kitchen

where I have been standing, drinking coffee, and staring at Avery.

Sky's name lights up the screen and I sigh, wondering why she's calling me right now. It's not even noon yet. And she usually doesn't call me in general. I let out a long sigh before pressing the green button and bringing the phone to my ear.

"You give up on me big bro? So easily? I thought I meant more to you than that." She sighs dramatically. "But, I guess I'm just not worth any more of your time. Oh, well. I assume I'll see you around eventually. You know, you were actually starting to wear me down and I am deeply offended you've decided to give up. I mean, really, Hudson...I thought mom raised you better than that." She says all of this in a very sarcastic, very mocking tone.

"Sky...is there an end to this ridiculous, clearly over dramatic speech where you tell me what the hell you are talking about?"

She laughs. She actually laughs and my chest tightens at the sound. I don't remember the last time I made her laugh.

"Oh, right. I forgot you're a love sick fool shacked up with a beautiful out-of-towner."

"I am not—" I start to lie, but she cuts me off.

"It's Sunday, Hudson."

Shit.

"And when you didn't show up in yet another pointless attempt to drag me off to Sunday brunch, I was a little hurt."

I place my pointer finger and thumb between my eyes and try to rub away the oncoming headache my sister has invited in with this conversation. "The first instinct you had was yourself and not worrying about me?"

"Self preservation, big brother. Anyway," she says, her voice further away now, the sound of boxes being shuffled around as she continues. "What are you going to say to convince me to come this week?"

I have been trying for too long to get Sky to come around again. I gave her space when she wanted it and then I suffocated her with my presence when she didn't want it. I suffocated her with Elias' presence, because I'm convinced she's always secretly liked him more than me. I *almost* dragged Ethan into it, but even I'm not that cruel.

We are at an impasse, but Avery might just bridge the gap. She already has, if I'm being honest. I can't remember the last time Sky called me instead of the other way around and the only thing that has changed is Avery's presence in my life—in *our* lives. I don't think I am the only one Avery is prying open.

I look over at her, a piece of toast halfway to her lips as she types with her other hand on her laptop. Sitting at the island bar, perched on the barstool, her hair is pulled to the top of her head, a ribbon tied around it. Red today. My face softens and I can feel the silence stretching between me and Sky, but the way Avery fits here hits me in the chest.

The image of her right now is perfect. She *fits* here. With Judy sitting at her feet, waiting for any scraps she can get, Bernard not far behind. Her shoes at the front door. One of her sweatshirts resting on the back of the couch, camera equipment spread out on the coffee table and suddenly, I don't want the coffee table to be clean ever again. I mask my features, but my eyes remain on Avery.

"Avery is coming."

The shuffling in the background stops and I hear Sky pick up her phone and take me off speaker. "Oh. *This* is gonna be good. Count me in," is all she says before she ends the call.

Avery's eyes shoot up at her name. They meet mine as she sneaks a few more crusts to the two beggars at her feet and fails. I noticed as soon as their whines no longer pierced the air, but I didn't care to stop her. Judy, Bernard and the rest of the dogs are completely wrapped around her fingers. Add in me and Sky and she's quickly running out of fingers.

"We going somewhere?"

"Sunday brunch." She glances at the clock on her computer and notes the time. "And we're late. So get dressed fast."

I reach across her and steal the last piece of bacon from her plate before heading upstairs.

"Hey!" she calls after me, coming up behind me to make a grab for it. I reach it above my head and she stretches up on her toes, but fails to get to it. I place a greasy, bacon scented kiss on her lips and turn back around.

"You would have had more if you hadn't fed some to the two beggars at your feet!" I call out. I hear her feet quicken behind me and I shove the rest of the bacon in my mouth and take the stairs two at a time.

She chases me all the way to the bedroom where I grab her around the waist and toss her on the bed. We're already late. Might as well enjoy being a bit later.

We stop by Fran's to pick up the usual pastries and I am thrown back to a week ago when I first saw Avery. How has it only been a week? Which means we have barely ten days left. Nine if you don't count the day she leaves. I don't waste time as I grab the pastries and ignore Fran's knowing look. She doesn't comment about my lateness, but the sly smile she gives me and her craning her neck to look around me to the truck where Avery is sitting, lets me know that she knows all.

I take the box from her and am thankful she doesn't say

anything else until I reach the door. She just can't resist. "Take care of her, boy!" I give her one of my charming smiles—reserved only for her and Cordie—and walk out into the warm air.

We pull up to my parents house a few minutes later and I can tell Avery has been digging her nails into her palms by the half moon indents now present on them. "When you said Sunday brunch," she starts. "I thought you meant at a restaurant or something. Like the two of us."

I realize my mistake too late and I understand the shapes on her palms now. "I forgot you didn't hear the whole conversation with Sky. It's Sunday brunch….with my parents and my family…at their house. Is that okay?"

She nods her head and shakes the anxiety out of her palms. "No, it's fine. I'll be fine, it's just…I wasn't prepared to meet your parents." She looks down at herself with analyzing eyes and I can see her picking apart her decision to wear leggings that cut off just below her calves and a navy blue tank top with a sport jacket over the top.

"Well, it's not really meeting my parents in that way, is it?" As soon as the words leave my lips, I want to suck them back in like the remnants of a milkshake.

"Oh," she says and I swear I hear a hint of disappointment in her voice. "Okay. Yeah, you're right. Let's go."

And before I can backtrack and take my words back from her, she leaves the truck with the box of pastries and heads for the porch toward the pristine, white front door.

I race up behind her and grab the box from her hands, plucking the other hand from the air poised to knock on the door.

"I'm not letting you go in there until I know you are okay."

She takes a deep inhale and lets it out long and slow, closing her eyes. I can feel her hands itching to do their familiar rhythm, but I hold them steady in mine, massaging her palms with my thumbs to keep her grounded. Another deep breath before she finally looks at me, her piercing blue eyes, shimmering beneath her lashes. Pools of glittering sapphire she's trying so hard to keep contained. To keep from overflowing. A tear escapes from one, leaving a trail of wetness down her cheek.

I lift our hands up and gently wipe the tear away with my thumb, her hand falling from mine. I wait until she is ready to talk, ignoring the sounds of Ethan and my mom getting out baking dishes from inside.

"Sorry," she says.

I shake my head and bend my head down so our eyes are level. "Never apologize for how you feel. If you don't want to go in there, we will go back to the truck right now and leave."

"It's Elias' truck though," she responds.

"I don't give two shits about his truck right now. I'll buy it off him right now if he asked and keep it for us if that's what you needed."

"I just wasn't expecting to be around your family," she explains.

"That's on me, Avery. I'm so sorry. I should have told you exactly where we were going. I get so caught up sometimes, I forget you don't know everyone's schedule in town. Sunday brunches are just kind of our routine. Do you want to leave?"

It's her turn to shake her head at me. "No," she says, taking her hands from mine to nervously wipe them on her pants. "I want to go in. I really do, I promise," she adds at the look of trepidation on my face.

"I just get nervous around a lot of new people and big families. I don't..." she struggles to find the words, looking down at her feet like she can pluck the words from there, weeds waiting to be tugged. "I don't come from a family like yours."

"I know," I say. I don't know the extent of it, but from what she told me on our hike, I know her relationship with her mom is not at its best. I don't think it has ever been in a great spot and from the way she talks about her, it doesn't seem like she's very interested in repairing anything. I don't blame her. Sometimes it's easier to cut things off, leave the people behind that don't have a place or even deserve a place in your life, but wanting to do that and actually doing that are two different monsters. One is just harder to slay than the other.

"I promise if anyone asks you questions, I will deflect. Plus, Sky actually showing up will be a huge distraction for my parents, so a lot of the heat will be on her. Not you," I reassure her.

She looks up at me, hope springing to her eyes. "Sky is coming?"

"Yeah."

"Wait, why is she coming? I remember the conversation in her store, not that I was eavesdropping or anything—"

"You *were* eavesdropping, but go on," I smile at her.

"Okay, fine. I was eavesdropping. But you were arguing about her never coming. So why is she coming now?"

"You," is all I get out before the door swings open and we are met by the biggest smile I have ever seen plastered on my mom's face. Her eyes widen at the sight of Avery and they fly to mine, questioning, but she doesn't ask what she really wants to.

"Mom," I greet her with a hug and turn back to Avery. "This is Avery."

She doesn't hesitate to step forward and wrap Avery in a hug. The Waters are nothing if not the biggest huggers in the world. When I was a kid I hated it—like Ethan does now—but these days I live for her hugs.

"Avery, the woman hugging you is my mom, Isabelle."

Avery is frozen, a statue of unmoving limbs and a shocked expression. Her hesitation passes and I see her visibly melt into my mom's embrace as she blinks back more tears. My heart aches at the sight of her putting up her walls and building a facade of warmth and happiness for my family when I know she is seconds away from breaking. The image of pulling her away and up to my childhood bedroom to let her cry and close herself off from the world fills my head and I almost step toward her to do just that before she pulls away with a genuine smile on her face and looks at my mom.

"It's so nice to meet you, Isabelle. Thank you for having me. And I'm so sorry we are late. It was my fault."

Mom pats her cheek affectionately and looks my way. "You don't have to lie to me, sweetheart. I know Hudson is the one to blame."

Avery laughs. "Hey, wait a minute," I say indignantly. "Why am I to blame?"

"Don't think I forgot that when you lived here, you'd spend over an hour in the bathroom trying to get your bun to sit just right on the top of your head." She grabs the box of pastries and heads back inside before I can respond.

"Oh, I *love* her," Avery says before following her through the threshold.

It's then I realize the combination of my mom, Avery, and Sky may be a lethal one I should have avoided.

CHAPTER TWENTY-EIGHT

AVERY

*I*f Hudson's house is the epitome of cozy and clean, his parents' house is the definition of a family home. With a huge wrap-around porch with rocking chairs, a porch swing and a hammock off to the side, it's easy to picture Hudson and his sisters growing up here. Walking through the door, I am met with three wooden stairs to the right that break off to a small landing and lead to a full staircase, heading to the second floor. I walk down the hallway adorned with pictures I vow to come back to later as I catch a glimpse of a baby Hudson in them. I almost do a double take when I see one of him hugging a fish to his bare chest, face angled down with his lips puckered, ready to plant a kiss to its wet lips. Hudson catches me looking at it and he covers the picture with his hand and puts the other on the small of my back.

He applies the lightest pressure. "Move along, Sunshine. Nothing to see here." I throw a grin back at him, puckering my lips like his are in the photo before we leave the hallway. We enter a spacious room with a long farmhouse table, chairs on one side and a bench on the other. Isabelle is already settled back at the kitchen island with Ethan rolling out some kind of dough. Flour is scattered on the countertop and Ethan is standing on a stool with a rolling pin in hand. I see him plant his full hand in a mess of flour before leaping off the stool to run to Hudson.

"Hey, kiddo!" Hudson beams and catches him as he jumps into his arms and hugs him tightly. Ethan giggles and places his flour-covered hand right in the center of Hudson's back. He glances my way and puts his pointer finger to his lips. I pretend to zip mine and smile back at him, heart warming at his mischief.

"Uncle Hud! We are making sugar cookies."

Hudson sets him down and a small, white handprint remains behind on Hudson's black flannel. I cover my mouth with my hand, unsuccessfully trying to hide my laugh.

"I can see that. You are covered in flour."

Ethan runs and takes his place back at the counter, Isabelle walking around him to grab the cookie cutters.

A man with thin graying hair and wire-rimmed glasses perched on his nose sits at the head of the table, a set of sliding glass doors behind him. He has a paper spread out in front of him, pencil in hand, the end of it pressed into his cheek.

"What's a nine letter word for a plant that gives you an irritating rash?" The man asks.

"Poison ivy," I answer without thinking.

"Really, Dad," says Hudson. "You couldn't figure that one out on your own?"

"Well, I must have two across wrong then, because those letters don't line up," he glances up, his eyes looking above his glasses and land on me. "Thank you for the help, darlin'."

I walk toward him and reach out a hand. "You're welcome. And it's Avery."

He doesn't move and I wonder if I already did something wrong. Did I walk weird? Should I not have approached him?

Should I have let him approach me? Is he a germaphobe? Does he not like hands?

Before I can let my thoughts spiral any further, he stands up and gives me a one-armed hug and throws his glance over to Hudson.

"Clearly Hudson didn't warn you we hug in this family," he squeezes my shoulder and I'm surprised his arm around me doesn't feel uncomfortable. A stranger I just met is hugging me and usually I would be a mile down the road by now, throwing paranoid looks over my shoulder to make sure no one is following me. But his hug doesn't feel like that. It feels like... well, like a dad's. A familiar feeling pings in my chest, the sound calling in my head, an echo at the edge of a cliff. I shove it down and wrap my arm around his back and return his affectionate squeeze.

"He didn't, but that's okay."

"Well, welcome to the family. I'm George," he says in a gruff tone that only men his age seem able to acquire.

At his father's words, I fully intend to ignore any look Hudson might be giving me now, the agreement coming to the front of my mind. The idea of us keeping this thing surface level for two weeks is fading fast. We have been plunged into the deep end and it's so dark, there's no telling which way we go to reach the surface.

George unravels his arm from around my shoulders and sits back down. Pencil in hand, he starts writing in the answer I gave him after erasing the incorrect letters he had before. There's a few more answers I could give him from glancing down at the boxes he already has filled in, but I refrain. I don't want to be a bother to anyone if I can manage it. I pull my eyes away from his Sunday crossword and turn toward the doors behind us.

Outside is the most beautiful backyard I have ever seen,

besides Hudson's, and I don't stop myself from sliding open the screen door and slipping out to look.

There's a large stone patio with a wood-burning fireplace a few feet over to the right, wisteria plants surrounding the stone wall that encircles the seating area. Shades of purple and blue hang from their small branches, stretching toward the stone. I feel like I have stepped into some kind of floral paradise. There are potted plants resting along the top of the wall, most of them succulents of various sizes. Bushes of hydrangeas line the side of the house and I wonder how Isabelle can possibly keep all of this alive.

I step down the wide stairs and make my way further to explore the rest of the backyard. I follow the stone path until I reach a fully fenced in-ground pool surrounded by concrete, pool chairs scattered on top. The rest of the yard stretches far enough to have plenty of space for dogs to run back and forth, even with a swingset back in the corner and a volleyball net off to the other side. This must have been a paradise for their children and I imagine Hudson and his sisters back here tossing a volleyball back and forth, the girls ganging up on him. He gets frustrated when he serves the ball and it continues to get caught on the net, because Sarah and Sky secretly raised it before their game.

My childhood flashes through my mind and I wonder who I would have been if I grew up in a place like this. A place with two parents who wanted to stick around for me, who wanted to love me for who I was and not who they wanted me to be. I don't even know who my dad is because Sharon never answered my questions in that regard. I always wondered if she ignored my question because she didn't know the answer. What would it have been like to have a mom who supported me? A dad who was present?

As if summoned by my thoughts, my phone buzzes in my jacket pocket. I reluctantly take it out and see her name flashing on the screen. I've been ignoring her calls and texts trying to focus on myself, but Sharon is a manipulative presence that is hard to fully ignore.

I take a deep breath and hit the green button, knowing the call is going to end with me feeling like I don't matter.

"Hello?" I can't muster my usual fake enthusiasm I put in my voice when she calls. I don't have the energy or the will to after seeing the home Hudson grew up in, mourning the childhood I never had the chance at having.

"Avery, why have you been ignoring my calls?" A harsh tone.

A part of me wants to be honest and tell her it's because I obviously don't have any wish to talk to her, but that would require a backbone. Something I don't have the energy to grow right now.

"Sorry. I forgot to pack a charger and my phone died," the excuse slips easily from my lips. As soon as it's out though, I know I chose the wrong one. I chose one that showed a flaw and Sharon doesn't like flaws. Flaws are unacceptable. They are like mosquitos on a humid day buzzing around your face no matter how many times you swat them away, seeming to multiply with every swing.

"You're so forgetful all the time. I don't know how many times I've told you to make a list to make sure you have every-thing, but you never listen. I swear, Avery."

The phone lands by my thigh as I crane my neck back, eyes staring at the stark blue sky. Birds are flying by in an organized formation Sharon would be proud of and I find myself wishing I could join them. Flap my wings and fly away with the wind, soaring above everything and forgetting my life below. Leave it behind and not worry about the mess I seem to leave every-where I go.

I bring the phone back up to my ear and realize she hadn't stopped talking. "And so I told him that if he couldn't provide for me, then he'd have to go because working isn't my style. I don't like it and I won't do it. And I can go out and find a man worthy of my time who wants to take care of me."

I roll my eyes, thankful she isn't here to see me do it and critique the fact that I didn't roll them correctly.

"Well?" she draws out. "Aren't you going to say something?" She doesn't want me to say what I actually think. She just wants me to offer her a place to stay while she finds a new guy that falls into her web of manipulation the previous men somehow found their way out of. This is what Sharon does. She takes and takes until the person she's taking from is nothing but an empty shell. She entices the hermit crab out of his shell only to make sure he isn't hiding any treasures behind him and if he is, she takes them for herself and discards him like the broken shell he leaves behind.

"I don't have much to say. I'm not home, so I can't really offer you anywhere to stay," I tell her, knowing what she's going to say next.

"Well, where are you staying now? I can just come stay with you, can't I?" I almost laugh, but I manage to hold it in. Telling Sharon where I am is the worst mistake I could possibly make. I can only imagine what she would be like sitting at that table inside watching Hudson's family in there actually *be* a family. She'd pass out from too many new experiences. I would like to see if George would smack her in the nose with the newspaper if she even thought of making a rude comment to one of his family members. That would be worth the trip. But I'm still not letting that happen.

I sigh, resigned at the state my apartment would be in by the time I get home. "You have a spare key. Just stay at my place until you can get back on your feet."

She scoffs. "I don't need your generosity and condescending tone, Avery. You should be happy to have your mother stay with you. I'll be able to fix the look of your apartment by the time you get back and then we can figure out what to do from there."

"Look, I've got to go. I'll be home in a week or so."

"Fine. Go be by yourself in your hotel room like I'm sure you have been for the past few days. Or hit the gym. You probably need to with all the junk you've been eating. I'll call you later and I expect you to answer."

I have no chance to respond before she hangs up and her words hit the mark she was aiming for. Dead center. Suddenly, I am wishing I had one of my oversized sweaters I could shrink my body into. I'm itching for my running shoes and wish I could take a few laps around the yard to ease my anxiety. My ankle is mostly healed, but I also don't want to look like a complete lunatic in front of a family I just met.

I hear the door slide open and quickly dry my face. Maybe I can play it off like the wind was in my eyes even though there isn't even a slight breeze. Hudson would be kind enough to ignore that fact though.

Instead of a tall figure coming to my side, a short one stands there and I am met with light hazel eyes and the sandy hair I have come to admire.

"Hey, Dory."

There's something about his kind features and the softness in his voice that lets me know what I say will stay with him. I sniff, not trying to hide the fact that I was crying anymore.

"I saw you out here on the phone and you looked upset. Are you okay?"

"Yeah, I'm okay, kid. Just mom stuff." I stiffen and glance down at him. His head no longer angled toward mine, but staring straight ahead, not really looking. "Sorry," I say, because I'm not sure what else to say.

"It's okay," he says, sadly. "It's been a while since she died. I get it though. I used to fight with my mom sometimes."

"Yeah?" I ask, letting him direct the conversation.

"Yeah," he smiles. "She used to chase me around the house with a towel every time I tracked in mud. I didn't get the big deal about tracking it in because it's always cleaned up later. I never got that she was the one who had to clean it."

I laugh at his memory and imagine a younger version of him giggling at the idea of escaping his mom. "She sounds like a fun mom."

"She was. What's yours like?"

"Not so much fun."

"What do you usually do after you fight with her?" He asks curiously.

"I run."

"So let's run."

I glance down at him skeptically. "I can't run. They'll think I'm crazy," I say, pointing a thumb in the direction of the house where laughter is spilling out of the open door.

"Not if they think I made you race me. C'mon, Dory. It'll be fun."

And just like that, my heart has completely melted. This kid, who lost a mother who loved him so much, is here beside me trying to help heal me without really asking why.

"I don't have my running shoes." I know it's a lame excuse, but I feel extremely self-conscious at the idea of running in front of anyone, much less Hudson and his whole family. Ethan starts to push off his shoes with the tip of his toes. When his bare feet touch the grass, he looks up at me with a grin I can't help but return.

"Running barefoot is better anyway," is all he says before he takes off running. I slip off my shoes and take off behind him.

"Hey! You cheater!" I call after him, ignoring the slight twinge of pain in my ankle. My longer legs start to close the gap between us until he reaches the edge of the yard fenced in by a tall white privacy fence.

He crouches in a runner's stance and looks over at me, waiting for me to do the same. I copy his motions and wait for him.

"Ready," my heart is pumping adrenaline in my blood and the feeling of being a disappointment has already started to lighten.

"Set," I tense, my body crouching lower, my thoughts only on the path ahead.

"Go!" he yells and we both shoot forward as fast as we can, sprinting across the yard. We each go around a side of the volleyball net and continue to run until I duck under one of the trees and feel the tickling, disgusting sensation of a huge spider web wrapping around my face.

I hear Ethan laughing somewhere ahead of me as I scream and try to get the webs off my face and out of my hair.

All I can feel are the webs sticking to my cheeks and I try to ignore the crawling sensation I feel on my neck and beg to whatever gods might be listening that it's in my head. Made up by my fear.

Fun fact: I don't like spiders. I *hate* spiders. I have intense arachnophobia from the many times I hid in my closet having panic attacks. There was always one or two making a home out of one of the untouched corners. They're gross, they have too many legs, and I don't like them. I try not to kill them, but if they find their way into my apartment, they will live under a cup or some type of tupperware until I get Charlotte to come over and save me from their numerous beady eyes.

James was always about killing them, even though I begged him not to. He made a sport of it, a competition between him and the spider. He would always win in the end and dangle its dead carcass in front of me, thinking my fear of them was irrational and funny. Meanwhile, I was hyperventilating at the sight of it, fighting off a panic attack much like I am now.

"Hey, are you okay?" Ethan's voice comes from somewhere to my right, but I can't tell because I have my eyes shut so tightly, all I see is red. But it's worth it to avoid any spider legs piercing my eye. Can that actually happen? I have no idea, but my anxiety tells me that it can so I keep them shut and continue trying to pluck the webs off of me while also attempting to calm myself down.

"No," I mumble. Spiders can also crawl into mouths. It's wet and dark. Spiders like wet and dark. "Afraid of spiders." That's all I have the ability to explain. I think back to the fake zipper I closed on my lips earlier and wish I could do that in reality, firmly zipping my mouth closed with no way to get in.

I hear quickening footsteps from behind and feel firm hands grasp my arms to turn me to him. The familiar scent of pine and salt rushes into my nose and I immediately feel a bit calmer knowing Hudson is here. "What happened?"

I shake my head at his words refusing to open my mouth.

"We were racing and she ran into the big spider web and I guess she's like really afraid of spiders," Ethan explains.

I can feel Hudson's hands tense on my arms. "Ethan, you knew that web was going to be there, why did you let her run into it?"

"I didn't know she would be afraid."

"It's okay… I'm fine…" I manage between panicked breaths. Ethan didn't know I would react this way. To his eight-year-old self, this was going to be a funny prank to play on a new friend, not a completely terrifying and traumatizing experience. I wasn't going to let Hudson be mad at him

"Listen to my voice, Sunshine. I am going to start pulling the webbing off of you, okay?"

I nod.

"Ethan come over here and hold her hand please." Within seconds, I feel a small hand become enveloped by mine. He squeezes hard and I am immediately grounded by the pressure. I take a deep, careful breath through my nose and let it out slowly.

"That's it. Breathe. Focus on my voice and Ethan's hand in yours."

I do as he says and I feel my heart start to return to normal as he pulls a web that was tangled in my eyelashes. Good thing I kept my eyes shut. Sometimes my anxiety-ridden thoughts can be beneficial.

"There are wind chimes above your head. Do you hear them?" I focus on the breeze sweeping across my cheeks and listen for the tinkling sounds above. Even though I can feel the other pairs of eyes on us, I don't feel as exposed as I normally do.

I feel...okay.

I'm okay.

Hudson is here. Ethan is beside me and something tells me that no one here is going to judge me for what's happening.

Once I feel the webs leave my face, I finally relax. Until I remember the crawling feeling from earlier and I tense up again. Hudson notices.

"What is it?"

"It's probably in my head. It's fine."

"It's not fine if it has your whole body seized up. Tell me what's wrong," he says firmly.

"I just thought I felt something crawl on me earlier, but like I said it was probably in my head. Or one of the webs. You got all those. It's fine."

He wastes no time in unzipping my jacket and peeling it from my shoulders. Ethan's hand briefly leaves mine, but his warmth returns as soon as my sleeve is off. I am grateful for his hand in mine and give it a gentle squeeze.

Once my jacket is off, Hudson starts circling me. A predator circling its prey except I am not the meal. Ethan's hand tenses in mine and I shut my eyes again at the fear creeping up my spine.

Nope. Not fear. *Legs.*

I am hyperventilating again as I hear Ethan say Hudson's name and I imagine him silently pointing to the creature on my back, crawling its way up to my exposed skin that is prickling at the surface.

"Stay still," is all I hear. Like I could even move if I wanted to. My body is petrified and I suddenly know what Captain America must have felt like in the block of ice he was stuck in for 70 years. A cold, suffocating pressure that is a constant presence. My chest tightens and the pressure of an anvil presses down, caving in.

I feel the quick motion of Hudson gently scooping the spider from my back. He immediately walks to the back corner of the yard. He opens his hand and shakes it off over the fence and the tension in my body rolls out of me. I am suddenly exhausted and feel like I could sleep for days.

Panic attacks are one thing, but being completely paralyzed by fear for a few minutes makes the energy seep from my body like liquid slowly leaking from a broken faucet.

I meet Hudson's eyes across the yard as he starts walking purposefully towards me. His eyes darken with something behind them I can't quite recognize. I want to ask him what he is thinking, but it's then I remember the other people around us.

I squeeze Ethan's hand again before letting go. "Thank you for lending me your hand."

"I'm really sorry," he says, looking down at his feet. "I didn't know you were afraid."

I squat down until my eyes reach his level. I tip his chin up meeting his gaze, misted over with unshed tears. "You didn't know. And it's okay. But next time, let's have Hudson be the one to go through the massive web, okay?"

He laughs and my heart warms at the sound. "Deal."

And just like that, he bounces back and is off running to grab a forgotten tennis ball to throw for the dog that must have come to investigate the commotion.

A strong hand pulls me up to standing and doesn't leave the small of my back. Isabelle appears in front of me with a glass of water in one hand and a pastry in the other. She reaches them out with a soft smile.

"Here," a quiet, kind voice. She nods her head toward the table on the patio where Sky is now sitting. Suddenly, I feel a wave of embarrassment swirl through me at the idea that all of these people just saw me have a complete meltdown.

"Thank you," I give her a sheepish smile. Grabbing the contents from her hands, I take her direction and sit across from Sky. I feel a light pressure on my knee and I notice Hudson's hand never leaves me. It goes from my back, guiding me to the patio, to my knee, concealed from view underneath the table, his thumb tracing slow, comforting circles in between reassuring squeezes. The intimacy of the touch rushes through me and my body seizes for completely different reasons. I drain half the water in the glass before I start to pick at the blueberry pastry Isabelle gave me. She is already back inside finishing up the cookies. George seems to teleport from the table inside to this one. He is positioned exactly as he was before, paper spread out and pencil in hand contemplating the next crossword clue.

Sky is watching Ethan play with the dog and looking around the yard like she hasn't seen it in years. From what I have heard over the past few days, she hasn't, but I'm not here to pry even though I really want to.

I like Sky. She's the complete opposite of Charlotte in the sense that Charlotte is colorful and loud where Skyler is darker shades with a more subdued personality. But she's not afraid to tell you how she feels and doesn't hold things back. Skyler is not a people pleaser and I find myself wondering what that is like.

"So," Hudson's voice pierces the air, his eyes fixed on Sky. "You came."

Sky quickly glances at their dad before throwing a sly look between the two of us. "So did Avery, I'd imagine," she says just loud enough for only us to hear and my cheeks are on fire. I want to dive headfirst into their pool and sink to the bottom.

Let me stay there for the rest of the afternoon hidden underneath the water. I'll find a way to grow gills if it means I don't have to navigate my way through this conversation.

Hudson's hand stalls on my knee and I can feel him stiffen beside me. I expect him to take his hand away and distance himself from me, but he doesn't. His hand stays and he bypasses Sky's comment.

"Glad you're finally around again," the words hit where they are supposed to and Sky turns her head away back to Ethan.

"Yeah, it's good to have you back, Sky. With you here, maybe your dad has a chance at beating us in volleyball." Elias comes around the table and sits next to her. She punches his arm softly, a sister messing with a brother.

When Elias sits, George finally sets down his pencil and removes his glasses. "Hey, just because you're on a winning streak doesn't mean anything." He points at Elias with his glasses in hand, "Just you wait, boy. You're going down." And he turns back to his paper. "Now, what is the answer to 'the disease in plants caused by excessive standing water' that has seven letters?"

"George, really," comes an exasperated voice from behind him. Isabelle sets the box of pastries down on the table along with a plate of what looks like lemon bars. She winks at me when she notices me staring at them. "Heard they were a favorite of yours."

If I had any energy left in my body, I might cry. Over lemon bars. I'm not used to this level of affection or kindness from a motherly figure and to receive it from someone I just met a few moments ago is baffling.

"C'mon, Bumblebee, you know the answer!" says George, playfully. "Tell me, I'm begging you."

She bends to wrap her arm around her husband and flashes him a loving smile. She sighs, giving in. "What would you do without me?"

"Without you?" He asks, returning her touch and pulling her in for a kiss. "Life wouldn't be worth living." His lips meet hers and I am waiting for Hudson or Sky to fake a gag or proclaim their disgust at seeing their parents being affectionate in front of them, but they do neither. They look at them fondly and even Elias' expression seems to soften.

There is so much love at this table between these people, I almost feel suffocated by it. It's easy to see how Hudson grew into the person he is with this family.

"Fine, the answer is root rot. But you have to finish the rest yourself," Isabelle tells George. "Ethan, come eat!" she calls and he runs to the table with the dog on his heels from across the yard.

"Is this dog named after an elf too?" I ask Hudson, putting my hand near the ground for the dog to come sniff.

"No, because we aren't psychopaths," Sky chimes in.

"Hey, just because you are a Grinch doesn't mean the rest of us have to be," he claps back.

"Ugh, you're annoying. And Christmas is overrated," she looks my way. "Avery, *please* say you think Christmas is overrated. Agree with me, I'm begging you." Her elbows go to the table showing off the tattoos that cover her left wrist and disappear into her short sleeved, dark blue shirt, her store's logo embroidered in the corner. Hands ruffle through her dark, cropped hair letting it show how much she takes this conversation seriously.

"Sorry, Sky. I am a sucker for anything Christmas related," I admit.

Her eyes go to Hudson who is focusing way too hard on the coffee in front of him. "Stick around then, Ave, and you'll fall in love...with the town."

She's good.

After we finished eating, we split up into teams for a volley-ball match which is apparently an ongoing thing they do throughout the year, even through the winter. Ethan explained they bundle up in all their winter gear and continue the game until their fingers are numb and their boots are soaked through. They go inside and spend the rest of the day with hot chocolate, s'mores by the fire, and Christmas movies playing in the background while they play Scrabble. The way Ethan talked about it made me want to stay to be able to experience it all with them.

A traditional family Christmas. The complete opposite of my childhood. We never really had anything traditional and to Sharon, Christmas was always a holiday "created by the greeting card companies" even though she was fully aware how ridiculous of an argument that was. She just used it as an excuse to forgo any kind of celebration or gift-giving. But being the hypocrite that she is, she always expected the man she was dating at the time to buy her some kind of gift. Preferably one she could pawn later when they inevitably broke up. Even though she didn't fully believe in the holiday, she still made a slim effort to be nice to me. But even that was surface level.

The weight of her expectations and criticisms sits heavily on my shoulders, a burden filled with a lifetime of insults that still ring through my head at the most inconvenient times. Usually when I'm getting dressed, trying to find things that fit, or picking myself apart in front of the mirror. There was even a time in my life that I physically covered up the mirror with a blanket, so I couldn't stand in front of it and criticize myself from every angle. My therapist was actually the one that suggested that, taking away the ability and the temptation to stand there before I got dressed and stare at myself looking for flaws I could pick apart.

"Avery, are you ready?" I shake my head and look at Hudson on the other side of the net, a volleyball stretched out in front of him, his body crouched, ready to serve it over. He must've said my name more than once because Sky and Isabelle have their heads angled toward me, a look of concern filling Isabelle's features. Sky's expression is stoic, but questioning.

"Yeah, sorry," I say, avoiding Hudson's gaze and squatting in a position to show him I am ready.

"Head in the game, Reid," says Sky. "I am not going to lose to these assholes the first day I come back."

We had decided to split up the teams guys versus girls, because Sky was sure that we could kick their asses. Her words not mine. I may run frequently, but that does not mean that I am coordinated, especially when it comes to a sport like volley-ball where you have to be constantly aware of what's going on.

I'm more of a baseball gal. Standing in the outfield, hanging out and kicking the grass, waiting for the ball to come to me. It's a more chill sport, more my speed. Volleyball is all about quick thinking. Something that I do not have a majority of the time.

Hudson serves the ball with a loud *thump*, and it comes straight to me. I put my hands together in the position he showed me before the game started. I hit it up in the air and it goes toward Sky who sets it up for her mom.

I had expected Isabelle to change out of her long skirt and button up shirt, but she insisted on playing in the clothes that she had on. However, she did copy me and Ethan by taking off her shoes along with everyone else. Everyone is barefoot and it is the weirdest, most wholesome thing I think I've ever seen.

But the most amazing thing is seeing Hudson's 50 year old

mother jump up in the air and spike the ball over the net like she is 20 years younger, scoring us yet another point, because we are indeed kicking their asses.

We huddle together in the center on our side and give each other high-fives. I pat Isabelle on the back and give Hudson a taunting look.

I can feel Hudson's frustration from here and Sky, turning around to verbally taunt him further is the cherry on top. Because he was cocky before the game. He and Elias were cocky bastards, and George...well, George didn't seem like he really cared all that much. Considering he is standing on the other side, the crossword puzzle still in hand trying to figure out the rest of the clues. It is almost comical, watching him step aside when the volleyball comes to him.

Finally, Hudson goes over to him, and kindly takes the crossword puzzle out of his hand, folds it up and places it and his pencil in his back pocket.

"You can have these back when we're done playing."

George just rolls his eyes and laughs at his son, but he does turn around toward the net, and prepares for what is now my serve. I may not be coordinated for the eye on the ball parts of the game, but what Hudson doesn't know is I did play softball in high school, so I have a killer arm. I throw the ball up in the air and serve it straight to Hudson, who only just nicks it on the tip of his clasped hands, but it goes wide and hits the fence with a satisfying *thwack*.

After a few more volleys, the game is finally over with Sky spiking it on the other side right in front of her dad who doesn't put much effort into reaching the ball. I'm pretty sure he's more worried about getting back to his crossword.

Sure enough, as we all trail back inside, George is already settled on the couch, deep in thought about the next clue. Isabelle and Ethan perch themselves on the bar stools at the island with the baked sugar cookies in front of them. Royal icing of varying colors sits in bowls lined up ready to be spread on the cookies. Sky picks up a cookie and starts nibbling at it as I grab the stool next to Ethan.

My phone starts buzzing in my pocket and a sense of foreboding enters my body. Luckily everyone is so busy grabbing cookies to decorate, they don't seem to notice me stiffening.

"You okay?" No one besides Hudson, apparently. He plays with my ribbon before placing a hand at the base of my neck, fingers kneading in circles.

I stare at my phone for a few seconds before hitting the red button, ignoring Sharon's call and then place it on do not disturb. Her call from earlier seems so far away and I had almost forgotten about it during the game and time with this family. Leave it to her to pull me out of being happy.

"Have you ever decorated cookies before?" Ethan asks.

I lean forward, Hudson's body moving in sync with mine and I immediately feel grateful for his presence and I suddenly wish we were back at his cabin, hidden from the world under his sheets, tangled in each other. My mind drifts to how his skin felt against mine as he moved inside me, hands guiding me and tangling in my hair before reaching down to—

Hudson clears his throat, startling me. I cross my legs and grab one of the cactus-shaped cookies along with a bowl of green icing, ignoring Hudson's smirk.

"I can't say I have. Will you teach me?" It comes out in a jumble. Ignoring Hudson's laugh from behind me, I keep my eyes on Ethan ready for instruction.

"Well, you can either spread the icing with a knife, or put it in a piping bag if you want to be fancier with it, or, my personal favorite, dunk the top of the cookie right into the bowl." He proceeds to do exactly as he said and dunks the cookie into his bowl of bright blue icing. Once he's done, he sets it on the parchment paper spread out in front of him and tops it with bright pink sprinkles, sinking into the surface of the icing almost completely hiding the blue underneath.

"One thing about cookie decorating, you can never have enough sprinkles," he says in a serious tone.

I copy his actions and top mine with dark green sprinkles to contrast with the bright icing and present my cactus to him for inspection. He twists his mouth to the side in contemplation before he grabs the sprinkles and proceeds to cover the top of the cookie.

"There," he proclaims. "Perfect."

Once the cookies are decorated and drying on the counter, I help Isabelle with clean-up and am at the sink rinsing out the icing bowls when the questions I have been dreading start to permeate the air.

"So, Avery," Isabelle wipes her hands on her apron and starts loading the dishwasher. "Where are you from?"

Okay, easy enough question.

"California. I live in Malibu right now."

"Do you like it?"

A more loaded question. *Do* I like it? I'm not so sure anymore. Especially after seeing the life that could be possible here. Or could it? I risk a glance over at Hudson who is in the living room with his dad and Sky, in the middle of a Scrabble game. Could I see a life here with him? With Sunday brunches and hikes in the mountains? Him working in the shop while I sit there editing photos? Coffee on the back porch, my feet in his lap, book in hand, snuggled under a blanket…a dream I am not sure could be real.

"Umm, yeah. It's okay, I guess," I answer, because there is something about Isabelle that makes me not want to lie to her. The comforting presence she gives off isn't something I feel like taking advantage of.

"You don't sound convinced," she states.

"It's not so much the place as it is the people," I say,

surprising myself. I look away from her and continue to rinse the dishes, handing them to her one by one. "I just…I have one really good friend there, Charlotte, but that's it. And then I come here and meet all of you and… I don't know. It makes me wonder why I still live there."

"Does California make you happy?"

"I used to think it did. But not so much lately."

"Well, if you don't find the joy in something, or if that something isn't treating you the way you deserve, sometimes you're better off leaving it behind. Even if it's hard to let go."

Her words sink in, rocks sinking to the bottom of a pool, creating a ripple on the surface. The words spread out, becoming waves that refuse to be overlooked. And I wonder if Ethan was the only one to overhear my conversation with Sharon.

Anxiety. It always comes back to Sharon. She is what triggers it and I can feel it starting to take hold with a grip I don't think is going to let go with my usual coping mechanisms. The last time I felt like this, I didn't show up for a week to anything. I skipped work. I skipped dinners with friends, not that I really had many. But the familiar cloud of depression is looming overhead and lightning is about to strike.

CHAPTER TWENTY-NINE

HUDSON

*I*t's been two days since brunch and Avery has returned to her reserved self that she was when she first came to town. She's closed herself off to me and everyone around her. Her phone hasn't been far away from her and I've caught her ignoring calls and texts from Charlotte and someone else I've been too afraid to ask her about.

As much space as I've been trying to give her, I find myself wishing she'd let me back in. Her walls have been built back up, tougher and thicker than before and I haven't found a tool strong enough to break them.

That ends today though. I am determined to break down her walls once and for all. This time into dust so they float into the wind, never to be built up again. I can't help but feel there is something more she isn't telling me though.

Sunday brunch went well. After her anxiety passed from being there in general and the whole experience with the spider, she seemed to have fun with everyone. She wasn't even afraid to go up against my dad in Scrabble later and I lost count at the number of times my sister laughed.

It ended with the cheesiest Waters family group hug ever,

with Avery smack dab in the middle, but when we enveloped her, her eyes fell closed and a soft smile tugged at her lips. It quickly turned sad though and I remember wondering what was going on behind her misty eyes.

I have a feeling whatever it may have been, it is still circulating there. A vulture circling its prey until it sees the perfect opportunity to fly down and peck at the exposed roadkill, picking it apart until there's nothing left but an empty shell.

Before we made it to the door, my mom pulled me to the side while Avery made plans with Sky for something later on in the week. I only caught the word "paint" and made a mental note to ask her about it on the ride back.

"You look happy, son," Mom had said.

I smiled down at her and saw her features softening as she placed a soft hand to my cheek. She gave it a gentle pat and said, "Don't let her go."

And made her way around me before I could deny her request. Her demand? Whichever it was, I'm not sure it matters. Avery has a life to get back to and so do I.

I head upstairs with a tray of food where I know she will be buried in the covers. With her staying in bed, I know she's not making sure she eats, so I'm making sure she does. I push the door open with my foot and she stirs lightly at the noise. When she sees me, her face doesn't light up like it normally does. It's solemn and stoic, like she can't make it look any other way. Or doesn't have the energy to.

"Hey, Sunshine," I say softly, closing the distance between us and gently setting the tray on the bed next to her. I shuffle myself in next to her and place the tray over my lap. "I brought you some breakfast."

A muttered, "thanks," is all she says, the bright energy drained from her. I hate seeing her like this. My sunshine dimmed and wounded.

"You need to eat, honey."

"I don't want to," she responds and she sounds defeated, like she couldn't sit up and eat if she wanted to.

I place the tray on my side table instead and reach out my arms for her. "C'mere."

Slowly, she moves out of her tight cocoon and wraps her body around mine, laying her head on my chest.

"What can I do?" I ask in a soft voice as I cradle her head. I press my lips into her forehead and hug her tighter.

"I don't know." Her voice is so small. So quiet.

"Do you want to talk about it?" While I don't know the specifics, I overheard Ethan telling Elias a bit of what happened before the spider incident. All I know is that it was something that involved her mom.

"I don't know," she repeats and sinks further into me, closing her eyes against the world.

"Can I ask you a question about this?" I want to help her, but I don't want her to talk about it if she's not ready. I don't even know if this is my place considering everything, but I have a need to be here for her. To help her get back to herself.

"Sure," she answers quietly.

"What about her makes you feel this way?" She sniffles and my heart aches with the knowledge that the question caused her pain.

"Everything," her voice breaks. I stroke her hair and let her cry into me, letting everything out that she needs to. "She makes me feel worthless. I'm a grain of sand and I don't matter to her. I don't matter to anyone," she sobs.

I sit both of us up, frame her face with my hands, and wipe the tears from her face. "You matter to me," I say firmly. "Avery, *you* matter. You are everything and I..." I hesitate. Afraid to admit anything, but looking at her now, her face streaked with tears, I realize I don't want her to go anywhere else. "She may not see it, honey, but I do. I see you just as you see me."

Her hands come to my wrists and she closes her eyes against

my words like she isn't sure she wants to hear them or believe them even.

"Your mom is wrong and she doesn't deserve a daughter like you. You are beautiful and kind, bright and courageous. You may think you don't matter, but you are wrong. You matter to your friends. You matter to the people you have met here. You matter to *me*," I say again before talking myself out of it, because it's the truth. And the truth is what she needs right now. "I am completely lost for you, Avery Reid. And I don't plan on finding my way back."

She finally opens her eyes and looks at me with a soft smile and I am not prepared for her to throw her arms around me, but she does and I am there to catch her. I'll always be here to catch her. She hugs me tightly and I embrace her back with everything I have, because what I said is true. I'm lost for her and the emotion in my chest is one I can't deny anymore. *I love you* are the words I do not say.

It's not the right time for them, but once I admit them to myself, there is no way I am letting her go. I squeeze her tighter before loosening my grip and bringing my forehead to hers. I brush the strands of hair sticking to her face and lean in to kiss her. She closes the distance quicker than I expect and I let out a small chuckle at her enthusiasm. There she is.

My sunshine.

We fall back, deepening the kiss before I stop her and tuck her back into me, letting her rest there. I remember my emotions being everywhere when Sarah died and it was always exhausting. Avery's tired eyes show that exhaustion. She needs sleep and as much as I'd like to do other things, her well-being is more important.

But we still have a week left before she leaves and I'll be damned if I let her spend them in a dark place. It is time to go find a flashlight.

As I roll up the gravel drive, I can hear 80's rock blasting from the garage, signaling that Axel is in there working. Typically, if his dad is working, there will be nothing but country music playing on the speakers, but with Axel it's always classic rock.

Once I'm close enough to the open garage, I honk my horn, which is followed by a loud clanking sound and a curse close behind.

Laughing with the knowledge that Axel probably just hit his head on something, he comes out and greets me with his middle finger.

"Come on man, how many times do I have to tell you not to honk your horn when you get here?"

"Well, if you turn down the music every once in a while, you'd hear me come up the drive."

"Your dumbass just wants to see how many times I can injure myself."

I shove my shoulder into him and he wraps his arm around my neck, trying to trap me in a headlock. I shove him off, wrestling him to the ground and we act like rowdy teenagers until his dad shuffles out from the corner office and yells from the garage. "Boys, knock it off! You act like you two aren't grown ass men."

"Sorry Mr. Wyatt."

He shuffles his way slowly back inside to the small office.

After he plants himself in front of the computer, I turn to Axel. "I need help."

"With?" He responds, motioning me to follow him into the garage. He grabs a wrench and goes back to working on a red Toyota car he has jacked up.

I rub the back of my neck and let out a sigh, bracing myself for his judgment. I fill him in on the last few days with Avery. From the first moment we met at Fran's to the brunch at Mom and Dad's.

"You gotta take her on a date, man."

"A date?" I ask stupidly like it's something I've never heard of before. "You don't think that would be crossing the lines of the agreement?"

Telling Axel about our agreement seemed like a good idea, but the look he's giving me now lets me know I maybe should have kept the agreement between Avery and me to myself. He scoffs and looks at me like I'm crazy. Maybe he's right.

"Screw the agreement at least for one night. You like her, right?"

"Yes," I don't hesitate. Lying to him would be pointless. I came for his help and he needs the truth to offer sound advice. He stands and takes a step closer to me and leans on the table of tools to the right of him.

"Then set aside the agreement for one night. Show her what it would be like if she stayed. Make her *want* to stay. Haven't you read any of the books Fran recommends? It's all about the grand gestures, man," he swats the back of his hand on my shoulder. "You need a grand gesture."

Out of the two of us, Axel has always been the hopeless romantic. He disappears back under the car, tools clanking here and there against the underside. Would something like this scare her off? The last thing I want to do is make her uncomfortable.

"What if she doesn't want to?"

He stands again and places a hand on my shoulder, grease stains streaked on his hands. "Look, I know you're afraid to put yourself out there." I go to deny it, but he holds up his other hand before I can get any words out. "Don't even try to make excuses," he says. "I know you better than anyone and I know you're afraid of her leaving. But not everyone leaves."

"It feels like that sometimes," I whisper.

"Sarah didn't have a choice," he says, sadly, gently squeezing before letting go and returning to his work. He stops himself before rolling back underneath the car and fixes me with a serious glare. "Seriously, man, get your head out of your ass and ask her out. You won't know what could be unless you try."

With that, he turns his music back on and goes back to work, promptly dismissing me. His words float around in my head like a hot air balloon slowly gaining height until it floats calmly in the air settling itself among the clouds. As much as I hate the idea, Axel is right. Chances are she will say no, but there isn't any chance at all of her saying yes if I don't try.

On my way back to the cabin, I swing by Fran's to pick up an order of lemon bars for Avery. Unfortunately, she is out of lemon bars, which explains why I am completely covered in flour at the moment. I should have put on the apron she offered me, but I always underestimate how messy flour is.

There are only a small selection of items that I know how to bake, and lemon bars aren't one of them, so Fran is barking directions at me in between customers and pulling her bread orders out of the oven. She apparently didn't have time to make the bars today, so I decided to take up shop and figure out how to make them for Avery.

I'm in the middle of combining the liquid ingredients, the mixer on the lowest setting when Fran comes from behind and bumps it up a few notches, the whisk in the center increasing speed. She instructs me to slowly add the dry ingredients.

I do as I'm told and try to carefully pour in the flour, but I lose my grip on the bowl and all of the flour is poured in at once and a big, puffy cloud of it billows out of the bowl, leaving white flecks on my shirt and face.

I let out a cough and Fran just turns around and lets out a shake of her head and a soft laugh. "You are hopeless, boy," she says.

"I may be hopeless, old girl, but you love me anyway."

"Who are you calling 'old girl'?" she asks, hands on her hips in a stance that could rival Wonder Woman.

"Old? I didn't say old. I said beautiful girl. Your hearing aid must be going out."

She points a wrinkled finger in my direction, but lets a smile break through her features. "You may be younger than me, and you may think you're smarter than me, but you are the stupidest man I know." I scoff at her.

"Okay, Fran, don't hold back. Go ahead," I challenge her.

"Love makes idiots out of all of you."

I roll my eyes at her and don't take the bait. I go back to mixing the batter for the lemon bars. I stop the mixer. Unlocking it to pull it up, I grab a spatula to scrape the sides. The color looks right...I think. And the consistency is right...I think.

After I mix the rest of the flour that remains at the bottom, I pour it into the baking dish. I get a few inches away from the oven when Fran yells from the front of the store, "Make sure you butter the pan before you pour in the batter!"

"Fuck," I mutter under my breath. I did not butter the pan. I shrug my shoulders and stick the pan in anyway. It'll be fine just this once. I start cleaning up and washing the dishes. By the time I'm finished putting everything away, the bars are done. I go to the oven to get them and set the dish on the counter to cool.

After I help Fran with a rush of customers, she comes back to inspect the bars and she's looking at them closely. I'm almost sure she knows somehow I didn't butter the pan. She looks up at me, square in the eyes. "You didn't butter the pan, did you?"

"Of course I did," I lie. "I listened to all of your instructions."

"You're a dirty liar, Hudson Waters. I've known when you lie your whole life. I don't know why you think you can get something by me now," she says, pointing a finger in my face.

"Oh, come on Fran. How did you know?"

"Because I know when you're lying, Hudson. You get a little crinkle in your eyebrow right there," she taps my left eyebrow with her pointer finger.

"You're too good, Fran. But you stick around anyway, don't you?"

"Yeah and you're lucky I do. You'd be lost without me."

"We all would, Fran. We would all be lost without you."

I give her a smile and collect the bars from the counter. I place a lid on the pan before picking them up and plant a kiss on the top of Fran's head before I leave. I take the coffee from the counter that she got ready for me and head out the door.

"Good luck scooping those out of that pan!" Fran yells from her place behind the counter, elbows placed on top, head resting on her hands. I let out a guttural laugh as I leave, the bells tingling in my wake.

Once I get settled in the cab of the truck and the coffee and bars are safe in a cup holder and in the front seat, I think about my conversation with Axel. I've never played racquetball before, but I imagine the sound the ball makes when it hits the wall is the same sound I hear in my head now as Axel's words bounce around inside.

Grand gesture. Like we are in some Hallmark Christmas movie, the guy trying to make amends with the woman he loves to win her back.

The woman he loves. The words seem so unreal to me no matter how true they are. I know I love Avery and I love having her around. I am better with her around. *She* makes me better.

I like the way my heart flutters at the sight of her untying her ribbons, her hair fanning out behind her, falling softly on her shoulders. The feeling of her presence in the room. When she's there, it's warm, comforting.

I wouldn't change where I live, but it has never quite felt like home until she moved in.

But she didn't move in. The voice in my head argues.

She was pushed in my direction because she had nowhere else to go. Would she choose to stay? Doubts start filling my mind, a dense fog over the hope I had moments before. I glance over at the bars I made and the coffee and focus on the smile they will bring to her face. I focus on the way her lips curve slightly when I enter the room and the light that brightens in her eyes when she has coffee in her hand. I clear the fog in my head and focus on her.

The thought of her leaving is one I push to the back of my mind to avoid the empty feeling it leaves in my gut.

CHAPTER THIRTY

AVERY

$\mathcal{T}$he bed is empty when I wake up, but there is a post-it note stuck to the window on Hudson's side of the bed.

Running errands. Be back later.
H

The significance of the act of leaving a note hits me in the chest and constricts like a python squeezing its prey. Tighter and tighter until the heartbeat slows and eventually comes to a stop.

Leaving a note feels too much like something a couple would do and Hudson and I are definitely not that. Are we? Small moments and almost touches come back to me like a highlight reel.

I'm overthinking, but something about the image of him in the early morning hours, writing a note for me as I slept feels... intimate. Something a husband would do for a wife or vice-versa.

I am completely lost for you, Avery Reid. And I don't plan on finding my way back.

Hudson's words from this morning echo through my head and I remember him pulling me to his body, cradling me until I fell asleep in his arms.

You matter to me.

His words healed a piece of me I've been missing for a long time. It's terrifying and I might not know how I feel, but right now, I feel like getting out of bed for the first time in a few days. One step at a time. I take a deep breath and stretch. Inhaling and exhaling, a sense of calm washing over me.

I take the note down and run my fingers over the indents in the paper. I imagine him sneaking out of bed and tip-toeing around the room trying to avoid the creaks in the floors. Slowly grabbing clothes and slipping them on before stopping to glance over at me dead asleep in his bed, hair tangled around my face. And then thinking I'd wonder where he was when I woke. Curious enough about his whereabouts, a wife wondering what time her husband would be home, to stop and write a note for me.

Placing the note next to the cold food Hudson brought up earlier, I maneuver around Buddy and Judy to climb out of the bed.

By the time I reach the kitchen all five dogs are at my heels ready for a treat (or two). I search through the cabinets until I locate the box of treats in the one next to the fridge. There's another sticky note similar to the one Hudson left on the head-board in the same handwriting.

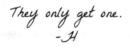

They only get one.
-H

I roll my eyes and look down at the patient animals that are giving me the most *desperate* puppy dog eyes. I dig out ten treats from the box and happily feed them two each. Hudson can get over it, plus, how will he know?

After the dogs are busy munching on their treats, I make my way to the coffeemaker to find it's already full to the brim with yet another note stuck to the counter in front of it.

Coffee is fresh. I made it stronger than usual for you. Mugs are in the cabinet to your left.

-H

I open the cabinet he indicated and grab a mug from the front. It is wrapped with colorful birds on the side, one orange and white, another with multicolored plumage, a black and white one, and one with a slight orange coloring. The words *Show me your tits* are written in orange letters across the top and I can't help but laugh and consider stealing it to add to Charlotte's mug collection. She would appreciate it. I make a mental note to ask him where he got it, so I can get one for Charlotte. Her birthday is coming up anyway, so another mug would be perfect.

My phone buzzes as I pour my coffee. My chest squeezes with anxiety before I see Sky's name come across the screen. I let out a shaky breath, thankful it's not Sharon. I don't think I can handle her before a full cup of coffee.

"Hello?" I answer, taking a sip of coffee, careful not to burn my mouth, something I do at least once a day because I am way too eager to get caffeine in me.

"Avery, what are you doing today?"

I glance around at the empty cabin, and find the dogs settled in the living room, Judy and Bernard playing tug-of-war with one of their ropes. "I thought of walking into town, maybe to take some more pictures. Why?"

Her tone perks up. "Oh good. Do that and then stop by the inn. I know we talked about it a bit at brunch about taking pictures, but I planned to help Cordie repaint the outside of the inn to spruce it up. Maybe you can do some before pictures and then stick around to take pictures when I'm done." I let out a chuckle without meaning to. "What?" She asks.

"You mean, you want me to take pictures beforehand, *help you paint,* and then take after pictures?"

"See, this is why I like you, Ave. You read between the lines."

"I'll be there in 30," I say.

"Bring coffee." She hangs up and I take another sip of coffee before heading back upstairs to change. I smile at the thought of spending the day with Sky. It'll be nice to have a day with a friend. Even if that friend is Hudson's sister.

And I find myself thinking about the childhood stories she could tell me about him.

I am completely lost for you, Avery Reid. And I don't plan on finding my way back.

His words scare me. But they also excite me? And even though I haven't been away from him for too long, I am ready to be back in his arms again.

I grab a pair of leggings, my running shoes, and a gray tank top. Without overthinking, I snag one of Hudson's flannels from his closet and put it on, wrapping myself in his scent.

The town will notice. Sky will notice. She'll ask why. They'll ask if there's more to us. What if they ask if we are sleeping together? There it is. Overthinking.

The thought of the town wondering if Hudson and I are together, doesn't bother me as much as I expected it would. I hug the flannel tighter around me and am comforted by his familiar scent. Let them assume.

I grab my camera before heading out the front door, stopping on the front porch to stretch. The urge to run after a few days of rest is creeping up more and more, but after my short run with Ethan Sunday, my ankle is back to being sore, plus running with my camera doesn't feel like the smartest idea. Walking it is. I roll out my muscles and stretch against the railing until I feel ready to go.

Something about walking down the gravel path away from the cabin feels...homey. Like the feeling you get when you're asleep in the car after a long drive and start to wake up the closer you get to home. The twists and turns feel familiar, the sound of the road something you've heard a million times before and you know you're almost home.

I remember feeling that way once. Sharon and I were in our small apartment, but this one had two bedrooms, so I was able to have a space of my own that felt safe. We drove for hours to pick up her boyfriend at the time, Phil, because his car had broken down and he couldn't get a tow. I didn't mind though. A long drive meant I got to see what was outside of our small neighborhood. I could see different streets and different roads.

Phil was her longest relationship in a while and I had actually liked him. They had been dating for a few years and he basically lived with us when he was in town, but he traveled a lot for work and could be gone for a few weeks at a time.

He always brought me back a present of some sort. Usually a snowglobe from whatever city he visited: Jacksonville, New York City, St. Louis, Nashville, Phoenix. They were my own little piece of the world I had yet to see and I kept them in my room along the top of my small bookshelf I had next to my bed.

I'm not sure what makes me think of them, but Sharon being so close to them feels wrong. Somehow they are on top of my larger bookshelf at home now and the thought of her stealing them or trashing them fills my thoughts. My only hope is she doesn't remember where I got them from. She never paid much attention anyway and always got offended if Phil paid more attention to me than her. She never did tell me what happened between them, why they broke up.

I don't even know where he is now. I wish I did. In some ways, he was like a step-father to me and I would have liked to stay in touch with him. Maybe when I get back, I can figure out where he lives. It would be nice to see him again. Talk to him.

I turn back to the cabin and realize Judy has been following me down the drive. I pat the top of her head and stop to memorize the details of the home in front of me. In just a week of being here, this cabin has felt more like home than any place I have lived before. The large windows on the second floor give a glimpse into the life I have lived since I have been here.

Grabbing my camera hanging from my neck, I adjust the shutter speed and the exposure. The sun is high in the sky, which is a striking blue, the mountains a dusty gray behind the cabin. All I need is a dusting of snow on the ground for it to be Christmas card material. Really, they could use Hudson's cabin for some source of advertising for Blue Grove. I take a few pictures before turning back to walk to town, Judy keeping me company the whole way.

We walk side by side all the way to Fran's, occasionally stopping to take photos of people outside their shops or of the shops themselves. They either stare at me as I walk or wait until I pass them to stare at the oversized flannel. Thankfully (and surprisingly) none of them ask any questions, but I can hear the occasional whisper behind me as I keep walking.

A few feet from the cafe door, a blond, short-haired familiar man in scrubs comes up to Judy and starts to pet her before noticing me. This Jacob is so much different than the one I met in the bar.

Judy's tail wags with enthusiasm as she sniffs his pockets for treats. "Sorry girl, I don't have any right now. Come by later and I'll grab some for you and your pack." He scratches behind her ears and talks softly in the baby voice I usually hear from Charlotte when she talks to her cats.

"Who's a good girl?" he draws out and my mind flits to

Hudson muttering those last two words. But to me. In bed. As he moves on top of me. "Hey Avery," he stands, leaving Judy begging at his feet for more pets.

"Hey, how's it going?" I stutter, trying to refocus my thoughts on anything besides the way Hudson makes me feel. In bed. His head between my legs.

My brain is a traitor.

"Just trying to get out for a bit. Sky said you were helping her paint today over at the inn?" He says, phrasing it like a question.

"Yeah, I'm excited to do something." Of course he already knows my plans.

"I'm glad. She needs a friend."

There's something more behind his eyes, but I don't press him on it. "I'm actually headed there now, but I'm grabbing coffee for us."

"And scones. Blueberry is her favorite. Bring her those and you're in with her for life," he says, rubbing the back of his neck. "Oh, and get extra vanilla in her latte. She says she doesn't like too much vanilla in her coffee, but she always likes it sweeter. She just doesn't know I order hers with the extra pump of syrup."

"Noted. Thank you," I glance down at his scrubs. "Do you work in the medical field?"

"Yeah. I'm a vet. I own the clinic combined with the animal shelter down the road from Frank's."

"Oh, right. Sky mentioned something about you being a vet when we went to the bar. So, you're the one who feeds Hudson's golden retriever addiction."

"Yeah, well, they're the best dogs and he takes good care of them. Every time I get one coming into the shelter, I make sure to call him first. So far he's five for five. It's nice knowing they're going to a good home. They deserve an owner who loves them the way he does."

"They do," I agree. I motion to the shop door, "I better get inside and get Sky her coffee before she calls wondering where I am."

"Sure thing. Stop by before you leave town. Maybe I can convince you to adopt one of the animals. I did just rehabilitate a cat that broke its leg and he's ready to find a home. Perfect timing," he winks like he knows I'll need some kind of companionship when I go back to California.

"I may take you up on that."

He reaches into the front pocket of his scrubs and pulls out a card. "Here, take this and give me a call before you go. We can set up a time for you to meet him or just come in whenever. I'm usually there. I live upstairs."

I take the card and stuff it in my back pocket. "Thanks, Jacob. I'll see you later," I say before opening the door, the familiar sound of the bells jingling above me. If I could hear that sound every day and smell the sweet aroma filling the air of the cafe right now, I would be a very happy girl. I wish there was a way to bottle up the smell of this place, take it with me to spray in my apartment. The bells, I could snag on the way out, but Fran might come at me with a broom or something.

Speaking of, "Avery!" Fran says a little louder than usual.

"Uh, hi Fran. I need some coffee and scones to go," I say. "Peppermint latte for me and vanilla latte with extra vanilla. And lemon bars please."

"Sorry, sweetheart," she says with a glance to the back. "All sold out of bars, but I will get the scones and the coffee for you and Sky."

"How'd you know that was for Sky?"

"Please. I know how Jacob orders her coffee. Plus I saw you talking to him outside so I figured he told you her order."

"Intuitive," I respond.

"I prefer observant," she says, eyeing the flannel suspiciously. She looks at me with a smile and lowers her voice. "But Cordie also just called to tell me you were going to help Sky paint after you take some pictures."

I laugh at the amount of detail those two women tell each other every day and watch Fran shuffle around making the drinks and bagging the scones.

She places them on the counter, "Here you go, dear."

"Thank you, Fran. When will you have more lemon bars?" I ask, because I have been craving more ever since I ate the last batch Hudson had bought for me.

"Later," she says with a smile that tells me she knows something that I don't.

"Okayyy," I draw out. "When later? Can I put in an order?"

"Orders are backed up right now, but I can call Hudson when I have some made."

"Okay, that works. Thanks Fran!" I turn to leave and ignore the light behind her eyes, because I am afraid of the meaning beneath it. I may have only been in this town for a short time, but it is long enough to know she's always up to something.

WHEN I ARRIVE at the inn, Sky is setting out the paint cans and paint brushes on top of a tarp she laid out on the side.

"About time you got here," she brushes her hands on her black cargo pants and reaches for the coffee I have stretched out in my hand.

She bends down and lets Judy lick her face. "Hey, Jude."

"Beatles," I say without thinking.

"What?"

"Hey, Jude. You know? The Beatles?"

Sky stares at me. "Huh. The number of times I have said that to this dog, and that never occurred to me. I always just think of the elf." Sky stands and flashes me a bright smile after taking a sip of her latte. "Holy shit, that's good coffee."

"The best."

"What are you going to do without Fran's coffee when you leave?"

I chuckle. "Honestly, no idea. I'm probably going to suffer from withdrawals."

"More than coffee withdrawals, I'm sure," she smirks and I roll my eyes in response.

"What's in the bag?" She asks, gesturing with her coffee cup to the bag in my other hand.

"Oh," I pull out the scones and she responds with the brightest eyes I have ever seen on her. "Blueberry scones."

She snatches in and takes a long inhale. "You are an angel."

"Thank Jacob."

"Jacob?" Her cheeks redden.

"I ran into him outside the cafe and he told me the scones are your favorite."

A smile tugs at the corner of her lips. "They are. Thank you."

She turns and I follow her to the supplies she has spread out. "So what's going on there?" I ask, because I have no sense of self control whatsoever.

"Going on where?" She shoves half the scone into her mouth and sets the rest of it on the table where she has an old fashioned radio set out.

"Between you and Jacob?"

"What? Nothing. We've been best friends since we were kids."

"Friends with benefits?"

She lets out a loud laugh. "No. Just friends."

"You guys have never dated? Ever?"

Sky stops pouring fresh, red paint into a tray and looks at me. "We've never dated. We've never thought about dating. We never will date. We're friends. End of story."

I should have brought her more scones, because I think I might have just landed on her bad side. Whatever is, or isn't, going on between Jacob and Sky, she clearly doesn't want to make it my business.

"Sorry, he just seems...smitten," I say hesitantly.

"No. Just really good friends is all," she grunts as she sets down the paint can and grabs a wide paint brush and the tray, moving them closer to the wall and starts covering the faded paint.

I copy her movements after another long sip of coffee and start painting a few feet away from her. The silence stretches and there is something strangely calming about the repeated movements of the paintbrush, slowly covering the dull red with a bright, new shade. A new beginning for an old building. I wonder what that feels like. Covering the old, faded memories with shiny, brand new ones. The same person, but changed. Brighter. Happier. A new chapter.

Is this my new chapter? Could it be?

"I didn't mean to get defensive," Sky breaks the silence, but doesn't look my way, eyes focused on the task at hand. Her movements are familiar and practiced.

"I didn't mean to pry."

"People do. It's human nature to be curious. We've just gotten a lot of questions like that our whole lives and sometimes it gets annoying having to constantly tell people we are just friends."

"Ah," I say in understanding. "I get it. The amount of times

I've gotten looks from everyone while walking in town can be exhausting. I can't imagine what it would be like to get that for years."

"Tired of people asking about you and Hudson?" She asks with raised eyebrows.

"Mmmm," I shrug my shoulders. "More like tired of the assumption? I don't know. It's weird. I'm not ashamed or anything, but I'm also just a more private person."

"This town is far from that."

"I've noticed."

"Soooo?" She raises her eyebrows expectantly.

"Oh so you can pry, but I can't?"

"Well, for starters, he's my brother. I'm protective. This is me asking out of protectiveness."

"That's a load of bullshit."

"I prefer horseshit." I laugh and feel myself relax. Before I can respond, Sky looks over and meets my eye. "Plus, I'm not an idiot. I saw you two at brunch. More importantly, I saw the way he looked at you when you weren't looking. It was obvious and you can't deny it."

"Fran isn't the only observant one," I mutter.

"No, she's not. But if you wanted to hide it, you two didn't try very hard."

"No, I don't think we're trying to hide anything, but I don't think Hudson wants your parents to know? I don't know. It's just a fling. An agreement. Surface level." She raises her eyebrows again, waiting for more of an explanation. "It ends when I leave."

"And when is that exactly?"

I don't answer right away. If I look at the check out date online, it says that I leave in one week. But if I ask myself now, I don't think I have an answer. It's not like I have anywhere to check out of since I'm living with Hudson.

Staying with him, I correct myself.

"About a week." There isn't a need to complicate things. I've had a lifetime of complications with my heart and mind always at war with each other. The two are never in sync and more often than not, I listen to my mind. Maybe this time I will listen to the other side. Raise a white flag and surrender the logical part of me that says leaving is what I need to do.

"And you're here with me?"

"You asked for my help!"

"You didn't have to accept."

I go back to painting, Judy settled close to my feet. "Well, Hudson wasn't home when I woke up and you called at the right time," I shrug my shoulders. "Plus, I needed coffee anyway," I lie. After being holed up in the house the last few days and allowing myself to wallow, I really just wanted to get out and talk to a friend. There's only so much FaceTiming I can do with Charlotte before I wish she was here with me. It's better to hang out in person and the idea of hanging out with Sky, getting to know her more was something I found myself wanting.

"Home?" The word is laced with a tone that says she can see right through me.

"Temporary home," is all I say in response.

We paint in silence letting the radio filter through the air, static interrupting the music here and there giving the moment a strange, comforting vibe.

"Did you know I paint?" Sky asks.

"No, I didn't. You mean paint buildings like this?"

She bends to gather more paint on her brush. "No. I do abstract painting. Lots of movement, colors, shapes, whatever comes to me in the moment."

"Do you sell them?"

"Nah," she swipes her hand in the air, waving off the idea of it.

"Why not?"

"I don't think they're worthy of that really. It's just a hobby."

"Do you want it to be?"

"I dreamed of being an artist while I was in school, but I went to business school instead to open the shop. Don't get me wrong, the shop was a dream too and I love what I do, I just wish I had the confidence to do more with painting."

"I can understand that. The idea of putting my pictures out in the world is terrifying."

"It is?" She stops painting to turn her body towards mine, watching me for a reaction.

"The most terrifying thing I have ever done," I mirror her movements and face her. "There is always that fear of judgment. It doesn't matter how good or perfect I think my photos are, there's always someone out there who will hate it so much, they will tear it down. Pick it apart until only bones are left. Imposter syndrome creeps back in and I lose my confidence all over again."

"How do you get it back?" She asks quietly.

"I don't. I just do it anyway. I'm proud of my photos no matter what any jackass thinks," I blurt out, thinking of the way James hated the photo of the fireman. A photo I was proud of until he shot it down.

"Is that what you're here for?"

"What do you mean?"

"Are you here to get your confidence back?"

I think for a minute before answering. "I guess so. That and to figure out what I want to do."

"Have you found it yet?"

"My confidence? Definitely." Hudson's face replaces James' and I smile at the memory of him praising my work. Praising me. The pride he showed in his features. "What do I want to do? No idea."

"You'll figure it out," she says.

"I hope so."

"You know," she starts, turning back to the wall and dipping her brush to grab more paint. "There is a vacant building for sale across the street from Fran's. It would be perfect for a photography studio," she shrugs.

"Or an art gallery," I give her a side-eye. "I ran past it the other day and it's a great space. But I would never be able to afford it."

We both smile at each other with mutual appreciation and my mind starts shuffling through ideas again and what I could do with my own photography studio.

ONCE WE ARE DONE PAINTING the wooden siding of the inn, we pack up the supplies into the back of Sky's truck. Does everyone here drive a pick-up truck? We make a plan to paint the shutters and the trim later in the week and before she drives off, she turns toward me, elbow hanging out the window, eyes squinting against the setting sun.

"Hop in," she says.

"For?"

"Come on, I have to show you something."

Before answering, I pause to take the after photos. I go to the passenger side and open the door and let Judy jump in before I settle myself next to Sky. We drive down the main road until we come to the vacant building.

"What are we doing here? I've already seen it."

"Just...give it a chance."

I sigh, relenting to the fact that Sky isn't going to let this go. I get out of the car and notice Elias standing at the front door with a key in hand. "What are you doing here?" I ask.

"Sky texted. Said you guys wanted to see the place. And I'm the one with the keys because I just so happen to be the one that owns it."

Of course. I almost say it out loud. "Mm, convenient."

"I originally bought it for Sarah to do something with, but she never got the chance and I never really had the heart to sell it to be honest."

My chest restricts at the pain still present behind his eyes when he says her name.

I give him a sympathetic smile and wait for him to unlock the door. Once it's unlocked, he steps back and opens the door for me and Sky. I walk in first and turn on the lights.

When Sky said it was vacant, she really meant vacant. The empty space brightens with a dim yellow lighting, and I am able to see more of the space than I could through the opening in the window before. I don't know what was in here previously but it looks like it could have been a boutique at some point or an antique store or something of that nature. There are no shelves lining the walls, no service desk in the middle of the room, no paint on the walls.

There are spackle marks on the walls covering the holes that were there before. The lighting could be updated. The old curtains covering the front and back windows are dusted over and I immediately go to the back ones and open them, letting in the natural light. It filters in through the windows and I turn and stare at the little particles dancing in the light.

I let myself imagine a full bank account and what it could accomplish in this space. There would be a desk to the left when you walk in with a logo of some sort behind it. The curtains would stay open or maybe I would tear them down completely to let in the sun. A fresh coat of light purple or blue paint, something fun and happy would coat the walls. A color that would make me smile every day. I could close off part of the space to make a dark room or a space where I could offer photography portraits or I could reserve an area for Sky to display and sell her paintings. There are so many possibilities with the space. It makes me sad that it has been empty for so long.

"I've been wanting to sell it for a while. I just haven't had a good enough reason to yet," Elias speaks up. "Or I've just talked myself out of it. But, for you, Avery, I think it would be a good enough reason."

I look over at him, wondering why these people who barely know me are willing to go to such lengths to include me in their lives. I am not worth all of this. I am not worth the trouble.

"Elias, there's no way that I could afford this place. Not on my own. But I appreciate you taking the time to show me." No matter how perfect the space may seem, I know the number in my bank account and there's no way it could cover a space this size.

"There is also a second floor," Sky mentions. "You could turn that into storage or a dark room or an office or whatever you want it to be."

"What about whatever *you* want it to be?" I ask, pointing in her direction.

Sky just shakes her head and shrugs. "I don't see it. The space doesn't feel like mine. At least not only mine."

"What do you mean?"

"Well, you say you can't afford it by yourself? Why don't you let me help you?"

"No way," I shoot her down. There's no way I can let her help me. I don't accept help easily and from a person I just met, I could not take her money. "I can't take your money," I tell her.

"Why not?"

"Because I just met you like two weeks ago. I can't accept your money. That's too much."

"What if I say it's not?"

"And what if I say it is?"

"Come on, Avery."

"Come on, Sky...not happening. End of story." I swipe my hand through the air, cutting her off. "Sky, please, I can't."

"What are you afraid of, Avery?"

Everything.

She raises her hands up in surrender at the look on my face. "Fine," she takes a step back. "I'll leave it alone."

"Thank you."

"For now," she mumbles under her breath.

I ignore her and head for the door, signaling for Judy to come with me.

"Look, I appreciate you two showing me the space and yes, opening a studio here would potentially be a great idea, but I don't have the money and... I have a life to get back to," I say unconvincingly. The truth is the more I look at the space, the more I can see myself here editing photos, scheduling clients, or working through the night with the mountain scenery in the background. A dream. That's all it can be. That's all it has to be.

After a few feet of walking, I hear steps behind me and turn to see Elias a few feet away.

"Elias. I'm sorry. I really can't afford it. Plus, I have a lot going on right now and I can't just pick up my life and move."

"Why?" he asks, simply, like the answer shouldn't be so complicated.

I sigh and let out as much stress as I can in one breath. There's something about Elias's presence that makes me want to open up. I feel calm around him and something tells me that he won't judge me or try to change my mind.

"I have a life in California. I can't just move."

"Do you?" He asks like he already knows the answer.

"Look, I know we talked about it before at the bar, but I have a really difficult relationship with my mom."

"Yeah, I remember," he said, falling into step next to me.

"It's just all my life she's told me that I wasn't good enough or pretty enough or smart enough and I've believed her. I still do sometimes. I don't even really see her as a mom anymore. She's just another person in my life that puts me down. Another person that makes me believe that I'm not worth it."

"Hudson thinks you're worth it," he interjects.

"He does?"

I am completely lost for you, Avery Reid. And I don't plan on finding my way back.

He lets out a sarcastic laugh, "Avery, if you don't notice that, then you are completely oblivious or just in deep, deep denial."

I laugh with him. "It's probably a little bit of both," I respond.

"Look," he says, "I know you don't know me very well, but I also come from parents who weren't the most supportive."

"Yeah?" I angle my head towards his and see him focused on the sidewalk in front of us.

"Yeah, I spent most of my life fending for myself. Once I was 18," he continues. "I was able to get away from my dad who could be verbally abusive towards me. He has anger issues so as soon as I could, I took myself out of the situation, and I haven't looked back since."

I remember him alluding to that fact at the bar and I wonder now what his breaking point was. What made him finally give up on them? Finally choose himself over them?

"How did you get the courage to do that? To just leave them behind? Even though they made mistakes, they are still your parents."

He shrugs, considering his words. "They are to an extent," he responds, "but, at one point I had to realize they didn't have a place in my life. They are the kind of people who only bring toxicity to it. Wherever they are, destruction and me feeling inferior or whatever is below that, follows. And I was tired of feeling that way and tired of letting them make me feel that way, so I cut them out. That's what I wanted to come talk to you about. It's okay to cut the toxic people out of your life. It's okay to leave them behind without guilt or expectations. You don't deserve to feel the way your mom is making you feel."

"I don't," I agree before thinking.

"And you never have deserved it, Avery. I already feel like I know you better than she does. You are a good person with a kind heart, and a kind spirit. You do everything for others, much like Hudson does, without expecting anybody to give anything in return. She doesn't deserve you and you shouldn't give her any more pieces of you. Be selfish. Take your pieces back and hold them close. Give them to the people that love you and appreciate you for who you are."

I let his words curl around me like a blanket, and I settle in, tuck myself into a ball and wrap them tightly around me. A cocoon of kindness and warmth. The kind I have only felt around Charlotte and this family.

Could I cut Sharon out? Could I leave her behind and never look back like Elias did with his parents? I take a deep breath and before I can second guess myself, I pull out my phone and call Charlotte, moving a few steps away for some semblance of privacy.

When she answers, I waste no time with greetings. "Charlotte, I need a favor."

"Anything," she says almost immediately. When I tell her what I need, she barely stops herself from cheering in the nicest way possible. "I'm so proud of you, Ave."

We hang up after discussing a few more details and I walk back to Elias and Sky, ready to go home. Taking Elias by surprise, I wrap him in a quick hug. "Thank you," I say softly before letting go. Glancing at Sky, I add, "Thanks for today. I needed it."

"So did I," she smiles. I wave as I turn toward the direction of the cabin, Judy at my heels and start toward Hudson's.

ONCE I GET BACK to the cabin, I immediately go upstairs to shower and realize Hudson still isn't back from whatever errands he had to do. I take my time showering, and for the first time in a long time, I don't feel the anxiety that creeps up at the idea of my phone vibrating on the counter wondering if it's going to be Sharon. Stressing over what she's going to say to me this time, or fearing how little she's going to make me feel.

All my life I have felt small and insignificant. I was the size of a citizen from Whoville. When I got here, I became the size of the dandelion and today, I'm Horton. I'm big and loud. I'm here and I'm not going anywhere, at least not yet. I still have a week.

Once I am showered and in comfortable clothes again, I make my way downstairs to find Hudson perched on one of the barstools, coffee from Fran's and a tray with what looks like lemon bars in front of him. He has a knife in his hand, cutting the bars into squares. He takes a small spatula and tries to lift one out, but it sticks to the bottom and comes up without the crust.

"Shit," he says, placing the top of the bar on a plate.

I giggle and he glances in my direction.

"Hi," eyes wide, mouth agape, he just stares at me, surprised

I'm out of bed most likely. My wet hair soaking his flannel shirt which is opened, revealing bare skin underneath, my breasts covered by either side of the shirt.

His eyes travel the length of my torso. Up, down, up, down again, until they land on my chest. He swallows and slowly puts down the utensils and turns his body fully toward mine.

"Are you wearing my shirt?"

"Yes," my voice soft, but confident. No more soft-spoken little mouse.

"Can you wear nothing else besides my shirts for the rest of your life?"

For the rest of my life.

"Yes," I respond, ignoring the feeling of trepidation spreading through my skin.

I point to the coffee and tray of bars next to him.

"What is all this for?" I grab for a coffee at the same time he does and our fingers brush for a brief moment. Something about the touch feels different. Something about him feels different.

"You," he answers, going back to his failed attempt at scraping the lemon bars out of the pan. "Fuck it." He stands and grabs two forks from the drawer next to the fridge and hands one to me.

I take it and smile at him, settling in the other stool at the island. When the first bite is in my mouth, I moan, a drop of filling landing on my chin. I close my eyes and lean my head back. "I could eat Fran's lemon bars for every meal for the rest of my life and never get tired of them."

"Technically Fran's."

"Technically?" I mumble, mouth full of food.

"They're Fran's recipe, but I made these," he says sheepishly, like he's unsure how to admit he did something for me, even though that's all he does. Like his mother, Hudson is a caretaker to his core. The nickname George gave her suddenly makes sense. Bumblebee. She spends her time caring for other people, going from person to person, child to child, giving pieces of herself to them like bees pollinating flowers. Giving them the things they needed to grow. Always making sure they have everything in each stage of their lives while creating a safe space to come home to.

His eyes are laser focused on the filling still on my skin, and before I can wipe it off with a finger, he reaches out and swipes it off with his thumb. Before he can pull it away, I turn my head and nip at it, pulling it into my mouth, until I feel the warm pad of his finger against my tongue. Mouth open, eyes wide like he's questioning whether or not to pull me in. I want him to, but instead I slowly take his thumb from my mouth and wrap my hand around his, moving closer so his knees land on either side of my hips.

"What's the occasion?"

He shuffles in his seat nervously, a child who can't sit still in school, impatiently waiting for the moment recess comes so he can run out all the energy he's built up throughout the morning. "I wanted to ask…" he clears his throat and meets my eyes. "Ifyoudgoonadatewithme," he says, but it comes out a jumble of words tangled together like the Christmas lights you leave yourself to deal with next year. I untangle them and play each word slowly in my head.

"Yes." I don't hesitate. "I will."

As much as the idea of going on a date with him scares me, not experiencing what it's like to *be* with him before I leave scares me more.

"But I don't have anything to wear. I just packed sweats."

"Nothing is an option," he chuckles.

"Not if we are going out in public!"

"Kidding. Plus, no one sees what's under that shirt but me." Territorial much? I think I like it. "But, I may have picked up something for you to wear earlier."

"Awwww, did you get me a flannel dress to wear?" I mock.

"Ha ha," he laughs sarcastically. "No, but thank you for the idea. It's over there on the couch."

I turn to find a brightly colored blue dress that flares out at the waist and a neckline that is lower than anything I would usually wear. Honestly this is something Charlotte would wear. Something bright, colorful. Something that would be noticeable in a crowd. I don't do noticeable. My colors are usually subdued. Dark, quiet colors that blend into the background. But the feeling brewing inside me at the knowledge that Hudson went to a store specifically to buy me an outfit is one I don't want to push down.

"There's shoes to match," he must have moved without me noticing, because his voice is near my ear and I can feel his breath whisper across my skin like a rock being skipped across a lake. I look down near my feet and sure enough there are simple blue sandals to match the dress.

"No heels?" I joke.

"No chance. If I carry you later, it'll be up to the bedroom, not to the hospital."

"You have a hospital in this town?"

He ignores my jest with a kiss on my neck as he trails higher to the base of my jaw. I lean my head back, lightly laying it on his chest and let out a sigh.

"Mmmm, you keep doing that and we will never make it to the date."

I bend over to pick up the shoes and dress, pressing my ass to feel the hardness of him. He is just as affected by me as I am by him.

"Not fair," he groans, pressing himself into me. He grabs my hips to hold me steady and continues his rhythm. I don't fight him and reach around to his ass and squeeze. I spank him playfully and am met with a surprised groan from him that I immediately want to hear again.

"Ohhh, you might have to do that again." The playfulness is gone from his voice as he positions me on the couch so my top half is leaned against the back, knees spread, him settled in the center of me. He leans forward and grabs both breasts with his hands and I gasp at his touch against my bare skin. The rhythm of his hips continues as I grind against him, begging for some sort of friction at the spot that is most sensitive. Hudson reads me and places a hand down there, circling as he lightly pinches my nipple with the other hand, pulling another moan out of me.

His hands leave my body quickly so he can pull down my shorts to my knees and he unbuckles his pants. I hear the ripping of a wrapper and he comes back to his position, my body ready for him.

He pushes himself into me slowly and smacks my ass, mimicking my action from a few moments before. New kink unlocked for the both of us apparently because he moans with me and we move together. I feel a tug on my hair as he unties the ribbon and tangles it in his fingers. He gathers my hair in his fist and pulls softly until my back is pressed against his, our knees digging into the couch. His movements never slow and I lose myself in him.

"I want to see you," he whispers against my neck. I turn to look up at him and meet his green eyes.

"Hudson," I moan and he silences me with his lips, tongues clashing, moving together. He pulls away and watches me as he puts one hand between my thighs and the other firmly on my stomach pressing me tightly against him. The pressure starts to release and he doesn't stop. His thrusts become more frantic as he reaches his peak and we both collapse together on top of the forgotten dress.

Our breathing fills the space and a sense of calm heaviness comes over my body and the idea of staying here with Hudson by the fire with take out sounds better than anything.

"Think you can move?"

I cuddle closer to him, "Not a chance."

"Pizza?"

I adjust my head to look at him. "What about our date?"

"Pizza and a movie sounds like the perfect date, plus what I really had planned was for after dinner so you aren't changing much." He grabs his phone from the coffee table and starts searching for the number.

"Are you sure?"

He places a gentle kiss to my lips, one I eagerly return and maneuver myself on top of him. Tucking a section of hair behind my ear, he cups the side of my face. "Anything for you, love."

My walls turn back into liquid and slide to the ground, a puddle slowly spreading, never to be built back up again.

"Plus," his tone is lighter, playful. "You can model the dress for me later."

By the time the pizza has arrived we are both clothed (mostly), with the rest of the lemon bars half eaten in front of us and *Elf* queued up on the TV because he insisted it didn't matter what time of year it is, it's always okay to watch a Christmas movie. I could only imagine Sky screaming "Bah Humbug" at the top of her lungs in protest of Christmas movies year round. I wonder why she seems to hate the holiday so much.

We settle next to each other after Hudson gets the pizza and lights the fire. It's warm outside, but the fire feels nice nonetheless.

The longer the movie plays, the more Hudson fidgets. I've noticed he does that when he's nervous. I don't think it's something he's aware he's doing, but his foot taps in a quick rhythm, or his fingers drum on whatever surface is in front of him.

I sit up and pause the movie. "Okay," I turn to look back at him. "Why are you nervous?"

He stills. "I'm not nervous."

"Yes, you are. You've been fidgeting the whole movie."

"I'm just...I want to show you what I had planned."

"Okay, let's go."

"Yeah?"

"Yes, we know how the movie ends. You're the hopeless romantic in this. Show me what you've got, Mountain Man."

CHAPTER THIRTY-ONE

HUDSON

"Okay," I respond, anxious energy coursing through me at the thought of her answering the question I have been dying to ask her all day. "But first, follow me." I grab her hand and go to the kitchen to grab two mugs and turn on the tea kettle for hot chocolate. Once it beeps, I pour the liquid into the mugs and add the mix.

"Did you just boil water for hot chocolate?" She asks like she can't believe I would do such a thing.

"Yes?" I say, confused with her offense.

"Hot chocolate with milk is superior. I can't believe you just made it with water."

"I've always made it with water. People make it with milk?"

Running a hand down her face, she laughs at my apparent ignorance. "Oh my gosh. You may know a lot of things, but in this you are clearly sheltered. Milk is *always* better."

I smile. "Then next time you can make it."

Next time. If she says yes.

I move closer to her until her back is pressed to the kitchen island with my arms on either side of her, keeping her close to me. "Thank you," I whisper.

"For what?" She looks up at me through her eyelashes, giving me a look that says she knows exactly where the rest of this night is going to go. I bend down to kiss her, pressing my lips to hers and moving my hands to either side of her face. Cradling her head here feels like the best kind of memory. Soft, warm, something I call to the front of my mind when I want to feel whole. When I want to feel like this life means something.

I break the kiss and lightly touch my forehead to hers. "For saying yes."

"Mmm," she responds softly, and fists her hands into my shirt to pull me closer. "Thank you for asking, even though we didn't go where you planned."

I shake my head. "This was better." She tries to pull me back down to her, but I stop her. "I have one more thing."

I grab her hand and guide her to the back porch, grabbing the drinks on the way, careful not to spill them. This is what I have been most looking forward to all evening.

"One of the best parts of the summer in Blue Grove is when it's warm enough to sit outside at night, my favorite thing to do is lay out here with the sounds of the night around me, and look up at the sky." We make it to the back porch where I take off my jacket and wrap it around her. The night is warm, but I know she is always cold. A few lanterns are placed on the railing where I left them earlier. I grab one and hand her the other, before reaching my hand back inside to switch off the porch light.

Her breath catches, and it reminds me of the first time I came out to this property when it was just an open field. I went once in the morning and once at night to see what the landscape was like. I stood where Avery is standing now minus the porch and stared out toward the trees. It was serene. Peaceful even then, but now, seeing her here, looking in wonder the same way I did, I don't think I knew what peace was until this moment.

I follow her down the few steps out to the middle of the

yard. She holds the lantern close to her chest like she's afraid of dropping it, causing it to shatter.

The glow from the lanterns light up features of her face in intervals. Her hair. Her cheeks. Her eyes. Her lips. A dance across her face I want to watch every night for the rest of my life.

"It's beautiful," she whispers.

"Yes," I say, my eyes never leaving her face. A blush creeps up her cheeks and she turns away. I pull her back with her chin between my finger and thumb. "Don't do that."

"Do what?" Her eyes are downcast, trying to hide.

"Don't hide from me. I want to see you. I *do* see you, Avery."

She leans in again, waiting for me to close the rest of the distance between us. A few more inches and I could press my mouth to hers, lean her down onto the blanket I laid out earlier. We set the lanterns down next to each other on the blanket.

We both stretch out next to each other to look at the sky, arms brushing against each other, our hands intertwined with one another. The stars glitter above resembling the flickering lights at our sides.

Bottled sunshine.

That's what Avery is. A jar just for me to warm my hands around on a cold winter night. A jar of love and warmth. A bright light filling a small space, her smile filling whatever room she walks into. I want more than just a bottle. I want the whole damn jar.

"This is perfect," she whispers.

I turn toward her propping my elbow underneath me, so I can see her face. My heart quickens to a speed that is probably dangerous as as I look at her and take her in.

"Avery, this last week has been...well, it's been more than I expected and I don't think I want it to end."

"I don't want it to either..." she hesitates. "But, what am I supposed to do, Hudson? I don't belong here. What would I do? I have a job to get back to, a life."

The way she says it doesn't convince me. "A job you don't like and a life you left to find something meaningful."

"I know, but I always planned to go back. You know that."

"Stay," I place my hand on her hip and pull her closer to me. "Stay with me. Live here. Build your photography studio. Hell, live out your dream and live above the studio if you aren't ready to live together. We can date until you're ready for that step. Whatever you need. I just want you in my life, Avery. Will you stay with me?" My voice cracks on the last two words and I can't help but sound desperate. The way people have left my life before may not have been voluntary, but it doesn't smother the feeling of desperation when it comes to the thought of Avery leaving.

"Sky told you?"

"She might have called me and filled me in on her idea," I admit sheepishly.

"Can I think about it?" She asks. "There's a lot I would need to figure out and I can't just," she sighs. "I can't just pick up and move my life without a plan."

I lean my head to hers, touching the pad of my thumb to her bottom lip. "Take the time you need, Sunshine. I will wait as long as you need me to. I'm not going anywhere."

I kiss her and we quickly shed our clothes, tangling our bodies in each other once again with the stars blinking above us, a slight breeze chilling our bare skin. The hope I feel in my chest swells as we move together, more hope than I have had in a long time.

CHAPTER THIRTY-TWO

AVERY

The doorbell rings mid-morning and I bury myself deeper into Hudson's comforter, breathing in his scent. Judy is snuggled up at my feet with Bernard taking over Hudson's side. After a morning of lots (and I mean lots) of orgasms. Hudson is nothing if not generous—and thorough. He left the bedroom earlier to make coffee. And apparently breakfast from the smell wafting up the stairs.

I reach over to pet Bernard behind his ears when I hear an all too-familiar voice piercing the air. A voice that sends my whole body into a panic. I shoot out of bed and dress as quickly as I can after running to the guest room. I may be sleeping—or not sleeping—in Hudson's bed every night, but my suitcase is still in the guest room. I rummage through my discarded clothes before throwing on leggings and the sweatshirt I got from Sky's store the other day.

Shit, shit, shit.

I don't know what to do. I don't know why she's here or how she even found me. I haven't been answering her texts or voicemails, because I didn't want to feel the way she always makes me feel when I am around her. Small and non-existent. To her I am a speck of dust that keeps coming back after it's swept underneath the couch. I am supposed to stay hidden, an unworthy particle. But I come back every time and when cleaning day comes around, I am swept right back where I belong. Where she makes me feel like I belong. I haven't felt like that speck of dust since I got here. Since my agreement with Hudson. He knows some of my relationship issues with my mother, but I never really gave him the specifics. I didn't want to scare him off with my baggage, and since I talked with Elias and made the phone call I did, I left her behind. I was done with her, but now she's here.

Now, she's here to ruin it; to ruin me like she always does.

Their voices carry up the stairs as I take a second at the top to compose myself.

Inhale. Exhale.

Clench. Unclench.

"I don't think she was expecting you," I hear Hudson say. I peak around the corner and he is fully clothed in his flannel pants and gray t-shirt. He's lucky he put something on or else Sharon would have tried to take advantage. Then again, a layer of clothes never stopped her before and now is not the time I expect her to show restraint.

"Oh, she is," is all she says with her nose high up in the air, a haughty look on her face like she is a prized mare and he is a stallion that should be begging for her attention.

She pushes past him, taking off the bright pink gloves that match her pantsuit. "Avery!" She calls. "Come down and greet your mother."

Dramatic much? I roll my eyes and take one last deep breath.

"Sharon, what are you doing here?"

Her eyes narrow at the name. She hates it when I call her anything but some form of the word mom. What she doesn't know is she lost that privilege a long time ago.

"I've been calling and texting you, and you haven't

responded. So I came to you. You had your friend go to your place when I wasn't there and move all of my stuff out *and* change the locks!" she yells, shrill voice piercing the air. The dogs run from the kitchen at the sound of it and hide behind the couch. Part of me wishes I could join them.

I can see Hudson look at me, questions swimming behind his eyes. I didn't tell him about the phone call to Charlotte. Only Elias knew and that was only because he was standing there when I made the call. As soon as Charlotte answered, she knew something was different and she didn't hesitate to go to my apartment.

She got up from her computer, left work in the middle of the day with James calling after her. She told him it was an emergency and when he yelled more, she finally yelled back, "You know what? Fuck you!" before promptly leaving, the brightest smile on her face as she skipped down the stairs of our office building. Well, my office building now. I doubt James will let her come back after that.

I look Sharon in the eyes and stand as tall as I am able. As tall as I feel, which is more than the few inches I am used to.

"You mean you stalked me…is what you did. I'm here for me and there's a reason I wasn't answering your calls or your texts. I don't want to talk to you. I am done."

She lets out a derisive laugh. "You're done? What does that even mean?" She stops to look around the space and her eyes land on the little pieces of me that I have left around. Clothes on the couch, a ribbon on the counter next to two mugs along with one on the floor that one of the dogs must have gotten a hold of.

"You expect me to believe you came here for *yourself*? When you are coming downstairs from a stranger's house looking like a whore who just spent the night in his bed? When did you meet him? Yesterday? And you're already jumping in bed with him? Looking like that? Really, sweetie? I raised you better than that."

Her words sting and Hudson speaks before I can. He places a

strong hand on my arm and pulls me back until he is standing in front of me, a protective wall of padding, guarding me from the beast ready to bite. He towers over her. "Absolutely not," is all he says in a voice I haven't heard before. Commanding and dark.

"You think you are going to scare me? Please."

His eyes darken and his voice comes out low and daunting, but calm. "Mmm," he scoffs. "It's funny you think I'm the one you need to worry about. But I'll be damned if I allow you to come in here and insult the woman I love."

My insides turn to ice at his words. He's never said them to me and I never expected him to. Our agreement ends in two days and I am going back to California. But when I look at him, standing there against my mother, speaking in my defense, my resolve shatters. He's picking up the pieces I came here to mend.

No, I tell myself. I am picking them up, but he is holding them together.

"*Love?*" she scoffs again. "I am her mother. *I* love her."

It's my turn to let out a condescending sound. She peels her eyes from Hudson, shock spreading across her features. "You've never loved me," I say. Hudson glances back at me and I nod, letting him know I'm okay. Letting him know I can do this. Stand up to her. Something I should have done years ago. "You raised me, but that's where your mothering ends."

"Av—"

I cut a hand through the air to silence her. "No. You shut up for once and let me speak."

She jerks her head back and her eyes widen in surprise. Never have I stood up for myself. Never have I talked back to her, not even when I was a kid being constantly belittled by her and her friends. But I will not shrink in her presence ever again.

"You have belittled me for *years*. You have treated me like I was nothing but a consolation prize and when I wasn't perfect enough for you and didn't live up to your impossibly high standards, you threw me aside." My eyes start to water and I can feel my voice straining with emotion, but I don't let myself break. Not in front of her. Not anymore. "Do you know what I go through on a daily basis because of your so-called mothering?" I ask.

Her features are stoic. Guarded and uncaring. I can tell she's just waiting for me to be done talking so she can resume whatever insult she is thinking of throwing my way. She crosses her arms, boredom shown in her movements and in her face.

"You don't. Because you don't care. You have *never* cared." My voice breaks, but I refuse to let her see me crumble. "I have no self-esteem because of you. I am in therapy because of you. I have hated myself and my body, because. Of. You. You are manipulative. You are childish. You are horrible. You are a monster and I could keep going, but I am a better person than you, so I won't. And you won't change. You have shown who you are. You are all of the things I just said and you will continue to be, but the one thing you will no longer be is my mother. So leave. Don't text me. Don't call me. Don't show up where I am. I never want to see you again and if I do, I will call the police. Don't think for a second I won't hesitate to get a restraining order against you, because I will. I had Charlotte move you out because I. Am. *Done.*"

I have never seen her look shocked before, but now her eyes are wide, tears forming behind them either out of panic at losing her daughter or panic at the fact that she doesn't have me to depend on anymore. I don't care. I try to look for a hint of compassion or regret, but I find none and my heart breaks a little bit more for the relationship I never had and will never have with her.

"As if I wanted anything to do with you anyway," she spits before she walks out and slams the door behind her.

I stand, frozen in place, staring at the door as I listen to her car starting. Her tires circle the gravel driveway and the sound fades from the air. The last words I will ever hear her say and they were said with such hate behind them, but I know I made the right choice. I am making the right choice. So why does it feel so shitty?

The house is quiet aside from Hudson's breathing and my quick breaths. He reaches his arms out to me and it's only then that I let the dam inside me break. I crumple to the floor and Hudson is there to catch me.

Strong arms and calm words, he carries me back up the stairs to his bed and lets me cry in his arms. His voice soothing me with soft lullabies and his hands tracing gentle circles up and down my back until I have nothing left in me and I welcome the darkness.

CHAPTER THIRTY-THREE

HUDSON

a very sleeps through most of the day and evening, only getting up for the bathroom occasionally. *The Princess Bride* has been playing on a loop on the TV in my bedroom and the only time I have left her side is to take care of the dogs or to bring her food..

We haven't spoken about Sharon since she left, or the words I said to her. I didn't plan on telling her like that. I wanted to do something special, something spontaneous to convince her to stay with me. To tell her I love her. I wanted to set up something good enough to give her an idea of what her life would look like here. She's supposed to leave in two days and we both have been avoiding the subject. That and talking about our agreement.

We gave it two weeks. What she doesn't know is it has been the best two weeks of my life.

Don't let her go, Hudson.

My mother's words have been echoing in my head since the first Sunday brunch we went to. I know I'm headstrong and not the easiest person to get to open up, but Avery makes me better. She makes me want to be happy. To *choose* happy. And I choose her. I just don't know if she chooses me.

The familiar feeling of anxiety crawls across my skin like ants scurrying to fix a caved hole in their home, rushed and frantic. What if I put myself out there, pour my heart out, and she decides she doesn't want to stay? What happens then?

I don't think my heart could recover. But, I think I'd rather take that chance than not and wonder what would have happened if I did. She's made no indication that she plans on sticking around the day after tomorrow. But that also gives me the rest of the evening and all night to find a way to convince her to stay.

My finger hovers over the FaceTime button but I realize she probably won't answer my phone call let alone a stranger Face-Timing her phone, considering I swiped the number from Avery's phone. I type up a quick text instead and hit send.

> Me: It's Hudson. I need your help.

I place my phone face down on the counter and grab the coffee pot. Before I even have a chance to turn on the faucet to fill it, my phone is vibrating with a FaceTime call from her.

I answer and as soon as my face appears on the screen she wastes no time.

"What did you do, Luke Danes?" Charlotte asks. The phone must be propped up on something because I can see her sitting cross legged at a table, going through a stack of papers. Her red hair is held up by a clip and her black framed glasses rest on her nose.

"Luke? And why do you automatically assume I did something?"

"Why else would you be calling me?" She says, ignoring my first question.

"Sharon," is all I say.

Charlotte drops the papers and grabs her phone. Her face

fills the screen and she stares into me. "What? How did she…..shit." She rubs her hands down her face and sighs.

"What?"

"James. Dammit. I kept telling Avery to delete her location app. Sharon came to the office the other day looking for Avery before I threw her out and I didn't say anything, only that she'd be back in a few days, but James must have found out because she went to talk to him after me. What did she do?"

"She just came to my house demanding to speak to Avery, but Avery told her off and told her she didn't want to see her again and she left."

"She left?"

"Yeah."

"Just like that?"

"Yeah. Avery let out a lot of things I think she's been wanting to say for a long time. Sharon didn't seem fazed, but I think she realized she was serious when she left."

"Good. Avery deserves better."

"She does," I agree.

"So, why are you calling me then?"

"Because….." I take a deep breath. "I asked Avery to stay."

Charlotte's features stay steady as if she expected this to happen. "Finally."

"What?" The pot of water stalls in my hand and I set it gently on the counter before looking at Charlotte.

"Hudson, don't act like I don't know how you two feel about each other. Avery has been complaining about you since day one."

"Complaining?"

"Yes," she says, like it's supposed to be a fact I know about. "And she's very easy to read. She loves you. You love her. I expected nothing less."

"I kinda….. told her I loved her. In a very unconventional

way. And we haven't talked about it. I think I may have scared her off."

"You'd have to do a lot more than that to scare her off."

"So what should I do then? I just asked her last night and then Sharon came and I think she's overwhelmed and scared. What can I do to make it easier for her?"

Charlotte quiets and her eyes start darting back and forth before landing on the ceiling like she's trying to solve a math equation in the air in front of her. "What's your sister's number?" she asks.

"Why do you want Sky's number?"

"Just trust me and give me the damn number, Lucas."

I roll my eyes and relay the number to her as she adds it to her phone. She hangs up shortly after that saying she will call me back with a plan. Whatever Sky has to do with this, I have no idea, I just hope it's enough. That *I* am enough.

CHAPTER THIRTY-FOUR

AVERY

I know I should get up. I want to get up. Or at least, I *want* to want to. But I don't. I want to stay in this bed forever. Hibernate for the winter and only come out when I am ready to feel the warmth of the sun on my skin again.

The bed shifts and Hudson's soft voice fills the air. A gentle hand coaxes at the hair covering my face and I inhale his scent. "Sweetheart, you have to get up."

"Is that a statement? Or a request?"

"Both," he chuckles. "C'mon...I have something for you," he plants a soft kiss on my shoulder. "Shower and get ready."

As much as I want to stay wrapped up in Hudson's sheets, I know he's right. I have to pull myself together and move on with my motherless life. Dramatic? Probably. But I think I'm allowed to be dramatic after everything she has put me through. "Can't you bring it to me in bed?" I beg.

"Unfortunately, no."

"Okay, I'll settle for just you then," I smile and reach over to grab him, but he quickly moves out of my reach. "Hey!" I protest.

"Nope," he wags his pointer finger in my direction. "No sex for you until you're showered and dressed."

"Being dressed defeats the purpose," I whine.

He backs away from the bed until he is nestled next to the door frame and he leans his bicep against it, crossing one ankle over the other. Finally, I make myself sit up in bed and let my tangled hair fall around my shoulders and take him in as he stares back at me.

He's wearing a pair of his nicer jeans. A pair that clearly hasn't seen his workshop given the fact they aren't covered with wood stain or have any holes in them. A plain white shirt hugs his torso and I don't think I have ever had a white shirt fetish before, but I most definitely do now. On top, he is wearing a pale green flannel that matches his eyes, the sleeves rolled up to his elbows.

"Clock is ticking, Reid. Shower," he points to the bathroom. "Now."

"Mmmm, I like it when you're demanding."

"If you don't get in that shower, I am going to come over and pick you up."

"The best kind of threat," I tease and sink my weight further into his mattress, strong in my resolve to stay here for the foreseeable future.

"There's lemon bars in it for you."

Nope. Not giving in for bars this time. This is my cave, my shelter for the winter and I am not leaving.

"Extra coffee?" he adds.

Caffeine is overrated, I lie to myself.

"Someone is here to visit," he says.

That gets my attention. I sit back up. "Who?"

"That information is only for women who are showered, dressed and ready to go in the next ten minutes." He turns and leaves the doorway. I hear his boots clunk down the stairs.

"Ten minutes?" I yell after him. "That's hardly enough time!"

"You had twenty when I came in to wake you. Not my fault, Reid!" He yells back.

I take the quickest shower of my life and dress in the clothes I threw in the corner the other day. More leggings and just to taunt him, his favorite flannel, but with a tank top underneath this time. Wherever we are going or whoever we are seeing, I'm sure they would appreciate me not showing up half naked.

I tie my hair up in a red polka-dotted ribbon and skip downstairs. Hudson is waiting by the front door with what looks to be a tie hanging from his right hand. He holds it up and it is indeed a tie. One that is decorated with multicolored Christmas lights and a blue background.

"Why are you handing me a Christmas tie?"

"Blindfold, sweetheart."

"I thought you said no sex? Are we living out some sort of fantasy of yours, Waters?"

"Only in your dreams, Reid. C'mon, turn around," he motions in a circle with his finger. I listen and he ties the makeshift blindfold over my eyes until I can only see darkness.

He does what everyone does when they blindfold someone and steps back, waving his hand a few inches from my face. At least, that's what I imagine him doing. "How many fingers am I holding up?

"Well, Hudson, I don't know if you noticed, but I am blindfolded, therefore, I cannot see how many fingers you are currently holding up in front of my face."

"Alright, good. Let's go."

I hear him walk in front of me and onto the front porch before he stops, remembering I am temporarily blind. His hand curls around my bicep and guides me down the steps and into his truck.

Once he buckles me in, he closes the door and makes his way to the driver's side. There are a million possibilities swimming through my head, waves of ideas flooding back and forth, dangerous waves in a hurricane I don't know if I am ready to face.

I hear the truck pull away and Hudson rests his hand on my thigh, a comforting anchor in the chaotic storm. "Where are we going?"

"You'll see."

"Is this the part where you take me to the woods to murder me?"

His laugh fills the cab of the truck. "If I wanted to do that, I would have done it ages ago when we went hiking. Much more remote. Easier cleanup too with the bears."

"That answer came way too easily to you."

"Don't dish it out if you can't take it, Sunshine."

"Oh, I can take it, Mountain Man."

"And you take it well," he says and I tighten my legs together. He feels my reaction under his hand and starts rubbing soft lines on my leg, back and forth. Higher and higher, until the truck comes to a stop.

"Not fair," I whine.

"Very fair," he says before he jumps out of the truck and back to my side to help me out.

"Can I take the blindfold off now?"

"Not yet."

He guides me a few feet forward and I hear a familiar jingle above the door he opens.

"Why did you have to blindfold me to go to Fran's?" I ask.

"Because we aren't at Fran's."

"Yes, we are. I recognize the bells above the door."

But when I step inside the familiar scent of old books and coffee doesn't hit me. Instead, it is a fresh coat of paint and a new, woodsy kind of smell. The kind of scent that greets you in a new store or a new space created in your home.

"Hudson, where are we?"

"Home," he whispers in my ear before finally removing the blindfold.

I open my eyes, blinking against the soft light from the strand of bulbs draping across the ceiling of the once empty space. We are in the space Sky took me to the other day, except it's far from empty this time.

A reception desk now sits to the left of the space and the curtains are gone. Near the back, there's a small desk with a pink chair in front of it accenting the soft purple color that now covers the walls. A color I know was chosen by my best friend who at that moment walks through the back door with Sky close behind.

"Oh finally," Charlotte says, making her way toward me. "We thought you guys were caught up in bed or something."

My jaw drops and I ignore her comment, wrapping my arms around her, tears filling my eyes. "What the fuck are you doing here?"

"Well, it's nice to see you too, babe."

"You know what I mean," I laugh through the tears.

"Well," she explains. "A certain someone called me," she glances at Hudson. "And we have a proposition for you."

I look between the three of them and my heart starts to beat hard in my chest. The image of a cartoon character seeing the woman he loves, his heart thumping literally out of his chest comes to mind.

"Who has a proposition for me?"

"All of us," answers Sky. "But you have to stay quiet until we explain it all. Deal?"

I nod my head because I'm not sure how to even respond to what's happening. And I am not even sure what that is.

"First off," starts Charlotte. "You probably know I got fired when I yelled at James as I walked out the other day."

"If I recall, you flipped him off and said 'Fuck you.'"

"Those were my exact words, yes. But when I went back to

your place to clean out that garbage woman's things, I had an epiphany."

"An epiphany?"

"Yep. And when Hudson called when Sharon left his house, I had an idea."

"An idea?" I ask.

"Stop repeating me and listen. I called Sky."

"And she told me her idea," Sky chimes in.

"And we agreed," Charlotte continues.

"Agreed on what?"

"You deserve to stay here," Sky says. "Make this your space."

"Well, *our* space," Charlotte corrects.

I am lost. Confused. And surprised?

"You said, you couldn't afford this place on your own. So we are making sure you're not on your own," Sky explains. "You wouldn't take my money and I know you won't take my dear brother's money either, but Charlotte came up with the idea of being business partners."

"Business partners?" I know I'm still repeating them, but my brain can't process anything else.

"Yes, the three of us," Charlotte gestures to herself, then Sky, then me.

"You run your photography studio, live out your dreams here. Take pictures of the moments that matter for the people that matter. Meanwhile, I can use the space upstairs to paint. Open a studio, maybe teach lessons in the future if I decide I want to deal with kids or even teach adults. This town needs some art culture in its bones, anyway." Sky explains.

"Meanwhile," Charlotte adds. "I will design the inside of the space for you. I can find work here with interior design. I've already talked to Cordie about redesigning the rooms at the inn and I can help you here too. Be your go-between, your assistant, whatever else you need me to be."

The tears are falling now, trailing down my face and

cascading to the dust-covered floor covered in dust and specks of purple paint. It's then that I notice the photos in frames lining the center of the walls.

They're... mine. All of them. They're the photos I have taken since I arrived in Blue Grove. I walk toward the wall and look at them, each one nestled in a simple wooden frame. Frames that I recognize from Hudson's shop. My mouth hangs open, amazed at the amount of work Hudson must have put into this to get them printed and framed.

There's one of Fran working behind the counter at *Books & Beans*. One of the shelves of books lining the other side of the store. A black and white one featuring Henry's book recommendations. Ethan helping Cordie at the inn. The town crowded into *Frank's* for a town meeting. Several are of the mountains behind Hudson's house and the field of wild-flowers that fill the backyard. When I come to the end, the photos become more intimate. A soft smile playing at the edge of Hudson's lips, one I took when he thought no one was paying attention to him. Another of him sleeping on the couch, his head propped on the edge with his legs stretched across me, mouth slightly open. The rest are a collection of him and the dogs, moments in time I wanted to remember of my stay here. Moments I wanted to burn into my memory. Lock them in a vault to take out when I needed to feel happy again. When I needed to remember what it felt like to be in the presence of someone who loved me uncon-ditionally.

I come to the last picture in the line, one I don't remember taking. Our feet are framed, legs tangled together on the blanket in his backyard, the picture he snapped on our date. The camera is focused on the glow of the lantern softly illuminating the area around it, creating a soft glow. The mountains are framed in the background, out of focus, but still prominent enough to be noticeable.

I chuckle as I notice a post-it note stuck to the bottom of the frame. I lift it off and read the words through blurry eyes.

Stay with me, Sunshine?
I love you.
-H

I look over at Hudson to see him looking back at me. He is quietly standing off to the side, hands in his pockets and shifting nervously from one foot to the next.

"What about California?" I ask Charlotte, my watery gaze still on Hudson.

"What about it? I have nothing there. No job. No family. I only have you and this place is what makes you happy. *He* is what makes you happy," she points to Hudson.

"So, that's our proposition," says Sky. "You go into business with us. Live your life here and be happy with my annoying brother."

My eyes don't leave Hudson's as I wait for him to say something. Anything. "You did this for me?"

Finally, he closes the distance between us. "I'd do anything for you, Avery. Two weeks with you was never going to be enough." He frames my face with his hands and leans his forehead against mine.

"That's our cue. I'm not staying to watch them make out," Sky says. I hear the bells jingle again as she and Charlotte leave us alone for a moment.

"Two lifetimes with you isn't enough, Reid. You're everything. My cabin and my life are dull without you. Without my sunshine. Come back home. Stay with me. Please."

Please... that word, his confession, the note he left on the photo. I know he's never been more vulnerable, more open than he is with me now.

And I can picture it. My life with him. His dogs. His family. His town. *My* town. In just three short, life-changing weeks it has become mine. *He* has become mine. And I have become his in more ways than I can even imagine. There's no doubt in my mind now that I am where I'm supposed to be.

Something brought me here. Fate, the universe...Charlotte. Whatever. It brought us together to heal each other. To find ourselves in the other. And suddenly, I can't remember my reasoning for going back to California in the first place. I hate my job. I have no family now that I have cut ties with Sharon. The only family I have is standing outside the shop and she's now moving here apparently. But, most importantly, there's Hudson. I love him. I am in love with him and the moment I walked in this room, I knew what my answer would be. I've known it since he asked me if I am being honest with myself.

"Yes," I say finally and he lets out a sigh of relief, his warm breath whispering against my skin. "I love you, Hudson." Saying it out loud sounds like the perfect mix of notes I have been trying to find for a long time. A melody that finally clicks. A crescendo in my head until a smile spreads so far across his face, it reaches his eyes. He lets out another sigh of relief and a small chuckle before pulling me to him hard. My lips crash into his.

He deepens the kiss, tongue invading my mouth and I feel his arms circle me. The heat travels with his hands as he plants them on my backside and lifts me up, my legs automatically closing around his torso. He spins me around like we are in our own romantic comedy movie at the end of the story, about to live our happily ever after. And I feel that last bit of me slide into place, my heart finally whole after years and years of it cracking and crumbling piece by piece.

He pulls his head back to meet my eyes and tucks a few loose strands behind my ear, his other arm wraps around me, holding me in place. His forehead gently touches mine and he breathes in, the smile never leaving his face.

"I love you too, Sunshine. Let's go home."

He gently sets me down, his hands never leaving my skin, his hand now tangled in mine. The smile stays on his face as he kisses me again and again like they are his oxygen and he cannot live for more than a second without his lips on mine.

I laugh against his lips and look around one more time, thinking of all the possibilities now in front of me, before pulling him toward the door. But he pulls me back so he is in front of me and drops my hand. He turns with his back to me and crouches down.

"Need a ride?" He says, looking back with a sly, knowing grin.

I roll my eyes with a laugh and put my hands on his shoulders. Bending down, I kiss him again deeply, his head angled back, his scent mixing with fresh paint, and stained wood.

"Always," I answer and hop on his back into a position wholly familiar to us.

The bells I love so much jingle above us as we make our way home. Together.

EPILOGUE

AVERY

FOUR MONTHS LATER

"'ll see you tomorrow, Charlotte," I say in a serious tone, telling her I'm actually leaving this time, which I have been trying to do for the past hour, but every time I try to leave, she has something else that has to be discussed immediately.

"But we still need to go over the dark room des—"

"Nope! Not today. I'm done! I have a date with Hudson, which he's kept secret and," I add, glancing at my watch showing 6 p.m. "I'm already late. Elias knows more about that anyway."

"But—"

I open the door and signal her to go through it. My keys are already in the lock ready to do their job and let me go home. "Tomorrow," I cut her off.

She groans and glances at her phone again. She's been looking at it every five minutes for the last hour. "Fiiiine," she finally says. "Let's go."

"Thank you."

She leaves the studio and I close the door, turning the keys to lock it. "I promise everything will be here tomorrow and we can tackle it then."

"Yeah, yeah," she says unconvincingly.

"If you'd just call Elias like a *normal* human being, you could get it sorted out sooner."

She scoffs. "*He* doesn't listen to me and just does what *he* thinks is best."

We still have a long way to go, because Charlotte can't seem to decide on what exactly she wants the space to look like. I don't either. I left the designing completely up to her since she was so adamant on doing it. She did, however, get settled in the space upstairs for now. We left the weekend after Hudson asked me to stay and came back with all of our things in one U-Haul. I don't know what it is, but there is something about seeing your whole life packed up in a truck to move it to a different state.

We both fully moved into our new spaces, with the help of Hudson's family—besides Elias since there were a few architect projects that required his attention at the time. I still haven't had a chance to introduce them in person. Both of them are always busy when the other is free and suspiciously, they haven't run into each other in town yet. They're clearly avoiding face-to-face contact and nobody knows why. I've tried to ask Charlotte about it, but she changes the subject every time, so I let it drop for a while.

"*He* owns the building. Can you just try to get along with him? You kind of have to considering he's doing all the architecture stuff for free. And you're the interior designer, so you have to work together."

"He's impossible."

"I think you both are," I mumble.

"What?"

"Nothing. Look, Charlotte, you two have to move past whatever you have going on and meet in person. Because we still have a ton of work to do on the studio and I was hoping we could have it done before Christmas."

Which is only two months away, I almost remind her.

She sighs, "Fine, I'll try. But only for you. *Not* him." She turns to walk around the building toward the stairs on the side leading up to her apartment above. "I'll see you tomorrow," she calls back.

I roll my eyes and they land on the sign hanging above the entrance. A lantern sits on the far right side of the wooden sign, a soft flame inside. *Pictures in Blue* is scrawled to the left of it in the loopy lettering I squealed at when Hudson showed me. Every time he revealed a new design, I would bite my lip in trepidation of telling him I didn't like the font. *Again.* And he would smile, plant a kiss on my cheek and start over. My corrections and idea changes didn't faze him, they inspired his creativity further, determined to make it perfect for me. Down at the bottom sits Sarah's dedication, something I suggested that I think finally allowed Hudson to loosen his grip on his grief a little bit more.

Fuck, I love him. My mind moves to a very different place as I get into Hudson's truck to drive home to him. Over the course of four months, we have only grown closer in every way we could. Emotionally, mentally, and definitely physically. I'm pretty sure there isn't a surface of the house that has not been graced with Hudson's ass—or mine—and I am not complaining.

I pull up to the cabin before I realize it, the time on the road passing with images of us in the kitchen, me sitting on the counter, Hudson's heads between my legs, hands bracing my thighs. Once on the stairs when we couldn't make it to the bedroom, him holding me up against the wall, my legs wrapped around his torso. The lazy mornings where we make love slowly, still sleepy from the night, making each other come in slow, gentle movements.

My favorite.

I smile and start walking toward the door, ready to jump him as soon as I get in, but the lights are off, which isn't unusual. I have been staying late at the studio the past week or so to try to help Charlotte get the layout right.

"Hudson, I'm home!" I yell into the darkness. Most of the time he falls asleep on the couch waiting for me, a Christmas movie or *The Princess Bride* playing on the television. I swear, he has seen that movie more than I have.

"Yoohoooo!" I call out. "I'm home and I am taking my pants off!" No answer.

"I'm home and I am stripping off my shirt!" Usually, by now, he comes into the living room from upstairs or from the spare room down the hallway that Ethan stays in every now and then, but this time I am met with silence.

I look down at Judy and our newest addition, Jingle, another golden named after a Christmas elf, who are at my feet, tails wagging, ready for a treat. "Where's he at girls?" I ask, and they seem to answer as they both trot toward the back door.

I follow them and my breath catches when I slide open the door. Hudson is standing at the bottom of the stairs, dressed for a hike, gear ready at his side.

"What are you doing?" I ask.

"We," he responds, holding out one of the packs to me, "are going on a hike."

"Right now?"

"Yes."

I roll my eyes, "I thought we were past one-word answers, Waters."

He lets out a low laugh. "Habit. C'mon, Sunshine. We are on a schedule."

"Hikes have schedules?" I ask, taking the bag from him and placing it on my shoulders.

His eyes meet mine, a softness behind them that never fails

to destroy me. "This one does," he responds. His hair is tied up in one of my ribbons –white with yellow polka dots– in a bun at the top of his head, giving me a full view of the wide smile that spreads across his face at the sight of me walking to him.

I take his hand and we head out to the trees, taking the familiar trail I've come to love over the last few months. I'm still using my therapy techniques some of the time, but mostly, if I have a particularly overwhelming day, I can depend on this trail. The slightly wonky tree at the entrance that provides just enough shade for the small sapling Hudson ripped out of the ground at the beginning of our agreement. We re-planted it shortly after I agreed to stay and honestly, it's a miracle we saved it. Even if it had died, I have a feeling Hudson would have found some way to preserve it for us, a full *Beauty and the Beast* move with a bell jar carefully placed over the top of it.

As we continue down the trail, Hudson takes a sharp right to an opening that wasn't there before. "Hudson, where are you going?"

"It's a surprise." Okay, he's being weird. I follow him through what looks to be a newly cut trail and wonder what exactly he's been up to back here over the last few weeks. According to him, he'd just been cleaning up our normal path because some trees were blocking the way from a bad storm. Clearly, he was doing way more than that.

He leads me to the opening we came to months ago with the horses except there's another trail that wasn't there before on the other side. Hudson glances at the sky and starts to pick up his pace, grabbing my hand and pulling me behind him.

"Hudson," I laugh. "Why are we almost running?"

"I thought you loved running?"

"Not when I don't know where I'm going!" I yell, laughing as the weight of the pack shifts from side to side with each step I take. He responds with a tug on my hand, almost dragging me behind him. I push my legs to catch up to him, matching his pace, practically running next to him. He keeps glancing at the sky, keeping track of something. We come to a hill and he starts climbing immediately.

"Hudson, I swear, if you don't tell me what is going on, I will stay at the bottom of this hill." He knows I'm not serious. I'd follow him anywhere, but this is getting ridiculous.

He stops halfway up and turns to face me, reaching out a hand. "Do you trust me?"

My gaze meets his and all I see there is warmth and excitement and I can't help but smile. After I roll my eyes. I start climbing until I am right in front of him and place my hand in his. "With my life."

Before he turns back to the trail, he places a firm kiss on my lips that I try to deepen, but he stops, breathless, and rests his forehead on mine. "C'mon, it's almost time."

"For what?" I ask, putting a dramatic flair to it.

"You'll see. Just a little bit longer." Kissing my forehead, he turns around, my hand still in his and we continue up the hill.

The sun has set, making it more difficult to navigate our way to the top, but Hudson pulls out a small flashlight to guide us. After a few more minutes we reach the top and come to a stop at an open patch of grass, a blanket spread out with two unlit lanterns on either side.

Reaching out a hand toward me, Hudson pulls me down to the blanket and we settle next to each other on our backs, reminding me of our first hike together.

Once we are settled, I turn my head to his. "Do I get an explanation now?"

His eyes meet mine, a wide smile reaching his eyes, the corner of them crinkling in the most adorable way. "Just look up."

So I do. And I am met with lights streaking across the sky, one after another, a light show just for us. "Holy shit, it's beautiful."

"Such a way with words," he chuckles. "I researched when the next meteor shower would be. I wanted to bring you here so you could see it. The Orionids usually peak this time of year at night and I couldn't have asked for a more perfect way to show you."

This man. I snuggle closer to him, laying my head on his chest, letting him wrap his arm around me, holding me tightly. These last four months with him have been a dream and my life has been so full with him in it, I am bursting. There have been struggles here and there with my self-esteem and anxiety, but he has done nothing but be supportive of me, helping me through whatever he can. As far as Sharon, neither of us have heard from her since that morning and I am better off for it. It was hard at first, getting used to the idea that my mother truly wanted nothing to do with me, but Hudson's family helped me realize that I deserve more than the very little she gave me throughout my life. I found my place. I found my home. My family. Everything.

A comfortable silence stretches as we watch the meteors streak by, their tails lighting up their path behind them. His heart beats beneath my head in a frantic rhythm and I have an inkling he didn't just bring me here for the shower. His chest rises with a deep inhale and his grip on me tightens.

"Avery," he takes another deep breath and shifts us into a sitting position. Reaching for the lanterns, he lights both of them, the flames creating a soft glow around us. My heart starts to mirror his, pounding in my chest. He bends down to kiss me, his body moving closer to mine until we are pressed against one another. I place my hands on either side of his face, attempting to lengthen the kiss, but he pulls away and continues.

"The moment you came into my life," he clears his throat and refocuses. "It changed for the better. I was lost before you and without you, and I don't think I ever would have been able to find myself again. I love you, Sunshine. I love the way you scatter your ribbons around the house, the way you willingly took in another dog, I love your passion and your creativity, and I love the way your eyes light up when you take the first sip of coffee in the morning or the first bite of a lemon bar. I love that you can kick my ass at Scrabble and can play volleyball way better than I can now. More importantly, I love *you*."

Tears stream down my face as he shifts, one knee planted on the blanket. He reaches out his arms, a pale blue pad of sticky notes resting in his palm. His familiar handwriting is on the top note:

Will you marry me?
-H

If you would have asked me five months ago, if I expected to be here under the gaze of a man who loves me with his whole soul, I wouldn't have believed you. And sometimes, I still can't believe I was lucky enough to find him. Someone who loves me for who I am; who loves me unconditionally, flaws and all. I look at Hudson. The man who has my soul. The love of my life. The man of my dreams.

I grab the pen I shoved in my back pocket earlier and gently peel off the first post-it from the stack, flipping it over. I write one word and turn it around so he can read it.

Yes.

As soon as his eyes read the paper, he takes the ring out of his pocket and places it on my finger. A simple gold band, an oval diamond in the middle, with two smaller diamonds hugging the sides. I hold it up in front of me and let it glitter in the soft light, tears now streaming down both our faces.

I grab his face again and bring him to me, whispering, "I love you, Hudson Waters." I crash my lips into his and pull us down on the blanket, the meteors streaking above us as we explore places we know so well, falling deeper than we ever have before.

ONCE THE PEAK of the meteors stopped, we hiked our way back to the cabin to continue celebrating. Once we get to the end of the trail however, Hudson stops us and pulls out the tie decorated with a string of Christmas lights he used months ago to blindfold me.

"Starting our games out here, Waters?"

"There's plenty of time for that later, Reid," his words sending a shiver down my spine. He spins his finger in the air between us, motioning for me to turn around. I do and I feel him tie the fabric around my eyes, blinding me.

"So, why are you blindfolding me then?"

"A surprise."

"Another one?" I say, spinning the new addition to my left hand around my finger.

I feel the press of his lips right behind my ear before he whispers, "Yes." The breath of his words igniting my body that is apparently not satiated from our time below the meteor shower.

He moves behind me and gently starts pushing me forward, the warmth from his hands bleeding through the fabric of my sweatshirt. After a few feet, we come to a stop and I feel the tie loosen as Hudson unties it from my eyes.

Suddenly, the yard blinks to life as lanterns around us are lit, glowing around the yard, revealing decorations, a table of food and drinks, and a stereo off to the side. I look around and see Hudson's family surrounding us along with Fran and Cordie, who are arm in arm, beaming at us. Charlotte, who's stalling earlier now made sense, stands next to them, smiling from ear to ear. She is dressed in the brightest yellow sweater, and bright red leggings, the epitome of the brightness in my life.

George's arm is wrapped around Isabelle's as she tries to hold back her tears. Ethan is on Elias' back watching with excitement, nervous energy coming out in the form of bouncing. Sky, in her usual black jeans, a gray tank and a plaid jacket with Jacob standing beside her, a lantern still in his hands as he struggles to light it.

Charlotte beams back at me and is the first to break from the group, running up to me, insisting on seeing my left hand. When she sees the ring she cheers and wraps herself around me. "You deserve everything, Ave."

"Getting soft on me, Char?"

She laughs, "Shut up." But when she pulls away, she wipes at the tears streaming down her face.

Everyone else comes to offer their congratulations and I feel Ethan's arms wrap around my middle. "Aunt Dory!"

"You've got that right, kiddo," I say, hugging him back in a tight squeeze.

"We made this party for you and I made mountain cookies!" He yells and pulls me away from everyone toward the table, the surface completely covered in food and a huge plate of mountain shaped cookies, covered in sprinkles signaling that Ethan did, in fact, make these cookies.

I hear Fran and Cordie a few feet away talking to Hudson.

When I turn back, they are on either side of Hudson beaming up at him. "We told you, boy," Fran says with a grin on her face.

"You owe us," Cordie says, nudging him with her hip.

"Careful, you don't want to break that."

"Be careful," says Fran. "We may be old, but we can take you."

"Oh, I don't doubt it," he responds and hugs them closer. I can't quite hear what he whispers to them but I do catch his lips mouthing, "Thank you," before he plants a kiss to the tops of their heads. I catch his eyes and we smile at each other from a few feet away, a moment for us, a sense of complete calm, knowing we will have a lifetime filled with moments just like this.

HUDSON

After hugs and a small celebration, everyone parted ways for Avery and I to celebrate on our own. The porch is illuminated by the soft lights above us and the full moon in the sky, lanterns we haven't picked up yet still stand in my yard.

Our yard, I correct myself.

Avery is bundled up in a thick blanket twisting her engagement ring on her finger, legs spread across my lap. I turn my gaze to the far-off mountains focusing on the stars and think of Sarah. There's one more lantern we didn't light sitting on the railing where I took the photo for Avery before. I insisted on having an extra one for Sarah as a way of finally letting go of my past.

I have come to realize that grief isn't linear. It comes in waves and rises like the tides. It stays and covers the shoreline until it's time to recede, moving to a calmer, quieter place. Leaving a path of foam and broken shells behind. But even the broken shells are worth seeing. The broken parts are worth living through because everyone is broken in their own way. It's the way we put ourselves back together again that makes life worth living. The people around us make it worth it. *She* makes it worth it. She stormed into my life at a time I thought my broken parts would never be mended, my grief over Sarah overbearing. Suffocating in the darkness.

She catches me staring at Sarah's lantern and nudges my arm. "Are you ready?"

I nod and stand, offering my hand to her and pull her up to me, chest to chest. I wrap the blanket around her shoulders and grab the lantern, leaning it toward her.

She gently unscrews the cap at the bottom and lights the long match, placing it inside until the wick catches. She rests her head on my arm as we watch the flame grow, joining the others among the wildflowers. I bend to place a kiss on the side of Avery's head and close my eyes, breathing her in, still unbelieving that she is mine.

She is the bright light that made me want to breathe again. Want to live again. She has soothed my soul in ways I never could have imagined and I am at peace. Finally, at peace with my bottled sunshine.

I breathe in the mountain air and for the first time in a long time, it doesn't hurt.

THE END.

ACKNOWLEDGMENTS

I am not even sure where to start with these. It has been five years since I published my last book and since then, I've applied and graduated from graduate school, had two kids, and re-entered the indie publishing world. I thought I was done writing books for the time being but seeing so many people succeed and thrive, I realized I could do it too! I'd done it before and this time around, I had so much more support.

So, first and foremost, thank YOU for picking up my book and giving it a chance. I know it won't be for everyone and that's okay! I am just appreciative you saw it and were interested enough to pick it up and I hope the inside reflected the outside in that it was just as stunning.

I can't go without thanking my people. So, without further ado, THANK YOU.

Kristen – Thank you for all the brainstorming, editing, proofreading, fact-checking, and most of all, your friendship. I am so so grateful to have connected with you and worked with you and I will forever be lucky to have you in my life.

Taylor – Thank you for everything you have done for this book over the last year. Between instilling confidence in me, always encouraging me, brainstorming, helping me figure out what works and what doesn't, beta reading, for always being honest, and always trying to figure out ways to help me with promotions. I am so happy we connected and formed a solid friendship. Thank you from the bottom of my heart, Tay!

Jessica (Gecka) – Thank you for reading another one of my books. Your everlasting encouragement and medical jargon are always a joy to receive. Thank you for beta reading and freely giving your opinions and thoughts on everything I obsessively send you. The mountains were all you. Thank you for helping me climb them.

Sabrina – Thank you for being a bottomless well of support. You hype me up in the best way. Thank you for your comments and insights during beta reading and everything thereafter. Your yelling gives me life.

Maria - Thank you for always encouraging me to follow my dreams and being my best friend over the years. Your advice and insight into this story gave me all the encouragement I needed to keep going. I can never thank you enough for always falling right back into our friendship no matter how long it had been since we had seen each other. Forever grateful to have you in my life.

Aleshka – Thank you for being my most thorough beta reader. A lot of this story developed from you and your suggestions and insights. It wouldn't be what it is without you and I am forever grateful you took a chance on my book.

Kelsey – Thank you for encouraging me to start my bookstagram account. And thank you for being the biggest supporter for us indie authors. It sounds cheesy, but it is truly because of you this book exists. Without you, I wouldn't have done this. From the bottom of my soul, thank you.

ABOUT THE AUTHOR

Kelsey Schulz is an indie author based out of Godfrey, Illinois where she is striving to work as a school librarian, while chaotically writing romance novels on the side. She lives with her husband and two sons who keep her active every day. This is her third novel and you can find out more about her future projects by subscribing to her newsletter through Instagram.

CONSIDER LEAVING A REVIEW!

Thank you for giving Pictures in Blue a chance! I would be SO appreciative if you left a review on Goodreads and Amazon. Tag me if you loved it, so I can share it and thank you!

CPSIA information can be obtained
at www.ICGtesting.com
Printed in the USA
BVHW041910010623
665240BV00003B/82